Apollo Ascending
Book 4

NICOLE BAILEY

This is a work of fiction. Names, characters, businesses, places, events, locales, and incidents are either the products of the author's imagination or used in a fictitious manner. Any resemblance to actual persons, living or dead, or actual events is purely coincidental.

No part of this book may be reproduced in any form or by any electronic or mechanical means, including information storage and retrieval systems, without written permission from the author, except for the use of brief quotations in a book review.

Copyright © 2022 by Nicole Bailey

All rights reserved.

Edited by Milly Bellegris and Natalie Cammaratta

Cover design by Stefanie Saw

Map design by Chaim Holtjer

"The Four Ages of Man" © 1934 by W. B. Yeats

"Ovid's Metamorphoses" by Ovid (18 AD) Translated by Brookes More © 1922

www.authornicolebailey.com

Content Warnings

Please note that these content warnings will contain spoilers for the book.

A Spark of Death and Fury contains some **dark content** including the portrayal of torture, ptsd, explicit violence, a child in perilous situations, an adult hitting a child, misogyny, and mentions of parental loss.

This story depicts battles, including the graphic death of gods, humans, and horses and the characters' emotional responses to these events.

The book also contains strong language and sexual content.

I hope readers will find that I've handled these topics with sensitivity. However, I wished to include a note for anyone who may find this content triggering.

Map

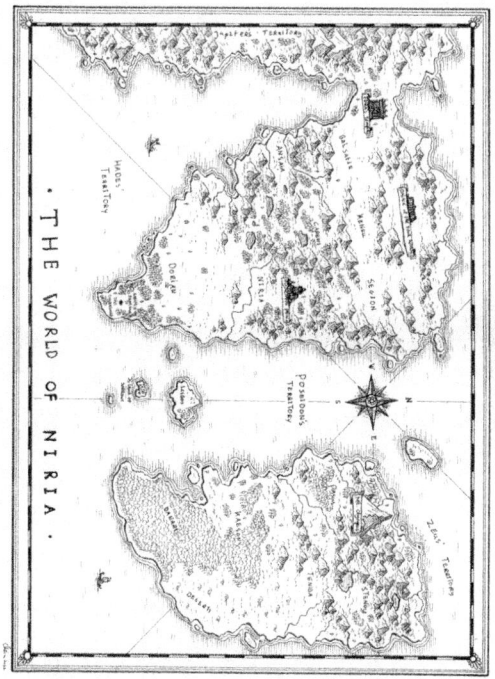

Character Review

Apollo
God of the sun. Hyacinth's husband and Temi's older brother.

Temi (Artemis)
Prophesied goddess of the sun. Huntress and Apollo's younger sister.

Hyacinth (Cyn)
Was the crowned prince of Niria before his death. A low deity. Apollo's husband.

Epiphany (Pip)
Princess of Niria and Hyacinth's younger sister. Valerian's partner.

Valerian (Val)
Master stableman at the palace in Niria. Epiphany's partner.

Emrin
Was the crowned prince of Niria before his death in battle.

Orion
A soldier from Segion and friend of Temi's.

Joden
Nirian high lord and political advisor.

Zephyrus
God of the west wind (spring). Hyacinth's past lover who killed him out of vengeance.

Other wind gods include Boreas (north wind, winter), Notus (south wind, summer), and Euros (east wind, autumn.)

Galeson
High lord from the country of Segion and a suitor of Epiphany's.

Delon
A high lord from a prominent Nirian family who grew up with Hyacinth. He became good friends with Apollo in A Crown of Hopes and Sorrows and died during a battle in A Shield of Fate and Ruin.

Zeus
Ruler over the deities of Mt. Olympus, god of the sky, and Apollo's father. One of the three major gods. (Married to Hera.)

Poseidon
God of the sea, Zeus' brother, and one of the three

major gods. Temi's father. Killed by Zeus at the end of A Shield of Fate and Ruin.

Hades

God of the underworld, Zeus' brother, and one of the three major gods. (Married to Persephone.)

Hecate

Goddess of the dark side of the moon, night, liminal spaces, and necromancy. She is Persephone's companion in the underworld and connected with Temi.

Ares

God of war, son of Zeus, and half-brother of Apollo. Father of Ixion. Died at the hand of Zeus at the end of A Shield of Fate and Ruin.

Arion

Temi's immortal, sea stallion Poseidon gifted her.

Tartarus

The realm of monsters and torment that Zeus locks his enemies in.

Ixion

Ares' son. A high deity that Zeus has kept frozen in childhood.

Leto

Apollo and Temi's mother. High priestess of her village in Danari until her death shortly after Temi's birth.

Jupiter

High deity of the gods from the west. Killed by Zeus in A Shield of Fate and Ruin.

Flora

Goddess of flowers and spring. Part of Jupiter's court. Married to Zephyrus.

Clothos

One of the three fates who determine the fate of mortals and gods alike. She forewarned Hyacinth of his death.

Review of Book 3

In **A Shield of Fate and Ruin**, Ares arrives to warn of Zeus' plan to send human soldiers to subdue Niria's rebellion. Ares agrees to turn on Zeus if Apollo and Hyacinth can get his son—Ixion—away from Zeus.

Temi joins the Nirian armies and leaves for battle with her horse, Arion.

Epiphany agrees to act as an ambassador for her father in the city outside where the army's camp will set up. Lord Galeson arrives and they work together, which puts Pip in an uncomfortable place of tension between her personal desires and the actions she must take for Niria.

Apollo and Hyacinth run into a variety of troubles on their journey. Their ship wrecks amid a battle of the sea gods, someone follows them, they're robbed, and they face a creature of Tartarus.

Temi reluctantly aligns with a soldier, Orion, to work on battle strategies. They become friends.

Emrin arrives to the war camp early and announces that King Magnes has died. Emrin enters a battle. Delon follows and dies while attempting to protect him. Emrin is injured by a weapon that gives him blood poisoning. He confesses to Epiphany that Valerian's father, Lord Lucien wrote and agreed to claim Val so the two could marry. But Emrin burned the letter. Emrin dies. Valerian tells Epiphany they should break off their relationship. Niria will look at Pip for guidance now.

Apollo and Hyacinth arrive in Pasus as the gods of Jupiter's court lay siege to Mt. Olympus. Apollo tells Cyn that he must face his father and asks Hyacinth to take Ixion back to Niria. Hyacinth is heartbroken but agrees.

Temi leads another battle against Ansair. As it begins, she sees Hyacinth's signal to move the moon.

After the eclipse, Apollo ascends Mt. Olympus to find Ares has turned all the gods against Zeus. Zeus kills Ares. Apollo pulls the sun into the palace, blowing up the spark, Zeus, and himself.

Temi sees the sun explode during the battle and panics, knowing Apollo has died. She's distracted and gets knocked off Arion. A horse tramples her leg, breaking it. She's realizes she's mortal now (after whatever Apollo has done) and is lying injured on the ground in the middle of a battle.

Epiphany decides the battle is the perfect distraction for her to speak with Valerian and tell him breaking up was a mistake. She sneaks out of the city and, finding the stables on fire, rushes in. She and Valerian get trapped as the flaming roof falls on them.

Hyacinth is at the docks with Ixion when he sees the sun explode. He's devastated but knows he has to keep it together for Ix. The captain tells him part of his crew has quit out of fear of the gods and he can't take them to Niria after all. Cyn struggles to decide what to do when enemies surround them. He fights back, but they cut Ix. The group force Hyacinth and Ixion onto a boat and lock them into storage. Cyn realizes he will have to do whatever he must in order to keep Ixion safe.

He with body waged a fight,
> But body won; it walks upright.
> Then he struggled with the heart;
> Innocence and peace depart.
> Then he struggled with the mind;
> His proud heart he left behind.
> Now his wars on God begin;
> At stroke of midnight God shall win.

THE FOUR AGES of Man
> W. B. Yeats

1

Apollo

Heat.

And fire.

And golden light.

My skin ached, and my mouth was so dry I struggled to peel my lips apart.

I had always wondered where the gods went when they died. I knew it wasn't the underworld like mortals.

Apparently, I'd landed in some hell made of abrasive dust and living flame.

A fitting punishment for a sun god.

I longed for water. A glass of it. A drop.

I'd trade my soul for a single taste.

I moaned and shifted, the gritty ground below me scratching my flesh.

The idea of eternity weighed on me.

I'd once thought being stuck as the god of the sun would make for a long ass existence.

Or losing Hyacinth.

My heart ached.

I'd lost him.

Again.

But he was safe.

And that was enough for me.

I closed my eyes and drifted off into a heat-infused nightmare.

2

Hyacinth

The boat lurched, and Ixion curled up beside me. His dark curls, damp with sweat, clung to his forehead. He whimpered in his sleep, and I drew an arm around him and rubbed his back. His lip trembled and then he took a deep breath before tangling my shirt in his fist, his features smoothing out again.

"It's all right," I whispered.

It was a lie.

That's all I knew how to do anymore, apparently.

But the child—for that's what he was despite being frozen at this age for hundreds of years—settled against our bed of coarse sacks over the rough planks of the ship's belly. I touched the damp strands of his hair once more.

It was my responsibility to care for him, to protect him.

And within a few hours of having that role, I'd already ruined it. I didn't know who these men were who'd captured us and locked us below deck on this ship, what they wanted from us, or where we traveled.

My heart fluttered into my throat, and panic coursed through my blood.

I struggled to draw in a breath.

It was only when Ix slept that I allowed myself to feel.

Anxiety.

Fear.

Hopelessness.

And, most of all, sorrow.

Like I'd never experienced before.

Apollo was gone.

I could feel the rough touch of his fingers grazing my spine, taste his lips on my tongue, hear his heartbeat thumping against mine.

He would be so disappointed in me, but regardless, I wished he were with us. He would have some idea of how to deal with this mess. His plan would probably be impetuous and terrifying, but it would be better than remaining frozen in place by fear, my nose flaring, as water drip, drip, dripped in the background.

No.

I took a deep breath.

I was a prince who had faced death and gods and the underworld and a giant serpent and shipwrecks and heartaches. And I could figure this out. I just needed a plan.

The hatch opened, allowing sunlight to flood in and illuminate dust motes. One of our kidnappers, a grizzly man with a shadow of a beard save for a spot where a long scar followed the length of his jaw, walked in with a tray of food.

I sat up. "Could we go outside today?"

He grunted and dropped the tray. The dried strips of fish fell off it and hit the filthy floor.

"The child," I said, raising my voice. "Needs sunlight and fresh air."

A Spark of Death and Fury

He sneered at me before climbing back up the stairs.

"He'll sicken," I stood and yelled, "if he doesn't get some."

The hatch landed with a thud. I clenched my fingers into my palms. They hadn't killed either of us, which meant we had some purpose—something they required us alive for. And I intended to use that against them.

"Am I going to get sick?"

I turned around. Ixion sat, his mop of curls mussed, his wide eyes fixed on me.

I bent down beside him and lowered my voice to a whisper. "No. You're too hardy for that. I'm just trying to trick them"—I winked—"to see if we can go above deck."

His shoulders eased, his worries washing away. Then he popped his head up, his features shadowed by the murky space. He was a high god, but had lost his powers, the silver glow around him, and the golden color of his eyes which had faded to brown when the sun had exploded. I swallowed back at that memory.

"Apollo is god of the sun, right?" Ix said.

"What?"

"Your husband." His brow furrowed. "He's the god of the sun, isn't he?"

He... was.

I nodded. "Yes."

"And so maybe if they let us out on the deck, he can travel with the sun and rescue us?"

His voice had pitched up several notches, his expression as hopeful and innocent as spring flowers quivering in the early breaths of a hurricane, unaware they'd soon lay ruined on the ground.

I straightened the bandage on his arm, which I'd tied on after a kidnapper had cut him. They'd used him against me, because I'd fought back. "Apollo had a task he had to do first, remember?"

The edge of Ixion's tongue pressed between his lips, and he squinted. "Was that him that blew the sun up?"

The boat lurched, and I tensed to maintain my balance. "I think so."

"But when he finishes, then he'll rescue us?"

My heart thundered, and tears stung my eyes. *No*, I longed to scream. *No, because he's dead, because he's an idiot and he left us to face his father.* Was Zeus gone as well? Was Apollo even successful? Did he achieve his purposes, or was his life senselessly laid to waste?

A knot formed in my throat, and I grazed my thumb over the ring Apollo had given me, my nail clinking into the grooves that made up the flowers, before I swept over the sun on the other side. The space sat too ensconced in shadows to make out the deep green of the stone, but I brushed over its smooth surface and remembered the day he gave it to me.

The day we exchanged marriage vows.

I'd had him—in my life and as my husband—for scarcely more than a moment. I'd barely had time to revel in the beauty of that before fate ripped it away... again. How could this happen? Apollo had said he would suffer an eternity for a day with me.

Maybe I was selfish, but that was not enough for me.

I wanted him forever.

I wished to see his golden eyes sparkle as we joked, to try to form with words things too impossible to capture as we talked, to listen to his moan and push into the rough touch of his hand as our bodies tangled together.

But... no.

He'd sacrificed everything.

The irony stung like thorns, gripping into me. When

he'd arrived in Niria last summer, I'd raged at how selfish I thought he was. And now he'd given himself up for the good of the world.

His selflessness didn't help—I was angrier with him than ever.

Ixion cocked his head to the side.

Right. He waited for my answer. Would Apollo come and rescue us once he finished his task?

No. No, he would not.

Tears prickled over my eyes. The anger was a cloak that blanketed the grief I didn't express. I couldn't break when Ixion's well-being rested on me.

I cleared my throat. "Perhaps so. For now, we have to stay brave and remain strong. You can do that, right?"

He clasped my hand, his palm soft and curved with youth. "I can. I'll be brave like you."

I forced a smile to spread over my cheeks, to squeeze his grip in return. But I wanted to say, *I'm not brave. Not at all. I'm terrified.*

The hatch creaked open, and I jumped up to place my body between the man stepping down the stairs and Ixion. The sunlight glared in, washing him in hazy light, and it took my eyes a moment to adjust. His sandy hair curled against the shoulders of a leather jacket, and he rested his hand on the hilt of a knife.

"The crew tells me you're worried about this one's health." He slid the blade out and gestured towards Ix with it.

Ixion leaned his head around my hip, but I pushed him back. I didn't doubt this man would stab him if it suited his purposes.

"The child needs to get out of the dust and shadows down here for a while."

The man considered me for a moment. "If you attempt to pull any shit, we'll kill the boy."

Ixion went as still as a rock behind me, and his fingers clenched into my clothing. I glowered. "Watch your language. He's a child."

The man twisted his lips before giving a nod. "All right. An hour on deck. And don't try anything."

"I don't intend to."

The man slipped the knife back into his belt. "If I thought you did, I wouldn't let you out of here."

I took a deep breath and crouched to offer Ixion my hand. He trembled and tucked his face against me the way he had buried himself in his nanny's skirts when we'd met. "I don't want to go. They might hurt me again."

"No. They only did that to scare me, so I won't use my powers on them, and I promise you, Ix, I won't do it. Because I'll keep you safe. I know these men are scary, but you can trust me, right?"

He lifted his face so that his eyes glistened like the dust motes floating around him. He sniffled but bobbed his head. "Yes."

"Then let's go get some fresh air."

He accepted my hand and marched with me up the stairs. My skin crawled as the man exited behind us. He could so easily harm either of us. I had my divine powers still, but Ixion didn't. The man could kill Ix… or cause him to suffer.

My palms broke out in sweat, but I kept my eyes ahead as we reached the deck. Ocean spray hit me, the cool saltiness of it refreshing. The sky stretched endlessly blue as it shimmered over the inky waters that rocked the boat. Men looked up from their stations where they rowed, some glowering, but continued their work.

Ixion lifted his face to the sun, and his dark curls fluttered in the breeze.

He didn't look like his Uncle Apollo, really. But he shared just enough features with him that my heart ached.

Our escort glowered at a crewman who approached us, but the sailor thrust his hands in the air. "No harm meant, I swear it."

The leader considered him before nodding. The crewman pulled out a bag and handed it to Ix. Ixion unwound the strings and marbles bounced out and scattered across the deck. "Oh," Ix said as he ran after them. "Thank you."

The sailor grinned and returned to his post.

"I suppose I don't need to offer you any more warnings," the first man said, his eyes darkening. "If you try to use your powers or any other unexpected moves, we'll slit the boy's throat."

A pit in my stomach grew, but I gestured out to the ocean. "What exactly could I do with my magic out here, anyhow?"

The wind held a bite to it that raked across my cheeks. So, we headed north, not south. He tapped his fingers against the hilt of his blade. "Maybe not, but I see the thoughts whirling through your head. I don't wish to harm a child, so don't do anything stupid. The name's Jax, by the way."

I turned towards him. The wind picked up, rippling my filthy robe around me. Ixion had poured the marbles out on the deck, and the breeze swept them forward. He scrambled after them. "I don't believe this is a first-name-basis relationship," I said, the words hissing through my teeth.

Jax shrugged and leaned on the railing. He wasn't

afraid of me at all. He must have realized that I wouldn't do anything to compromise Ixion's well-being. After all, I could travel out of this situation with my magic in a blink... but I couldn't take Ixion with me. My powers only allowed me to travel, not to carry others. And with Ix's powers gone... I held back a sigh. We were stuck.

"Figured I'd share since I already know yours, Prince Hyacinth. It doesn't please me to hold a royal and a child, but with the wars on both continents a man's gotta do what he must in order to feed his family. And I don't intend to piss off my employer."

"Who would that be?"

He chuckled darkly. "I'm not stupid enough to share that detail, but I have some information for you."

"What's that?"

"Niria destroyed Ansair in their last battle. Apparently,"—he leaned in, his eyes sparkling—"they had gods on their side. Who'd have seen that coming, eh?"

A spark of hope pierced through me. The country was safe. I imagined Father and Emrin buoyed by the win. Our alliances strengthened. It emboldened me. They had faced a war and overcame it. I could do the same. "Thank you, Jax."

He tucked a strand of hair behind his ear. "Half an hour and then you both return under deck. We can't spare the crew to watch you for longer than that."

I nodded and pressed against the railing but kept Ixion in my peripheral vision. Perhaps it was stupid to turn my back on these men, but it didn't seem likely they would harm me. They delivered Ix and me somewhere.

More ocean spray whipped up and speckled my cheeks. The sun stretched above in the distance, already starting its descent for the day. I suppose after its explosion, and whatever Apollo had done, it returned to its regular pattern as it had before he ascended. Soon it would disappear behind the water, gone, its light and warmth leaving with it. Grief garbled through me again, but I clenched my hands against the rail until it hurt enough to block out the emotional pain.

3

Epiphany

I slipped out of my room as the gray light of morning trickled through the windows. My arm ached from the burn and I needed to let the physician clean and bandage it again. I winced, but it was a minor thing considering Val and I had nearly burned to death. Soldiers had brought him back to Lady Antonia's house with me after Hecate had saved us, and he had a room in the attendant's quarters. I knocked quietly, barely tapping my knuckles against the door.

Val inched the door open and at the sight of me pulled me in so fast I squeaked in surprise. "How badly are you hurt?" he said before he finished latching the door back.

"Not bad."

Valerian's frowned, and he lit an oil lamp to a dim flicker that bled a wash of warmth into the room. "Epiphany," he whispered, his back still turned to me, heartbreak in his voice. "Why did you come to the stables and put yourself in so much danger?"

I stepped over to him and wrapped my arms around his waist. I still felt as sure as I had when I'd raced after him. He stiffened but then clasped his hands over mine. "Because we made a mistake, Val."

He twisted in my arms. "A mistake?"

I nodded to the bed, and we both sat on the narrow cot, the mattress creaking with our weight. "I realized that giving you up is too high a cost."

"What about Niria?" His eyes darted to the bandage. "What happened?"

"A minor burn. Don't worry over it." I pulled my sleeve down. "It's true I must stand in for Niria right now, and things are insecure and terrifying; you were right." I grabbed his hand and curled my fingers around the rough edges of his fingers. "But, Val, I love you."

He swallowed, and his throat bobbed. The light flickered over his skin I knew so well, had pressed my mouth to and run my fingers down a thousand times.

"I love you fiercely," I continued. "And I don't know how everything will land right now, but I can't give you up. I can't give us up. Please, give us a second chance."

"Epiphany, I never gave up on us." He leaned in and grazed his nose over my cheek, which sent a shiver down my spine. "I'm trying to consider what's best for you. And I'm not that."

"Let me be the one to decide what's best for me. Please... just... give me time to figure this all out."

He scraped his thumb along the edge of the bandage that peeked out beyond the sleeve. "I'm sorry you're the one who got hurt." He stared at it like he saw our future. My attachment to him would harm me. It had already. And I didn't care. Maybe that's what love was, the willingness to risk burning if it meant doing so at his side.

"Please, Val. We'll figure it out. But I don't want to end us... yet, at least. If we have to because of Niria, we'll face it when the time comes. But I refuse to give up prematurely. That's what I came to tell you that morning."

"Oh, Pip." He sighed into my neck. "I'm not good for you. You know that don't you?"

"I disagree."

He kissed me, and his lips lingered against mine.

"Is that a yes?" I asked.

"I should say no."

"But you're not."

"I guess I'm not."

Later, I winced as a physician rubbed a salve over my arm and pulled me out of the memory.

"Apologies, Princess."

"No, it's fine. Thank you." I clenched my teeth down as he pressed the medicine deeper into the burn that glided up from my elbow, a blistering streak of marred flesh that would scar and leave a reminder, for life, of everything that had happened.

Tears stung my eyes, and I closed them, blocking out the high ceilings and painted walls of Lady Antonia's estate.

Father was gone.

Emrin was gone.

I currently stood as the proxy ruler of our country, per my father's orders with my role during the war. But that would change soon.

"A nasty injury there."

Hecate loomed in the doorway, her eyes—a deep emerald color now that her high god's magic had fallen—skimmed over the physician where he wrapped my arm in gauze. The man trembled and picked up his pace with shaking fingers before securing the ends, rising, and bowing to us both as he skittered out of the room.

Hecate grinned.

A Spark of Death and Fury

Even with her powers gone and the snake she loved to carry with her elsewhere, the entire house found her disconcerting. She'd even dressed demurely, wearing a standard gown in an unassuming mauve color.

But her posture, the way she held herself, her expression, made it clear she didn't fear anyone.

And a woman unafraid was a truly terrifying sight.

She stepped beside me and lowered onto the seat the physician had worked in. "Hello."

"Hecate. I... I'm glad you came by. I wanted to thank you. If you hadn't saved me and Val... we would have..." My words ended in a puff of unspoken anxieties.

We would have burned to death in that stable.

Hecate shrugged and draped her arm over the back of her chair. "When I lost my powers, I wished to make myself useful in some other manner, and then I saw your young mortal running into the stables. Though I wonder"—she glided a long, creamy finger over the carvings in the wood—"how often my family will need to save you two."

My cheeks warmed. "I'm sorry. Or thank you. Or..."

She chuckled, a soft sound that buzzed in the air. "It's fine, dear. I wished to check on you as Hades and I leave for the underworld today."

"You're going back?"

She nodded. "We still have work to do. Clothos forewarned us of this, and our place is to return home. How is your lover?"

My face heated again at how casually she said that word, but I shrugged. "He's awake and doing fine. It seems unfair"—I narrowed my eyes at the bandage on my arm—"that he walked out unscathed."

Hecate rose so smoothly it was like an unseen hand pulled her up. "Well, that's what happens when another being uses their body to shield someone. The latter is protected, while the first is harmed."

I stood as well. "I suppose so."

"I have counsel for you, young royal."

As I stared into the piercing intensity of her gaze, a tremble ran down my spine. "That is?"

She grabbed my fingers, her touch icy and firm. "Stop letting the world dictate who you are." She pressed her hand against my chest, right above my beating heart. "In here, you already have everything you need. The Fates formed you for greatness."

I stumbled over a few words before giving my head a shake. I didn't know how to respond to that. Hecate pursed her thick lips before cocking an eyebrow and walking out of the room, the energy of the space deflating as she left.

Well, that was... weird... and slightly terrifying.

I licked my lips, pushing the loose gauze of my sleeve over the bandage. I wanted to go check on Temi, but she wasn't awake yet. The physicians had to do surgery to set her broken leg again. Her first surgery hadn't healed well. Anyway, I had a meeting to attend.

I stepped out and walked down the hall to the sitting room, where various advisors scattered around. Asher paced in front of the marble fireplace. Joden stood clustered with a group of men who all had furrowed brows and spoke in hushed whispers. He lifted his face towards me. "Princess Epiphany."

"Forgive me for the delay. Thank you for waiting for me."

The men bowed.

One with kind brown eyes took a step closer to me. "We're all glad to see you well, Your Highness."

"Thank you."

The advisors nodded, though a few gave me censuring

A Spark of Death and Fury

looks. *Why had I been at the camp during the battle? Why wasn't I safely ensconced in this estate instead of inside a burning stable?* Joden's lips pinched like he tasted something sour. He likely suspected the reason.

I cleared my throat. "Let me not delay this meeting any further."

"The closest male heir of your line is a cousin of yours, Your Highness," Joden said. "A Lord Demetri of Carens. Perhaps you remember him when his family visited a decade ago?"

"Carens? He's not even Nirian?"

Joden frowned. "I'm afraid not."

A man in Joden's group scuffed his foot across the intricately patterned rug. "I don't understand why our country didn't make closer connections with this cousin?"

Asher stopped pacing. "With King Magnes having two healthy sons nearly grown before his brother died, who would have thought we'd be in this position without an heir?" Asher clasped his hands together and bowed towards me. "Forgive me my callousness, Your Highness."

Sorrow pulsed through me, but I waved his words away. "I think, for the time being, bluntness is necessary. At present, the good of the country comes before any of our personal feelings."

A round of hums of agreement passed through the room.

"The families were never close as King Magnes took issue with his cousin, Demetri's father. Presently, per the king's orders," Asher pushed on, "Princess Epiphany is the royal in charge. King Magnes explicitly left her with full authority for the sake of the country during the war, and that extended even if he were to pass. We have, according to the law, six months that we can delay the ascension of this cousin after the death of one family line. So, I propose that as many of us who can return to the capital, invite this Lord Demetri, and get acquainted with him as quickly as possible. And we should send out messengers in search of Prince Hyacinth. If he's on another continent, it could take weeks to pass a message, and that's assuming we locate him."

Joden readjusted his jacket. "A wise plan. Princess Epiphany?"

"Yes?"

"You must return as well, first thing in the morning. Niria stands without a ruler currently and needs one now more than ever. That lot falls to you."

My breath caught, but I could do this for Father. For Niria. "Of course. I'll make plans to return home at once."

The men bowed and shuffled out. Once the room emptied, I sighed, and my shoulders slumped. The entire country looked to... me. My internal voice came high and trembling. I wasn't sure I could manage it all. But I'd find a way.

Gods, I hoped we'd locate Hyacinth quickly. He would come up with a better plan than some Carens stranger who my parents hadn't liked taking Father's throne.

"Epiphany?" I turned. Galeson stood in the doorway, his blue eyes heavy, pale locks silhouetting his face. "May I speak with you, if you have a moment?"

"Of course." I gestured to a couch, and we both sat.

He cleared his throat and fidgeted his fingers together before twisting a ring around. "I know you're grieving, and I feel terribly selfish for bringing this up right now." He pushed himself up straighter, the silk of his clothing glimmering alongside the rich fabric of the furniture.

"It's fine," I said. "Whatever you need to discuss with me, please do."

"The thing is..." He sighed and gave his head a shake.

"I don't understand. Why were you at the camp during the battle?"

A breath whooshed out of me.

He lifted his face expectantly. Gale was the last person I wanted to explain this to.

"The man you spoke of to me." He cleared his throat. "The... the one you were in love with?"

I nodded, still unable to come up with something intelligible to say.

"Is he with the army?"

He shifted those kind blue eyes to me again. His hurt echoed in my body, causing my heart to give a painful lurch. "Yes," I whispered.

He released a breath that shifted him away from me as his eyelashes blinked rapidly against his cheeks.

"I'm so sorry," I said. "I never planned to..."

"I see... Was there anything between us at all?"

"No. Or, yes... But..." I pressed my face into my hands. "Gale, I'm sorry. I've been in love with him for years. I didn't mean to lead you along. Spending time with you was enjoyable, and our countries were going to war together, and..."

"Did you actually believe"—the hurt in his voice pierced through me—"that I would harm the connection of our countries if you didn't return my feelings? Do you think so lowly of me?"

"No, but..." I stumbled over a sob, the misery in his expression stalling me. "I'll stop speaking. You're right. I've been wretched to you. I thought I could push past my emotions and do the honorable thing."

"And the 'honorable thing' you speak of with such disdain is marrying me?" His nose flared.

I stared at him, my mouth gaping unceremoniously. "I suppose so."

"I'm sorry that prospect was something you felt duty-bound to."

"It wasn't. Or it was… but… I also liked you… but…"

"Not as much as your soldier." His eyes fell into shadows.

I wanted to find words to patch this up, to undo his hurts, and apologize for my choices.

None came.

Galeson rose. Tears streaked his cheeks, and he wiped them away with his fingers. "You have my promise, on my honor, that no harm will come between our countries over this. I hope"—he stumbled on the word, and I bit my lip—"you maintain a high enough opinion of me to believe that, at least."

I stood. "I do, of course."

He sighed and bowed before exiting the room.

I dropped back against the couch and clasped my hand over my mouth to muffle my sobs.

4

Artemis

I screamed. A pain seared through my leg so bright and hot my vision went white for a moment.

"Get the fuck off of me."

"Artemis, we need you to lie still."

I smacked at the hands reaching for me. He dropped a dish, and the copper tang of blood filled the air. A blinding light flooded in through a window and my head pounded so achingly I could scarcely see. But I knew where that blood had come from. It's what had woken me. "Do not touch me."

"She's awake?" This voice was low and familiar and comforting.

"Yes, for all the good it will do if she won't allow us to set that bone again."

People moved back. A shuffling sound echoed, and then a chair creaked as the person sat down, his warm, earthy smell filling my senses.

"It's good to see you alive."

I cringed and kicked the leg that didn't ache against the frame of the bed I lay in. "I can't agree."

"Temi."

Dark smudges curved under Orion's eyes. Behind him, a group of physicians stood and watched me warily. One held a jar, and the contents of it splashed as the creature inside moved. Leeches. Because they'd bled me.

I grabbed a pot off the table and hurled it towards the man. It smashed against the wall by his head. His color drained, and he took an uneasy step back, clutching the life-suckers to his chest.

"Temi," Orion's voice grew harder.

"Did you know?" I sat up and cringed as my body shuddered with the motion. "Were you around when they were bleeding me?"

"They were trying to save you."

"I don't need saving." I turned to the cluster of physicians at the doorway. "So leave me the fuck alone."

Orion frowned and waved his hand. "Give us a minute."

"Commander, it might be best if—"

"That wasn't a request."

His voice hung in the air for a moment before the group shuffled out of the room, and I swallowed before dropping back against the bed. The exertion left me shaking, sweat breaking out across my brow. Why was my body like this—weak and useless?

Then I remembered.

The weight of it sucked the breath out of my chest, like it physically landed on me.

Apollo.

My lip trembled, and I turned my face away from Orion.

Once the echoing footsteps disappeared, Orion leaned against his seat, and it groaned again. "I'm glad you're awake."

A Spark of Death and Fury

"You clearly haven't slept."

"You're right." He shifted, and the feet of the chair clacked against the tiles. "After I dragged your ass off the battlefield, I stayed by your side while these physicians attempted to pull you back from the edge of death."

I took in a shaky breath. "Thank you for that."

He stood, lifted a pitcher, and poured water into a cup before bringing it to me. I turned away again. "Take it, Temi. You don't have to be so godsdamn stubborn at every moment."

I scowled but snatched the cup as I sat up. My muscles screamed and ached as I took a sip. "Arion?"

"Is fine." He leaned against the wall and crossed his arms. "He's being pissier to the stableman having to care for him than you are with the physicians, if you can believe it."

"Are they trying to bleed him, too?" I choked on my water. "Wait. Why isn't Valerian caring for him?"

Orion took his seat in the chair, his shoulders covering the back of it. "He's here at the house so physicians can monitor him after he was injured while clearing the stables." I startled and jerked my leg, causing pain to shoot through me, and the gash in my side grew warm. "Damn it, Temi. He's fine. But look at you." Orion took the cup, set it down with a clink, and then grabbed my elbow to ease me against the bed. He pulled the blanket down and lifted my tunic. The cool air against my bare skin caused goosebumps to rise where bandages didn't cover. He clicked his tongue. "You've reopened the wound. And you're not healing like you would when you had powers. You've…"

I sniffled, and he stopped speaking as he raised his crystal blue eyes up to focus on me.

"Have the high gods fallen, then?"

He scratched his thick fingers over his beard. "That's... the belief at the moment."

I nodded and turned away from him again. He fumbled through the items on the table next to me then peeled the old bandage off before pressing gauze against my side. "I've found that the best way to deal with grief is to face it, rather than avoid it."

"I didn't ask," I said through gritted teeth as the pain whipped through me.

He sighed as he pulled strips of cloth out. "Fine. But listen to me." His expression held a heaviness, his brow furrowed. It didn't suit him. "You're going to channel this hard headedness into getting better."

"I don't want those physicians touching me."

"The first surgery didn't go well. They have to reset the bone, or you'll never walk again. You can forget about hunting or riding Arion. And if you don't stay still and stop fighting them,"—he gestured to the gash on my side—"you're going to end up with blood poisoning or a festering wound and you'll die." I parted my lips to argue with him, but then his shoulders dropped, his voice lowering to a whisper. "I don't want you to die."

The air seemed to thicken, and I took several aching breaths, letting my eyes close. I'd been selfish. I hadn't cared if my life ended, but I hadn't thought about who it might affect. The women relying on me, Epiphany, Valerian, and... maybe even Orion.

He pressed a fresh cloth against my side, and I winced, struggling not to pull away from him. For several minutes we said nothing, the whispering sound of the bandage Orion wrapped over my broken flesh only punctuated by sharp breaths.

He finished, placed the blanket back over me again, and dropped into the chair. I took a slow breath, letting the air raise my chest. Everything hurt so much it was hard to focus and my vision wobbled, but I wouldn't give in to the pull of sleep. Molded flourishes outlined the edges of the ceiling, so we were in a house in the city. That had to be Epiphany's doing.

Epiphany.

Who would need me now more than ever.

I hadn't even considered that.

I squeezed my eyes closed. "I think..." I whispered, choking over the consonants I needed to form. The thought hurt so much my throat squeezed as if to shut them off. "I think Apollo is dead."

"I know."

I opened my eyes to find Orion twisting his fingers together.

"You know?"

"You've been talking in your sleep. You've called out for him."

"Oh."

He clamped his massive hand over mine, his callouses scraping my skin. "I'm sorry."

I sucked in a shaky breath, and tears broke forth and tracked down my cheeks. One rolled over my lip, and I licked it away. "This wasn't how this was supposed to go. He was supposed to grow the fuck up and take his mantle. We were supposed to have our fucking lifetimes"—my voice shook—"together. Not... this."

Orion's grip tightened. "I understand."

And he did. He'd lost his sister, and she'd been much younger. I laced my fingers into his. "And my body feels like death. Everything fucking hurts."

"Yeah, well..." Orion's voice came gravelly, and he cleared it. "You've fought the physicians like the mistress of death"—he smirked at me and the reference to Hecate I'd made before—"had a hold of you. She visited, by the way."

I wasn't sure how to feel about that. On the one hand, I appreciated her consideration. On the other, she'd probably already left before I'd gotten to speak with her. I shifted and winced as my side screamed at me. "Apollo and I belong together. I'm not supposed to go on without him. He's... he's all I have."

Orion bowed his head and his golden hair glimmered in the sunlight. "I understand that feeling. It's terrible to be the only one in your family left." He quieted for a moment. "But he's not all you have."

Our eyes met, and I drew in a shaky breath.

"Now." Orion disentangled his fingers from mine, clapping his hands against his thighs. "Let these physicians reset your bone and get some sleep. That way tomorrow we can travel with the party to the capital."

"The capital?"

He filled a second cup with water and took a swallow. "Mhmm. The princess heads back tomorrow, and I'm assuming you'd want to go with her." He nodded to my leg. "You can't ride yet, but I'll join you in a carriage. I'll convince these physicians I can care for your bandages, and it won't overtax you. With the way you're treating them, it probably won't be difficult to talk them into letting you leave." He grinned.

"That's... generous of you."

"It's nothing."

"What of the war?"

Orion scoffed. "What of it? Ansair has retreated. The world is up in flames at the moment. No one knows how to handle the gods falling. Unrest is ripping through the countries like a spooked sheep in a herd. All the leaders want to return to their seats of power until things settle."

A Spark of Death and Fury

I gripped my fingers into the blanket, and the fabric pressed under my nails. "Don't you have a troop to oversee?"

He leaned against the chair and crossed his arms. "If you don't want me to go with you, just tell me. I'll stay."

He cocked his head to the side, and I shuddered. "No, I'd like you to travel with me, and I want to leave with Epiphany if I can manage it."

"All right. If I have the physicians return, can you not threaten to kill them?"

"No promises," I grumbled.

He chuckled and jumped up to march out of the room.

I sank against the mattress. My body hurt. Losing my brother... that hurt far more. But Orion was right. He wasn't all I had. There were others who relied on me, who I needed to live for. I would just have to learn how to redefine myself without Apollo.

5

Apollo

The blanket I lay on bumped over a rock.

I gasped, and my eyes flew open.

The sun beamed above, bright and hot and miserable.

The shushing sound of sand blared. I turned my head to watch the world as it passed by. Something dragged me.

I lurched forward.

I may be in in some afterlife punishment—or gods, maybe this was Tartarus, full of monsters—but I wouldn't go down without a fight. A stick snapped out and hit my leg. I winced and fell back against the blanket.

"Sit down before you injure yourself further."

I licked my dry lips, and my eyes dashed about for an exit. I pulled my elbows into my chest, winced as some injury in my arm screamed with the motion, and rolled off the blanket.

My knees hit the burning sand, and my skin shrieked. The world blurred into a swirl of gold and cerulean as my head spun.

Hands yanked me up onto stumbling feet. "Now look at what you've done." I pulled away, but the fingers, long and strong and deeply calloused, tightened. "Come back to the pallet and lie down. You've split your wound open again." She clicked her tongue. "Mama Hiscu is going to be furious."

"What..." My throat ached as I spoke, the words rumbling out of me. "What are you talking about?"

My vision cleared, and the woman lifted her chin, her dark skin luminescent in the sunlight, her gray braids bundled back away from her face. She took the stick and snapped it against the lower part of my left bicep. I winced and held the stinging skin. "You've torn your burn open again. It's been festering, but Nedia has tended to it. She's clever with healing, that one." She gave her tongue another click. "But you're testing our patience, boy."

"I... I don't understand." I took a step, but dizziness swept over me.

The woman scoffed and led me back towards the blanket. "Lie yourself down before you kill yourself out in this heat. You're only half alive at that. Zeus' hatred, you'd think you have a death wish."

I lowered to the pallet, helpless to fight against her, but remained upright. "Aren't I already dead?"

She burst into a laugh that caused her walking stick to vibrate, and I winced, wary to receive the painful end of that again. "No, honey, unless I've passed to the other side in the last few minutes with ya, you're still as alive as I'm standing here."

"But..." I lifted my hands and stared at them. "I thought..."

"That you'd blown up the sun? Yeah." She wiped sweat off her brow. "We saw that."

"You... saw it?"

Her expression contorted, like she wasn't sure what to make of me. A group of women walked around a grove of palm trees dressed in swathes of brightly colored fabrics. One scowled as she leaned heavily against her walking stick. "So, he's awake."

"Yes, Mama Hiscu," the woman standing at my side said.

Hiscu's frown deepened. "Opened his arm again, though." She tutted, her wiry gray eyebrows pulling together. "How old are you, boy?"

"I'm..." I paused, my thoughts muddled. "Twenty-one."

She scoffed and the women with her bit their lips. "Hear how he hesitates?" She swung her stick at me, and I shifted to avoid it. "Doesn't even have enough years on him to count and yet he stumbles over the answer. And I overheard him talking. He thinks the god of the sun could be killed by the sun." She threw her hands up towards the heavens. "And this is what the Fates leave us with."

"Go easy, Mama." One woman from the group stepped forward, and placed her hand on Hiscu's shoulder. "He's disoriented, yet. Let me tend to him."

Hiscu pursed her lips. "Pfft. Do your best, Nedia. At least we won't have to drag him along with us anymore." She pinched my arm hard enough that I winced. "You don't look like you should weigh as much as you do, boy."

She turned and the rest of the group followed her to the shadows of the palm grove. Nedia bowed beside me and pulled a pouch from the layers of her burgundy wrap. "Forgive Mama Hiscu. She's..." Nedia gave her head a shake as she let her words trail off, her halo of curls bouncing with the motion. She pulled a cloth and salve out of her pouch, brushed the blood away from my arm, and unscrewed the tin before gliding the medicine over the injury.

"I'm alive?" I said, my voice hoarse.

A Spark of Death and Fury

"You are."

Emotions clogged the words in my throat. I'd survived. Hyacinth and I could be together, I only had to find him. Nedia returned the cap to the jar with a jangle and tucked it back into her pouch. I nodded to it. "Thank you for helping me."

"You're welcome."

"Could you tell me where your village is?"

She lifted her face, and a smirk touched the edge of her lips as her brown skin glimmered in the sunlight. "My village?"

"Or city." Shit. Had I offended her by assuming? "Wherever you live."

She chuckled before pressing the cool back of her hand against my brow. "Your fever has broken. That's good." She stood and gestured to a patch of shade. I followed her on unsteady feet and sat beside her. "You won't find any mortal city near here, young god."

I jerked my face in her direction, and my head swam with the motion. "Are you a deity?"

"Of a sort."

"Not a high god, then?"

Her chuckle grew warm and low, and it vibrated through me. Her fingers brushed along the mottled patch of marred flesh that made up the burn on my arm. I realized she was beautiful, and I found her attractive, but somehow it registered to me as a logical fact, separate from any spark of feelings. There was only one being that could elicit that for me anymore, and I had to get back to him.

"Your idea of high and low deities is part of the problem, Apollo."

"What do you mean?"

She pulled out a waterskin and offered it to me. I took a long swallow as she spoke. "You ask if I'm divine." She brushed a group of curls behind her ear. "I am... but not in the way you understand divinity. We are the old gods."

"The old gods?"

She gave a quick nod. "Zeus once was one as well. The All created us as guardians of the world. But they imbued us enough humanity so we could empathize with the mortals." Her eyes glimmered and the sand in front of us jumped and molded into formations, jungles with swaying leaves, winding rivers, creatures that prowled about, a human tossing a child into the air. "But it backfired when some of the old gods grew ambitious and leaned into the human's emotions of greed and jealousy."

The sand shapes changed form, a man rising, lightning in his hand.

"My father," I whispered.

Her features tightened. "Yes. Among others. But it was Zeus who learned how to steal the essence of humanity and channel that magic into powers The All did not intend for our kind to have."

A bird cried out as it flew from a tree and into the bright glare of sunlight. "You say *our kind.*"

"Oh, yes." She looked over her shoulder to where the other women had spread out mats and sat cross-legged in the shade, unpacking a basket of food. "All deity were once like us, you see. We were created to be servants, of a sort."

I reached to my shoulder for my knapsack strings before remembering I didn't have it. Hyacinth did. I had to get back to him and Ixion. "The gods were supposed to serve humans?"

She waved her hand and the sand dropped back against the ground, the burgundy fabric of her clothing rippling in the wind. "No. Humans were never meant to know of us, much less worship us. We are bound to the elements and maintain balance in this world."

"But Zeus changed that?"

She unscrewed the cap to the waterskin and took a swallow. "He did. He stole magic from humans, creating what you know as the spark. It enabled some gods to have unimaginable powers and the ability to live forever, but also required them to rely on human dedications to keep the spark ignited."

"Wait." I jerked towards her again, which caused me to sway, and my vision blurred. "We aren't supposed to live forever?"

"What actually lasts eternally, Apollo?" She nodded to the women. "You've met Mama Hiscu. She closes in on her tenth century. And the end of her life."

I considered that. "So, we'll all die now that I've broken the spark?"

"You haven't broken it."

"I blew it up."

"He actually thinks he destroyed the spark," Mama Hiscu said, her voice carrying on the wind. "And this is the being Clothos had us drag halfway across the desert."

Nedia looked at her and then shifted to me, arching an eyebrow. "Yes, but the spark will form again around whichever god exerts the most power." She wrapped her fingers over my wrist. "And it must be you, Apollo." The intensity of her expression grew. "Gain authority over it so you can disperse it. Every deity who's sat in shadows and longed to take Zeus' role will come after you now. It's rumored that you killed Zeus to become the new reigning high god. So, you must fight for your powers again. With the spark gone, all the high deities have fallen and will need to ascend once more."

"You want me to regain the powers—while other gods will do the same—so I can cause them to fall as soon as they've gained everything again?"

"Not fall." She released my arm. "Return to their place. We were never supposed to be heavenly beings, elevated above each other or the humans. The 'high gods' experience earth sickness as a punishment for ascending above your station. We belong to the earth, and it to us. We must come back to that."

I gave my head a shake. "Some of these gods will not agree with that."

She swept her fingers through the sand between us, creating a pattern of swirling lines. "Then they will have to fall. The spark and its stolen powers must be dispersed. The gods must return to mortal beings that prioritize maintaining balance in the natural elements."

I stared at her for a dozen heartbeats before I sighed. "Can you tell me where we are? There's someone I must reach."

She cocked her head to the side, her hair bunching up on her shoulder. "Are you very much in love with this person?"

I closed my eyes and Hyacinth came to me, the sharp lines of his features, the steadiness of his touch, the glimmer in his eye when something caught his exacting gaze. My heart ached. "Yes, I am."

She considered that. "Very well. But don't forget your fate, young god. Find your lover, but you and your sister must act when the time is right."

"My sister?"

She rose to her feet and offered me a hand, which I accepted. "For all of Mama Hiscu's complaints, do you really think the Fates would leave the destiny of the world in your hands alone?"

I stared at her. "I feel like I should be offended, but I'm honestly too tired."

"All right. Let's get you back to this lover of yours."

"You have the ability to do that?"

She laughed, and Mama Hiscu muttered something behind us. "No, Apollo. But you do."

"I do?"

"For too long, what you call the 'high deities' have relied on the power of the spark. When you ascended you did so with the sun, but through your connection to the spark in lieu of leaning on your elemental powers. Your magic is inherent in you, though. It's like an under-used muscle, weak and flabby." She squeezed my uninjured arm. "But it's there. You must exercise it. The sun is unanchored once more." She glared at it in the sky. "It has no guardian now. You must rise again to your magic."

"Do the old gods ascend?"

"In a way, but not how you think of it. We don't come into our powers in one tremendous sweep like you did with the spark. We connect with our magic as children, and it slowly builds in us until we are synced with it. You'll do the same. The powers of the sun—of a deity—still live within you."

"You mean I can still travel instantly?"

She nodded, curled strands of hair brushing across her cheeks.

I took a deep breath and leaned back in my body, the way I had hundreds of times before. And... nothing.

"He won't be able to do it," Mama Hiscu yelled from the grove. "That boy's never worked an honest day in his life and doesn't know his powers from a piss hole in the ground."

"I know how to use my powers."

Nedia's lips pinched like she fought a smile. "Try harder."

I lifted my arm, and the burn ached through my muscles, winding around my bones, and I clenched my teeth hard. These women implied I hadn't ever had to do the work of using my magic. They didn't know how right they were—I spent most of my life avoiding my powers, even when they were simple.

But if this would get me back to Hyacinth.

I closed my eyes and reached for the glittering heat of my powers.

Nothing hovered there.

It was like a dried-up well, echoing around with the promise of what once was.

"It will not be easy, Apollo. Try again."

I sucked in a breath and clenched my fingers into my hands as my feet pressed divots into the sand.

"You're too much in your physical self." I opened my eyes, and Nedia stood with her hand on her hips. "Separate from that. Remember your divinity is not within this body. This is only a form you wear, a mask."

A mask.

How many times had Hyacinth and I discussed wearing those?

I lifted my face to the sun. If what Nedia said was true, my magic formed through some connection to that star. It glared against the blue of the heavens and shimmered bands of light ahead of us. Somewhere in this world, the sun shined down on Hyacinth flowers, the ones we'd sown on our journey, or those growing free in the fields of Niria, or the ones Cyn's father planted in the atrium to keep them protected from the elements. Somewhere the flower reached out for the rays of sunshine.

I was that light.

A spark of magic glittered within me.

The tiniest flicker of my powers whispered to life.

I startled, grabbed hold of it, and leaned into it hard.

The sun wrapped me up, heat, and warmth, and

A Spark of Death and Fury

sparkling powers. But it felt different than it ever had, like my body burned, and my muscles pulled apart.

I pushed forward across the deserts, past the jungles, over the sea, and tumbled down onto a patch of soft grass in Niria. I hunched over, and my stomach heaved as I threw up, retching for several minutes. When I stood again, I wiped my arm over the back of my mouth. Nedia leaned against a tree, smirking. In the distance, the palace walls lay shrouded by the boughs of trees.

"You see," Nedia said. "Your magic remains. But you must learn how to actually connect with it and use it. And you must do so quickly, young god. Others will soon rise against you."

"How did you follow me?" I choked out, still wobbly on my feet.

She laughed and pulled the tin of salve out of her bag. "How could I have not followed you with the unsteady, slow path you made here? Your magic is weak, but the power lies there dormant. Here, take this." She handed over the medicine. "Twice a day on your injury. In some ways your body is more mortal than it's ever been with your powers suppressed. That could scar." She readjusted her wrap. "Best of luck to you, Apollo." She nodded and then dissolved into sand that swept out on the breeze.

I remained still for a moment, my filthy tunic stained from dried sweat rippled in the wind as trees in the distance danced together, like they performed for the palace. I was here. And I would have Hyacinth in my arms soon. I clenched my hand around the tin and started down the path to approach the massive gates.

A guard lifted his face and his eyes doubled in size before he bowed. "Lord Apollo."

"Please. Can you take me to see Prince Hyacinth?"

The guard exchanged a look with his partner before speaking. "He hasn't returned, my lord."

My body froze. "He hasn't? Wait... How long has it been since the sun burned the skies?"

The other guard, a man with glistening hazel eyes, spoke. "Not quite a week, my lord."

A sigh of relief swept out of me. "Prince Hyacinth traveled by boat to return to Niria just before that happened. He won't have arrived yet, but he should be here soon."

The guards looked at each other again and their postures loosened. "It is comforting to hear that, my lord."

Something about their tone bothered me. "Why?"

The first guard gripped his fingers tighter around the hilt of the sword on his hip. "Have you not heard that the King has passed?"

I stumbled back a step on trembling legs. "No."

That couldn't be true. Hyacinth's father was... dead?

Cyn would be devastated.

Tears bit at my eyes as if his heartbreak ripped through me.

"I'm..." Words seemed unable to form for me. "So sorry to hear that. Could I wait for the prince here at the palace?"

The guard bobbed in my direction. "Of course, my lord. We'll have you shown to a room."

I followed him, but a numbness flooded through me. Magnes had died? And soon Cyn would arrive and experience a heartache that would crush him. Hyacinth's father meant the world to him. Gods, this would tear him apart. It ached through me so much that for a few minutes I forgot everything Nedia had said to me.

6

Artemis

I lifted an edge of the bandage and winced as the wheels hit a dip. I sat in the seat with my splinted leg propped against the lip of the carriage, and every jostle pulsed through me. Dark clouds swept across the sky, gliding over our group of a few dozen. Epiphany sat, shoulders back, the skirt of her riding dress sweeping out in the air, her curls tumbling. Valerian rode a few paces apart from her, his emerald eyes darkened by the low light never left Pip's form.

Our carriage edged too far off the road, and Orion clicked his tongue, attempting to steer us onto the smoother path again. Arion pressed his ears back.

"Ack, we need to ease up, boy," Orion said.

Arion huffed and flicked his seaweed-like tail.

"For me, Arion," I said.

He took a deep breath before giving his head a shake and drifting up along the path where Orion tried to direct him. I longed to sit on his back, to lean over and scrape my fingers over his neck in gratitude.

But that would have to wait.

My leg ached as we trundled over the uneven ground.

Arion had the strength to pull the carriage alone, and he didn't get along with other horses adequately to have a second stallion hitched with him, but he'd been temperamental, Orion struggling to keep him on track.

"What's next?" I said, my voice hoarse. I sucked in a breath that ached the wound in my side, but if I remained still enough, it almost didn't hurt between heartbeats.

"For who?"

"I don't know. Niria, you, me, the world?"

He shrugged. "For what it's worth to me, the high gods falling…" His eyebrows pulled together again, and he frowned. "Well, aside from you having to recover from these injuries like a mortal… doesn't really affect me."

I kicked my head back. "Right. Maybe I'll join you in revering the stars. They seem a hell of a lot more consistent than deities."

He chuckled. "I suppose with the war, everyone is going to crawl home to their countries and see how things settle. Unrest isn't good for cities. Some people will use it to loot businesses, break the law, and cause damage because they think they can get away with it."

I'd met my fair share of people like that. "I suppose Niria—and other countries—may need their soldiers in place to hold their cities."

Orion nodded.

"Does that mean you'll return to Segion?"

"Nah. I'm a free agent, not contracted with the army."

"You are?"

His laughter grew, the corners of his eyes crinkling. "Of course. Why do you think my men and I could do whatever we wanted?"

I hummed a reply. The horses ahead of us whinnied, and

A Spark of Death and Fury

I thought of the creatures who had gone out to battle and never returned, of Valerian and how that had ached through him. "What do you plan to do with the world upside down?"

"Well, right now I'm escorting a goddess to a palace. That sounds important enough."

I snorted. "You know what I mean."

"I'm not that worried about the future. I'll take today. And until you don't have need of me anymore…" He gave me a look that made me feel every inch of the injured, aching mess that my body had become, but somehow not weak or broken. "I'll stay with you, if you can tolerate me that long."

I rolled my eyes but couldn't fight the smile that peeled up on my lips. My gaze darted to Epiphany again. Even after several days of travel, she kept her face on, her shoulders pulled back, her tone with the guards and other leaders of Niria upbeat and authoritative.

But I knew.

Beyond that, she held down a canyon of emotions.

"Want to talk to her?"

I startled at Orion's voice, jerking my leg and wincing. "I wish I could. I haven't gotten to speak with her alone since before the last battle."

"What do you think, Arion?" Orion said. "Can you behave yourself well enough for your mistress?"

Arion flicked his tail again, but Orion smirked and pulled him to a stop. Several of the guards yanked their reins to join us and then the entire party froze. "Everything all right?" A guard said.

Orion jumped down and gestured to Epiphany. "Artemis wonders if you would ride with her for a while, Princess."

Epiphany's expression broke, and she tucked a curl

behind her ear before nodding. "Of course. You'll take my horse?"

Orion accepted the reins and bowed to Epiphany. She walked over, climbed into the carriage, and eased into the bench beside me. "Do you think Arion will listen to me?"

"I hope he will." The group trundled along again, some guards pulling in tighter to Arion now that Epiphany rode with us as well. "Thank you for joining me."

She reached out and squeezed my knuckles. "I feel like we haven't really seen each other since…"

Since she'd lost her father and brother?

Since I'd lost Apollo?

Since the sky caught on fire, and the gods had fallen, and the world had shifted into chaos?

"A lot has happened in the last few weeks."

She grazed her thumb over the stitching on the leather reins. "We'll make it to the palace before nightfall."

"That's good."

She remained quiet for a moment, but her throat bobbed, her eyes gaining a sheen. "I don't know what comes next, Temi."

"Me neither."

She turned to face me, the sweet scent of the oils she wore filling my senses. "I'm so sorry… about Apollo, I mean. I heard… Well, I saw… and…" She bit her lip. "I'm shutting up now."

"No. Don't." I clenched my fingers into the fabric bunched up around the splint. "I just… I have no idea what to say, either."

Her nose wrinkled, the tan of it darkened in the low light. "Everyone keeps telling me how sorry they are." She choked on the words. "I'm so sorry, Princess. My condolences, Princess." Her curls whipped around her. "And here I am, doing the same thing to you. I guess it's just what we say when we don't know what to offer instead."

"Orion says it's best to handle grief face on."

Epiphany's gaze darted to Valerian, a pulse of longing in her expression before slipping back to me. "And what do you think?"

"That he's full of shit." She laughed, and I joined her. "But I've thought that since I met him and he somehow gets through, so maybe he has a point."

A smile still lingered on her lips, and her cheeks gained some color. For a moment we let the thunder of the horses' hooves sit between us, but then her shoulders dropped. "I don't know what happens next for Niria. The high advisors have invited the person in line for the throne to visit."

"Who's that?"

"Some cousin who doesn't even live in our country."

I frowned. "They're missing the ruler right in their midst."

"Who?"

I clicked my tongue and gestured at her. "You, obviously."

"Oh, Temi. I'm not a leader. I..."

"Grew up receiving the same education as your brothers, stood as the ambassador for the country during the war, faced endless trials with grace, and care deeply about the people of Niria? Should I go on?"

"But I'm a woman."

Exhaustion kept me from arguing with her. I struggled to keep my eyes open, and she knew what I had to say, anyway. Instead, I rested against the back of the bench and sighed. Epiphany reached for my hand, and I tangled our fingers together, grateful for her friendship and presence even as the world fell apart around us.

When we arrived at the palace grounds, and Valerian

ushered Arion to the stables, I leaned against Orion as we hobbled alongside Epiphany.

"You know," Orion said, "I could carry you. Just inside so that—"

"I would rather die."

"Ah." He grinned. "There's the Temi I know. Glad to hear you're feeling better."

I rolled my eyes, Epiphany laughed, and for a bubble of space, a breath of time, life felt normal. Then I banged the splint against a paver and warmth drained from my face.

Orion tightened his grip. "You are going to stubborn yourself to death."

"I'm... fine." I gritted through my teeth.

"Yeah, and I'm Hades."

A buzz of annoyance whipped through me, but Epiphany laughed again, and it warmed me. We made it nearly to the doors when they flew open.

Apollo walked out, and I trembled back a step. Orion braced me. The gold of sunset rimmed Apollo's curls, his brown eyes wide and focused on me. "Temi. You're hurt?"

"Apollo?"

He walked over and cocked his head to the side at the three of us. Epiphany's guards stared at him.

"You're dead," I finally said, my words coming garbled. "We... we saw the sun explode after I moved the moon... and I thought..."

"Me too." He swallowed. "Are you hurt badly?"

"Not too bad."

Orion clicked his tongue. But Apollo took another step closer. "Too injured for me to give you a hug?"

I stumbled into his arms, gripping his shoulders. My side screamed at me, but I didn't care. Apollo was alive, breathing and warm and smelling of grass and summer days, and I wanted to cry and yell and smack him for doing whatever the hell he'd done.

"My brother?" Epiphany whispered. "Hyacinth?"

Apollo leaned back. "He's okay. He traveled by boat with my nephew from Pasus, and they should arrive any day now."

Epiphany's entire body sank, and she dropped her head, her curls draping down her dress. I pulled an arm around her and hugged her to me but spoke to Apollo. "You managed to get Ixion?"

"Yes, he's safe."

Apollo's relief was palpable and I nodded but then remembered he didn't know Orion. "Apollo, meet Orion."

Orion thrusted one of his massive hands forward, and Apollo clasped it. "Nice to meet ya," Orion said. "I've heard a lot about you."

Apollo side-eyed me. "I'm afraid I can't yet say the same."

Orion's grin broadened. "I'm the only mortal who has ever put your sister's knife skills to the test."

Apollo's eyebrows shot up, and I gaped. "That's... not true."

Orion smirked and elbowed me gently in the arm. "I thought you didn't like to lie."

"I thought you denied being an arrogant shit."

"Nope." He crossed his arms. "That I never did."

Apollo and Epiphany both smiled, whether at Orion's comment or my eye roll, I didn't know. The sun hovered low against the sky, and I had so many questions to ask Apollo. Like what the hell happened? And why was he here when Hyacinth wasn't? Had Zeus fallen? But before I could voice any of them, he spoke. "Did Delon and Len travel with your party?"

I froze, and Epiphany tensed beside me. None of us

said anything for a moment. Wind whispered through the gardens and fluttered over fields where only a few months ago discus games were played when everyone was still alive and present and had a future stretching ahead of them. "Oh, Apollo."

He grazed his fingers over his collarbone, as if he reached for his knapsack though he had no bag on him, before dropping his arm again. "What is it?"

"Delon." I swallowed, looking to Orion and Epiphany as if they might have words I couldn't form, but Pip had drawn into herself, and Orion placed an arm behind my back, steadying me without offering words. "He went into a battle and… he didn't return."

Apollo's expression crumpled, and his eyes shimmered. "Oh."

The guards shifted behind us, and we all stood there, bathed in grief and loss. Pip sniffled, and Apollo closed his eyes and took in a deep breath that raised his shoulders. Tree limbs chittered together as none of us spoke. I altered my weight and winced as I put pressure on my broken leg.

"Come on," Apollo whispered. "I believe I can heal you."

"How?"

He lifted his hands. "Magic."

"But the high gods' magic is gone, isn't it?"

"Let's go inside where we can talk. I'll tell you everything."

We walked to the door, the pace slow as I hobbled along. Before we stepped in, Apollo paused and pressed his palm against the stone wall. His face shifted out towards the fields, and I could almost hear half a dozen young men laughing, their feet slapping against the ground, joy ringing around them.

Apollo sighed and walked through the doorway.

A Spark of Death and Fury

Later, I stretched out on a couch and listened to Apollo's story. Orion sat in a far corner of the room restringing a bow, his attention drawn into it. Epiphany had gone to attend a meeting with her advisors which left the three of us alone. When Apollo finished speaking, I huffed. "So, Zeus and Poseidon are both…?"

"Dead. Yes."

I took a deep breath. I'd suspected as much for Poseidon when he didn't answer my call before Emrin's death. The echo of grief that rippled through my body surprised me. I'd never even known my father. That had never bothered me, but now the chance to get to know him was gone. And Ares had died as well. The sting of sadness on that account was more for Apollo's sake. I'd barely known him, but he was the only other sibling Apollo cared for.

And the news he'd brought: The spark would reform around whoever exerted the most power. Other gods anticipated it to be Apollo. And we needed to ascend again. Well, again for Apollo. I'd never reached that point.

Apollo pressed his fingers above the bandage on my leg, and I winced, remembering how it hurt if something grazed the injured part. He closed his eyes.

Nothing happened.

For a long time, I remained still. Orion lifted his face, and I met his gaze.

Maybe the powers were truly lost.

Orion cocked an eyebrow as if challenging my unspoken worries, and I scoffed before shifting away from him. He had no right to know my thoughts as well as he did.

Brightness flashed over Apollo's body, golden and glittering. I jerked against the couch. Warmth flooded through my body, loosening my muscles, and the pain washed away as a tide of heat raked down my bones.

Apollo tumbled back from me and tripped over a table. Orion jumped up to steady him and helped him find a seat. He trembled, sweat suffusing his brow.

I unfastened the splint and peeled it off before gingerly pressing my foot against the rug. Nothing hurt. I snapped my face up. "It worked."

Apollo draped against the chair like a wrung-out cloth, contrasting against all the finery of the room. "It did."

"So, the magic isn't gone?"

"Apparently not."

"We have to regain it, then."

Apollo parted his lips to speak, but a woman's voice, steady and deep, broke in over his words. "Yes, you must. Your time has come, Artemis."

Orion and I both jumped forward, but Apollo threw a hand up to stop us as he stood on unsteady legs. His eyes pierced the woman standing in front of the unlit fireplace, her gray streaked hair resting over her silvery cloak, her skin as smooth as porcelain though deeply wrinkled at the corners of her lips.

Apollo frowned. "Clothos."

She didn't even shift her gaze towards him. She remained focused on me, unblinking, her shoulders so still I wasn't sure if she breathed. "The time has come to rise. Claim the spark and disperse it. Return to what you once were."

I looked at Orion and Apollo before answering her. "Aren't other gods trying to gain the spark as well?"

"Yes." She paused for so long Orion shifted, the crinkle of his clothing breaking the silence. "You and your brother must destroy any who resist. They will look for you." She skimmed her gaze over all three of us. "Whispers of your

A Spark of Death and Fury

prophecies have spread. And every divine who has sought to unseat Zeus will look to destroy Apollo—and anyone with him—in order to gain the spark. You must stop them."

"I won't do it." Apollo turned towards me, wobbling, his shoulders still slumped. "I vowed to Hyacinth to be a better man. I won't kill anymore."

"Even if it's for the good of the world?" I asked.

"I refuse to be used as a weapon in other's plans anymore," he yelled and stormed out of the room, the door thudding behind him. I turned to Clothos again.

She stood close enough to touch me, her unnaturally smooth skin and silver eyes both glowing. I startled and stumbled back a step. But she lifted her hand slowly, brushing it in an arc between us. "A prophecy for you, moon goddess."

My eyes transfixed on her as though I was incapable of looking away. "Yes?"

"*WHEN YOU LOSE what you've gained*
　And arrive at a fight too late
　Your brother will ascend only to bow

WHEN THE SUN *overtakes the moon,*
　And the trio stands guard
　That is your moment to rise."

I LOOKED at Orion with a *'what the hell does that mean?'* look. He shrugged, and I shifted back to Clothos to ask.

But she was already gone.

Only shadows remaining.

7

Hyacinth

The boat lurched, and Ixion's marbles swept across the wood floor of the belly of the ship. He scrambled after them, but I stood and pressed my hands against the wall of the vessel as it screeched and wobbled again.

My heart thundered.

Could we have wrecked?

Gods, that would just be my luck. Two shipwrecks in a season.

And locked below deck, how would we get out?

Ixion tumbled to his knees with another sway of the boat, then jumped back to his feet to chase after the lavender form of a marble that rolled around with the motion.

The men above yelled but didn't sound panicked, just focused.

So, we probably hadn't crashed.

I scraped my hands down my face, avoiding the compulsion to scratch. I hadn't shaved in over a week, and the gritty growth on my jaw endlessly irritated me.

The hatch opened, and Jax stepped down. "All right.

We've made it." He thrust two coats fashioned from coarse material in my direction. "You'll want these."

Ixion had gathered the marbles and walked over to my side. Though he'd grown less fearful of the men on the ship over the course of the week, he still clung to me. I pulled the coat on and bit down to avoid grimacing as the scratchy cloth crackled over my arms.

I knelt by Ix. "Here, you need to put something warmer on."

"Are we getting off the boat?"

I looked back at Jax, who I didn't quite trust but also didn't believe he intended immediate physical harm to either of us. He gave a sharp nod, and I turned to Ixion. "Yes. And you can feel how cold the wind is today." The breeze rippled through the hatch, causing my cheeks to ache.

Ixion offered his arms, and I pulled the coat on, but it drooped over his wrists and puddled in a pile of fabric at his feet.

"This is far too large for him," I said.

Jax shrugged. "I'm afraid it's all we have."

I brushed my thumbs over the lapels. The material wasn't fine enough to make any adjustments without potentially damaging its integrity. Then I sucked in a breath. "Can I have my bag back?"

"We can't risk you having knives or…"

"You've already searched it, I'm sure, and removed any weapons. But there's a coat in there I could give him."

Jax stared at me for a minute before sighing and trudging up the stairs. He returned a few minutes later with Apollo's knapsack and handed it over to me. The braided material of the strap under my fingers made my heart ache again. This bag had meant everything to him.

I bent down, pulled it open, and rifled through the

contents, ignoring my miserable heart as I touched the items that held so much significance for him: his lyre, Temi's bracelet, the poetry folio. My poem was missing from it, as he'd given it as an offering at my death.

I swallowed past a lump in my throat and withdrew Apollo's gray coat, the one I'd had commissioned for him when we traveled to visit the wind gods, before everything had happened.

I have excellent taste, I'd said.

He'd laughed, his eyes sparkling, his body so young and close to mine, and said, *I'd like a coat with terrible taste, then.*

I snapped the material out. He'd gotten it, too. This jacket had no style about it, but it was made of fine cloth. At the bottom edge, a rip jagged its way through the hem. I wondered what he'd done to tear it; now I'd never get to ask him. It hurt like a physical blow as I grabbed the material and ripped it more, yanking off several inches of the hem.

Apollo had treasured this coat.

But Apollo was gone.

I clenched my teeth and pulled it over Ixion's frame.

The sleeves were long but lined with silk and less bulky. I rolled them up, and the jacket nearly fit him. Certainly better than the one Jax had offered. I closed the clasps and rested my hand on Ix's shoulder.

Apollo's nephew.

Clothed in his coat.

Protected by me alone.

I needed room for grief, for tears, for my pain to spill forth.

But there was no space for that.

I stood and nodded at Jax, who turned and led us up through the hatch. He hadn't taken Apollo's bag back, so I pulled it on, hoping they would let me keep it.

A Spark of Death and Fury

Outside, the world stretched icy blue and brutally cold. The land glistened in shimmering shades of white. I didn't know where we were. There was no plant life or magic I could call on, anywhere I could reach. I released a breath that puffed out a cloud.

The boat hadn't docked at an official harbor but moored against a rocky coast where waves beat relentlessly.

Ixion slipped his fingers into mine.

We didn't have gloves. A coat alone wasn't enough. Did they mean for us to walk in this weather? I had my divinity protecting me, but Ixion didn't anymore. Cold like this could kill him.

A carriage appeared on the horizon, and its horses kicked up snow in puffs. Jax raised his chin. "A word of advice for you, Prince Hyacinth?"

Ixion squirmed in my grip, and I drew him closer to me. "Of course."

"I share this because I like you and don't wish to see your harm." He yanked his cloak tighter, gripping the top closed. "You're smart enough to know that we didn't want you harmed on this journey."

The carriage pulled up and a group of men jumped down from it. I nodded.

"Don't fight and give them a reason to hurt you or the boy. The goal is to have you both delivered whole, and they won't harm you if they don't have to."

Ixion trembled, and I tightened my grip. "Thank you."

Jax studied me for a moment before disembarking from the boat and jumping to reach the cliff. He shook hands with a man from the carriage and I tucked Apollo's bag under my coat.

Jax gestured for Ixion and me to come. Everything in me wanted to fight against them. But between the two groups, dozens of men watched us. We stood in some icy land where my magic held no sway. What could we do? Jump off the ship and swim? They'd likely catch us, plus Ixion would freeze to death. Fight? What little I knew of my powers wouldn't help me here, and I didn't know how to fight. I doubted even Apollo and his sister could get themselves out of this mess alone.

Apollo.

I promised him I'd protect Ixion.

It was some of the last words I'd said to him.

I tightened my grasp on Ixion's hand. "Come on, Ix. We have to get off the boat."

He looked up at me with his wide brown eyes as his dark curls trembled in the breeze. He trusted me. Though I'd already failed him so much.

Sailors set up boards between the deck and the cliff, and Jax secured one side while a sailor held the other. Ixion bit his lip. The water beat against the rocks and freezing spray splashed on us. Falling likely wouldn't kill him, but it would severely injure him.

"Just keep your eyes on where you're going," I said, my voice strangely calm. "You'll be fine."

Ixion frowned before stepping onto the planks and walking across. I followed him. Gods, Apollo would hate this, balancing on wooden boards that enemies held above a fall to potential death.

I had to stop thinking about Apollo.

Was that even possible? He'd said he was notched into my soul. Maybe that wasn't poetic sentiment. Perhaps it was true.

He seemed to seep into my essence, flood my thoughts, ache through my bones. I wanted him with us so desperately. I would never have him again. All that was left of us was the promise I made to care for this child.

We reached the other men where our feet sank into the

A Spark of Death and Fury

snow. Ixion wore soft moccasins, and the ice must have been seeping into the sides. Damn it. As much as I had fought against the idea of getting into the carriage with more strangers, I suddenly hoped we would soon do so. Ixion couldn't tolerate exposure to these elements dressed for a different climate.

The man who stepped forward from the horses had thick arms, which he crossed as he surveyed Ixion and me. "This is them, then?"

Jax nodded. "As agreed."

"Prince," the man said, his pale skin cool in the reflection off the snow, "I'll need to send your ring ahead of us for identification."

I stumbled back a step and pulled Ixion with me.

The man reached for his weapon, and my heart buzzed into my throat, but I didn't care. They could have anything. Except for Ixion. Except for my ring.

It was my last connection to Apollo.

The only thing I had that he'd given me.

It had passed from his hand to mine, his lips had pressed upon it, and it had glided over his form as we made love. My thumb clenched into the sun etched on one side. "No."

The man scowled. "I thought you said he'd be complaint?"

Jax cut his eyes to me, willing me to give in.

"Not my ring," I said.

Jax turned to face me, his cloak whipped out on the breeze as his breath puffed golden in the sunlight. "For the child," he whispered.

I stared at him for half a dozen heartbeats.

I wanted to scream and cry and rage and fight and tear the world apart.

How could fate demand this of me? The ring was all I

had left. Aside from Ixion, it was the only thing that truly mattered to me.

Jax's jaw tensed. He wanted me to acquiesce. He'd offered advice to try and help me. The man pulled the blade from his side. I yanked the ring off and gave it to Jax as tears bit at my eyes. He nodded, like he understood.

But how could he?

He couldn't understand what it was like to have your soul ripped from you, and then the remnants scraped away.

Ixion looked up at me, but I didn't meet his eyes.

I couldn't.

My composure sat on the edge of breaking, and he needed me to stay strong for him.

The man slid the knife back into its sheath as he accepted the ring and handed it to another, who took a horse and galloped off.

I watched the rider and his mount disappear into the creamy landscape as the first man handed Jax a bag that clinked with the sound of jangling coins. When the horse that carried my ring disappeared, I released a breath that seemed to send my soul out with it.

What more could they possibly take from me?

I ran my thumb over my naked finger.

I noticed you didn't have your rings anymore, Apollo had said when he'd given it to me. *You don't have to wear it if you don't want to.*

As if it meant nothing.

When it had meant everything to me.

That was done. Protecting Ixion was the only thing I had left.

Jax turned towards me, his voice a whisper. "I'm sorry. Look out for yourself."

I nodded but couldn't find words. It didn't matter,

A Spark of Death and Fury

anyway. What more could they take from me? My husband was gone. The ring, the only physical thing reminding me of our bond, was gone.

But I had Ixion.

His nephew.

The son of the brother he'd loved fiercely.

As I followed the man to the carriage, stepped into the back—which was crafted for storage and scarcely big enough for a grown adult and a child to fit into, and clutched Ixion against my side—my mind solidified.

My wants and needs were done.

Keeping Ixion well and protected was all that mattered.

As the carriage rattled forward over the soft banks of snow, I took a deep breath and drew Ix closer. He curled into me and clutched his fingers into my coat. He would be safe. No matter the cost to me.

8

Epiphany

I pressed my face into Father's robe and curled deeper into the chair. His room rested in shadows, stale from lack of use. An ache pulsed through me. I wanted desperately to have my family with me for another day, another hour, even.

And I wished I could tuck into Valerian's arms. He was the closest thing I had left that felt like family in the palace. But I couldn't risk sneaking around with him while the entire country looked at me. Instead, I grieved alone.

My foot rested against Father's desk, which sat neatly organized in a corner. Father had a pressed Hyacinth flower resting on a stack of parchments that bore Emrin's handwriting.

I needed to sort through the papers in this room. The advisors may need some information from them. But not today.

Being home again flooded Father and Emrin through my mind.

Their loss, the finality of it, hammered my heart.

A Spark of Death and Fury

A knock caused me to jump from the chair, my hands still clasped into the silk of Father's robe. "Please come in."

Tresson, with his kind eyes and soft waves of gray hair, walked in. "Forgive me, Your Highness, but your cousin arrives within the hour."

I sniffled and set the robe down, my fingers lingering on the fabric. "No. Of course. I shouldn't have stayed so long."

We stepped out of the room together. Staff bowed to us and scurried down the carpeted hall. "Another thing, Your Highness, the advisors wish to know the plans regarding your father and brother's funerals. Do you want to continue to delay them?"

Having to discuss my family's demise and make arrangements for them would drown me under the weight of grief. As the only person at the helm, I had no choice. I had to keep it together. "Yes. Apollo says Prince Hyacinth should arrive any day now. We'll wait for him."

"Very good, Your Highness." He bowed and turned a corner. I stopped and stared at my reflection in a mirror. My face bore splotches from crying. I pinched my cheeks and fluttered my eyelashes before smoothing out the heavy, intricately decorated fabric of my dress. I readjusted the crown, making sure no smudges took away from the gleaming jewels on it.

Today I had to represent Niria.

And I would make Father proud.

I would make our people proud.

As I stepped into the throne room, Temi and Apollo waited, wearing outfits in glittering metallics, circlets of gold leaves in their hair. I appreciated the gesture of them dressing as gods standing on our country's behalf. I pulled Temi into an embrace before walking up to the throne.

The advisors stood evenly split on either side of the

thrones with their best robes on. The entire palace prepared for this meeting with my cousin who would inherit the kingdom. A bad feeling sank into my gut as I approached Father's seat.

My steps trembled.

I took a deep breath and sat, my body rippling with heartache again. But I blinked hard and kept my posture upright, my expression schooled.

Father would be proud.

Apollo and Temi stood to the right. Temi laced her fingers together in front of her. A few of the advisors gave them wary looks. They may have lacked the glow of divinity, but the way they carried themselves, the expressions they wore, marked them. Since Apollo had brought news that the high gods would regain their powers, those who didn't respect them feared them at least.

My fingers clenched into the armrest, and I remembered sitting here not so long ago, waiting to greet Apollo and Temi. Hyacinth had sat noble and kingly in Father's seat, Emrin on his other side.

So much had changed in so little time.

The doors at the front of the room opened. A man walked in. His gaze darted to the pools of water lining the walk and then up along the tall windows until they landed on the grand chandeliers. As if he was assessing.

I stood. "Lord Demetri, it's an honor to welcome you to Niria."

He bowed, his dark curls bobbing with the motion. "The honor is mine, cousin." His eyes swept over the dozen individuals in the room. "I must say, I was more than surprised when I received the missive."

I swallowed.

The letter explaining that two of the people I loved dearest in the world had died. He spoke of it so casually.

A Spark of Death and Fury

Of course, he didn't know them well. I couldn't expect him to feel the way I did.

"Please let me introduce you to our royal advisors, who will help during this time of transition."

Demetri nodded to the men, his gaze lingering on Apollo and Temi. "I expected more of a welcome, were I to be honest." He shifted back to me, his lips twisting.

"Pardon me?"

"Well… I'm the king, aren't I? You think there'd be more fanfare."

The advisors shifted so that their robes crinkled and it echoed in the beat of silence that followed Demetri's remark. My teeth clinked together and I straightened. "You are to be the king in six months' time; once the period of grieving for my father and brother"— I rolled my shoulders back despite my shaking voice—"has passed."

Demetri frowned and crossed his arms. "Am I to take the orders of a woman in the interim?" Temi hissed and took a step forward, but Apollo caught her arm, stalling her steps. Demetri shifted towards the first advisor to my left, Joden.

Joden eyed him before speaking. "You'll find that we honor protocol and the laws here in Niria, my lord. And you can use the interim period to learn the work required to lead the country."

"Work?"

Joden looked like he might speak again, but I cut in. This was my audience. "Yes. The role of king is a laborious job, as there is much to do directing the well-being of an entire country."

Demetri's mouth gaped, and he sputtered as he gestured to the men, causing the ruffles along his sleeve to ripple. "For what purpose do we have advisors if the king must do the labor?"

"They are here to provide input on their areas of expertise. We are blessed to have intelligent, hardworking, and thoughtful advisors, at that." The men raised their chins. "But decisions rests on the king's shoulders. The fate of traders, the arts, religion, politics, wars, and much more will be yours to direct, Lord Demetri."

He looked over his shoulder as if he could walk out of the room. "I... I must say, this is more than I expected."

A sick feeling pooled in my gut. What had he expected? For my family's tragedy to hand him a palace and a life of luxury with no work? I wanted to stomp my foot and scream. An outburst wasn't something I could afford as the current leader of our country. "Allow some of our attendants to show you to a room so you can rest after your journey and have a chance to assimilate."

He nodded and stepped out. Once his echoing footsteps quieted, everyone broke their positions and huddled in the center near the thrones.

"This is a disaster," Fen, the court historian, said.

"He's young and hasn't grown up for this." Dune crossed his arms. "But I agree. He doesn't inspire confidence."

Apollo and Temi exchanged a look.

"Well spoken, Princess." Asher inclined his head to me. I nodded back.

Dune's dark eyes glimmered in the light spilling in from the high windows. "We should reconsider the precedent of Prince Hyacinth taking the throne. He should arrive any day now." Dune looked at Apollo, who inclined his head, though his eyebrows pinched. Cyn was behind schedule, and it left a current of anxiety running through us. "We've never considered a deity to rule before, of course, but he is a prince of our nation first. King Magnes raised him for this role, and he's an honorable leader."

Fen clicked his tongue. "Prince Emrin made it clear that Hyacinth no longer wished to maintain his role and intended to live with Lord Apollo separate from the palace." Apollo crossed his arms. "And I cannot imagine a reality where the people accept us handing the kingdom over to a deity, regardless of who he was in his mortal life. We need to consider alternatives."

Joden scowled. "If Lord Demetri is the alternative, I'd prefer a god leading part-time myself."

"How can we legally crown a god as king?" Fen spread his hands out. "What kind of precedent does that create? And, further, no one has heard from Prince Hyacinth. There's a chance he might not return." Apollo and I both winced. "Forgive me, Your Highness. I understand what a difficult time you've had lately, but for the sake of the country, we need to consider all possibilities."

"Of course, Lord Fen. Niria first."

"In the likely scenario that Prince Hyacinth isn't able to rule, we must start training Demetri at once. He won't have the decades of education our princes had."

Asher's jaw worked. "Or the mentorship under a ruler like King Magnes."

The group bowed their heads, and my heart lurched into my throat, but I fisted my hands. "We don't have to ordain anyone for six months. There's a grace period. We can use that to learn more about Demetri. Perhaps he started on a poor foot. We all know how tiring travel is."

Many members in the circle hummed their agreement.

"Why can't Princess Epiphany take over?" Temi said, and I gasped.

Dune laughed. "Well…" He waved to me. "She's a…"

"Incredibly competent leader who is currently holding

this meeting together, led the country's direction during the war, and has the benefit of having grown up under the tutelage of her father with the same education as both of her brothers?"

The group sat in stunned silence for a moment before Dune turned to Asher. "Explain to Artemis why that isn't a possibility."

Asher shrugged. "I actually think it's a good idea, as many of Artemis' plans are."

Temi grinned, but I spoke up as the reflection of my dress rippled in the tiles as I shifted. "It's a gracious nomination. But Lord Fen has a point. It's not how the laws are written."

Temi's gaze bore into mine, a spark of a challenge in her eyes. I'd seen that look plenty of times to know whatever was about to come out of her mouth would push me out of my comfort zone. She swept braids behind her shoulder. "Then change the laws. You"—she pointed at the advisors—"all just considered doing so to allow a god to become king. Why is it more ridiculous to give the authority to a competent, hardworking woman who loves this country and was raised by the leader you respected?"

Apollo shrugged like he agreed, but I struggled to form words. The expressions on the men in the room varied from considering to angry.

"This is absurd," Dune said.

"Is it?" Asher scoffed. "We must consider what is best for this country."

"And you think it's a woman leading?"

Asher, who still bore the faint line of a scar along his cheek from a recent injury in battle, paused before speaking. "Many of you know that after my father died in service to our nation, it was my mother alone who raised me. I've never held to the belief that women are inherently weak."

Joden scowled at me. His face probably said all he needed to. But he gave his head a shake. "Artemis has made a valid point. Princess Epiphany, despite her shortcomings"—I clenched my teeth—"was cultivated alongside her brothers with the same education and she proved herself competent during the war." He eyed me as if he wasn't certain if that was fully true. "Perhaps she could act as an intermediary until a male heir is born."

Temi's lips parted like she intended to speak, but I cut her off and gave her a warning glance. These men's minds were already stretching a great deal. Whatever she had to say would shove them off the cliff.

Dune leaned in with a jerk, his dark robe rippling around his shoulder. "Even if the princess married tonight and had a child within the year, it would be decades before we could have her son prepared to sit on the throne."

Temi looked prepared to murder them all, but I took a deep breath. "Lord Dune, I understand Niria must come first. However, I ask that you not discuss my marriage or childbearing as if it is solely a political move."

A few others seemed ready to speak, but Asher pressed his hands together. "We should all take a step back and think through things before any of us lose our ability to bring our best to this conversation. In the meantime,"—he gestured to me—"we can consider what position the princess may hold and what is best for Niria."

Everyone's eyes pinned on me.

The expressions varied so much it left me dizzy. A few of the men in the room thought I could do this. They believed I could become a queen. A queen ruling a kingdom by herself. Who had ever heard of such a thing?

Temi gave me a subtle nod. She believed I could do it

—thought I should.

"Wise words, Lord Asher," I said. "We're all under a great deal of pressure. And, as I said, we have a grace period. Let's take time to consider all our options and get to know Lord Demetri better before we discuss major changes."

The tension broke. Some men scowled, others pulled at their beards or whispered to each other. They bowed to me and dispersed out of the room. As soon as they had cleared out, Apollo leaving with them, I turned on Temi. "What was that?"

She pulled the golden circlet out of her hair. "What?"

"Nominating me to run this country?"

She lifted her face, her lips pursed. "I was just thinking of your father and if he was here, what he would want. Your cousin"—she waved to the door he had exited through—"cannot do this job."

"And I can?"

"Yes. You can."

I swallowed at a knot in my throat, and she drew an arm around me. I melted against her, resting my head against her chest

That anxious feeling didn't leave later as I walked into the stables, passed by Meadow who nickered at me, and approached Valerian. He was working alongside another man, but I couldn't put off speaking to him. "May I have a moment, please?"

Valerian nodded towards the stableman, who bowed to me before exiting. As soon as he disappeared, Val shifted to face me. "What's wrong?"

I pressed my hand over my stomach. I must have tied the dress too tight because suddenly I couldn't breathe. "Val, something has happened."

"What is it?"

"I may have been nominated to become the next leader of Niria."

He froze for a moment, his dark hair plastered against his forehead with sweat. His gaze darted around the stalls to the horses, who tossed their manes and huffed hot breaths. "That's good, Pip."

"You think so?"

"Of course." The emerald of his eyes sparked with a new energy when he lifted his face. "There are murmurings of unhappiness over this cousin of yours taking over. People loved your father." He gripped the stall beside him. "They trusted him. There's disquiet with losing your family amid all this chaos."

"And you think the people would accept a woman as a leader?"

Valerian took a deep breath and rolled his head towards his shoulder. "Maybe. There would be some unhappiness over it, certainly." He met my gaze again. "But you could turn their opinions. I know it."

I twisted my fingers together and loosed them to brush a piece of hay off my skirt. The heavy fabric pulled on me. If I became a queen, this would be my whole life.

But what of Niria?

"Why does everyone else seem to think I can do this, but I don't?"

Val chuckled and placed his hands behind his back, as if he had to resist the urge to pull me against him. How I wished he could. But someone could walk in at any moment and with everything so precarious we had to be more careful than ever. "Because we all see how capable you are. You just need to catch up."

I bit my lip and considered that.

And I had thought I'd stumbled into a mess during the war.

9

Apollo

I paced by the open door of the sitting room, waiting for the runner who reported twice daily on the ships that made it to port. I fidgeted with the fabric of my jacket. The palace's tailor had designed it for me. It wasn't something I'd choose for myself, but having opinions about clothing was low on my list of priorities. Temi lifted her gaze to me, then returned it to the scroll in her lap. Orion sprawled out on a settee across from her.

I'd never seen this compact sitting room before with its burgundy furniture and unremarkable paintings.

Perhaps that was the point.

Memories didn't linger here like in the rest of the palace. Ghosts didn't sit in the corners, waiting to whisper things.

I'd attended Delon's funeral the day before, shaking hands with his father and offering my condolences to his mother. My own goodbye was later, on a rooftop overlooking the city, a mug of ale and a stack of cards in hand.

"You promised not to do anything stupid or dangerous," I'd said to the sun-streaked sky. "But Temi told me you died being noble, godsdamn you." Tears slipped over my cheeks, but I pressed the pile of cards down and left them to flutter out in the wind.

The runner stepped in and bowed, breaking into my thoughts. "Lord Apollo."

"Well?"

He shook his head. "I'm sorry, my lord, but no new boats have docked today."

I stared at the boy, anger coursing through me, and his eyes widened before I cleared my throat. "Thank you."

"Of course, my lord." He inclined his head and exited the room.

Damn it. Where the hell were Hyacinth and Ixion? It had been weeks since they'd left, and they should have arrived by this point. The boat couldn't have had troubles, could it? Or maybe something had gone wrong with him getting aboard a ship. Could he still be on the continent, traveling by land? Fuck. I didn't even know where to look.

I hadn't been able to tap into my powers to travel since Nedia had left. Even if I could, I wasn't sure where to go. It wasn't like I had the ability to locate Hyacinth even if my powers were at their full strength. Chances were I'd leave, and they'd arrive. Luckily, I didn't have to make that decision as I couldn't travel at all. The magic felt impossible to reach.

"Interested in a game, Apollo?" Orion stood, stretched, and pulled a stack of cards from his bag.

The bad feeling deepened. "I don't play cards."

Temi frowned at me but kept her thoughts to herself. "Dice, then?"

I prepared to turn him down again as Temi rose. "Join us. It's a chance to take your mind off things for a while."

I'd have said no to anyone other than Temi. I walked over to a table by a window that looked down on the gardens. A pear tree's emerald leaves tangled together and bowed over a bed of flowers that stretched flush with color.

Temi joined me as Orion set a cup and half a dozen dice onto the table. "I don't believe any of us"—he gestured between the three of us—"are designed for this much idleness."

"I can't leave until I get word on Hyacinth."

Temi gripped my arm. "Of course. Once he returns, we can discuss what our next step should be with this information you got in the desert."

Orion looked up at Temi. "Are you joining us in the game as well? It's been a few weeks since I've bested you at something."

Her grip stiffened. "You've done no such thing ever."

He grinned. "Knives."

"No."

"Weaponry in general."

"Absolutely not."

"Horseback riding."

She froze and her mouth gaped. "Maybe it's time for you to return to your troops, Commander."

He cocked up an eyebrow. "Maybe I will."

"Maybe you should."

Orion scoffed, rolled his eyes, and gave the cup a rattle. The dice spilled out and he snatched a few up to toss them back in. I wasn't sure what the relationship between the two of them was, but Temi trusted him, and I didn't need more information than that. If he was trustworthy in her eyes, then I liked him on principle.

Temi licked her lips. "I've been practicing calling my magic again." Orion handed me the cup, and I gave it a shake, letting the dice clatter across the wood. "It's much more challenging than it was before."

I nodded as I scooped all six dice into my hands.

A shitty roll.

My luck.

I threw them out again and scoffed as another poor set landed on the table.

Temi leaned closer to me. "We need to exercise those powers if we're to gain the spark."

I handed Orion the cup. "I'm not going to attempt to regain the spark."

Temi jerked towards me, and her braids slipped over her shoulder. "What?"

I closed my eyes, taking in a breath filled with the smells of the polishing oils and floral scents of the room. "Nedia and Clothos have both said I would have to kill others who had ambitions for it themselves." I pushed my chair away from the table, stretching my legs out under it. "I won't do it."

Temi frowned. "Why?"

"Because..." I thrust my hands out, smacking one into a vase that I steadied before turning back to her. "I have always seen myself as a killer, a divine set on destruction. Hyacinth sees me differently, and I want to live up to that. I won't kill to gain something."

Temi gestured to Orion. "We both struggled with that during the war." Orion nodded his head to the side in agreement. "I promise you I take no pleasure in killing, however we must gain the spark. I agree with Nedia's perspective on divinity. It would be a service not only to the gods, but mortals as well. Haven't you always cared about that?"

"Of course I have, but..." I huffed a breath. "I won't be a murderer anymore. Not for any cause."

"Not even if it achieves the purpose we've spent our whole lives fighting for? Accomplishes the promise you made to Hyacinth?"

I gritted my teeth. "I don't expect you to understand. You're better than me and always have been. If you killed someone, it was for a damn good reason. I've always had some of my father within me, and I'm afraid that if I give into it, it will consume me. I'll become what I hate."

Temi frowned. "You can choose to do what is right regardless of the circumstances. You define who you are. I've told you this your whole life. And this isn't as black and white as you want to make it. You don't fulfill one prophecy and then you're done for life. You have to choose who you're going to be every day."

I closed my eyes. Temi didn't understand and I wasn't sure I could help her to. "You know the destruction and heartache Zeus wrought on mortals. You didn't see what I've seen, though. The way he slaughtered gods to maintain his role as the high god. He killed"—my voice choked—"his entire family for that purpose, and I will not retrace his footsteps." They both stared at me, but I didn't care. "I'm going to be the man Hyacinth sees me as. Now, excuse me, I'll go ask if they have any more news from the docks."

Temi huffed in frustration and slapped her arms against her chair. As I stepped out of the door, Orion chuckled. "He's as stubborn as you are."

"Oh, shut up."

His warm laughter trailed me as I kept moving.

They couldn't understand. They hadn't traveled with me and Cyn. They didn't know how many times he talked me down from doing things that would have weighed on my conscience for life. Abandoning the girl on the road, raising my bow to slaughter a group of human mercenaries who posed no immediate danger, threatening the god. I would have killed him without hesitation if he hadn't vowed not to go to my father.

A Spark of Death and Fury

Every single time, Hyacinth had looked at me with love in his eyes.

He'd seen more than the vengeful god in me.

He saw good.

And, damn it, I could be that for him.

I turned down a hall past a group of attendants who bowed to me and hurried off. With the way I swept down the carpets, I probably terrified them. A sigh built within me.

I was tired of being terrifying. What I wanted was to be the man Hyacinth believed I was.

But I needed him and Ixion here.

Where the hell were they?

They should have arrived by now.

I turned another corner and realized where I had walked to. Not the attendants' offices. Despite what I said to Temi, there was no point in asking about more ships. They wouldn't have news.

I opened the door and stepped inside.

A small bed sat beneath a row of massive windows that held a view of the north side of the gardens. Roses scrambled up the stone outside of the palace, some of their blooms draping against the windowpanes. The stuffed rabbit Temi contributed leaned against a pillow, and a wooden chariot was tucked against a wardrobe in the corner. Epiphany had told me the toy belonged to Hyacinth as a child.

The chamber stretched open and fresh and carefully prepared with little touches from those in the palace who cared about Cyn and me.

A room for Ixion.

Who should be here.

I dropped to the bed, clamped my hands together, and bowed my head.

Something wasn't right.

I knew it as intimately as the sun's movements that colored the sky in deepening peaches. As much as I knew the steady beat of Hyacinth's footsteps and the spread of his smile when his lips split with laughter.

Gods, what had gone wrong?

They'd made it to the docks.

That was the deal. He would arrive and then call on Temi to shift the moon.

What had transpired beyond that? I had to go look for him. He might arrive right as I left and with my magic scarcely tangible, no one could summon me to make me aware. It made sense to wait at the palace, but not having information about what had happened to them was like an itch beneath my skin that I couldn't reach.

I fell against the bed and closed my eyes.

After an hour, I rose, straightened the blankets, and walked out. Pacing through the halls made the staff nervous and I felt bad for that. I couldn't help it, though. I could hardly sit still with Cyn and Ix out in the world somewhere. The gardens brought back too many memories to be a sanctuary. More ghosts haunted me there. Ares had stood in those gardens once and told me he loved me. He'd seen good in me too, even before Hyacinth had. I'd vowed to protect his son. When I'd watched Zeus rip his soul from him, grief had pulsed through me. But I knew it wouldn't last long. I assumed I would die, and Hyacinth would take Ixion safely home. Now here I was in this palace, and Cyn and Ixion were somewhere in the world alone. It made me so miserable I felt nauseous with it.

Temi walked up. "There you are."

I sighed. "I'm sorry about earlier."

"I am too."

"I'm just so worried about them."

A Spark of Death and Fury

She pulled me into her arms and hugged me so tight it sucked the breath from me. "I know."

For several minutes we held each other, then I drew back to turn towards the window. The mausoleum of the palace grounds sat in the distance, a gray dot on a hill shrouded by trees. The King and Emrin's funerals would soon take place. It would crush Hyacinth. I needed him to arrive here safely, so I could hold him in my arms, share in his grief, and love him fiercely through it.

I tucked my hands behind my back. "If you wish for me to practice my magic more, I will."

Temi shifted her weight to her other foot. "Well, it doesn't hurt anyone to work on regaining your powers. It might make use of the time while you wait."

"You're right. I'll do it."

She leaned in closer to the window, her breath fogged the glass, and her gaze swept over the heavens and the waxing moon that already rested in the pink of the early evening sky. Then she jerked back, and her muscles tensed. I followed her gaze, to the deity that stood outside, skimming his eyes around. They landed on us, and he grinned before disappearing and then reappearing in the hallway before us. "A letter for you, Apollo."

Temi pulled a blade from her belt, but I accepted the letter, nearly yanking it from the god's hand and flipped the parchment over. The god disappeared again before we could ask questions. A wax seal imprinted with curls held the parcel closed. The wind gods. I slid my finger under it. A ring fell, hitting the tile with a clink, clink, clink, and rolled across the floor.

Temi grabbed it and handed it to me.

The green of the stone glimmered in the soft light.

The etchings of the sun and the flower had dirt caked in them.

Hyacinth.

I clutched it in my palm until it ached and lifted the letter.

IF YOU WANT THEM, *come and get them. -Zephyrus.*

COLDNESS SLIPPED DOWN MY LIMBS. Ice I'd never felt before. Like the sun had died, and I stood fully in its absence. My hand trembled, and the paper shook with it.

No.

My mind had only that word. Everything else was just a roar, my entire body screaming. Of anything that could have happened to them, not Zephyrus. Why? He'd already killed Hyacinth. How did he even find them?

Temi's brow furrowed.

She had questions, but I couldn't form words.

My fingers curled slowly, swallowing the paper until it scrunched into a ball.

I turned and bolted down the hallway.

"Where are you going?" Temi said, running after me.

"He took them."

"Who?"

"Zephyrus took Hyacinth and Ixion."

She gasped and stopped walking for a heartbeat, then jogged to catch up with me. "Wait. Where are you heading?"

I ceased moving and turned to face her. "I'm going to the Palace of the Four Winds. Zephyrus will regret the moment he crossed me."

"Apollo, every god that's ever had a desire for power will hunt you if you're traveling and they discover you.

A Spark of Death and Fury

You've only been safe here because no one knows you're here presently. That's the point I was making earlier."

"Then I will kill them. Every single one. I'll litter my path with the blood of the gods."

"I thought you didn't want to kill? You didn't want to be like that?"

Heat coursed over my skin, magic skittered to the surface without me calling for it, and my words came as barely a whisper. "Yes, because Hyacinth saw me as something better. He believed in that and said he'd be my compass." I growled. "But Zephyrus took him. I will coat this continent in blood without hesitation if I must to get him back. Zephyrus wants me to face him, then I will fucking face him."

Temi sucked in a breath, her eyes growing glassy, then her posture straightened. "I'm coming with you."

I considered that. It would be dangerous. There was no point in fighting her if she set her mind to something, however. I doubted I could magically travel again without Nedia's guidance or my full powers. "Very well. I leave before the moon sets."

"All right. Don't go without me, Apollo, please."

For just a moment, the fury and worry washed away from me, and I saw my younger sister with wide eyes and pursed lips looking up at me. I cupped her cheek with my hand. "I won't, Temi. You have my word."

She nodded and turned down the hall.

10

Hyacinth

The carriage rumbled along, horses' hooves trundling into snow. Ixion rubbed his sleepy eyes and sat up. Days of travel over an icy expanse, the men stopping only for Ix and I to eat, left me sore and more anxious than ever.

Magic fizzed through my blood and fluttered through my heart.

Because I could travel out of this situation.

I could return to my palace in a breath.

But I couldn't take Ixion.

Divine powers didn't work like that.

He ran his fingers through the tangles of his hair, and I pulled a comb out of Apollo's bag and gestured for him to sit closer to me. He moved over, and I brushed through his curls, starting at the ends, using my other hand to keep it from pulling. He winced anyway.

"I hate having curly hair," he grumbled.

"Do you?"

"It always gets knots, and they hurt."

I hummed a reply and tried to slow down, pulling the strands of his hair more gingerly.

"Does Apollo like having curly hair?"

My hands stilled. "What?"

He looked back over his shoulder. "Your husband. He has curls like mine." He patted his head. "Maybe thicker. Does he get tangles?"

Not anymore.

Grief swelled in my chest again, and I swallowed it back. I thought of Apollo's fingers combing through his curls, the same hands brushing over my hair, down my cheeks, over my chest. My nose flared but I sucked the emotions back hard.

This burden didn't belong to Ixion.

"He likes to keep his hair long, so I'd say this part of it must not bother him too much."

Gods know he'd complain about it if it did. I smiled at that.

"My hair has grown." Ixion pulled a strand and released it so that it bounced against his forehead.

"Has it?"

"I don't ever remember that happening." He slid a lock between his fingers. His curls did seem to drape closer to his eyebrows than before. He was growing. Zeus' curse must have broken. Did that mean Zeus had died? Or had he just lost his connection to his magic when Apollo did whatever he'd done with the sun?

The carriage creaked to a stop and the horses snorted.

Valerian would have opinions on how hard they had run the creatures with so little rest. I wondered about my friends and family as well—Val and Pip, Father and Emrin. What did their lives look like during the war and what happened to them all now? How I wished I could stand at their side and help them with whatever reality the country faced. I longed to spend an afternoon with my siblings, try to make things right with Emrin, and discuss things with Father, hear his warm voice.

First, I had to get us out of this predicament.

The doors swung open, and I tugged Apollo's bag on before grasping Ixion's hand. We stepped out, the ice of the wind bitter cold and stinging my bare cheeks. Ix huddled against me, tucking under my coat, and I wrapped an arm around him.

Then my heart lurched.

The snow was deeper than the last time I'd been here, the sun dimmer somehow.

But I knew where we were.

The Palace of the Four Winds glimmered, its towers piercing the blue sky. I took a step back.

No.

No… not Zephyrus.

He'd already killed me.

He had stolen my life and place and family from me.

Now he had Ixion and me in his grips.

One of the men prodded me in the back with the butt of his knife, and I took a step forward, my feet sinking into the snow. Then I stopped again. I would not go into that palace. I had to have some power that would be useful here.

I pulled Ixion in closer, and he squeaked but I didn't loosen my grip. I leaned into my powers as deeply as I ever had, calling on the bowels of the earth, the sleeping plants that lay there, any limb or vine or plant that might heed my call.

The ground rumbled, vibrating.

Another jab in my back. "Move."

I would not.

The doors to the palace opened.

Zephyrus stepped out, his pale hair fluttering in the

breeze, his wings pulled in tight, his crystal eyes narrowed to slits. "I would not do that if I were you, Hyacinth."

I took another step back. Sweat broke out on my forehead from the effort. If I could push hard enough, I could rip this world apart if need be. I could get us free.

Zephyrus nodded to one of the men who'd captured us. He lunged forward and knocked Ixion and me into the snow. Ix screamed, and the man ripped him from my arms, yanked his knife around, and pierced it into the tender flesh of his throat.

Ixion's brown eyes welled up, and tears trailed his cheeks. "Cyn," he said, his voice wobbling.

I dropped the connection to my powers.

I would hand them over forever, give up my divinity, before I'd allow him to come to harm.

"Very good." Zephyrus walked over. "Listen to me. I will hurt this child." Fury filled his expression. His voice dropped to a hush of a sound, a wind that promised devastating storms. "Not kill him quickly. But hurt him. Slowly. Do I make myself perfectly clear?"

I swallowed as my filthy coat rippled in the breeze. "Yes."

"Do you doubt I would do so?"

I studied him.

The man I'd slept with.

Manipulated.

Aligned with.

The man who had betrayed me. Killed me. He was prepared to do much worse, now. And, like me, he was a low deity. He still had his powers.

Did I doubt he would or could do worse?

"No."

"Good. Then you will follow me and not pull any other

bullshit. Every misstep you make will come out of the child's flesh. Do you understand me?"

I clenched my fingers into fists. I longed to tear him apart. I would gladly die again if I could take Zephyrus with me. But Ixion... He stood a few dozen feet from us, trembling in the man's arms as the blade reflected the crystal of the world.

"Why?" I said to Zephyrus.

He took a step closer to me, his breath warming my cheek. "Oh, Hyacinth." He swept his eyes down me. "You and Apollo took everything from me." The feathers on his wings ruffled in a breeze, as if his emotions urged his magic forth. "I will admit killing you was impulsive. I regretted it because"—he leaned in closer, his arm brushing mine, and I struggled against pulling away—"better retribution would be to hold you and watch as I destroyed your life piece by piece. But the Fates blessed me. I get a second chance."

"You've already killed me. You've had your vengeance. Let the boy go. He's only a child."

Zephyrus grinned. "Oh no, Prince." He spat the word. "I intend to keep him while I use you to achieve my purposes. The spark you tried to steal from me shall be mine, and I'll have the pleasure of wrecking everything you care about in the process."

My heart thundered. I felt the urge to send a warning to my father for Niria. Alongside fear, another emotion trickled through me. For the first time since the sky had exploded, I was grateful Apollo was gone. Zephyrus couldn't hurt him, at least.

Zephyrus waved to the man holding Ixion, and he lowered the knife but kept his grip around the child's arm. "Imagine my surprise," Zephyrus said, "when those I'd set to monitor Apollo..." He clenched his teeth as he snarled.

A Spark of Death and Fury

"Boring Apollo who did nothing day after day but sit on his throne and guard your kingdom like some sort of watchdog. Until one day my informants tell me his mortal prince had returned. And then, better news, that you both traveled to destroy Zeus."

I shivered as snow slipped against my ankles but couldn't break his gaze. "It was you who followed us in Danari."

"Oh, yes." His eyes sharpened. "The wind hears everything, Prince. It wasn't like you two were very subtle. Luckily, Apollo succeeded in killing his father." I sucked in a breath. I'd longed for any news of my husband, of his ill-fated journey, and what might have happened to him. He'd brought down his father. Apollo had died but achieved his goal. That took a drop of the sting out of it. Zephyrus scoffed. "And that bastard god of war went down with Zeus, too."

I turned to face Ixion, but he must have stood too far away to hear Zephyrus' cruel words. Ares was dead if what Zephyrus said was true. Apollo would be heartbroken. But he was gone, too.

Maybe it was a mercy. He avoided suffering and pain and hardships. I could feel gratitude for his sake while still missing him desperately and wishing he was there.

Zephyrus' feet crunched into the snow. His lips brushed my ear as he whispered, and I cringed. "And watching you suffer as I tear apart your entire life and achieve my purposes will be the highlight of my existence. Far better than fucking you was."

Disgust rippled over me, like salt that lingered after a dip in the sea. "What do your brothers think of this plan?"

Zephyrus stared at me, and a cruel smile slipped up on his face. "They did not approve. You were not the last to try to subvert me, but I brought that to an end."

My breath puffed into the air. "You killed your brothers?"

"I did. So, think, Prince. Do you doubt I will hurt you or this child if you get in the way of my plans?"

My nose flared, but I didn't respond.

"Now, will you behave yourself, so we don't have to harm the boy?"

My eyes darted to Ixion again who whimpered, his large eyes fixed on me.

"If you do not harm the child, then yes."

Zephyrus pasted on a fake smile and swept his arms out before raising his voice so the others could hear. "Please show our guests to their room. The prince has given me his word to abide by our rules."

He strode back to the palace, and his jacket whipped out behind him.

Everything in me wanted to fight. To run behind him and pull him down. To strangle him.

I'd always told Apollo I didn't believe in killing.

That we were better than Zephyrus.

I didn't care anymore. I would kill him without hesitation.

Except Ixion would suffer.

I walked over to Ix and took his hand. The soft pillows of his fingers squeezed mine. We followed a man into the palace and up a set of steps into a bedroom. Inside, a fireplace crackled with warmth and two large beds lay covered with rich fabrics. The only difference from a royal guest suite were the bars covering the windows. Saving the last fact, the room was much like the one I'd stayed in during my last visit to the Palace of the Four Winds. The room I'd made love to Apollo in and held him as he slept in my arms.

A Spark of Death and Fury

I swallowed as the man gestured to another door. "A washroom is to your left. Guards are posted at the exit."

He slammed the door, and I dropped on my knee in front of Ixion. "Are you okay?"

"I don't know," he whispered. "I'm... I'm not brave like you."

I'm not brave, I wanted to say. *I'm just angry.*

I brushed my fingers through the silk of his hair. "You were very brave out there. I bet a lot of grown men would have wet themselves with a knife at their throat."

He stared at me before a smile peeled up his lips. "Have you seen that before?"

No, because it isn't normal to see people held at knifepoint. Gods, what kind of childhood was Ixion having? I had to find a way to get us out of here.

"Why don't you get washed up?"

Ixion nodded and walked to the doorway but then looked back at me. "Would you stand at the door? I feel afraid."

I stared at him. At that clever, curious, sweet child who didn't deserve this. "I will."

Later, once we'd both cleaned up and received dinner, I tucked Ixion into bed, but he sat back up. "Will you please sleep with me?"

"Of course," I whispered and eased onto the bed beside him. He curled into a ball, pulled his fists against his chest, and rested his head on the crook of my shoulder. My heart melted. As much as I wanted to destroy Zephyrus, I couldn't. For Ix's sake. I was the only person he had in the world.

The next morning, so early the light outside had scarcely changed to navy, the door barged open, and I woke with a startle. Zephyrus walked in, shadowed by four men. "Wake the child."

"Why?"

Ixion sat up, his hair tousled and eyes bleary.

"This way," Zephyrus said, gesturing with his head to armchairs in front of the fireplace. Unease swept through me, but I nodded. Ixion and I walked over with him. Zephyrus patted the chair beside him, and Ixion looked at me before accepting it. "My source tells me that as Ares' son you are likely to inherit his role now that he's dead."

Ixion flinched. "My father is dead?"

I hissed through my teeth at Zephyrus' callousness, but he ignored me as he continued speaking. "You need to start learning your magic again. We have need of your powers."

"The high gods have fallen," I said.

Zephyrus looked up at me. "They will rise again. The child must lean into his powers before too many regain their magic."

Ixion trembled and leaned back against the chair. "I don't know my magic. I was forbidden to use it."

Zephyrus stared at him like he would rip his heart out if he could possess his body. I gripped the back of Ix's chair, anxiety coursing through me. "Sometimes," Zephyrus said, "intense feelings help." He pulled his arm back and slapped Ixion hard enough to knock him against the chair and bring a slash of color to Ix's face as he screamed.

My heart stopped pounding.

Fury, like I'd never felt before whipped through me.

I jumped on Zephyrus and knocked him to the ground. The chair fell with a clatter. I clenched my fingers into his face and tore flesh away. Ixion cried out again. Zephyrus growled and flipped me over, pulled back, and punched hard. My nose crunched, the impact blinding my vision for a moment as blood poured down my chin.

Other men in the room jumped forward and secured

Ixion who shrieked and kicked against them as he reached for me. Two yanked me up by the shoulders.

Zephyrus rose and wiped his hand over his cheeks. "You said," he whispered, "that you wouldn't pull any bullshit like this."

"And you said you wouldn't hurt the child."

The flickering oranges of the fire rippled over his features. "Plans have changed. The child's magic has purposes for me."

"He may not have even inherited his father's magic. You can't know that."

"There's one way to find out."

"You will not touch him again," I roared.

He rubbed his cheek against his tunic, the blood sopping into the fabric. "Or what, Prince? Have you considered that you're far outnumbered? We will kill you."

I didn't so much as blink. "If you wanted me dead, you would have already killed me. Which means you have a plan for me. You need me alive."

Zephyrus glared at me, and his fingers curled into fists. Then he sneered. "I need you breathing. Nothing more. Keep that in mind." He slammed his shoulder into mine and knocked me against the men who held me. "And have that child work on his powers or I will do so myself."

He turned and strode out of the room, his group following him. I wiped blood off my chin as I scrambled towards Ixion. "How badly are you hurt, Ix?"

He wept as he burrowed into the cushion of the chair. He turned to face me. An angry crimson mark marred half his face. I stopped a breath mid inhale and brushed curls behind his ears. "There's some medicine in Apollo's bag that will take the sting out."

I retrieved it, unscrewed the jar, and brushed it over Ixion's cheek.

My hands shook from anger, from a desire to harm Zephyrus.

I forced a deep breath to slow my heart.

"Thank you, Papa," Ixion whispered.

My arm froze. "Ixion, you know I'm not your father, don't you?"

Ixion looked at me from beneath his curls, his brown eyes still wet with tears. "Ares is my father. But Nanny Essie told me my Papa was who looked out for me and kept me safe from the bad gods who might want to hurt me." He sniffled and clamped his small hand around mine. "That's what you're trying to do, isn't it?"

I stared at him. "I am."

"Then you're my Papa, right?"

"I…" My hands trembled again but not from anger. He looked at me like his hope rested on my response, and I swallowed. "Of course, Ix. And I'll keep you safe."

He hugged me, and I wrapped my arms around him.

Everything solidified for me.

Zephyrus lacked a moral compass and he'd stop at nothing for his purposes. Ixion had no powers. The shimmer of magic has disappeared from around him. I wasn't even sure I believed the high gods powers would return. But Zephyrus did. And If slapping Ixion across his face was his gentlest attempt of drawing those powers, I wouldn't allow him to take it any further. It had already passed a line it never should have crossed.

I squeezed Ixion tighter as the fire crackled beyond us.

I had never known if I would be a father, but this child saw me as one. And I knew about good fathers. I had one of the best. A good father would not allow his child to suffer when he could do something to prevent it.

"He won't hurt you again, Ix," I said.

The magic of my divinity ripped off me, unwinding

and untangling, shielding him. As it had once done for Apollo as we tumbled through this dark world. We'd tried so many different variations with the shield and I knew how to make Ixion disappear. It didn't solve every problem. It was temporary, at best. Zephyrus had a reason to hold us, though. Which meant someone was likely coming for us. The shield could protect Ixion until help arrived, at least.

Even if it left me as weak and vulnerable as a mortal.

"You're safe, now," I said, my voice shaking.

"Thank you, Papa."

Tears bit at my eyes as I held him close to me and silently promised that I would keep my word to him.

No matter the cost.

11

Artemis

Epiphany pressed her hand over her mouth. It trembled before she pulled it away. "Does he intend to hurt him? I mean, Hyacinth can die, can't he?"

The advisors studied me, concern painted over their features. Tapestries behind them sat dull in the light of candles and oil lamps.

"He could, yes. But I don't believe Zephyrus would go through the trouble of capturing him and luring Apollo with them both if he intended to kill them before Apollo arrived. He wants to force my brother to move against him. I believe he'll keep Hyacinth alive to goad Apollo." I hesitated for a moment. Apollo had already left the palace and waited for me outside the gates. He'd attempted using his magic to travel again and failed. I was glad for that. I didn't want him going alone in his state. Apollo and I could take on Zephyrus, but what if he harmed or killed Hyacinth or Ixion before we could rescue them? I shuddered. It was a loss none of us could endure. That I was sure of. "We'll get them both and return them safely to Niria." If I had to die trying.

A Spark of Death and Fury

Epiphany straightened. "There's no one else I would trust. Would you want military support?"

I shook my head. "Mortals can't stand against gods. It would be a slaughter. We'll bring him home, I swear."

I just hoped it wouldn't be for a funeral.

"Very well," Epiphany said, and she cleared her throat. "Joden." The advisor turned his sharp profile towards her. "We'll move forward the timeline for King Magnes and Prince Emrin's funerals. As much as I would like to wait, the country deserves to mourn and to see we'll carry on beyond this."

Joden studied her for a moment, a spark of admiration in his eyes, before bowing. "Very good, Your Highness."

The other advisors nodded and turned out of the room.

Epiphany's curls draped over her gown as she clasped my fingers. "Please be careful."

"I will."

I shifted to move, but she tightened her grip. "I'm serious, Temi. Please. You... you mean everything to me, and... I'm not sure I can lose one more person."

"Hey." I hugged her to me. "It's all right. I swear to you that I plan to return. Promise me something as well?"

She sniffled and leaned back. "What is it?"

"Stay strong and don't let these men make you doubt yourself. Understand?" I trailed a strand of her hair away from her face. "Soon we'll be back, and we can break down over all of this together."

Tears broke free and spilled over her cheeks. "We'll eat comfort cake together?"

"Until we're sick."

She laughed through another sob as she patted my shoulder. "All right. I'll make you proud."

I shook my head. "Make yourself proud."

"I love you, Temi."

"I love you, too. I'll see you soon."

She brushed her thumbs under her eyes and took a deep breath before walking out of the room.

Heaviness swept around me, like all the worries and fears had bundled onto me. There was no time to reflect on that. Apollo's agitation would only grow the longer I delayed leaving. I stepped out of the room and started jogging as soon as I made it outside.

Valerian met me as I reached the stables. We walked up to Arion's stall, and I tangled my fingers into his seaweed-like mane. "You'll make sure he's cared for?"

Val crossed his arms as he eyed Arion. "I will. Though I hope he *lets me* care for him."

"Arion." I bowed my face against his, and he released a hot breath that warmed my chest. "I have to leave for a while, and you can't come." He knickered and twitched one of his ears. "I know, but it's important. I'll be back. While I'm gone, listen to Val."

Arion looked at Valerian before butting his nose into my shoulder.

"Hopefully he'll behave himself." I patted his side. "I'll miss him, though."

Valerian pulled a carrot out of his pocket and offered it to Arion who snuffed at it for a moment before huffing a sigh and accepting it. "I assure you the feeling will be mutual."

"I'll see you soon, Val."

He offered a half-hearted smile, and I pulled him into a hug. He startled before pulling his arms around me. "Stay safe, Temi."

"Don't worry." I leaned away, readjusted my bag, and pulled my bow out. "I'll be back to annoy you and encourage Pip into questionable decisions in no time."

A Spark of Death and Fury

He laughed. "I look forward to it."

I nodded and stepped out of the stables and into the navy of night.

"So, we're not taking horses?"

I turned to Orion. "We?"

He shifted a pack across his shoulders. "Yup."

"This will be dangerous."

He cocked an eyebrow. "We've faced danger together before."

"That was mortal-level dangerous. This will be deities set on death and destruction."

"You're heading to the Palace of the Four Winds, right?" I clenched my jaw and gave a quick nod. "That's only a few hours from where I grew up. I know those mountains like I know how to wield a knife. Meaning, better than you do."

I scoffed and stopped walking. "Do you plan to offend me until I concede and invite you?"

He grinned. "Is it working?"

"No."

Orion frowned. "I can help on this trip."

"Fight gods?"

"Yes."

"Again, no." I shifted my bag. "You could die."

The stars sparkled behind him. The moon had already reached its zenith and it kissed the mountains in the distance. "I could have died in the war."

"That was a human fight. This isn't."

"With the spark's power gone, aren't you currently as mortal as you've ever been until you ascend?"

"Well... yes, but—"

"All right, then. Feels like we stand on level ground."

I crossed my arms and rubbed down the gooseflesh that had risen there. "And if you die?"

"I could ask you the same question."

I huffed. "Fine."

A smile slashed his face. "So back to the question at hand. No horses?"

"We're taking a hired carriage as far as it can get us. Apollo can't ride horses, and I think he's worried about me losing Arion now that the immortality of the spark is gone." Crickets picked up their jumbled chirping. "He doesn't want me distracted, worrying about those I care about on this trip." I shot him a look.

Orion's grin broadened. "If I'm reading your implication right, then what you're saying is you care a lot about me."

I clicked my tongue. "That's not at all what I said."

"I think it is." He punched my arm gently. "I care about you too."

"We're not having a feelings talk. That isn't a thing I do."

"You already did."

"You assumed."

He chuckled as we reached the gate and passed through it to where a carriage sat gleaming in the torch lights along the wall. He slung his knapsack into the back. "I'd worry about you too. Now we can cover each other's asses."

I hummed a reply and jumped inside with Apollo, before scooting over to make room for Orion.

"Before I die"—Orion eyed the ceiling that his head nearly reached—"I'm going to get a sincere compliment out of you. It's what I now live for."

"I'm glad to know you plan to live for a long time."

Orion smirked, gave his head a shake, and then pressed his fingers against the ceiling as if to test the integrity of it. I didn't like feeling walled in either, but it was a good way to stay inconspicuous. Apollo sharpened a knife against a whetstone, his gaze unfocused. He barely acknowledged us and didn't even comment on the addition of Orion before returning to his thoughts. As soon as we sat, the carriage rattled forward, taking us to our destiny.

12

Epiphany

I paused behind a wall and slipped into the shadows of it as my cape rippled around me. Getting spotted visiting Val's apartment at night had always been a risk, but when Father lived, I had his authority to shield me. Everything would fall on me if I got caught now.

That wasn't enough to stop me.

I stepped onto the slivery grass that glimmered in the moonlight, reached the building, and stopped behind a tree. Holding my breath, I listened for any movement before continuing. I pulled my hood tighter around my face before clacking up the steps and pulling a key out of my pocket.

I pushed it into the lock, hurried into the room, and pressed the door closed behind me.

Valerian sat up in bed, his eyes bleary. He rubbed a palm over his face before jumping up. "Epiphany, are you okay?"

"I'm…" The word shook as it left my mouth.

He stood and opened his arms. I fell into them and

A Spark of Death and Fury

melted against the warmth of his body, the rumble of his half-awake voice.

"I'm sorry to wake you."

"No, don't be." He kissed the top of my hair and tightened his embrace. "What's wrong?"

I shrugged my cloak off, hung it on a hook, and gestured to the bed. Valerian nodded, and we dropped on it together. I lay down and allowed the warm, earthy scent of him to cocoon me. If only I could hide in there with him forever.

Val rubbed his hand down my back. The limited light of the moon washing through the small window of his apartment highlighted the curves of him arm. "What is it?"

I bit my lip. "The palace is full of ghosts. And I'm so worried about everything. I know I shouldn't have come here tonight, but I can't sleep, and I miss you terribly."

He kissed my cheek and brushed a strand of curls behind my ear.

There weren't any words. How could I express all the pain of the losses I'd experienced? The concerns I had over Demetri and Hyacinth. Or about Apollo and Temi traveling to rescue Ix and Cyn. Of gods who might act vengefully towards our country. Of Ansair sitting in the eaves, considering more battles and war.

My life and country were a wreck. The worst aspect was I didn't know how to fix any of it.

Valerian's chest rumbled like he might speak again.

I didn't want words.

I needed the safety of him, the comfort of his touch, the warmth of his body next to mine.

Before he could speak, I kissed his collarbone and ran my tongue along it. He shuddered as his hands froze on my waist. I continued my trail down his rib cage, over the rise of his muscles, along the firm planes of his stomach. I grazed my tongue under the waistband of his pants, and he groaned. "Epiphany."

I sat up. "What?"

"I..." He rubbed his hand over his face again. "It's been a while. If you do that, there's no way I'm going to last." He rose and shifted me on his lap where the hardness of him pressed into me and made my heart race. He brushed the curtain of my hair back and placed kisses onto my shoulder while his free fingers untied the ribbons of my dress.

I freed myself from having to make decisions or be in charge. And allowed myself to surrender to the steady, warmth of Val's touch, the passionate press of his mouth to mine, the comfort of being in his arms, and the release that wiped every worry from my mind for a glorious few minutes as I pressed my face into a pillow to muffle my whimpers.

When we finished, I curled against him, and his hand draped down to my stomach where he brushed circles with his thumb.

I found my voice. "A day is going to come when we can do this, and I won't have to be quiet."

He laughed, the warmth of his breath tickling my back. "I don't know if that's a good idea."

"Why?"

"I can barely maintain control now. If those little noises you make get any louder, I'll be useless."

"I have a fix for that, too."

He hummed against my neck, the vibration of it echoing through me. "And what's that?"

"In this future reality, we'll also have more sex."

He chuckled again. "Well, I won't argue with that."

We remained quiet for a moment, the heat of our

bodies slowly cooling, though the warmth of us curled up together tucked us in like a blanket. I doubted I would ever lover another person like I did this man. I couldn't have secrets standing between us anymore. "Val," I whispered, the wobble in my voice giving me away.

He clutched me tighter. "What is it?"

"There's something I need to tell you. Something... I did... that was disloyal to you."

"You have to do what is right for the country in your position. Sometimes that may mean not being loyal to an individual. That's okay."

"No, it's not like that." I scrunched my fingers into the pillowcase and my hands trembled. "I kissed Galeson."

Valerian's body froze and his breathing stopped for a moment. "Is he visiting?"

"No. I mean... during the war. I kissed him. It was a mistake. I was just... overwhelmed. I need you to know about it, though."

Val sighed again and pulled me tighter against him, his chin resting against my shoulder. "You mean you kissed him when I was encouraging you to marry him?"

"Well..."

"Epiphany, you don't need to apologize." He brushed his nose along my neck. "I don't... enjoy the idea of that, but I was pushing you towards marriage with the man." He released an anxious chuckle that raised gooseflesh on the nape of my neck. "Don't let this become one more worry for you right now. I love you. I understand, and I don't hold it against you."

I curled in tighter to him. "You're who I love, Val. I'm sorry if—"

"Don't apologize anymore. I promise, it's okay. Here, get some sleep. I'll stay up and wake you before sunrise so you can slip out."

I wanted to argue with him. He needed rest, too. But my body had already grown warm next to his and for the first time in weeks, I felt safe. Sleep dragged me down.

A few hours later, it was still the warmth of Valerian's laughter, the coarseness of his hands, the love and forgiveness in his eyes that buoyed me as I met Demetri for breakfast. He sat at a table with a parchment in hand, his curls slicked back, his food ignored. As I walked in, he lifted his face. "Ah, Princess Epiphany. Please have a seat." He gestured to the chair but didn't rise to mark my arrival. Well, perhaps he didn't know the rules of decorum among royals. Except he was a high lord. Though he wasn't raised in Niria, so maybe that explained it.

I sat, took a piece of bread, and spread jam over it. "I hope you're finding your way around the palace well, and the advisors are proving to be helpful."

He lifted the parchment again and groaned. "Yes, they've given me a great deal to think about. Nasty bit of business, your brother, isn't it?"

He didn't even look up. I stared at him as anger shook my hands before setting the bread down and clasping my fingers together in my lap. "I have full faith in Apollo and Artemis to rescue him."

His hair glimmered in the sunshine that poured in through the tall windows. That same light gave everything in the room, the long table, the rich carpets, the silks hanging over the ceiling, a touch of gold. "It seems fate won't release your family from punishment." I gasped, but he didn't notice as he plowed forward. "I never assumed all of this would fall to me. When you have a king with two young, healthy sons, who would? But here we are. After speaking with the advisors today, I agree with a suggestion a few of them made."

It took me a minute to find my voice, but I straightened

my back—because damned if his lack of decorum would force mine. I'd make my family and country proud. I poured myself a glass of wine and lifted it to my lips. "What was that?"

"That you and I marry."

I choked on my drink and coughed as I set the cup down on the table. "What?"

He snapped the parchment out and lowered it so he could meet my gaze. "I see the idea of that arrangement does no more for you than for me. There is some sense in it, though. We're both unmarried, Niria needs stabilization, and…" He paused to take a bite of food and chewed it excruciatingly slowly before swallowing. "The advisors suggested that since you grew up with the education and experience you did, you could run the country as my proxy. That suits me fine. I'm a man of leisure, and I don't have any desire to change that. We'll have a few heirs, and our lives can otherwise be uninterrupted."

My mouth gaped. "Did you think to discuss that with me?"

He frowned and studied me for a moment before laughing and disappearing behind his paper again.

I sat in silence with my nails biting into the flesh of my palms and my mind whirling.

This was how those old men, stuck in their traditions and bullshit, would turn this. They'd get the benefit of a child raised by my father while still crowning a king. They wanted me to do all the work, to marry this man and have his children while he got all the glory.

No.

No, I would not do it.

I rose, the chair shrieking across the floor.

Demetri looked up at me again.

"Excuse me, please. I won't interrupt your leisure further."

He waved me off, and it took every inch of my desire to represent my country well to resist pulling the tablecloth off and spilling breakfast into his lap. He thought he could just use me. I would not stand for that.

I clipped out of the dining room, turned down hallways, scarcely noticing those who passed by me until I reached a door and knocked.

"Come in."

I stepped into Joden's office, a chamber dominated by emerald furniture and a painted mural of gods overlooking a human court. Joden inclined his head. "Princess."

"I wish to speak with you."

"Please have a seat."

I took a chair in front of his desk. Fury wanted to spill out of me, but I sucked in a deep breath to temper myself. I was the daughter of King Magnes, one of the best leaders who'd walked this world. "I've spoken with my cousin this morning and wish to inform you I am no ox to be yoked to the most convenient cart. I will not act as a proxy. If I'm running this country, then I intend to run it myself."

Joden cocked his head to the side, and his sharp nose caught the light.

The weight of his disregard hovered over me, but I maintained my posture and my gaze. I would not agree with this. If they looked to me to do the work of leading the country, then they would not have a man sitting on the throne to cover for it.

"And I'm the one you come to speak with about this?"

"I know you don't care for me, but I thought we had formed an alliance of sorts during the war, and I'm not stupid." I clenched my fingernails against my palms until it

A Spark of Death and Fury

hurt. "If I can't get you on my side, it's unlikely I'll get most of the other advisors, much less the high lords."

"I'm certain I don't have to explain to you that your family and I have not seen eye-to-eye throughout your father's reign—"

"Yes, but—"

"Please, let me finish." He clasped his hands together, and his rings reflected over the surface of his desk. "That said, I respected your father. It's the only reason I stayed on his board of advisors despite our contentious personal relationship. He was… a strong leader."

I swallowed, emotions rising within me again. "He was."

"I actually disagree with the advisors who put the foolish plans in your cousin's mind. That man"—Joden gave his head a shake—"does not have a kingly bone in his body. And what if a day comes when he doesn't wish for a proxy and wants to rule this country himself? I believe it could be a disaster for Niria."

"I agree."

"But there has never been a ruling queen."

"There's never been a mortal who died and returned as a deity, either."

Joden pursed his lips. "Point well made. And I will back your move." Despite coming to speak with him, I hadn't expected that. "On a few conditions."

Wariness flooded through me. "What are those?"

"First, that you will compromise. You cannot expect those under my realm of influence to acquiesce to a ruler who doesn't consider their needs."

"My loyalty is to Niria as a whole."

Joden nodded. "Second, you must conduct yourself as a leader if you wish for others to perceive you that way. You're already at a disadvantage, as everyone is aware of your poor reputation growing up." My cheeks flamed, but I lifted my chin. "You'll need to change the way you dress, something feminine but strong. The high lords and people of influence of this country will judge every step you take."

I swallowed. I'd never done well under the expectations of others. But this was for Niria. And I wasn't the frightened girl I'd been as a child. "I can do that."

"There's also the matter of your partner."

"I will not marry Demetri. That's not even a consideration."

Joden steepled his fingers. "He's not who I reference. I speak of the man you share a bed with."

The blush deepened and spread over my nose. "I won't apologize for that."

He sighed and leaned forward. "You will never get the high lords' support if you're having an illicit affair with a man well below your station."

I dropped my face to search the intricate marbling of the floor like it would offer answers. Then I snapped my eyes up again as I remembered Emrin's final words to me. "What if he wasn't below my station?"

"What do you mean?"

"If his father, Lord Lucien of Carens, claimed him and we went through the process officially?"

Joden leaned against his chair. His gaze shifted to the windows where an expanse of blue sky reflected in the panes. "If we're able to negotiate so that trade is improved between the countries because of the connection, and if it's sanctioned, then perhaps we can make it work."

My fingers trembled, and I placed them into my lap to still them.

"However, this must happen officially. You cannot get caught in a scandal. No more late-night visits to the stable apartments. No more private conversations between you two until we are certain this will work. That is non-negotiable if you want me to align with you. Am I clear on that?"

I stared at him.
I hated to agree.
But for Niria.
For Val's and my future.
"Perfectly."

13

Hyacinth

My magic called to me, wanting me to pull it back and remove the shield from Ixion. He bowed his head over the marbles, sticking his tongue out before shooting and knocking half a dozen of the glimmering balls out. "Yes," he exclaimed as a grin curled over his face.

I didn't know how he was being so resilient.

He'd left his nanny, had men threaten him with a knife multiple times, been cut, injured, taken on this long journey, and held prisoner.

He wept at night, though.

So maybe he wasn't dealing with it as well as he seemed.

He gestured for me to go, and I flicked my marble forward. It scarcely knocked into any other and none of them slid out of the boundary.

"Too bad," he said.

An attendant arrived to build up the fire again. Its reflection gleamed over the wood floor, adding warmth to the room that the stormy day outside withheld. She peered at the closed washroom door before leaving. Hopefully she assumed Ix was in there and it bought us a few hours.

"Ixion."

"Yes?"

"The men won't recognize you when they come back in here and they'll probably be angry. It's very important that you listen to me and follow my instructions now."

He stilled but nodded.

"You're shielded. No one will be able to see you. I'm fairly certain they won't be able to hear you." Frustration crept through me. I wish I understood the powers more. "To be safe, it would be best if you kept your voice low and not speak when anyone else is in the room. You can't eat or play games when others are in here, either, because they'll see the movements. Do you understand?"

He stared at me.

"Also, they could still touch you even if they can't see you. If many of Zephyrus' guards come in here looking for you, crawl under the bed or hide. Don't let them reach you, okay?"

"Will they hurt me again?"

"No," I said so fiercely that he leaned away from me. I gentled my voice. "I've shielded you. They won't hurt you again However, I need you to follow my instructions carefully."

"I can do that, Papa." Ixion's eyebrows drew together. "Might they hurt you, though?"

I took a deep breath. Because yes. Yes, they might. "I'm very strong. That is for me to worry about, not you. Okay?"

He stared at me, fear welling up in the browns of his eyes that seemed brighter than normal against the bruise marring his face.

"I have my magic to help me, remember?" I didn't, of

course. Not with it covering Ix. That wasn't for him to worry about, though. We only needed to keep this up for a few days, hopefully. Just until whoever Zephyrus wanted to use us against arrived. It was a messy, slipshod plan and I had no idea if it would work but it was all I had. So much relied on Ixion following through and I prayed he would. "It's your turn to shoot."

He returned to the game. Worries permeated my mind as the morning wore on. When an attendant arrived bringing breakfast, and quickly realized Ixion wasn't present, he scrambled out of the chamber. After various attendants and guards had searched the room and missed the child that sat and watched them the entire time, they all left.

A few minutes later, the door burst open. I took a deep breath but kept my gaze on the fire as I sank farther into a chair.

Zephyrus walked around until he faced me, his arms behind his back, his blue irises darkened with fury. "Where's the boy?"

"What boy?"

He cocked his head like he considered slapping me, too. "This is not the game you wish to play with me, Prince."

I lifted my eyes to meet his. "My greatest regret in life is ever playing anything with you. Your games aren't even interesting."

He jumped in front of me, his wings stretched out to their full length, brushing against the chair Ixion sat in. Ix whimpered but Zephyrus didn't seem to notice so my theory about them not being able to hear him seemed to be true. Zephyrus snatched my arm, and his spit speckled my cheek. "Think for a moment, Prince, because I can assure you, I will add new regrets to your list if you do not bring the boy forth at once."

"Please, Papa, tell him I'm here," Ixion said between sobs.

My heart rippled with grief at his pitiful cries, but I ignored him. "I don't know who you're speaking of."

Zephyrus dragged my sleeve up and twisted my arm into the light of the fire, exposing the dull color of my flesh, the lack of glimmer my magic gave it. He laughed. "Oh… so you're shielding him. And you've rendered yourself mortal to do so. I believe we can handle that."

My heart beat so quickly that it buzzed, but my voice remained steady. "You underestimate me, Zephyrus."

The blue of his eyes turned to ice, and he tightened his grip on my arm until I winced and had to hold back a grimace as the pain shot through me. "Are you certain you wish to test the mettle of your strength today, Hyacinth? What are you made of?"

I swallowed before I could push past the aching misery and speak with an even voice. "Stronger stuff than you are."

Zephyrus growled and jerked me up out of the chair before shoving me into the guards. "Take him downstairs."

Blood rushed back into my arm, tingling and painful, but I pressed my tongue to the roof of my mouth hard to avoid expressing any emotions.

"Don't take him!" Ixion shouted. "Please, please don't!"

The door muffled his cries.

I was the only one to hear them. I didn't know who would look out for him, comfort him, make sure he had food. He wouldn't become a victim to this monster, though. That was all I had control over for the moment.

We marched to stone steps that led to a basement lit

with two torches while most of the room lingered in shadows. The men shoved me against a wall hard enough that the breath knocked out of me. They forced my hands into manacles, and Zephyrus loomed in front of me as he yanked a cloth rolled bundle from a shelf.

"You can leave us," he said to the guards, and they turned to walk up the stairs. Zephyrus brushed his hand down the bundle. "I brought you into my home and treated you as a guest."

I stared at him. He couldn't possibly believe that. I had long thought him foolish and dangerous. Perhaps he was beyond that. "Against my will."

He continued speaking as if I wasn't in the room. "But you thwart me at every turn." He unwound the cloth package, metal blades and lengthy sharp-edged tools within reflected the orange of the flames. "And I've had enough, Prince."

My heart raced. I pressed my feet hard against the floor and forced my voice to stay even. "You need me alive. You never would have gone through this much trouble to get me here if you planned to kill me."

Zephyrus smiled, something wicked and sharp in the turn of his lips. He leaned in so close to me I could see the gritty texture of his jaw, the navy dots speckling his irises. "I need you *breathing*, Prince. Your physical condition is negotiable." He leaned back and pulled an instrument out, twirling it between his fingers. "There is a great deal of pain that can be exercised on a body before it dies. Do you wish to find out, or will you unveil the boy?"

My heart galloped against my chest like it intended to break free, but I raised my chin. "What boy?"

Zephyrus growled then took a deep breath. "The hard way, then. Very well."

He slipped the end of the metal under my fingernail. I

A Spark of Death and Fury

jerked my hand back, the manacle cut into my skin, and ripped up flesh.

"Last chance." He grazed his thumb over my knuckles gently, and I cringed as I pulled back again and tore up more skin. The coppery smell of blood filled the air. "How I'd hate to mar someone so beautiful. I need the boy. Release him to me. I won't hurt him again; I swear it to you. We'll just talk."

I licked my lips. I wanted to believe him. Zephyrus was a liar, though. The minute I freed Ixion they'd take him from me and do gods knew what with him. Harm him, for certain.

I would not allow it.

If honoring Apollo's memory meant protecting Ixion, then the gods themselves would not break my resolve.

"I still don't know who you're speaking of."

His expression turned bitter. He slipped the tool under my fingernail and jabbed it forward, separating the nail from the soft flesh there. I attempted to bite down, to swallow my sound, but a whimper peeled out of my lips. The pain washed along my arm in a wave and radiated until my entire body ached.

This could be Ixion.

They could torture him to force his powers. I would endure this burden for his sake.

Zephyrus spread his wings out causing the torch on the wall to flutter. "I can stop at any time, Prince. Just let me know."

I sucked in a shaky breath and dropped my gaze.

My magic screamed for me. Gods, did I want to pull it back, wrap myself in the earthy comfort of it, let it heal me.

I wouldn't.

I believed what I'd told Zephyrus.

Bravery may not define me, but I was made of stronger stuff than him.

I shifted and the manacles jerked against the hand that ached with pain.

If my powers had taught me anything, it was how to mentally separate from my body. Even though I didn't have that magic available, I could remember how it felt to slip away and follow the length of a vine, my physical form disappearing.

I tucked back into the recesses of my mind as Zephyrus positioned the tool under a second finger. I trembled as I centered myself.

I didn't have to be here mentally.

I could be anywhere.

Next to Apollo as his curls fluttered in a breeze and the lights of a million oil lamps flickered on through the city. His mouth on mine, his eyes wide and vulnerable.

Zephyrus jammed the weapon forward, and I winced.

I didn't make a sound, though.

I had to drown myself. Forget that I existed. Find some place in the corner of my brain where I could disconnect from everything around me.

The day provided a great deal of opportunities to practice that. The only time my concentration shattered was when Zephyrus broke my first finger.

For a moment I returned to the chill, damp of the basement, the leering craze in his eyes, and the aching pain of my hands.

I shoved back down, down, down.

Past reality.

He couldn't break me if he couldn't find me.

When Zephyrus finally escorted me to the room where Ixion waited, my hands shook so much they vibrated my arms, and I took slow, painful steps towards the bed. I was just glad to return so that I could make sure Ixion had his needs met.

"Consider if you wish to repeat this tomorrow, Prince," Zephyrus said, before slamming the door.

Ix jumped onto the mattress, his face puffy. "Papa! Are you okay?"

"Don't touch me." I took a deep breath. "For just a moment, all right?" He bobbed his head, his cheeks swollen from tears, and I looked to the door. It remained closed. I pulled my magic back. The powers flooded my senses and mended broken bits as it bloomed through me. My lips trembled before I removed my powers again. They clung to me, like vines twining around my legs and wrists, pleading with me not to lose them.

I forced it off and onto Ixion.

He sobbed, and I pulled him into a hug and kept my voice low. "It's all right."

"The bad gods hurt you."

"Yes." I brushed curls away from his forehead, taking in the bruised section of his face. "I'm tough, Ixion. And I think someone is coming for us." It had to be true. Zephyrus kept us hostage for some purpose. Probably to trade us to Niria for some gain. He wouldn't keep me alive for no reason. I had to believe that, because otherwise there was nothing but hopelessness and pain. "We just need to stay brave a few more days. Someone will come get us."

"I did what you said today. When the bad men came in here I hid and didn't touch anything. I tried to be brave like you."

My heart ached at the tremble in his voice. "You're being so brave, Ix. I'm proud of you."

He brushed his hand over my cheek, the gentlest gesture I'd ever received, and then pushed himself up to place a kiss there. "Nanny Essie always kissed me to make me feel better. Does it help?"

I studied him, that fiercely sweet little god-child. "It does. Thank you." I patted the bed beside me, and he curled up on my arm. "Why don't I tell you another poem and you get some sleep? Try not to worry, okay? This won't last much longer."

"I bet when Apollo gets here, he's going to be so mad at the bad gods."

I shuddered. "I'm sure. Now get still, and I'll share a story."

"How about more of the Heracles stories? I like the one where he faced the lion."

I clenched my teeth. Heracles. Apollo's brother. I started speaking and my voice deepened or slowed or rose as the narrative called for. But my hands never stopped trembling.

14

Artemis

The carriage rattled along, swaying the three of us in the compartment. The driver we'd hired—after explaining the dangers of the trip and paying him richly enough to set his family for life—occasionally called out to direct the horses. I'd switched to sitting by Apollo and my shoulders rocked against his and the wood of the wall. Apollo remained stoic, facing the window, his arms crossed. He'd barely spoken more than a few words.

Orion, who sat across from us, kept a stream of conversation flowing as his blue eyes sparkled in the sunlight that glittered in through the small windows. When a pause happened, leaving only the unspoken worries to press into the space, I readjusted my bow. "Do you think we're the trio that stands guard?"

Orion shifted towards me as the carriage rocked. "The trio?"

"Remember, Clothos' prophecy for me? When the sun overtakes the moon, and the trio stands guard, that is your moment to rise."

Orion tilted his head. "I guess that'd make sense. The

sun and the moon have to be you and your brother." He nodded at Apollo. "When do you think he'll overtake you?"

"Never."

Orion laughed. "Then I guess you don't have to worry about it. Wasn't there also a part where you don't show up to a battle?"

"When you lose what you gain, and arrive at a fight too late, your brother will ascend only to bow. That's the first half."

"Well," Apollo said, his voice scratchy, "Clothos knows me well. I have no interest in ascending to reign over others."

I sighed, longing to stretch my legs, wishing I could wash away Apollo's worry and pain. "I wouldn't miss a battle that needed me, anyway. So, I agree with Orion. This prophecy will never happen."

Orion grinned at me, but Apollo said nothing, lost to his thoughts again. He tossed a sheathed blade and caught it with a steady thump, thump, thump.

"At the rate we're going," I said, trying to keep the conversation moving, "we should make it in a few days. Maybe the trip itself will be uneventful."

Apollo readjusted, his voice holding an edge to it. "It's not like you to be naïve."

I clicked my tongue but ignored him. He was terrified for Hyacinth and Ixion and rightfully so. Zephyrus had killed Hyacinth once before. I worried he might have done it again already… but no. If he didn't have Hyacinth alive, how would he compel Apollo to fight him, to attempt to overpower him and gain the spark? That had to be his aim. Apollo had suspected he wanted to overtake Zeus when they'd visited the Palace of the Four Winds last year. And now rumors spread that the only way to gain that power was to end Apollo. True or not, Zephyrus didn't strike me as one to ignore it.

I hissed through my teeth. We should be riding horseback and working on our powers during this part of the journey. Then again, no. At least we'd be at the mountains and out of this damn carriage soon.

Orion rolled a short spear on this lap and tapped a rhythm on it.

"Are you trying to accidentally stab all of us?"

He grinned. "Nah. The spear is my favorite weapon and if we're riding in this death trap"—he eyed the enclosed walls of the carriage as his lips pinched—"then I plan to stay prepared."

"Not a fan of being boxed in?"

"Are you?"

I crossed my arms. I hated it. But it was the fastest and most discreet mode of transportation short of magically traveling which I couldn't do yet or horseback riding which Apollo couldn't do. Apollo's failed attempt to use his magic to travel proved we needed to figure out our powers, and quickly. With the carriage, we'd already covered half our journey in a short time even if all three of us—prickly, and restless, and anxious—trapped in a compact box together proved for an interesting drive.

Apollo crossed his ankles, his hand going to the straps of a new bag he'd packed for the trip. It lingered there as if he thought of his old one which he'd left with Hyacinth.

Orion bent down to look out the miniature windows. "At least we're going now and not in a few months. Winter storms in the north can be fierce."

I considered that. "Do you think Boreas could have aligned with Zephyrus and might stir up bad weather for us?"

Apollo shook his head, his curls bobbing. "Boreas

doesn't want to be involved in the gods fighting or the politics. Further, why would Zephyrus delay us when his purpose is to draw me to him? No... I think the weather for our journey will be clear, at least."

It was the most he'd said since he'd received the letter and I was glad to have him talking. "But what about Euros, could he—"

A creaking of the carriage cut me off, a horse whinnied, and the driver shouted something.

For a moment we stared at each other and held our breaths.

It was probably nothing, I lied to myself. The horse stumbled or there's a downed tree on the road or... Clunk, clunk, clunk. Arrows peppered into the side of the carriage. The horses screamed, a high-keening sound that I'd hoped to never hear again after the battles.

Orion snatched up both of his spears, yanked his bow free from behind the seat, and tucked it over his arm. "Going to complain about me keeping my spear in hand now?"

I rolled my eyes as I freed several knives from the belt on my hip. My bow rubbed my shoulder as I jerked our bags free. "You *would* be in the middle of a battle and saying you were right."

Another smile spread over his cheeks. "I would, wouldn't I?"

He shoved the door open and jumped out. Dust rose at his feet as his arm swept into motion.

I joined him and pulled my bowstring back.

Then I hesitated.

Hundreds of people—gods I had to assume—stood around the flat expanse with weapons aimed for us, arrows sweeping in our direction, magic rumbling the ground.

So at least some of them were low gods who had full access to their powers.

I thrusted a knife forward, and it caught in the neck of a nearby being. They yanked it free, hissing.

Right.

These were gods.

We could kill them but not easily.

Magic whipped through the air, and the earth shook. Apollo leaped, rolled, and lifted his bow to fire off arrows.

I froze.

"Temi," Orion yelled. He yanked my arm and jerked me away from a crack that split open where I stood. It sucked our carriage into the earth with a thundering crash and the screams of the horses and driver.

"Oh shit," I whispered.

"Come on." He grabbed my hand and pulled me with him behind a boulder.

I jerked my bow loose. "Thanks for saving me."

He grinned. "It's becoming a habit of mine."

A huff of a breath peeled through my lips, but we said no more as we sent arrows soaring. One after another, they hit their marks. The gods growled, yanked the arrows free, and turned in our direction.

Gods, this was easier when we faced a human army.

Apollo didn't take shelter. He plowed into the group, taking them by surprise, and sliced his knife around to stab through ribs, cut necks.

He fought with a vengeance I'd never seen on him.

Still, he was one being standing against hundreds.

He was going to get himself killed.

Dozens of the fighters ran in our direction. The earth trembled again. Whisps of clouds trailed in the blue sky, and I wondered if it would be the last sight I'd see. Already sweat soaked my brow, and my arms trembled.

Orion licked his lips as he yanked his spear up.

"Why aren't you shooting?"

He winced. "I'm out of arrows."

"How?"

He thrust the spear forward and it knocked three of the approaching enemies at once. Orion dragged his sword free, his last weapon, right as my fingers grasped the final arrow in my pouch.

In every scenario I'd imagined, facing a group of deities this large hadn't crossed my mind. I released a shaky breath. Half a dozen gods pounced on Apollo and pulled him to the ground. He kicked and slashed and fought against them.

Those approaching us climbed up the boulder we were behind, and there was no way to hold them back. One jumped up and threw a knife. Orion shifted then winced as the blade struck him.

"Orion!"

He jerked to slash his sword forward and knocked the man from the rock. "I'm fine. It just grazed me."

More of the gods climbed onto the boulder, their eyes dark, their bodies laden with weapons. They leaped down on us and pushed us against the ground.

I kicked and pulled weapons off them, used my legs to roll them over, punched and scrabbled and fought for my life.

They so vastly outnumbered us, though.

There wasn't a chance we'd get out of this.

Someone threw me down hard enough that a crack echoed, and my vision blurred.

Which was why I wasn't sure if I was seeing things when the earth ripped open again, wider, splitting the ground into two planes, and a gush of water flooded forth,

A Spark of Death and Fury

covering us. I released air in a trail of bubbles as the water washed us apart.

I coughed as the wave receded, stumbled up, and pressed my hand to my aching head as I tried to locate Orion and Apollo.

A boy with glimmering cerulean eyes leaned back, and more water rushed up from the earth, knocking down the deities who attempted to regain their footing.

Three others stood beside the boy, and they tapped into their magic. Fire flashed and burned the gods, the earth opened and closed to suck them into the belly of the world, wind knocked them down whenever they tried to stand.

A few minutes later, Orion and I stood surrounded by the hundreds of dead bodies, staring at four teenagers.

One with a copper braid and freckles across her nose walked up and grinned. "You're Artemis and Apollo, right?"

I turned to face Orion who ripped a piece of fabric from his tunic and tied it over the worst of his injures—a gash that showed the pink of his muscle. I winced and turned back to the girl. "No. That's not Apollo."

She blanched. "Oh gods. We didn't kill him, did we?"

Shit! I dashed around to look for him among the fallen.

"Oh," one of the teenagers with gray hair and bright eyes said. "No. He's not dead. Sorry, I had him." A bubble of air burst, and Apollo tumbled out, bruised and cut, but alive.

"Damn it," he growled.

My mouth gaped for a moment as the sun beat down on the endless bodies lying scattered across the dusty ground beneath the expansive blue sky. "Who are you?"

"I'm Kama," the girl with the freckles said. "We're gods, if that isn't obvious."

"Thank you, for…" I gestured at the destruction around us.

Apollo walked over to Orion and grasped his arm, his eyes focused as he tapped into his magic. Orion sighed with relief as it flooded through him and healed his injures. Apollo didn't even look at the group as he spoke gruffly. "Yes, thank you."

"We appreciate the help," I said. "I'm afraid we can't stay and thank you properly. We have to go."

"We know," Kama said. "We'd like to come with you."

Apollo wiped blood from a blade. "No."

"But we saved you. We could help."

Apollo didn't even look at them. "It's not up for consideration. You could get yourselves killed."

The quiet one with the giant stature and soft eyes spoke. "Or, worse, we could do nothing and allow Zephyrus and others like him to take control."

"That's right," Kama said. "We want to fight for a better future. We're good. You've seen that."

"What do you know about Zephyrus' plan?" I asked.

She shrugged. "He wants to be the new high god and everyone knows he'll be as bad or worse than Zeus.

I walked over to my brother. "Apollo."

He lifted his face. "Yes?"

"They make some valid points."

"They're children. They're like twelve years old."

Kama crossed her arms. "Nero, Mia, and me are fifteen. Chares"—she nodded to the boy with the gray hair—"is sixteen."

Apollo scoffed. "Sixteen." He shifted back to me. "Kids. They'll get themselves killed."

"We were younger when we faced the roads alone." I gripped his arm. "When you wanted to do something meaningful and not just sit back and watch the gods

A Spark of Death and Fury

destroy things from afar. And, in case you're not aware, they just saved all our asses. We would not have come out of that alive on our own. Do you want to be successful at this or not?"

He stared at me, his brow furrowed. Then he sighed. "Fine."

"Yes," Kama crowed as she slapped the other girl's arm.

Apollo jerked his bag open and dumped the cleaned weapons in as he grumbled. "Why do I always have someone wanting to add random travelers on these journeys? And I always agree. Because I'm an idiot."

"Did you and Cyn have someone travel with you?"

The lines of his face grew hard, and he swallowed his expression back down. He slung his bag over his shoulder. "There's a stream. I'm going to go clean up."

"We shouldn't separate."

He ignored me as he turned and walked down the path.

I fisted my hands and held back my desire to punch him. Orion stepped up beside me. He didn't say anything, but his gaze remained on Apollo's receding form, and I knew we both thought the same thing. Grief and anger clouded him. "Come on," I said. "Let's get everyone settled and find some place reasonable for a campsite. Do you want to take first watch or would you rather I go first?"

"You."

"Oh, you decided that quickly?"

"Your ass will be up working on your powers with the moon either way. Hopefully, if you take first watch, by the time second watch comes along you'll be tired enough to actually sleep."

I rolled my eyes.

There was no arguing against the truth, though.

Apollo and I needed to regain our footing with our magic. And now we'd lost our supplies for the trip other than the basics we carried in our bags. I turned to watch Apollo disappear on the horizon, my heart aching for a moment, before I shifted back to Kama. "Do you four know anything about hunting?"

15

Valerian

I brushed Arion's back, and he swished his tail irritably, swiping a fly away before shooting me an annoyed look. He scarcely tolerated me despite me bringing him apples every night and allowing him as much freedom as possible. Clouds puffed across the sky like smoke.

A stableman, Garrison, walked across the pasture and handed over a sealed parchment. "A letter for you," he said. I accepted it and before I could reply he bobbed his head and turned back to the stables.

Rumors which had started as whispers, had risen into a gale of wind that whipped over me. Barely any of the stablemen would speak with me beyond the basics now. I'd always stood out in some ways. I was Hyacinth's closest friend and that alone kept me from fitting in. I'd worked just as hard as any other, shared in their jokes, stayed quiet, and eventually they'd forgiven my connection with royalty. After all, how could I help it that I'd been picked as a companion for the prince? They saw it almost as something to pity me for.

Now, however, staff around the palace suspected there was something between me and Epiphany.

That, in their eyes, was unforgivable. I was an opportunist rising above his station and doing so by manipulating the princess—now the leader of our country—at that.

I dropped the brush and patted Arion to release him into the pasture. I could finish grooming him later. Most of the jobs around the stable were not that pressing since the war. They could wait. It left me restless and worried. It was a strange thing to have spent so much of my life sheltered here and then leave for a war where death and suffering were so visceral. I woke in the middle of the night sometimes smelling the copper tang of blood, hearing the cries of horses as they died, or feeling the warmth of fire as the roof fell against Epiphany and me, trapping us for certain death.

Gooseflesh rose on my arms at the memory. Suddenly I wished Hyacinth was there, safe, and not in danger. What I longed for more than anything was a friend. We could spend a day riding horses and mulling over the last year. Though I'm sure he'd love to hear the story of how his sister nearly burned to death because she came to speak with me. I cringed. Besides, he had bigger issues to face than I did at the moment.

I broke the seal and peeled the parchment open.

I recognized the handwriting, the slant of it, the curled edges of the letters, before reading the words.

Thank gods it was sealed.

The men I worked with would never speak to me again if they knew Pip wrote to me directly. Though her letter held a touch of formality I wasn't used to from her, even in writing. She wouldn't put intimate or personal touches to paper. Her father had raised her to consider the political implications if a note ended up in the wrong hands, after all. But still... normally a touch of her voice shone through.

I read the words again.

YOUR PRESENCE IS REQUESTED *at the king's office directly after lunch.*
Dress accordingly.
-Epiphany

SHE MUST HAVE SENT SUCH a formal letter out of worry that someone else could see it. What was my presence needed for? I folded the note back up. Well, only one way to find out.

I washed as best as I could, though the earthy smells of the stables would linger on me, and donned my best uniform. I stared at my reflection in the window of my apartment. Should I wear the insignia? On one hand, it indicated loyalty to Niria, on the other, it marked me as a servant.

I wish I had more information about this meeting. I sighed and decided to leave it off.

As I walked through the palace, I could feel the eyes of the attendants I passed piercing into me. The gossip would only continue to grow. Mother would bear the brunt of that. I couldn't ignore a summoning from a royal, regardless of the gossip it may stir up.

I paused outside of King Magnes' office and knocked.

For a moment the world stretched intensely quiet, and the sweet smells of the palace halls filled the air.

"Come in," Epiphany said, and I pressed the door open.

She stood, radiant and golden, silhouetted by the sun

that poured through the windows lining one wall, wearing a dress of a deep peach that followed the ample curves of her body and gave a glimmer to her tan skin.

For a moment I remained so fixed on her I didn't notice the others. Joden stood in the corner, eyeing me like I was an unfortunate horse he got saddled with that he didn't have the heart to put down. Asher waited at the far window and he cocked an eyebrow up as I met his gaze.

I bowed. "Your Highness, my lords."

"Please shut the door," Epiphany said, before turning. I pulled the handle, and the latch clicked in place, but my focus remained on her where she twisted her fingers together.

No one spoke and the sunlight dappled across the rugs as trees swayed outside. I longed to say something, to ask why they'd call me to this meeting. It wasn't my place, though.

"Your Highness," Joden said to Epiphany.

She took a deep breath and shifted back to me. Color warmed the curves of her cheeks. "I'm sorry about… this." She waved around the room. "We need to have an uncomfortable conversation."

I tucked my hands behind my back and clenched my fingers together. I'd really rather not have Joden and Asher present for any discussion with Epiphany, much less an uncomfortable one, but here we were. Maybe she planned to end our relationship publicly in front of them. I didn't think she would do that without discussing it with me first. Wariness swept through me, anyway. "I'm listening." Joden frowned at me, and I cleared my throat. "Your Highness."

She gave him an exasperated look before she turned back to me. "Do you want to marry me?"

My lips snapped apart, but I couldn't form words for a minute. Of all the dozens of things I'd anticipated her saying, that was not one. For one thing, this was not how I imagined a proposal happening between us. Foolishly, if we ever made it to that point, I'd imagined proposing to her in the hayloft where we'd become friends and quietly fallen in love.

Joden clenched his fingers into the carved back of King Magnes' chair. "Well?"

"I do," I said as I met his gaze, my words tumbling together. I turned back to face Epiphany whose complexion had reddened further. "Yes, of course."

She swept her palms down her skirts. "We're"—she gestured to Asher and Joden—"working on me taking over the kingdom."

I stared at her. Was I supposed to act like this would be new information for me? She'd already told me some of the advisors considered that, of course, but I wasn't sure if Asher and Joden knew she'd told me that. I managed a nod.

Epiphany cleared her throat and took a step forward. "I want, very much, to marry you. But…" She gave a frustrated shake of her head.

Joden rolled his shoulders back. "The country will not accept a bastard, stablehand as the reigning monarch's spouse."

"Lord Joden," Epiphany snapped, and even Asher gave him a dark look.

"Don't expect me to apologize," he said. "We agreed to be blunt in this meeting and that's the state of things. I'd far prefer to see you with someone who has an existing reputation, Lord Galeson, for example, but if this is the situation we find ourselves in"—he skimmed his gaze along me and his nose wrinkled—"then, very well. We will not sit here and speak in pleasantries, however, when the reality is Nirian high lords, much less the gentry of other countries, will never tolerate this union. I'm only entertaining this because I'm trying to consider the best course for our country, and I believe King Magnes' child to be that. This path we walk is a delicate one."

Asher sighed and bobbed his head. "It's true."

Epiphany frowned, and I longed to walk over to her, brush my thumb over her cheek, kiss her until she smiled. "Which is why," she said, "we need your father to officially claim you."

I took a deep breath. I'd never even laid eyes on my father. "Has he written again?"

"No." Joden tapped his fingers on the edge of the chair. "I've sent a missive to him as has Princess Epiphany with the hope that he will agree. Even then, it's a precarious business." He looked to Asher who nodded again. "Lucien is well connected with many of the noble families here. If he can convince them, it might just work."

Epiphany's eyes welled with so much longing and hurt. I'd face anything, go anywhere, do whatever I must to stand at her side, to love and support her.

Joden's sharp nose wrinkled again. "However, we must stay above board in every aspect of this until all goes through. A scandal would ruin all our plans and possibly tip Niria into more of a crisis than it already is with the high gods fallen and war lingering at our borders. You two"—he pointed between me and Epiphany—"are not to speak alone again until this is all settled. Princess, I do not even want you to so much as visit the stables until then."

"Surely," Epiphany said, "we could speak for just a moment now."

"No." Joden frowned at me. "If someone saw him walking out of this room with you alone in here, what might happen? Already the gossip about you both is unacceptable. It's a wonder you haven't been discovered yet.

Your father..." His voice softened. "He wished to have Valerian claimed and you married, quickly, to avoid such issues."

Epiphany sniffed quietly and shifted away from them for a moment. Her eyes glistened.

Damn if I hadn't suffered through too many times watching her break from across a room and unable to do anything about it. She straightened and looked at me. "Would you go to visit your father and see if he'd follow through on claiming you?"

"Of course I will."

"Good," Joden said. "There is another issue, though."

"What is that, my lord?"

He sniffed, as if annoyed he had to waste some of his time on me. "Your mother. A future relative of the queen cannot work in the kitchen."

"My mother cares deeply about her work," I blurted out before I had time to pause.

Asher stepped forward. "It is honorable to take pride in one's work, but you must understand politics and how precarious it would look for the grandmother of your children to work as an attendant in the palace kitchens. You understand, if you marry and we succeed at crowning the Princess, your children will one day rule this country."

My heart skipped a beat. I guess I hadn't really thought that far. For all my worrying about the future, I suppose I'd never let myself imagine us actually marrying. If this all worked out, I'd have a child who might rule Niria in the future. Holy shit. I swallowed. But my mother. She would be devastated to be pushed out of her role. And it would be my fault. I'd already caused her so much grief, and this would only add to it. "What would become of her?"

Joden steepled his fingers. "We'd remove her quietly."

"To what?"

His eyes narrowed at my lack of propriety. "She would have a room in the palace, and we'd outfit her as a lady. As the mother of the future queen."

Mother would... hate that. There was so much I hadn't considered, other lives being affected. Epiphany's eyebrows pulled together so tightly they creased her flesh. She stared at me, her eyes saying what she wouldn't put into words in front of Asher and Joden. Could I do this? Could I take my mother's greatest source of pride from her?

Epiphany's lips pressed together, and she mouthed one word. *Please.*

My heart broke.

I couldn't tell Pip no. I loved her too immensely for that.

I wanted this, desperately. Even if it was turning out differently than I had expected. There would be no forgiving myself for this choice. "Of course."

"I can speak with her," Epiphany said. "If you'd like."

"No." I said the word so fast she startled. It was my responsibility. "I'll tell her."

Epiphany's nose flared and an apology welled in her expression. "Very well," she whispered.

Joden gestured to me. "You and Lord Asher leave for Carens at sunrise."

Asher cocked his head to the side. "I wish to touch in with the military leaders of Carens as they border Ansair."

"Right."

"We'll send you," Joden said, "with all the markings of a prince consort." He stepped in closer to me. "You no longer represent yourself. You represent Niria. Do you understand the weight of that?"

My heart pounded.

I wasn't sure if I did.

A Spark of Death and Fury

I'd never set my sights quite that high.

Epiphany looked at me. Wrinkles swept across her brow as she twisted her fingers together. She understood more and more what it meant to stand for Niria, to fight for the people of our country, to try and fill her father's place. And I knew what it meant to support her at any cost. Maybe that was an underappreciated but important aspect of representing Niria in its own way.

I turned back to Joden. "I do, my lord."

He kept my gaze for half a dozen heartbeats before answering. "Good."

"I should speak with my mother, then," I said.

Joden nodded. I shifted towards the door but not before meeting Epiphany's gaze again. How I wished to have two minutes alone to speak with her. I wouldn't even touch her if propriety wouldn't allow it, but I longed to hear the burdens of her heart and reassure her. To tell her that I would race the wind for a chance with her. That she didn't need to feel sorry as she did. That I loved her like the moon loved night.

Asher and Joden watched me, the first with his hands clasped together, the latter with pinched lips. I bowed and stepped out of the room.

I found a servant's door and walked down the steps that ran within the belly of the palace, sparser than the formal sides, but brightly lit and well maintained. It was then that I realized they hadn't shared what my role would be after we were betrothed. Afterall, the Queen's spouse couldn't be a stablehand, could he?

I stopped walking and leaned against the wall. My head spun. So much had changed in a breath, in a moment. I was afraid of the ramifications.

"You all right, Val?"

I opened my eyes to find an attendant with bright

brown eyes and a basket of laundry on her hip standing in front of me. I pushed off the wall. "Yeah, I'm fine, thanks."

"Going to see your mother?"

"I am."

"Tell her I said hello."

"I will."

I continued down the stairs, but the bad feeling sank deeper in me. Mother had an entire network of people in this palace who she would lose. Because of me. Damn it. Maybe I should have said no. Perhaps it would have made the most sense for Epiphany to marry Galeson. Anger, hot and sluicing, whipped through me. No. I loved Epiphany desperately, stupidly, as was evident from every choice I'd made in the past year.

I reached the kitchen but worry hung on me like a millstone. Mother walked up, the deep wrinkles of her face crunching together. "Valerian, what's wrong?"

"I must speak with you… privately."

She sucked in a breath and nodded. "Delsa," she called over her shoulder. "Take over for me? And make sure the fruit is sliced this time. Lord Demetri is very particular."

Mother hooked her arm into mine and walked us back through a pantry filled with onions that hung from the ceiling and hundreds of jars of preserves and into a small office in the back. Her office.

"What is it?" She gestured to a chair.

I sat and waved for her to do the same. She lowered into the only other chair in the tight space. It was small, but it was hers. And I was going to take that from her. I cleared my throat. "Epiphany called me to a meeting earlier."

"Has she ended things? Are you in trouble? I have some money set aside and—"

"No… No, it's not that."

She sighed and one of her dark curls fell free of her headscarf.

"It's worse, in some ways." I winced and the worry came back to her face. I explained the situation to her, watched as disbelief and fear and anger worked its way over her. When I finished tears streaked her cheeks and dripped off the end of her chin. "I'm sorry," I said. "I didn't consider how this would affect you."

She wiped her face with the towel hanging on her apron. "Is this what you want?"

I looked at her, the woman who had birthed me, raised me, fought for me against all odds. "I don't want to hurt you."

"Is marriage to the Princess truly your desire?" She licked her lips. "It would not be an easy role." She looked over her shoulder as if someone might come into the office. "Especially if she becomes the reigning authority. I remember the strain it caused Queen Diomede. She died young, at that."

"I know."

Mother reached out, her touch gentle. "You want this, don't you?"

"I… I do. I'm in love with Epiphany." I gave my head a shake. "I'm just so sorry."

She sniffled again, wiped her nose with the towel, and then balled it up and tossed it into a basket of laundry. "I am too, if I were honest. What kind of mother would I be if I stole your own happiness for mine?"

She swept her fingers over recordkeeping lists on her desk.

"I thought you hated me being with Epiphany?"

She blew out a breath and pulled her headscarf off. "I hated the idea of you getting hurt or ending up in a scandal. I will not sit here and say"—her voice broke—"that this isn't a blow to me. But I love you, Val. I want the best for you. If you're willing to face everything you will endure in order to achieve this, then I will sacrifice too, happily. I've always done so for you."

Tears broke free over my eyes and dripped down my jaw. "Your entire life has been sacrifice for me. Now I'm asking you to give up even more."

She stood and pulled her arms around me. "Let me worry about myself, Valerian." She brushed her hands over my hair like she'd done when I was a child. "You don't concern yourself with me, all right?"

I wiped my face, scraping over the coarse edges of my beard, brushing away the tears, but nodded.

"Now, go on. You have preparations to make, I'm sure. Say goodbye to me before you leave?"

"I will."

She nodded and sat in her chair again. I stepped in the direction of the door but looked back over my shoulder. Mother leaned over her desk, her eyes gleaming, her shoulders hunched. The image of her sitting so miserable in one of her last days in the role she'd fought and worked hard for seared into my mind. I would never forget it.

16

Apollo

The young gods chattered endlessly as we walked into the rapidly cooling world. Colors dulled as we approached the mountains where the Palace of the Four Winds rested. Orion pointed to trails off the main road that we could move through more quickly on foot. His directions were the only breaks in the endless conversation.

Kama, with her copper hair and bright green eyes, spoke the most, only pausing when she intertwined her fingers with Mia, a quiet girl with short, ebony curls who possessed magic that shifted the earth.

Every time they touched bitterness rang through me. It was no mystery why. I was jealous of them. A bunch of teenagers finding a spot of light in a dark world. I'd dropped to a new low. My mood remained sour, and I walked in front of the group, avoiding the young gods' questions, Orion's appraisal, and Temi's worried looks.

Wind breathed down the side of the mountain that stretched ahead of us, and I adjusted the collar of my jacket up along my neck. It wasn't my coat, the one Hyacinth had made for me. That was with him... if he still had my bag, which was unlikely. Gods, I hoped he and Ixion were okay. Zephyrus wouldn't kill them, I didn't think. Otherwise, he'd have less ability to manipulate me. He might get me to fight him if he killed them both, but there was always a chance I wouldn't. However, if he had my husband and nephew, I would die trying to save them.

I leaned into my body and pressed for my powers.

Despite what Temi thought, I was actually working on getting them back.

It was exhausting. Without Nedia's guidance, it felt more difficult than ever. Like sinking in mud and trying to pull myself out with no leverage.

"So, anyway," Kama said, her voice a bright chirp against the crisp air of the day, "that's how we ended up here."

"My story is similar," Orion said. "I wasn't much older than you when I took to the roads myself."

"How did you learn to fight?" Temi asked the girl.

Kama laughed, a sound too happy for my bleak mood. "We had to. We're elemental gods. The high deities who rule over the magic we have don't like us having powers connected to what they control. Gaea, for example, attacked Mia."

I fell back into the group. "The goddess of the earth?"

"Yup." She kicked a browning clump of grass. Mia's gaze followed it but her color had paled and a crease had formed between her eyebrows.

"But she never comes out of the belly of the world. She doesn't even attend the high gods' events."

"Well, she came for Mia. Didn't like that she can move the earth. Oh, and Nero had an issue with Poseidon before, too."

Temi's posture went rigid. I cleared my throat. "What issue?"

"He wanted Nero to join his court, and when he refused, he threatened to end him."

"Didn't do it, though," Nero said, his voice low and rough as if he didn't use it much.

Kama rolled her eyes. "Nero doesn't think Poseidon is so bad, even though he tried to kill him." She grinned at Nero and his pale skin took on a touch of pink. "He's our forgiving one and too gentle to be out here with us vagabonds."

Nero's color deepened, but Orion chuckled. "There's nothing wrong with being both strong and tender."

Kama looked up at him. "Would you consider yourself to be tender?"

"Well, that depends on what your measure is. If you're comparing me to the boy I was a decade ago, not really. If you compare me to a bunch of prickly gods." He nudged Temi with his elbow, and she scoffed. "I'd say I'm fairly soft-hearted."

"Albeit arrogant as f—" Temi cleared her throat. "Stuff."

Kama laughed. "We're not that young. You don't have to watch your language in front of us."

We stepped into a narrow part of the path, the sides of the mountains closing in and sloping down to meet us. "You're not that old either," I said, ignoring the fact that they were actually only a few years younger than Temi and me.

Kama scowled, but Temi picked up the conversation. "We're on this mission to rescue Apollo's husband and nephew. Zephyrus has them."

Tears bit at me, my heart aching at the words. I swallowed and took a step ahead of them. I couldn't discuss it.

"Oh," Kama said, her expression taking on a tinge of pity.

"Zephyrus is the one who has it out for me," Chares said, his dark eyes shifting to me with sadness as well.

I couldn't deal with sympathy from a bunch of teenagers. Kama brushed a strand of hair behind her ear. "We thought your mission was to gain the spark and remove the division of the gods. Well, that's what Clothos told us, anyway. She said every god that longed to gain the power and authority of the spark would come after you during this journey, and we had to help end them so things could be set right again."

I whirled back around. "Fucking Clothos."

"Apollo," Temi chided as she darted her eyes to the young gods.

"No. She's caused all of this trouble."

Kama arched an eyebrow. "You don't have to watch what you say in front of us. We aren't babies."

I ignored her as I kept speaking to Temi. "She knew! She fucking knew Hyacinth would end up in this situation. I…" My voice broke and my lip trembled. Temi's expression softened as I continued. "I asked her if he would be in danger traveling with me, and she evaded the damn question. She could have spared him all of this."

Temi bowed her head. "I'm sorry."

"So,"—Mia thrust her hand on her hip—"are you guys fighting for a better future or not?"

"Mia." Kama raised her eyebrows. "He's hurting."

"And we're out here risking our lives and killing others. There needs to be a good reason."

I wiped my hand over my face. How did we end up with these tagalongs? I sighed. *Might as well tell them.* "Our prophecy is—" A clattering sound cut off my words. A shadow passed across the sun. Temi whipped her bow out and Orion tightened his grip on his spear and crouched lower, his eyes sharp.

A Spark of Death and Fury

A chariot driven by four winged horses landed on the cliff above us. Half a dozen gods stepped off, and spread out along the edges of the surrounding bluff, their faces expressionless. I pulled my bow off my shoulder, nocking an arrow.

"Apollo," a man with golden, wavy hair and broad shoulders said. "You were far too easy to hunt down. Predictable and foolish." His eyes skimmed the ravine we stood in, and he grinned a bright smile. "How lucky for me."

My fingers tightened. "I don't believe we've met."

He gave his head a toss and pressed his hand over his tunic. "Helios, god of the sun."

Temi narrowed her eyes as her arrow remained trained on him. The young gods waited, hunched and focused, and their magic hummed through the ground, rattling my feet.

Helios frowned. "Oh, wait, I forgot. That can only be my position if you're dead." Temi's arm pulled back, ready to strike. Helios gave a dramatic sigh. "It seems rather unfair that you're the golden one, does it not? Considering who your father is? The slaughter he just committed." Helios took a step on the path leading down from the precipice, and Orion snapped the spear in his grip. "Have you heard of it, or do you not care?"

"I saw it," I said. "And I agree with you. It was a slaughter. and I don't regret ending my father."

Helios continued walking and pebbles skittered down the side of the cliff. "Forgive me for not believing you. You brought him down to become the new high god. Killed your own father to achieve your ends. The world knows of your ambitions, *Apollo*." He spat my name.

Frustration gnarled within me. What ambitions? My only life goal was to get away from the politics and troubles of the gods. It wasn't by choice I was constantly thrust into the middle of it. How many gods believed this to be true? How many would attempt to kill me for the position they believed I was trying to take? "I don't care about being the sun god, but I can't die right now."

Helios clicked his tongue. "Would you prefer I put it on my schedule?"

"We don't wish to harm you or your party. Let us pass, and we won't hurt you."

Helios laughed, the sound ringing against the side of the mountains. "It's endearing that you think you could do us harm."

The other members of his party lifted weapons. Shit. I nodded to Temi as I released an arrow that whistled as it swept towards its mark. Helios dodged then disappeared.

My fingers froze on the bowstring.

A dozen arrows rained over us, and Chares whipped his hands up. Wind rushed through the valley we stood in and knocked the weapons aside.

Temi yanked out more arrows. They soared at the gods standing on the cliff.

Then half of the targets flashed out of view.

Temi faltered, lowering her bow.

What the fuck was happening?

An arrow sliced against the edge of my arm, and I winced.

"I'm sorry," Chares said. "I didn't see it coming."

I shifted in the direction it had come from. One god flickered into view and then out. It wasn't like he was invisible, but as though my eyes struggled to perceive what was obviously there. "They're shielding each other."

"Fuck," Temi said. Apparently, near death situations made cussing in front of the teenagers appropriate again. "How do we fight enemies we can't see?"

"Helios wants me, right?"

She nodded, and Orion frowned.

"I'm going to separate from the group." Temi parted her lips to argue as Chares sent another blast of wind around us that whipped us into a tunnel of protection. "The rest of you try to take out the others as I distract Helios," I yelled over the roar of the wind.

"But…"

"I'll go with you." Nero raised his chin. "We can't perceive them, but their bodies don't disappear. I could use water to expose Helios' form."

Temi licked her lips. "That's a good idea."

Nero spoke to Mia. "Will you help us?"

She nodded and squeezed Kama's fingers before trailing behind us. Uncertainty rippled through me. I wasn't sure if I should drag these two into a fight separate from the group. But Nero had a valid point. I was sure if we could bring Helios down, we'd end the fight. It was his ambitions this group fought for and if we ended their leader, they'd scatter as well.

"All right."

I gripped my hands around my bow as Chares dropped the wind and crouched into a defensive position beside Kama, Orion, and Temi.

I jogged up the edge of a cliff that provided us shelter until I reached a plateau tucked against a wall of boulders. A perfect spot to protect us. Anyone who wanted to fight would have to come to us.

We waited. Below, Orion snapped forward. His spear hit its mark and knocked a god down. The deity tried to rise again, but Orion whipped around with a thrust that sank the weapon into his throat, and his blood poured out onto the dusty path.

The young gods beside me bounced back and forth on their feet and shook their hands out.

I remained still.

Nothing could unnerve me like Hyacinth being in danger.

These were just obstacles. Marks in my way.

I would end them without hesitation to get to Cyn and Ixion.

The glowing sunshine in front of us shimmered, as if something had passed by. "Mia, now," Nero said.

She clenched her fists, and the ground cracked, splitting and screeching as the earth moved and rumbled beneath our feet. Nero yanked water out of the crack, pushed it forward, and outlined the form of three beings.

I sent arrows out, one after another, that hit their marks. A god screamed, tumbled backwards, tripped, and fell into the valley with a crunch. The water continued gushing from the gap, exposing the forms of the two others. I yanked a knife free and marched towards them.

Guilt no longer plagued me.

I'd kill whoever I had to.

I sliced the blade into a man who screeched. His body crashed with a thump to the ground.

The shield that had covered Helios ripped away, and he looked at his fallen companion and then back at me with fury in his eyes. He lifted a spear. I ducked to block it, but he shifted it in the other direction.

It swept across the precipice we stood in.

I reached for it like I could stop it.

The weapon had already reached its goal.

Nero stumbled as it struck him in the throat. He gagged and dropped to his knees. Mia screamed and lowered beside him.

A Spark of Death and Fury

I turned back to Helios, and the heat of the sun rushed through my veins. "You bastard."

He grinned and lifted another spear.

He wouldn't get a clean death. I was not about to give him such a mercy.

I dropped my bow and pounced on him. We tumbled together. Rocks cut my arms, banged my shins, bruising every inch of me. I didn't care. I clasped my fingers around his throat. He hissed and punched me in my stomach. It knocked the air from me, then he hit me a second time that ached into my spine.

I didn't release him. "We had no fight with you," I choked out, my voice gravely. "He's just a fucking kid."

Helios kneed me in my gut, and I tumbled back from him. He jumped to his feet and gasped for breath. I scrabbled up to jump in his direction again.

"He's a kid," Helios said as he ducked my punch, "who has chosen a side in this battle for the spark."

"No one here," I growled through my teeth, "cares about the damn spark."

He spat blood out and knocked me down. I hit the ground hard and the impact thundered through me. Helios jumped on top of me and held a blade aloft. He wiped ichor off his cheek with his shoulder. I jerked to get myself free, but he pressed against me. "You're pitiful for a sun god, Apollo."

Anger swelled and reminded me of those powers that lingered in my veins, waiting in the eaves.

I grabbed his face, dug my nails in, and swept into my powers as intensely as I ever had. It was like drowning and forcing myself to the surface. The magic whipped out of my hands, fire laced over my fingertips, and Helios screamed.

The smell of burning flesh arose between us, and I clenched my teeth hard to hold off a gag. Helios tumbled away from me and held his palms against his burnt face. I snatched the blade he'd dropped. He reached for his belt, but I flung the knife before he could reach for another weapon. It struck him in the chest, and he growled as he pulled it free.

Temi would have comments on my aim.

He lifted his arm back, and the weapon glittered under the sunlight.

The earth rumbled, shaking us, and boomed as it split apart, before swallowing him into the chasm.

Then it smashed together with a crunch as it covered Helios' cries.

Mia stood, covered in blood, tears creating tracks over the dust on her cheeks. Her hands trembled as they reached out to the gap in the earth.

The rest of Helios' party lay dead on the ground, surrounded by our group who stood coated in sweat and grime.

Mia ran back up the path to where Nero had fallen. My shoulders heaved as I followed behind her. The walled in space echoed with Kama's sobs. Chares drew her beside him and she pulled her knees against her chest and wept.

I dropped beside Nero who lay still. His eyes stared blankly ahead.

I reached out to him but already knew.

There was no healing the dead.

He'd died because he'd followed me.

My heart gave a lurch, but I stood and used my magic to restore everyone else who needed it. The intensity of exercising my powers wasn't enough to drain the anger thrumming through me, though.

Orion pulled out a cloth to clean up Nero. Temi looked at me before speaking to Kama. "I'm so sorry for your loss.

A Spark of Death and Fury

We will honor him. We can't linger here much longer, however. It's dangerous."

Kama's mouth gaped. "You want us to just leave him?"

"I am sorry," Temi said. "We'll bury him, of course. But we've used so much magic, and the shifting of the earth might attract other gods."

"We can at least pause for one night, can't we?" Kama asked.

I kicked a rock, and it tumbled, clattering against the wall. "Let them stay."

Temi gaped. "You want us to leave them after what just happened?"

I slapped my hand out, the ichor of the gods still fresh enough that it flickered off my hands. "These *children* should not have been with us in the first place."

Temi jumped up, her braids flying. "Now is not the time."

"No? Really? When is the time, then? When the rest of them are dead?"

Kama looked up from her position by Chares, her face red from crying.

Temi growled. "Not in front of them when they are grieving."

I lowered my voice to a whisper. "They are grieving because we included them in this. Because I allowed them to join us."

"They wanted to help, and they have. They've saved our asses twice now."

"At what cost?" My voice rose again, echoing off the rocks. Orion frowned at me from his position by the young gods.

Temi grabbed my arm and dragged me out, away from the group. She turned and bared her teeth. "What is this about?"

"A child has died because I allowed him to join us."

She studied me before lifting her chin. "This is about Hyacinth, isn't it?"

I shifted away from her.

"You agreed for him to go on your trip, he's in trouble now, and you blame yourself."

I clenched my teeth so hard it ached. "It's about nothing." I stomped in the direction opposite the group, away from Orion with his careful eyes, and Temi with her frustrated growl. I climbed higher, to the top of a cliff, just out of sight of the others. The world blurred, and I didn't care.

Temi was right.

It was about Hyacinth as much as Nero.

I'd selfishly wanted Cyn with me, had allowed him to shield me, had tasked him with caring for Ixion. Now he was in trouble. And it was my fault. I had tried to be the man he saw me as. The god who didn't kill without thought. I'd attempted to diffuse Helios, and it'd done nothing.

I pulled Cyn's ring out and grazed my fingers over the etchings on it, smoothed my thumb over the gem.

What did it matter? I'd lost Hyacinth, anyway.

Now Nero had also followed me, tried to help me.

And he was dead.

The time for a soft heart and a good man was gone.

I would cloak myself in stone if I must.

I would become everything I hated if it's what I had to do to save Cyn from the same fate.

The world could burn, for all I cared.

17

Hyacinth

I woke long before the sun did and lay in the bed watching Ixion's chest rise and fall. The bruise on his face had begun to heal, and his features looked so young and innocent as he slept. His lips pursed with his gentle snores. The curves of his cheek and the soft curls laying on them reflected the silvery light of dawn.

My hands held phantom aches from the previous day's torment.

Still, it was my heart that hurt the most.

The sun winked over the horizon, gleaming the condensation on the windows with drops of gold.

"Apollo," I whispered, just to hear his name.

My chin trembled, and I clamped my teeth down to fight tears.

It was in the quiet moments when I didn't have to put on a brave mask in front of Zephyrus or a calm one for Ixion that the heartache rippled through me. In some ways, focusing on that was better than the fear that dripped in the back of my mind, slowly wearing down my resolve.

What did Zephyrus want me alive for? It had to be a

trade of some sort, but with whom? Not knowing how long I might have to keep this all up suffocated me.

Instead, I remembered Apollo.

The coarseness of his curls tangled around my fingers, him rolling his eyes and scoffing, his lips pressed against mine.

I took a slow breath.

The door opened, and I jumped to my feet.

Zephyrus walked in, his expression unamused, his blond hair slicked back. "Have you reconsidered releasing the boy?"

Ixion sat up, his curls a jumbled mess, his eyes welling with tears. He froze though and nodded at me. He'd follow the plan. He'd stay still and try to be brave.

My breathing picked up, but I raised my chin and kept my words steady. "I don't know what boy you're talking about."

Zephyrus hissed and stepped closer to me, dropping his voice to a whisper. "I'll give you this much, Hyacinth. You're stronger than I would have guessed. But I assure you, yesterday was the smallest taste of what I will do to you. Think carefully if this is the road you wish to choose."

I met his eyes, the piercing blue of them, and frowned. "I have no choice here. There is no boy. You're delusional."

Zephyrus yanked his hand back and slapped me, hard enough that my vision blurred for a moment. I stumbled as the coppery taste of blood flooded over my tongue. I opened my mouth and red-tinted saliva dribbled out over my aching jaw.

If he thought that would change my mind, he was mistaken.

It only solidified my decision.

He'd done the same to Ixion—a child.

A Spark of Death and Fury

Zephyrus had hurt him like this.

He would have to kill me before I let him so much as look at Ixion again.

I straightened and looked him in the eyes. He stared at me, his chest heaving. I would not drop his gaze, and finally he shook his head. "So be it, then. Everyone can be broken, Hyacinth. Stubborn princes included."

He gestured to the door, and I hesitated for a moment. Ixion remained still but cried out, "Please don't go with them again."

I didn't turn towards him, didn't respond. Instead, I gave him another quick look and hoped it expressed more confidence and calm than I possessed, before walking to the door. I wouldn't make a scene in front of Ixion.

We made it out to the hall with Zephyrus walking ahead. Guards followed us, but no one held me. Zephyrus didn't even think I was that dangerous. Fury ached into my gut.

We turned another corner, and I pounced to yank my arms around Zephyrus' throat, before slamming his forehead into a wall. He grunted at the impact, and we tumbled to the floor as his wings smacked against me. I searched his hip with my free hand for a knife or a weapon of any sort.

There was nothing.

A guard jerked me off him and threw me against the opposite wall. Another smashed the back end of a spear into my side, and a crunch echoed. I moaned and bent over to hold my ribs where I was sure something had broken.

Zephyrus righted himself and brushed hair out of his face. He ran his wrist under his nose and pulled it down to examine the glistening crimson of his blood. "You"—he lifted his face—"are going to regret doing that."

A guard yanked my hair to force me upright. I whimpered as pain tore through my side. I refused to show more weakness than I had to, though. "You're a coward and a monster, Zephyrus. And one day you'll pay for all your crimes."

He came closer to me and grabbed my jaw. I attempted to jerk away, but the guards held me fast. "You do not know how much of a fool you are."

"I disagree. I've slept with you. Only the worst kind of fool would do that."

He clenched his fingers hard enough that the inside of my cheeks cut against my teeth. I winced, my eyelashes fluttering, before he released me. "Take him downstairs."

The guards half-ushered me, half-dragged me, and affixed my hands in the cuffs. My fingers flexed, and I trembled. For all the bravado I'd offered Zephyrus, I wasn't actually brave. I was terrified. My body already ached. Every time I drew in a breath, my chest pierced with pain.

Zephyrus walked in, and spread his wings wide, blocking out the torchlight along the wall which made his feathers gleam. His face was cast in shadows, like some sort of demon that came for me.

He dropped his roll of weapons and brushed it open. "This can stop any moment you want it to. Pull your magic back and release the boy."

A tremble ran down me, and I clenched my fingers until they bit into my palms. "There is no boy."

Zephyrus growled and slammed a knife into the soft part of my hand hard enough that the blade sank into the wall. I screamed.

I drifted into my mind, into memories and places away from there. I thought of the gentle kindness of my father, the spirited laughter of my mother, the sweetness of growing up with my siblings. Apollo was the best distraction, though.

Remembering him allowed me to draw my spirit out of the moment and drift far from my physical form.

I was never a badass, Apollo, I'd said to him.

He'd snorted. *You're the bravest fucker I've ever met.*

Tears dripped down my cheeks.

I wasn't sure if it was from the pain or the memory of him.

But I would try to be brave for him. For Ixion.

Hours passed, or maybe only minutes.

My body hurt so much, time had lost its sense of meaning. They'd locked me in that cellar forever, as far as I could tell.

I was slumped against the manacles when someone came and unlatched them. I hit my knees with a bang and blood from my face fell with a drip, drip, drip against the stone. There wasn't a section of my body that didn't have some damaged piece. The world blurred as they directed me back to the suite. Everything hurt, but all I could think as they unlocked the door was that Ixion couldn't see me like this, injured and broken. It would scare him.

They shoved me inside, and Zephyrus said from somewhere in the distance, "I want a guard in the room the whole night. And, since there's no boy, only deliver enough food for one."

I wanted to fall to my knees, to give into the lack of consciousness dragging on me. I stumbled to the bed and fell onto it. Ixion scrambled up beside me. "Papa." He sniffled. "You're hurt." He trembled against me and caused every cut and injured part of my body to ache.

Blood stuck my fingers together, and it hurt my side to speak, but I forced my voice out in a whisper and prayed the guard that shuffled in through the door didn't hear me. "I'm not. It's an illusion, a trick."

"A trick?" he asked, his voice trembling.

"Zephyrus wants to scare you. But it's just pretend. You have to try and stay still, remember?"

He hovered his hands over me like he wasn't certain if he should touch me. Gods, I wished he wouldn't. I wasn't sure I could hold back the wince if he did. The guard settled in a chair by the door and crossed an ankle over his leg.

Ixion lay down beside me and whimpered. "Papa?"

"Hmm?"

"I'm so scared."

"It's okay to be scared," I whispered. "I'm going to be brave for us both."

He remained quiet for a dozen heartbeats, and my eyes grew heavy. The room turned into a fuzzy mass of gray and peach.

"Do you want food?" Ixion asked, breaking into my drifting. The guard was distracted with a parchment in his lap, and Ix could finally eat a few bites without his notice.

"No. I'm not hungry. You eat."

Ixion said something else, but I didn't hear it. My last thought before everything faded was that I hoped Ixion could remain away from the guard's notice before I slipped into darkness.

18

Epiphany

"Who makes the offerings?" the priest said from beneath the shade of a tree that stretched over the palace's mausoleum. I stepped forward, carrying gold and oils and dedications not just for Father but also for Emrin. An endless crowd undulated around, and gray clouds hovered over it all. Everyone present—high lords, prominent Nirians, friends and connections of Father's and Emrin's—all looked at me to close out my family's life. My private grief was a national affair.

I'd buried too many people in the last year.

My mind drifted to Hyacinth, and I wished he stood with me instead of facing whatever danger he endured. Worry was a heartbeat in my body. I had to trust that Apollo and Temi would see Cyn home safely.

I placed the offerings on the ground before each sarcophagus, the maroon panels of my dress chuffing against the grass, then I rose before grazing my fingers over the gritty stone. I remembered Father doing that at Hyacinth's funeral, the grief that had weighed him down.

I stopped, leaned over Emrin's sarcophagus, and whispered. "I remember the good, Em. And I won't let others forget you."

As I approached Father's, my heart galloped. The design that workers had crafted on the stone was one he'd selected. It depicted Father, not on a throne or before the nation, but sitting on a bench beside Mother, with me and Hyacinth and Emrin at their sides.

I grazed the depiction of him, my fingers bumping along the edges of his nose. "I love you, Father. And I will fight for this country you led so well."

The priest waited for me. I found my place next to him and crossed my hands. The crowd of thousands watched me. I longed for one friendly face in it. But Valerian had left to meet his father. Delon had died. Temi traveled to rescue my only remaining relative. My family was broken and I stood alone. The last time I'd felt that way, I had Galeson at my side. Now I faced a grieving nation and political upheaval entirely on my own.

I straightened my spine and met the gaze of people in the crowd. A woman with soft brown eyes pressed her lips together and inclined her head. A man holding the hand of a child with wispy curls bowed.

The looks of grief and pity and heartache hurt.

I didn't drop their gazes.

I held them. I wanted my people to know that I was with them.

That while I shared in their heartbreak, it had not broken me. They didn't stand alone.

After the ceremony ended and the crowd cleared out, Fen approached me. "Forgive me, Your Highness, for being so callous as to bring an issue to you at the funeral of your family."

I took a deep breath as the trees rattled above me. "It's all right. The circumstances are unusual at the present."

"Just so." He placed his hands behind his back, and we started walking down the path in the direction of the stone fortress of the palace, which rested against a cushion of darkening clouds in the distance. "The issue is with the war widows, Your Highness."

I clenched my fingers. So many lives lost and so many families harmed from it.

"Yes?"

"We're receiving many complaints that some households cannot make ends meet on the pittance offered for the men's service."

"Do the advisors believe that to be true?"

"We do." He stopped walking and steepled his fingers together. "The gods have blessed Niria with peace for well over a century. When the laws were last written, the value of gold was far less than it currently is."

"I see. Can we change it?"

"We can." He nodded. "With your approval. It will take weeks to pass, though."

"Weeks." A bird swooped through the sky and crossed where the sun peeked out behind a building storm. The creature's shadow passed in silhouette before it trembled into the branches of a tree. "Are these families able to make ends meet until then?"

Fen's hair fluttered around his ears in the breeze, and he frowned. "Some very well may not, Your Highness."

I rubbed my thumb in a circle over my palm. "We recruited most of our soldiers from here in the capital, didn't we?"

"Well... yes."

"Good. We'll open a daily meal that the kitchens will provide for anyone in need."

Fen bobbed his head, but his voice came warily. "How will we cover the expense, Your Highness?"

We reached the palace, and I turned to meet his gaze. "We'll have to cut extras, so our people won't starve. Can you work with Lord Haven and Lord Eliga to discover any extra expenses we could draw back without harming the temples or artists excessively? The first one can be my personal money."

Fen pressed his fingers together. "Begging forgiveness for my bluntness, Your Highness, but do you not wish to maintain your income and save it... should things not go well with your cousin?"

A wind whipped through the gardens and tumbled petals free from flowers, scattering them across the pathway. I understood what Fen meant. If Demetri took the throne and I displeased him, he could banish me. I might find myself in a place of limited finances, with no family, and minimal connections. I gave my head a shake. "It's the people of Niria that are the priority to me right now. I'll just pray things work out for me as well."

"Very well, Your Highness." He bowed and turned back down the path.

That's how I found myself a day later standing and handing out cloth wrapped bundles of bread as Nirians moved through the line, my guards shadowing me and watching the entire group with narrowed eyes. Some people stepped back when they realized who I was. Their gazes darted to the crown on my head and widened. Others wept. A few refused to accept the portion of the meal I offered and bowed nervously as they backed away.

When the line had dwindled to only a few dozen people remaining, a woman grasped my hand. My guards shifted in, and a few drew weapons. She gave my palm a squeeze before dropping it. Her eyes watered as her gray hair wisped out from under her cloak, matching the sky behind her. "Thank you, Your Highness. I can't say how much this means to all of us."

"Of course. It's the least we could do."

"It's a great deal more than many would. We know it, Princess." She sniffled and a few tears broke free to spill down her cheeks. "You're compassionate like y'er mother and have a good head on y'er shoulders like your father did. Niria is proud of you."

Words tumbled through my mind that I struggled to form. Finally, I choked out, "Thank you."

"I'm sorry for the situation you find yourself in, but I believe you'll be all right."

"I'm sorry that this"—I waved to the group of palace workers handing out food—"is necessary. I know we will overcome hard times together."

"Seeing you here," she whispered, "makes me truly hopeful for that, Your Highness. Forgive me, I'm holding up the line."

I offered her several loaves of the bread, and she tucked them into her bag that already stretched heavy with the cheese, fruit, and dried meat she'd already gathered. She clasped my hand once again before moving on. My heart soared with opposing feelings. I was heartbroken, of course. I had lost most of my family. So many Nirians had died. Grief throbbed through me. Another feeling bloomed in me as well, wrapping into my bones alongside the sadness. Hope. Seeing the people of my country, their bravery and endurance, reminded me of who I was, where I came from, and what I fought for.

The line finally dispersed as the sun sank slowly down behind dark clouds, as if it was as exhausted as I felt. My guards tightened around me. They wanted me back within the safety of the palace walls. They were right. I wished to help clean up, but I should go in. It wouldn't help Niria if something happened to me. My wellbeing wasn't just about myself anymore.

I set a pile of towels into a stack, then a woman in a plum gown caught my eye. I abandoned my post and walked over to her. She folded cloth bags into neat squares, and her dark curls that had slipped out of her headcloth stuck against her forehead. Valerian's mother.

"Hello," I said.

Her lips thinned but she bowed. "Your Highness."

"Really, that's unnecessary." I cleared my throat. She stared at me as if she waited for a command. I gestured to the kitchen staff who stacked bowls and utensils together. "I see you came to help."

A breeze picked up and whipped her skirt around her. Her eyes darted to the trees, the other workers, the palace. Anywhere but me. "Attendants informed me it was an acceptable activity being as you took part yourself, Your Highness, but if it displeases you, I won't attend again."

"No… No, I'm glad you came." My lips parted to speak, but I wasn't sure what to say. This was Valerian's mother. I wanted us to see each other as family. But my relationship with her son had cost her everything. "I'm so very sorry… I never thought… Well…" I clasped my hands and bowed my head. "I should have considered how my choices might affect you and…" My chin trembled, and gods, I wouldn't cry here in front of her. She didn't strike me as a woman who would respect someone breaking. When I lifted my face, her eyebrows had pulled together, her lower lip caught between her teeth. I sniffled and brushed down my gown. "I should have thought about you, I mean."

She stepped in closer to me and lowered her voice to a whisper. "The palace staff shouldn't see you crying like this, Your Highness."

A Spark of Death and Fury

I lowered my chin again.

She hated me, of course. She'd been abused by high lords in the past, had always disdained mine and Val's relationship, and now lost her position because of it. I'd hate me too if I were in her place. I don't know why I had expected anything other than disregard or a scolding. I nodded and turned to leave.

"You aren't the only one deciding things," she said. I stopped, meeting the intensity of her dark eyes. "Valerian has, and I have as well. You don't need to apologize to me."

"I'd really like it if we could have a relationship."

The wary expression returned to her face. "I'm uncertain how I might serve you."

A drop of rain plunked against my cheek, and I looked up at the sky that trembled, ready to burst. My guards shifted beside me, and their weapons clattered against their armor. They wouldn't break propriety to tell me to head back, that soon this storm would begin, and we'd all get caught in it. Their expressions said enough, though. "I should go in. It was good to see you…" My words trailed off as I remembered I didn't even know her name.

Valerian's mother folded her hands together as I turned. "It's Isadora."

"Pardon me?" I shifted back around.

"My name." She rubbed her arm and looked over her shoulder, as if she'd been caught somewhere she shouldn't. "My name is Isadora."

"That's a beautiful name."

She bobbed her head.

"I would really like it if you'd call me Epiphany."

The wind picked up, trailed our skirts back, and whipped my hair off my neck, cooling the flesh there. Isadora winced. "I'll try."

"Thank you. I'm sorry, but I really should go now."

"Of course."

I turned, and my guards circled around me as I started moving in the direction of the gates. Another complicated emotion burned through me. I wanted Valerian's mother to like me. I didn't want to be a burden to her. But who knew if that was a possibility. I'd caused so much trouble for her life. She was the only thing like family I had anymore. And she was Val's mother. I wanted us to have a good relationship, as hopeless as that felt.

When we made it back, I eased through the halls of the palace, weary but still blooming with hope and compassion for my people. Those feelings tangled in with the confusion over my connection with Isadora.

I turned down the hall towards my bedroom. The hallway had settled into the silver light of a stormy early evening. Demetri pushed off a wall, his cape rippled out behind him, and he frowned. "Where have you been this afternoon?"

His voice came like a scolding, and I took a deep breath to keep my words even. I was not about to stand here and allow this man to reprimand me. Especially since he'd apparently waited in this corridor he had no business being in to speak with me. "We're hosting free meals for the widows and families affected by the war. I'm sure you might have heard something about it. I was helping."

He scoffed. "It's not proper for a lady to be out working in front of the people like some sort of attendant. And, yes, I've been informed of your decisions. Is your plan to drain the coffers before I take the throne?"

A coolness flooded through my arms. "I'm making careful judgments under the counsel of the advisors, and I assure you, Niria is wealthy. A month of generosity on our part will not harm us."

"I hear you've canceled the palace's plays."

Annoyance pinched at me. "Then you've heard incorrectly, my lord. We've only put off new performances that require fresh costumes and scenery. The actors, however, will still receive their salary and they plan to repeat past productions in the interim. Now, if you'll excuse me, I'm tired."

I took a step closer to my bedroom, but Demetri cut me off and the scruff on his jaw creased with his frown. "Don't think, Princess, that I'm unaware of what you're playing at."

"What do you mean?"

He leaned in closer, and his brown eyes darkened in the shadows of the hall. "You believe you can usurp the throne? Do you truly think that the high lords will accept a woman as their leader?"

My fingers curled into fists, and my guards stepped forward, but I raised a hand to stall them. I could handle this. "If their only other option is a man who refuses to work and has no concern for this country at all, maybe they will. Why do you care? You don't even want this role."

"It is publicly known now," he hissed. "What am I supposed to do? Leave here and let everyone know that my baby cousin, some... woman"—he laced the word with so much venom spit speckled from his lips—"stole my rightful position from me?"

I clenched my teeth and drew in close enough I could slap him. "If you think your insecurity over your reputation will play any role in my decision making when considering the good of this country and the people in it, then you are mistaken."

I ducked past him and my guards and grabbed my door handle.

"I'll fight you on this," he said without turning around. "I won't stand back while you take the throne from me."

The knob rested cool and sturdy against my palm. I took a deep breath to keep my words calm. "Then I hope you came prepared to battle, my lord."

I walked inside my room and closed it firmly behind me.

19

Valerian

Arion gave a jerk of his shoulders. I lost my balance and yanked on the reins to keep from tumbling off him. Some of the guards side-eyed me, and I forced my expression to remain neutral. They returned to scanning the mountainous path around us, the lilac forms of hills in the distance, the sunshine glittering down across a valley where clouds dappled parts of a lake into shadows.

Wind rattled Arion's seaweed strands of hair. He huffed and flared his nostrils. I clenched my legs tighter, so he didn't throw me. The guards on this trip already didn't respect my choices, and I couldn't blame them, really. But the one bit of pride I'd always had was that I was a natural with horses.

Of course, on this trip, Arion had fought against me so much, even that looked suspicious anymore. The stallion reared up, and I clenched hard against him. "Arion," I growled.

He tossed his head like I could get the fuck off his back if I didn't like it.

A sigh slipped through my lips.

Asher trotted up beside me. His gray mare complied to every small tug of the rein.

I'd trained that damn horse and now, I was stuck with Temi's unwieldy creature.

"Having troubles?" Asher said.

I clacked my teeth together and shrugged. I didn't like to complain. It wasn't my place and especially with me publicly aligned with Epiphany now. I'd overstepped my station, and everyone knew it, me most of all. "It's fine."

Asher cocked up a dark eyebrow. "Certain of that? We'll reach Lord Lucien's estate today and I don't think you wish for this"—he skimmed his gaze over Arion and frowned—"to be his first impression of you." If there was one mercy or scrap of my pride saved in all of this, it was that the rest of our group was terrified of Arion. No one else would even approach him, much less ride him.

"I couldn't leave Arion. No other stable worker could handle him." I paused as I realized that I had included myself in that group. I didn't belong to it any longer, however. I'd always balanced the two edges of a chasm. Suddenly the gulf had widened, and I'd landed on one side. How strange to find myself longing for the other as well. "I promised Temi I'd take care of the creature." My voice pitched with annoyance. "Even if he's a moody pain in the ass."

Arion snorted again, and I tensed my legs in case he attempted to toss me another time. My thighs and stomach ached from all the effort it took to remain on him as we journeyed.

Asher nodded as the cape he wore rippled out in the breeze. I readjusted the silk robe I wore and the discomfort in me deepened. This type of clothing belonged to Hyacinth and Emrin. Not me.

What was I playing at?

A Spark of Death and Fury

"If he can't behave better"—Asher gave Arion a censuring glare—"we may need to leave him with some guards. We can't have Lord Lucien's first impression be your horse tossing you."

Arion sank his hooves into the path, rocks skittered with the abruptness of the motion, and the horse behind him whinnied as it pulled up short.

I clenched my teeth and kicked his side to urge him forward. His only response was to press his ears back against his head. The sun splashed out, peeking behind clouds that glided through the sky, making Arion's aqua coat sparkle.

"Can you give me a minute?" I asked Asher.

He frowned again and gestured for the group to go around us. They paused farther down the path, though the guards watched us carefully. After all, I was escorted as a prince like Joden has said. This was my whole life now, guards following me, freedoms gone.

I jumped off Arion and brought Epiphany to mind.

She was in the same place. Trapped. And currently alone.

Gods I hoped she was okay dealing with her cousin and the advisors. She could handle it, but sometimes she let her self-doubts get the best of her.

I did this for her.

Epiphany.

And for myself.

To do something meaningful.

My entire life I'd wanted to matter, to serve our country well, to find a place for myself. That's why I'd gone to war. I'd found that disappointing, though. It left me with nothing but haunting nightmares and regrets where I replayed events and wondered if I could have done something different to save lives and create a better outcome.

Maybe this was my opportunity to make a difference and help.

Those thoughts filled me like a breeze that rippled the sails of a boat, and I peeled the robe off, folded it, and hung it on a tree limb that stretched near the path. I turned on Arion and placed my hands on my hips. "Listen, Arion, this meeting I'm about to go to is important."

Arion eyed me before lowering his nose to the ground and grabbing a bite of grass.

"If you don't behave yourself better, you're getting left with the guards."

He bared his teeth, pressed his ears back, and released a sharp whinny that fluttered my hair around my temples.

"Temi wanted you to stay with me, so you were looked after."

He stomped a hoof before returning his nose back to the vegetation on the side of the path, his eyes dropping.

"I know you miss her. Damn it, I miss her too, and not just because I wish she could be the one to deal with you."

Arion flicked his tail.

"You don't belong here with me. Just as I don't belong pretending to be a prince worthy of marrying the Princess of Niria." I crossed my arms. "But here we are. Sometimes we have to make the best of situations. This may not be helping a goddess in battle, but I'm facing my own fight right now. I could use someone in my corner. Please, Arion, behave yourself today?"

He considered me for a moment and swished his tail back and forth before he heaved a great sigh and turned to the side where I could mount him again. I wasn't sure if we'd actually come to an understanding or not. I knew he comprehended what I'd said. Temi talked to him like she spoke with an equal. I pulled the robe down and the rich burgundy silk unspooled as I slipped my arms back into it.

I jumped onto Arion's back and grabbed the reins, half-expecting him to toss me. He started into a trot at a nudge of my foot. We caught up with the group again, and for an hour I remained tense, certain Arion would start fighting me again. By the time we reached the red-tiled roof of Lord Lucien's estate, I had relaxed and patted Arion's neck as he held himself with the dignity of a godborn horse.

As our group arrived, attendants opened the gates and my posture tensed. I'd spent my entire childhood wondering what this place looked like. A mountain range sat shrouded in fog in the distance. The courtyard we rode into stretched out the length of the house with six massive fountains on either side. At the head of the yard, painted tiles glimmered in light, forming a patio around the entrance that was defined by massive windows. I gripped my fingers tighter into Arion's reins. This estate was every bit as luxurious and elegant as I'd imagined.

What I had to assume was the family, all dressed in rich velvets and rippling capes stood ahead of us. They assessed our group, the navy Nirian flags that fluttered in the breeze, the dozens of guards, Asher with his uniform on and his chin lifted. And me. Dressed like a prince when I was anything but, seated atop a creature clearly not of the human world.

The expressions ranged from curious to sharp eyes and pinched lips. I tugged Arion's reins to draw him to a stop as we reached the group.

A man with a sharp jaw, emerald eyes, a ghost of a salt-and-pepper beard, and thick dark hair with streaks of gray at the temples stepped forward. "Lord Asher." He bowed.

Asher dismounted, and I joined him, standing at his side.

Asher removed his glove and thrust his hand out. "A

pleasure, Lord Lucien." They shook hands and Asher gestured to me. "Let me introduce you to Valerian."

Lucien's gaze darted to me, and his lips pressed together. The thin woman with sharp cheekbones and arched eyebrows behind him frowned, her fingers curling into fists, but she took a deep breath and remained silent. Lucien cleared his throat. "Our attendants will take your horses."

"I'll see to my own horse," I said. "An attendant can lead him to a stall, but I'll care for him."

Lucien eyed Arion and then scowled at me. "Don't trust my staff to manage your beast?"

Asher laughed. "That *beast* would gladly take the hand off one of your staff. He's god-born and headstrong. Few men can manage him." Asher squeezed my shoulder. "Valerian is quite the horseman, however."

Lucien remained quiet for a moment but then nodded.

I walked over to Arion and gripped my fingers into his mane. "Please," I whispered. "Go with these stable attendants and don't put up a fuss." His muscles twitched like he prepared to kick up. "I'll steal you a dozen apples later. I swear it. And I'll visit in a few hours."

Arion snorted, but his shoulders loosened, and he joined in with the other horses as stablemen ushered them to the back side of the courtyard. I turned around to face Lucien again.

"Let me introduce you to my son," Lucien said. "He can show you to my office where we can have a private conversation. I'll meet you there once I have all our guests" —he surveyed our group, his lips pinching down— "settled."

"Of course," I said.

Lucien turned and gestured to a man who had to be half

a dozen years older than me at least. He had the same green eyes as Lucien. The same ones I had. I swallowed past a knot in my throat as Lucien spoke again. "This is Lord Evander, my firstborn, and heir to my estate." He narrowed his eyes at me, as if to make it very clear that I was none of those things.

My heart lurched.

I'd always known this man hadn't accepted me, hadn't wanted anything to do with me. Standing here, facing him, and receiving so little decorum brought up all my childhood insecurities and sadness and made it a struggle to force my expression to remain unaffected.

King Magnes had raised me. I'd taken all the classes Hyacinth had on deportment, manners, and politics. I knew how to play the game. I bowed deeply. "It's a pleasure to meet you, Lord Evander."

He nodded and pointed to the doors. We passed by others I had to assume were my siblings and Lucien's wife who glared at me.

As we stepped into the estate, the light dimmed, and polished tile floors glimmered with streaks of silver and gold. Tall walls covered in intricate murals defined the hall. A grin slashed across Evander's face that stretched out his pale cheeks. "So, you're Father's bastard, huh?"

I faltered for a moment, missed a step, and stumbled slightly before matching his pace again. "I suppose so."

Evander's eyes twinkled and he grinned as he opened a massive door that had jewels worked into the detailed carvings of it. "I'm sure you understand the discomfort. I mean if you're fucking the Princess of Niria"— my blood ran cold, and I struggled to force myself to continue into the room with him—"you have to know how bad it looks for others to find out about your indiscretions. Gods, I honestly didn't believe Father was foolish enough to leave some attendant pregnant with his bastard, but the two of us couldn't look more alike."

He gestured to burgundy chairs with rich, brocade fabrics, and I lowered into a seat even as I longed to leave this room and never return. I was here for Pip and for Niria. I'd entangled myself with royalty, fallen in love with the standing leader of our country, and I would do anything to help, no matter the discomfort it caused me.

Evander perched against the edge of the desk. "Fair warning, my mother hates you." He shrugged. "Understandably. I mean, men are supposed to be more discreet, you know?"

"Right," I whispered, even though I didn't know.

I would never betray Epiphany.

Not if it cost me my soul.

Perhaps Lucien's marriage wasn't a love match. Still, he'd made a commitment and she clearly wasn't comfortable with his 'indiscretions.' Evander has said that in the plural. How many other children did Lucien have in the world? How many siblings did I possess and not know about?

Evander kicked his heel against the desk, studying me like I was an oddity. "Do you mind me asking how you ended up fucking around with the Princess? I mean, that's pretty on course for the men of this family." He laughed. "That would be ambitious even for me, much less a... you're a stablehand aren't you?"

He stopped speaking long enough for a gap to stretch that required me to fill in the quiet. "I was a stablehand, yes. The Princess and I grew up together."

"A strange way for King Magnes to raise his children. I suppose it isn't my place to say so. Anyway..." He waved around the room, the rich greens and golds of it, the tall windows and heavy curtains, the thick rugs that stretched over more gleaming tiles. "I'll leave you to it. Good luck."

He pushed off the desk and stepped out of the office, clicking the door shut behind him.

I dropped against the back of my chair. So many emotions whirled through me that I struggled to make sense of them. He'd called me a bastard so casually, as if it was nothing. Then he'd asked about me "fucking around" with Epiphany... as if I was using her.

I'd seen so much crassness in the previous year—horses that suffered to death for men's gains, political maneuvers that disregarded the people they affected, humans slaughtered like chattel in a war driven by greed—to realize I'd grown up sheltered. I'd seen so much good in Magnes and his family. I'd believed that was the reality of the world, that most people were honorable or well-meaning at least.

The past year had soured my opinions on that.

Maybe the world was actually cruel and good people were the anomaly.

Epiphany was good.

I didn't know if I qualified. I wished to. And I was willing to help her fight for Niria. If that meant facing more vulgarity and selfishness, then so be it.

My teeth clenched as the door pulled open again. I sat back up and brought to mind Magnes. He'd prepared me for this moment and thought me worthy of his daughter. Regardless of what these people said, I would live up to that.

Lucien walked in, dropped in the same spot his son had, and leaned against the desk to tower over me. He frowned and it sank into me that I looked like him. I'd always thought I must have been a mix of my father and mother, but now, looking my father in the face, I couldn't deny it. Mother looked Nirian with her dark curls and brown eyes. I favored Lucien, had the same jawline and green eyes that always made me stand out. I bet we even shared expressions. It was a mercy I wasn't aware of mine enough to know if that was true.

Lucien clicked his pinky finger against the edge of the desk with a loud tap, tap, tap. He crossed his ankles. "You've put me in quite an uncomfortable position."

It was the first words he'd ever truly spoken to me, aside from his annoyance over Arion, and I hesitated a moment before speaking. "Forgive me, my lord, that wasn't my intention."

One of his brows rose as he pushed off the desk and walked behind it to drop into his seat. "I suppose you're aware the disagreement King Magnes and I had over you caused trouble between traders in our country. Niria, being wealthier than Carens, fared better in that dispute, and it did not add to my popularity among the high lords here."

I kept his gaze, made my breathing remain even and steady, and stalled my words so they didn't rush out. "That must have been troublesome."

"Let me make this perfectly clear. This estate belongs to my *son*." He emphasized the word as if to say, *which you are not*. "Even if I do claim you—and it would only be for the purpose of not further sullying my name and the benefit a connection to the royal family may have for me— you will not touch a single coin of my wealth. You will not be invited into the bosom of my family. You'll have no reason to set a foot on this estate again. Do you understand me, boy?"

My chest burned and I longed to snap out a sarcastic remark. But for Epiphany, for Magnes, for Mother, for Niria… For my own damn self I would control my words. "My only desire and purpose in coming here, my lord, is to

A Spark of Death and Fury

obtain a title so that I'm able to marry the Princess. I ask nothing more of you, I assure you."

He sighed but stood and gestured for me to do the same. "Very well. You'll stay for a few days while Lord Asher travels to meet with his military connections. In the meantime, we'll work on the paperwork and I'll sign it"—he skimmed his eyes over me and his mouth twisted into a grimace—"*if* I feel it's a wise choice at that point. Some attendants will show you to a room." He gestured to the door.

I rose and stepped out of it, followed an attendant who waited for me.

My heart sank, though.

For whatever reason, I thought he would sign the papers, and that would be that.

Apparently, I had to prove myself to him.

Great.

20

Hyacinth

Consciousness came and went for me in waves. Zephyrus smacked my face, and I barely felt it. Everything hurt so much, I couldn't draw a breath without every inch of my nerves lighting on fire like someone took a torch off the wall and pressed it into me. I shuddered at that. I wouldn't put it past Zephyrus, and I didn't want to give him any ideas.

My breathing came raspy and painful. I could scarcely close one of my hands anymore. I coughed, and the coppery bite of blood filled my mouth.

I hadn't eaten for several days. Or I thought it was several days. It was hard to tell. Time seemed intangible. The number of times the sun had set and the moon rose all blurred together. I was woozy from hunger, that I knew.

Zephyrus combed the blond strands of his hair out of his face with his fingers. "Enough of this, Hyacinth. Release the damn boy."

I parted my lips to say there was no boy.

Words didn't come.

My body was broken, and my spirit was going with it.

A Spark of Death and Fury

I whimpered, and my head dropped against the wall.

What was I even fighting for? If Zephyrus killed me, the shield would lift, and he'd have Ixion, anyway. I felt like I edged up against my demise so perhaps he'd soon have Ixion and what could I do about it? Perhaps no one was coming for us.

Maybe my entire life would consist of torment for the rest of my limited days.

For a moment, I regretted returning after my death.

I could have stayed in eternal peace, never feeling pain, never suffering, or wishing it would end.

Except then I never would have seen Apollo again.

I thought of the last time we'd made love, the feel of his skin warm against mine. He told me he'd suffer the pain of losing me a thousand times for a single day with me.

I felt the same.

Everything I'd endured had been worth it for the time we'd had together. My heart, for one painful lurch, hurt more than my body. Until the coursing pain streaked through me, and I shuddered.

Zephyrus grabbed my face, and I whimpered again as his touch shot pain through my jaw. I gasped, and my side burned. "I only need you barely alive, Hyacinth. In fact, I think Apollo seeing you like this might work even better than just having you as a prisoner."

I lifted my eyes, ignoring the sharp burn that swept through my body. "Apollo?" For another heartbeat, I forgot about my agony and every miserable second since I'd arrived here. "He's alive?"

Zephyrus frowned, dropped my jaw, and turned away from me. The feathers on his wings appeared to flutter in the flickering torchlight. "It won't matter, Prince. You won't live long enough to reunite with him."

I drew in another painful breath as guards unlocked my chains and dragged me to my feet. Every muscle screamed, and each time I stepped on my left foot, it pulled the breath from me and made my entire body run cold.

But...

Zephyrus had said Apollo lived.

Could that be true?

Maybe he lied to me.

Of course, I'd thought that before when he'd shared rumors about Apollo's ascension, and his words had been true.

Apollo had survived the blast? My mind whirled as they returned me to the room. I stumbled towards the bed and fell against it. Ixion clambered onto the mattress and came to lie down beside me. I didn't know why Zephyrus kept returning me to the room. Maybe he hoped I'd break with Ixion nearby. If anything, it strengthened my resolve.

Ixion had gotten used to this routine, to not moving around much because of the guard and not touching me because of my injuries. *Ixion,* I mouthed. He sniffled and ran his fingers over the tattered hem of my shirt.

Gods, this was going to damage him for life. In attempting to protect him, I was causing him harm in another way. He'd spent the last few days terrified and cowering, worrying over me and afraid of the men who kept us here.

I started reciting a poem, one I knew so well I didn't even have to think as I whispered it. Ixion settled in beside me, and his anxious movements stilled.

That left space for my mind to wander.

If Apollo had lived and he was on the way here... there was hope. He would be here soon. Gods, he'd tear the world down to get to us; I knew that. All I had to do was survive a few more days, keep Ixion safe for a few dozen more hours, and this misery would end. Apollo could take over care of the child, whether I survived or not.

Maybe I'd see him at least one more time, the golden radiance of him, the strength of his body and love in his eyes.

Hope buoyed through me.

Like it burned me.

As if Apollo's sun nestled into my heart, scorching away the broken bits.

I knew it was true.

He was alive.

And he'd be here soon.

"Papa," Ixion whispered.

I shifted to face him, and dried blood peeled away from the blanket and pulled my skin. "Yes?"

"The guard is asleep."

I turned again, despite the pain it caused me.

Zephyrus' posted man had drifted off, his head lolling against the wall.

"Take your magic back so you can heal."

I hesitated, because what if the man sleeping was a ruse? My injuries screamed at me to take this chance. It might be my only one. I called my powers back to me, and they rushed into my veins, wrapping into my bones, knitting broken parts back together so quickly I slammed my teeth down hard to stall the groan that wished to press out of me.

The guard snored softly and readjusted on the chair.

A sigh of relief whooshed past my lips.

I sank beside Ixion and drew him against me. He clung to me and sniffled against my filthy shirt. The energy of my powers thrummed through me, and I hated it as I peeled them back off. It grasped to me harder than ever, vines of power that curled around my heartbeat and whirled through my mind.

I whimpered as I forced it off and back onto Ixion.

He shivered and pressed his small head tighter against me.

"You knew my injuries were real?" I asked.

He lifted his large brown eyes that welled with tears. "Yes, Papa. You didn't want me to be scared, so I tried to be as brave as you. I don't like you being hurt."

I swallowed. "I'm sorry, Ix."

He brushed his soft fingers over my cheek. "We'll be rescued soon, right? We just have to stay brave a little longer?"

I took a deep breath, thankful it didn't hurt to do so, and pulled Ixion into my arms, felt his heartbeat race against my chest. "Yes, Ix. You were right. Apollo is coming for us."

Ixion's voice turned cold and hard. "He'll kill Zephyrus."

The vengeance in his tone frightened me. Though he was the son of the god of war, he'd always seemed so innocent. This entire experience was ripping his childhood from him. However, what he said was true. We just needed to survive another few days.

"Yes," I said. "He will."

21

Epiphany

I brushed my hand over the dark, heavy fabric of my skirt. The mirror in my dressing room reflected my image back to me, but I had a hard time accepting it. My curls had disappeared into a tight, low bun. The makeup was darker than I preferred, and the clothing was stiff and linear.

Joden had advised the royal dress maker to form a new look for me.

It worked.

My appearance held a maturity I didn't feel.

I agreed with him, though. I needed to convey that I was taking this role seriously. I had to get our citizens—high lords included—on my side if I was to have a chance of claiming Father's throne.

There wasn't time to worry about that. I had a meeting to attend, paperwork that needed sorting through, my role in serving the widows in the afternoon, and a dinner I was hosting for the high lords that evening.

I took a shaky breath.

Hyacinth had handled this before.

He'd struggled… but managed it.

Father had balanced the work as well.

I could too.

I gave my head a toss like I could shake off the weight of those thoughts and stepped out into the hallway. In the meeting room, I approached Father's seat. Several of the advisors already waited, standing behind their gilded chairs, and they scowled at me. A few narrowed their eyes.

My fingers slipped off the furniture.

The men had never loved me stepping into Father and Hyacinth's place, but they had accepted it for what it was... a necessity. I'd never received scorn like this before.

I sat, and the advisors dropped into their places.

"Princess," Dune said, his eyes tight. "I feel it's imperative we begin this meeting by discussing a rumor Lord Demetri has heard."

I scraped my nails into the seam of the chair where the softness of the fabric met the sturdiness of the wood. "What rumor?"

"That you're attempting to usurp his inheritance by working around the laws."

The advisors shuffled. Joden lifted his face, his sharp nose catching a glint of morning light. Fen gaped, and his curls shifted over his jacket. Frowns deepened on several other faces.

Joden met my gaze and cocked up an eyebrow.

So, this was up to me. Great.

I cleared my throat. "I am considering what is best for Niria, and that drives all of my actions."

"Is it true, then?" Dune huffed a disgruntled laugh. "Do you actually think the Nirian high lords would accept a *woman* running the country? Do you believe you can work around this council?"

Anger sluiced through me. "It's funny to me, Lord Dune, that you have such a problem with the idea of a woman running the country. You appear close to my cousin, and someone advised him he could wear the crown while I ruled in his place if we married. Clearly, no one takes issue with me doing the actual work."

Dune looked around as if to gather support. "It solves this conundrum we've found ourselves in, does it not? King Magnes was an excellent leader, but he has no remaining sons and—"

"Hyacinth is still alive," I said with more heat than I intended.

Eliga steepled his fingers together. "He very well may be dead." I winced. "I'm sorry to speak so coarsely, but it's a reality we *must* face for the country. Besides, we've determined that a deity cannot lead. It sets a dangerous precedent. As far as legality is concerned, Prince Hyacinth died a year ago."

I struggled to not fidget and lifted my chin. "So, you thought you can have King Magnes' daughter sitting in this chair without having to admit to your peers that a woman is ruling."

"A woman," Dune said, his words heavy and punctuated, "will never find acceptance among the high lords."

Fen smacked his hand against the table. "Princess Epiphany has done more than admirably under the pressures of losing her entire family and guiding the country through this troubling time."

"I agree," Joden said.

"Are you seriously giving in to this nonsense, Joden?" Dune leaned back, as if to separate himself from the thought.

"What's nonsense to me"—Joden straightened the parchment in front of him—"is the idea of handing this country over to a stranger solely because he's the closest male relative. We all know Lord Demetri has no capability to run Niria. Otherwise, you never would have concocted such a scheme, Dune."

"Is it a scheme for the Princess to marry to form an alliance that would benefit the entire country?" His thick eyebrows pressed together as he turned back to me. "Your role wouldn't change either way. Why do you wish to commit treason by overturning the laws and—"

"Treason?" Fen screeched.

I stood. "Gentleman." The entire group lifted their eyes to me. "Enough. I am not a horse. You will not sit and discuss how much you can gain from trading me." A few of the men ducked their faces, but Dune and Roan stared at me, unimpressed. "I will not marry Demetri. It's not even up for negotiation. That man has no loyalty to anyone but himself."

If I had to make a political marriage, it would be to someone like Galeson. I winced internally. I may be in a better position to bargain if I'd made that alliance. But no. This was a game of cards, and I'd already chosen my hand. Now it was time to play it.

"My father and brothers cared about this country deeply. It runs in my blood, beats in my heart." I met each of their eyes. "And if you think I will stand back and not do whatever I must—treason or otherwise—to see to the well-being, prosperity, and good of Niria, then you are severely mistaken. I know my father would have done the same."

Roan rubbed a hand down his face. "If you had a better reputation, Princess, then of course—"

"I understand my reputation." A silence slipped through the room like a chill. "I mean to make a new one. All the gossip about me: *the princess creates her own path, the princess doesn't know her place, the princess is stubborn.* Those are the same attributes you have praised in my father. I won't stand here and let you shame me for it anymore." My arms trembled with fury, and I curled my fingers into fists. "I can do this job. It's a lot… It was a lot for Hyacinth. But I have the education, the tenacity, and the passion for the well-being of this country that I can assure you my cousin does not."

Dune scowled at me. "Those are not the only rumors about you, Princess. What of the others? You struggle with reading. You don't know how to comport yourself. You're fornicating with a bastard stableman."

An uncomfortable shuffle passed through the room as the men suddenly became deeply interested in the papers in front of them.

I rolled my shoulders back. "The only people that don't have others talking about them are those who aren't taking any chances. Who aren't attempting things and, yes, failing at some along the way. Tell me, Lord Dune, are there any rumors being whispered around about you?"

A muscle around his jaw jumped.

I pressed my fingers to the table and leaned down to survey the group. "Let me make something clear to everyone in this room, as it's obviously needed. I have spent my entire life hearing rumors about myself. I lost my whole fucking family in the past year." Eyes widened. Eliga coughed and red crept up his cheeks at my language. Hypocrites. "I don't give a damn what anyone says about me. I will prove to the people of this country—traders, high lords, and commoners alike—that I will work and fight and sweat and bleed for them. Your job currently is to help me with that. Unless you don't actually care about Niria." I stood and slammed a hand over my heart, feeling the passion of my words thump against me with each beat. "I, for one, would rather die than see our nation fall or suffer. What about you?"

The energy in the room had shifted. A few of the men who had eyed me when I walked in studied me like they'd suddenly realized I was more than just the unfortunate daughter of a man they respected.

I dropped into my seat. "Now, let this meeting carry forward with something important. There are topics we need to discuss for the good of Niria."

As the advisors grabbed piles of parchment and left a few hours later, I waited until the room cleared out, except for Joden. He tucked a stack of parchment under his arm. "You did well today, Princess."

"You didn't step in to help at all."

His lips pinched. "You are a bird learning to fly. Out the nest you go, and you'll either soar or crash. If you intend to lead this country, you'll have to find your wings and quickly."

"I thought you intended to support me."

"I am. I assure you that me speaking up in your favor surprised more than a few of the men in this room today. However, we are not friends, Your Highness. We are unlikely allies. If you intend to take this country, it will be on the weight of your own abilities. You're continued pursuit to marry a bastard with shaky connections is hindering you. If you married Lord Galeson of Segion, your life would be far easier."

I raised my chin. "I'm not here for easy. I plan to marry Valerian."

He studied me for a moment, censure in his expression, and then bowed and exited the room. My breaths came heaving and my stomach pressed against the stays of my gown. I longed to rip the heavy fabric of it off. I wanted to jump onto the back of my horse and run until we left the continent.

This was my damn country, though.

I loved it fiercely and would fight for it.

But now that I stood alone, their words peppered into my mind, echoing through it. *You struggle with reading. You're a woman. You're fornicating with a bastard stableman.*

Gods, I had no allies here.

Joden and I weren't even that.

We had a common purpose.

I opened the door into an attached sitting room decorated in sunny yellows and ivory molding. I screamed through my teeth, turned, and kicked the wall. My foot ached, and I didn't fucking care. Tears broke free, slipped down my cheeks, and caught on my lip.

I missed my father.

And Hyacinth.

And Emrin.

And Valerian.

I missed my freedom and Temi.

I missed horseback riding.

My life was a mess, and I wasn't sure what the hell I was doing.

Destroying myself for people who didn't appreciate it.

I screamed again and whipped around, my skirts whirling between my ankles.

An attendant stood in the corner. Her large brown eyes fixed on me, and she held a dusting rag pinched in her fingers.

"Oh," I said.

"Forgive me, Your Highness." She bowed and turned to walk out.

"No. Wait."

She paused, and I walked over to her, took in the sharp angles of her chin, the dark curls loose from her head wrap framing her cheeks. "I know you," I said.

Her eyes darted back and forth around the room, but she didn't answer.

"Your name's Brina, isn't it?"

She lifted her face. "You remember my name?"

"Of course. How could I forget the person who told me off?" She'd done so when Temi and I were sneaking out with Valerian to practice shooting arrows. Back when Apollo had first arrived in Niria. Gods that felt like a lifetime ago.

"That was… inappropriate of me, Your Highness, and—"

"It was entirely appropriate. I was causing trouble for Valerian and hadn't fully considered the risks I took for his sake." My voice dropped to a whisper as I rubbed my hands together. "I never meant to harm him, though."

"Yes, Your Highness. I didn't realize…" Her fingers trembled as she worried the rag. She raised her face again, and that spark of defiance she'd worn when she chastised me glimmered over her eyes again. "I didn't know you actually cared for him, that you wouldn't just use him."

"I'd never—"

"I see that now." She swallowed. "The entire palace staff does, Your Highness. We support you with what you're trying to do."

This woman knew more about the feelings and thoughts of the palace attendants than I did. Probably the city populous in general. She lived in that world in a way I didn't. "Brina, I could use your help."

"Your Highness?"

"I need the people on my side. If I've learned anything from Val and Temi, it's that the high lords and royalty are often separated from the thoughts and needs of the citizens of the country. I want to know what people honestly think. Do you… Could you possibly help me with that?"

A Spark of Death and Fury

Her mouth gaped, and she looked over to the fireplace like she could escape up it. She licked her lips. "You may not like everything you hear, Your Highness."

"That's fine. I don't have an excess of vanity at the moment. I need honesty. You can give it to me. You have the connections and you've not been afraid to tell me the truth before."

"I... I could do that."

"Good. Also, call me Pip, or Epiphany if you prefer. No more of this 'Your Highness' every five minutes."

"You want me to call you by your name?"

"Yes." I rolled my eyes. "Well, not in front of my advisors or the high lords. They'd lose their shit if they heard it. But, otherwise, yes."

Brina's eyebrows rose to her hairline, and then a peal of laughter pushed past her lips. "All right... Epiphany..." She stretched my name out like she tried it out.

I smiled.

A spark of hope burned alongside the anger and passion the meeting had kindled. The advisors didn't believe me capable of fighting for this country. They were about to learn just how wrong they were.

22

Artemis

The moon sank towards the earth, and the blush of morning blossomed across the horizon that stretched above the cliffs we moved through. We'd walked all night, and everyone's postures drooped. The young gods had remained quiet since Nero's death. Orion had lit memoriams for him and offered prayers for his soul. The three deities had remained close to him since.

I'd spent the night tapping into my magic, focusing on the moon.

My muscles trembled, and I felt nearly faint as exhaustion whipped through my body.

Orion had chatted on and off with me, sometimes making verbal jabs when he could tell I was discouraged, other times remaining quiet when I needed to concentrate.

Having someone at my side who could read me so well was a comfort amid all the chaos we'd encountered.

He ran a large hand over his face and smoothed it down his beard. Dark circles under his eyes contrasted against his pale skin.

"Apollo," I said. "We should stop. We all need to rest."

A Spark of Death and Fury

Apollo turned, his eyes shadowed and void of expression. Whereas everyone else in the group had huddled together, shared tears over Nero's death, and drew closer, Apollo had pulled away, shoving his emotions down.

"I think we should try and make it out of this valley we're in." He lifted his face to the cliff edges. The ones that had given Helios an advantage.

I looked at Orion and he took a deep breath that raised his shoulders before he nodded. "We're probably less than an hour from reaching the mountains and getting out of this gulf."

Mia shuddered and Kama rubbed her shoulder. Chares didn't react, but his body wilted. Everyone was exhausted and discouraged, but we could make it an hour and we'd all feel better to be out of the craggy path Nero had died on. "All right," I said. "But then we stop for sleep."

Apollo continued forward. He stepped with a confidence I'd never seen on him before, his shoulders rolled back, his fingers grazing the edge of his weapon.

Like he had nothing holding him back anymore.

I worried that was true, and what it would mean for him.

A quiver rippled through the chasm, and I stopped walking. Orion paused as well and placed a hand against the trembling cliffside.

Kama pulled Mia tight to her side. "You okay?"

"It isn't me."

The shaking of the earth picked up and rattled our feet. Orion crouched down and pressed his fingers against the earth to balance himself. The shimmer of magic that had slowly returned to Apollo's form glowed brighter as he pulled his bow free.

Mia's forehead furrowed, and she closed her eyes.

The crackling of the earth picked up until we all shook and struggled to keep our balance.

"I... I can't stop it," Mia said.

"Is it Gaea again?" Kama clenched her tighter, like she'd keep her safe.

"I don't know."

Apollo swept around and parted his lips like he might speak. A roar swallowed whatever he intended to say.

A chunk of the mountain ripped away and fell towards us.

Orion pounced and yanked Mia and Kama back from where they stood. A boulder landed in their spot a minute later, smashing into the ground with a thud. He curled his body over theirs to shelter them.

Chares.

I lifted my face to him.

Rocks pummeled my back, and I winced. The slide grew, and as rocks piled up, they blocked the sunlight, shifting the world into dust and shadows.

Apollo grasped his arms around Chares. A golden shield glimmered around them that falling shrapnel peppered against.

I could shield too.

And I needed to.

Pebbles fell like raindrops in a thunderstorm, cutting my skin and bruising my arms. I pressed into my magic, but exhaustion dragged on me. I called for the moon, for night skies and stars, and the cool whispering surety of those powers.

Magic glittered down my veins.

A rock banged into my shoulder and knocked me onto my face. Another landed on my legs and pinned me to the ground. I screamed, and Orion and Apollo both turned towards me. "Temi," they both yelled.

The clattering of the stones falling finished with a massive crunch. The rocks had slid into a pile, ensconcing us in a slim pocket between the mountain and the path. A rock smashed into the stack of those hovering above us and swallowed the last ray of morning light. We sat in a small cave formed by the landslide. I pulled to shift the boulder off me, but it pinned me in place. My body ached, and I wasn't sure I could feel my feet.

Apollo's powers glittered over him, lighting the space as he jumped away from Chares, leaving the boy unsteady on his feet as he moved in my direction. Orion rolled away from the girls. He winced as he stretched out on the ground, and blood trickled off his trembling arms.

Apollo reached me and pushed into his powers, his eyes turning golden, his flesh lighting up and casting a glow over the dark cave we'd found ourselves in. He shoved the boulder away, and I whimpered as feeling came back into my lower half, tingling and slicing through my muscles.

Apollo kneeled down and stretched his hands out to heal me.

"No, Orion first."

"Temi."

"Apollo," I whispered, my voice trembling from pain. "He's mortal."

Apollo's eyebrows drew together, but he nodded. He'd loved someone mortal before. The concerns that come with it were familiar to him. He healed Orion and then returned. His magic surged through me, licked along my bones, and burned so hard I clenched my teeth.

The injuries disappeared, and I stood beside Apollo who wobbled. I clutched my hand around his hip, and he leaned against me. Using so much magic after walking all night had wiped him.

"Is everyone else all right?" he said.

The young gods all nodded except for Mia who seemed lost in her powers, her gaze faraway.

"Okay. Let's see if we can move these rocks and get back on the path."

"You're exhausted," I said. "We're stuck here for now. It's a good time to take the break and leave one person on watch in case anything falls again."

Apollo jerked out of my arms. "You want to just stay here?"

"I want you to rest. You're tired. I'm tired. We can't fight gods or deal with natural disasters in this condition. It's a wonder we both didn't die."

"And if this damn mountain falls again?" His voice echoed against the walls.

Orion watched us both, his arms crossed but I shifted my focus back to Apollo. "Hence why we have someone stay up to watch. This provides some cover. We aren't limitless, Apollo. We're all exhausted right now. We need rest. *You* need rest."

"Fine," he hissed and turned to trail farther into the cave, back against the mountain side.

I growled through my teeth. That's just what we needed, for him to part from the damn group. I turned to the young gods. "Sleep. I'll keep the first watch."

Kama looked ready to argue, but Mia grasped her hand and pulled her next to Chares who drew a sleeping roll out. I sat cross-legged in a corner where I could watch them as well as the rocks stacked precariously above us. Orion lowered beside me.

"You should sleep too," I said.

He shrugged and pulled his pack off. "I'm not as tired as I thought I was."

"I think it's something about Apollo's healing. It's left me feeling more energized."

A Spark of Death and Fury

He nodded. "I'll stay up. Keep you company for a while."

I smiled. "Thanks."

We remained quiet until the breathing of the young gods grew heavy. Even Apollo had fallen asleep. I could just make him out in the distance, laying underneath a jut of the mountainside where more falling rocks wouldn't have the ability to harm him. We'd spent so much of our lives surviving we didn't know how to do otherwise.

"What'd'ya think you'll do when this is over?" Orion said, his deep voice humming through me as it echoed off the rocks we leaned against.

I dropped my head back. Sunshine gleamed through slivers of space between rocks. That's probably how we needed to get out. Test the integrity of the pile, climb to the top, and push off the rocks closest to the surface. Apollo would just love that with his fear of heights. "What do you mean?"

"When you're done with this whole fight the gods and rescue your brother's family business. What are you going to do?"

I slipped a knife off my leg and pulled a whetstone out of my bag. I could just make out the form of the blade in the soft gray light, but the scraping sound of the work soothed me. "Well, if Clothos and all her prophecies are right—and despite Apollo's dislike of her, they have been so far—Apollo and I will be the new reigning gods. So, I guess we'll… do leadery god stuff."

Orion chuckled, pressing his lips together to keep the sound low. Kama rolled over in the distance and readjusted on her mat. "So, you're going to be a *leadery god*, and you once said I was born into a family of cheese farmers. I'm glad you're not the god of bequeathing titles."

"Naming things is hard, okay?"

His teeth glinted in the light as he grinned. "All right. What does being a leader of the gods look like?"

"Well…" Heat rose to my cheeks. I had an idea of a plan I'd like to implement, but I hadn't shared it with anyone. Something about saying it out loud felt foolish to me. I met Orion's gaze, the way his blues eyes had darkened in the low light. It wasn't ridiculous to share with him. There was no one I trusted like him. That thought slammed into me. It was true. "If we get rid of the spark and the curse of earth sickness that goes with it…"

I drifted off and Orion nodded, his attention focused on me in that steady way he had.

"Well… the gods won't need dedications anymore. So, I thought I could repurpose the temples."

"For what?"

I slid down against the rock and put my knife back into its holster. "I don't know… Maybe people could still provide dedications, but we could use them to help those who are struggling. And I thought… if I had a temple one day… maybe it could act as a safe house for women who… needed protection." I sighed. "That doesn't make sense when I say it out loud."

Orion rested his hand on my arm. "It sounds brilliant."

I lifted my face to find him looking at me with so much admiration and acceptance, I almost felt embarrassed. "Well… I've always wanted to help those who get left behind by laws or culture or circumstance. I just thought… if I'm one of the high gods, maybe I can."

"It's a good idea."

"And what about you?"

"Me?"

I scooched back up to sit at eye level with him. "Yeah. When you're done helping me and my stubborn ass brother,"—he chuckled—"what do you plan to do?"

"Du'nno." He picked up a pebble and tossed it back and forth between his hands. A breeze rippled across the top of the cave, whispers of it reaching us. "Since my family died, I haven't had much purpose, if I were to be honest." He turned towards me. "Until I met you."

I cocked an eyebrow. "Until I led you down this path of slaughtering gods."

He laughed again. The warmth of it vibrated through me. "We've had this conversation. There's a reason we're doing this. I hope to not kill in the future, though. It weighs on my conscience." He brushed his hand over his bag that held the little, crude candles he lit in memory of others.

"Well, that will be a damn shame if you still carry the burdens of this life when you become a star. Maybe you'll blink a lot. Stress astronomers out."

He rolled his eyes. "I never should have told you about that."

I knocked my shoulder into his. "How would I burn memoriams for you one day if I didn't know about it?"

He smiled but the expression dropped quickly, and his voice came out low and gravely. "I would appreciate it if you did." He raised his face. "I have no one left who will. For... my people, we burn the memoriams to keep a person's spirit alive. The candle reflects the light of their star. And well, I fear my star might dim with no one here to do so."

I gripped his arm and paused for a long moment to let the weight of the loss of his family and his people sit in the air, not speaking over it or sullying the grief. "Of course, I will. Honestly."

He nodded.

"So, what would you think of guard work?"

He dropped the pebble. "Like at the palace?"

"I was thinking more like at the temple of the goddess of the moon."

Another giant grin snaked over his jaw. "Aww. You don't want me to leave after this, do you?"

I made a sound in the back of my throat. "You're good with a weapon and personable. You'd make an excellent temple guard. That's what this is about."

"I think that's the closest you've ever come to complimenting me. I'm getting closer to pulling real praise from you."

"Enjoy it," I grumbled.

He sank down again. His shoulder leaned against mine and his laughter vibrated through me. "All right. I accept."

"Accept what?"

"Your offer to guard your temple. If you'll take a heretic star-worshiper, that is."

I scraped my braids back. "Once we survive all this, I don't plan to apologize for my choices ever again. I can have a heretic star worshiper guarding my temple if I want."

"I have a feeling you'll have whatever you want in your temple, other's opinions be damned."

I hummed a reply. My gaze flitted over the three sleeping young gods where they huddled together then shifted to Apollo where he curled up, just the dark edges of his curls showing.

"Worried about your brother?"

I pulled my knees against my chest and rested my chin on them. "Yeah. I guess so. What do you think about him?"

"He's your brother. I don't need to think anything else."

I grazed my thumb down a ripped hem of my shirt sleeve. "If I asked you to tell me the truth, would you?"

A Spark of Death and Fury

He took a deep breath and the whooshing sound of it filled the empty space between us. "I think Apollo is currently driven by anger and fear." He kicked a leg out and pebbles skittered. "I've been there before. It makes a person unpredictable and dangerous."

My eyes darted back to Apollo's form curled up on the cliff edge.

My heart ached.

I knew what Orion said was true.

He readjusted his pack and laid his short spear on his lap. "What did Clothos' prophecy say about him again?"

"When you lose what you've gained, and arrive at a fight too late, your brother will ascend only to bow."

"Could his bowing be a humbling of sorts? Perhaps it means his anger has him unfocused and Zephyrus will use that to his advantage."

A cold chill slipped down my spine. "Maybe. But the next part is: When the sun overtakes the moon, and the trio stands guard, that is your moment to rise. You said you thought the sun and the moon stood for me and Apollo. If he's overtaking me, how could that be true?"

"Maybe it simply means it'll be sunrise. The sun overtakes the moon's place in the sky."

"Oh."

Orion scraped his hand down his beard. "Do you know what's one thing star worshipers don't have?"

"What's that?"

"Prophecies. Thank the moon goddess for that."

I chuckled but rolled my eyes. "How are you going to thank a goddess who's part of the religion with prophecies for that?"

He nudged me with his elbow. "I know her personally. She's the one deity I truly believe in."

For a moment I stared at him. Despite the teasing I knew his words rang true. "Thank you, Orion."

He smiled and returned to studying the sleeping forms of our group and the silvery outline of the rocks. Our conversation ebbed to a peaceful quiet as we sat in companionable silence together.

23

Epiphany

I knocked on the sitting room door. Ixion's bedroom was only a few doors down. The proximity stirred the worry about him and Hyacinth. That concern was always there like a thrum that echoed beneath all the other problems that blared around.

Isadora opened the door, and her eyes widened as she took me in. It was strange to think of Valerian's mother by name. Just the sight of her made me miss Val desperately. He'd been the steadying presence my entire life. Now, in this moment when I felt adrift at sea, more alone than ever, he was gone. Of course, he was doing it for both our sakes. He sacrificed a great deal for me. Standing here staring at his mother dressed in a maroon silk gown, her face wrinkled with worry, was proof enough of that.

"Would you like to come in?" she said.

Right. I was here for a reason, not only to miss Valerian. "Yes, thank you."

She stepped out of the way and allowed me to walk in before she latched the door back. I waited for her to offer me a seat, but she remained standing with her hands crossed in front of her skirts.

As if she waited for me.

Waited on me.

"Should we sit?" I asked.

She nodded, and her eyes dashed about the high ceilings and rich carpeting of the room. I found a chair and lowered into it as she eased into a couch across from me. Next to it, a basket of sewing supplies nestled against the foot of the furniture, a variety of threads scattered on the table at her side.

Perhaps that was how she passed her time now that our relationship had taken her position from her. Her wrists bothered her. It seemed a strange occupation in that condition.

"Is there something you need from me?" She shifted in her seat, the fabric of her dress crinkling and filling the quiet between us.

"Yes. I have a small group of women meeting in the morning after breakfast. I was hoping you might attend as well."

She brushed her hand over the table and fiddled a strung needle between her finger and thumb. The string spiraled in front of her before she set it down. "What is the purpose of this meeting?"

"I'm trying to form an accurate picture of the feelings and needs of the people in our kingdom."

Isadora's curls, styled and free from the headscarf she'd always wrapped them in while working in the kitchens, spilled over her shoulders. "Is it true then?"

"What?"

"That you intend to take over the country instead of your cousin?"

A bird sang beyond the window, dampened by the

panes, its notes trill and resonant. I straightened my spine. "I am."

She scrunched her fingers into the thick layers of her skirt. "I don't think matters of the kingdom are something I can advise you on. I believe it would be best if I stay out of it."

Suddenly I wanted to cry. My mother and father and Emrin were dead. Hyacinth was gone. Valerian and Temi had both left. I had no allies, and this was the closest person I had to family in the palace anymore.

And I couldn't determine how she felt about me.

It was possible that she hated me.

Maybe I'd just convinced myself we'd had a moment of connection while volunteering together. My heart thudded with a painful ache. Damn it. I needed someone on my side. I pinched the skin on the back of my hand to stall tears.

Isadora shrank against her seat. She appeared small and vulnerable. She'd intimidated me the few times I'd seen her in the kitchens with her commanding attitude and quick responses. Here, dressed in clothing that clearly made her uncomfortable, stuck in a room in the palace that seemed ready to swallow her, her light had dimmed. Maybe it was a mistake to ask something of her. We both were like lost boats, bobbing on uneasy waters.

"I'm not capable of being a strong ally for you, Your Highness." She said the words gently, but her switching back to my formal title sent a shiver down my spine. My belief that we'd had some spark of connection was apparently just that, a feeling. "I'm going to speak bluntly with you, if you'll allow it."

"Of course," I said.

She raised her chin and the sharpness I'd remembered in her expression returned. "I'm the mother of the bastard you're sneaking around with." My mouth dropped open, but she kept speaking. "My connection would hinder you more than help you, Epiphany."

I met her gaze when she used my name.

She pressed her lips together before speaking. "I want to see you successful, but this task you're taking on is nearly impossible to begin with. Marrying a man with no title is an added obstacle. Even if his father claims him—and I don't believe he will, if you want my honesty—he's still going to be a scandal and a mark against you."

I swallowed hard. "You speak of honesty. If I married solely for political connections, if I denied Valerian and everything between us, how could I ever look my people in their eyes and promise them integrity?"

She sighed. "High lords and royals marry for political connections all the time. It wouldn't be uncommon."

I rolled my shoulders back. "Well, I am uncommon. I've never fit the mold. I won't apologize for that. I care about this kingdom, and I think I'm able to do this job, but I can't do it alone. I need help."

Curls tumbled forward as she bowed her head again. "I'm sorry, but I'm not the person who can help you, Your Highness."

That conversation pierced through my mind the next morning when I met with Brina and two others she'd recruited. We stood in an unused attendant's bedroom where dim light slipped in between drawn curtains, the space tight with the four of us crowded in it.

Brina crossed her arms and clenched her fingers into her sleeves. "The issues are, Your Highness…" I cocked up an eyebrow, and she looked at the other two before clearing her throat. "Epiphany." She drew my name out like it was something foreign. "The people of the city like you, but they're not sure a woman can lead.

It's not been done before. And"—she shifted on her feet—"you have a shaky reputation. A lot of the women don't care about that. They think people just love to gossip."

One of the other attendants, with ruddy curls tucked beneath a headscarf, nodded. "It's a different situation with the men, though. Most of them don't believe women possess the constitution to run a business, much less a country. Begging your forgiveness, Your Highness."

I curled my fingers over my lips. The heat of my breath warmed my palm. "Okay, so I need to prove that I can be a competent leader. I should be out amongst them more. My guards want to keep me in the palace, but that's not how Hyacinth or Father did it. They toured the city weekly."

Brina nodded. "I think that would help."

"Good. I'll arrange that. And I'll find some way to show them I'm taking this seriously."

Brina started to speak again, but the door slid open and cut her off.

All four of us tensed and my mind whirled with excuses for why I was meeting privately with attendants if it was Demetri or some advisor who'd sided with him.

Excuses weren't needed, though I hardly calmed when Isadora stepped in, dressed in a navy gown, her hair braided into a low bun. The three attendants bowed, but she shook her head. "None of that. I'm not your superior anymore."

"I think you're a bit more now, my lady," Brina said.

Isadora's brow furrowed as she took in the three women before she shifted to me. "Could we speak for a minute, Your Highness?"

"Of course. We were just wrapping things up." I nodded to Brina and the others, and they filed out of the room and shut the door behind them. It left Isadora and me standing alone in the shadows.

"I'm here to tell you I've changed my mind," she said.

"You'll help me?"

She fiddled with the embroidered sleeve of her gown. "I will, yes."

"Can I ask what's spurred this change?"

She turned away, but even with her face farther into the dark, I could make out the color that rose to her cheeks. "I'm afraid your cousin came to speak with me today."

"Did he?"

"Yes. He threatened to use my reputation and rumors about me using Valerian to rise above my station against you. He advised me to talk sense into you." Her dress swept across the floor as she turned back into the light. "It was then that I realized you were right. He has no concern for this country. If I'm going to be used as a weapon against you, I can at least try to help as I'm able."

Anger burned into my gut. Demetri threatened Valerian's mother. He truly didn't care about people like I did. His reputation was all that mattered to him. Here I was laying my weaknesses and flaws and reputation bare to do the best for Niria. The fury gave way to desperation again. I wished Father was there, Hyacinth, Emrin, Mother. Anyone who was on my side.

"How do you believe I can help you?"

I looked up at Isadora.

She was there.

Maybe our relationship was rocky, but I knew she wouldn't betray me. "You can read well, can't you?"

Her dark eyes twinkled with a spark of irritation. It was so familiar—something I'd seen in Valerian's expression when he tried to shove back frustration that he didn't feel he had a right to voice. "I can."

She must have thought I meant that judgmentally. I stepped in closer to her. "Well, I can't. Or not easily." She cocked her head to the side as I continued speaking. "It gives me headaches and causes me problems. I've not been able to stay on top of all the paperwork, which is, of course, not helping my case with the advisors. That's what I need your help with. If you could work with me during my office hours and read the documents out loud to me."

She stumbled back a step and her hand reached out as if to steady herself. "You want me to read official documents?"

"Isadora," I whispered, "you are the only one who I truly trust here. You're the mother of the man I'm in love with. I know from what he's told me that you're a good person." She bit her lip, but her expression softened. "My advisors have their own schemes and ideas and plans. It's beneficial for the kingdom to have different points of views. My father championed that. It's beneficial, but that leaves me with no one I can rely on to remain neutral."

"I'm just a kitchen attendant, Epiphany. I'm not an advisor."

"You were the head of the kitchen, which makes you a leader. You're intelligent, and you've raised a wonderful person, and I trust you. It would mean the world to me if you would help me."

She looked back over her shoulder at the door. Then she returned her gaze to mine and hesitated for only two heartbeats before speaking. "All right. If this will really serve you, I'll do my best."

Relief crashed through me, and I jumped to pull my arms tight around her. The way her muscles went rigid underneath my touch made me realize my overstep. I had just felt so exuberant that she would assist me. I truly needed her.

I stepped away, but she placed her arm behind my shoulders and patted me awkwardly.

"Sorry. I just really need the help, and I can't say how much I appreciate it."

"Well, you have it. All that I'm able to offer to you, at least."

A glimmer of hope bloomed in me.

She thought this was an impossible task. It felt like one.

But maybe we could achieve it.

24

Hyacinth

I woke up in some loamy part of a forest where the blue light of early evening wrapped up the long forms of the trees and muted the color of moss that crawled over dark soil. A gentle wind whisked through the bushes, fluttering leaves together.

I took a step forward.

I should have felt afraid and worried.

Only peace lingered around me, though.

It reminded me of the underworld—how it suppressed negative emotions.

For a minute I wondered if I'd died.

My heart rate spiked, and a sharp sting of worry for Ixion pierced through me and that was confirmation enough that I was alive.

I took another step, and my bare feet sank into the pillow of the ground. Lightning bugs glittered in the wood line where a soft mist rose and permeated everything. A silk robe, finely crafted and covered in intricate embroidery, rested on my shoulders. My body was clean, and the jasmine smell of my oil filled my senses.

Someone stood between the shadowed outlines of two pines.

He turned, his tunic and curls rippling.

I froze as a chill ran down me.

Apollo walked towards me, his steps quiet and sure. His golden eyes sparkled. There was the lilt in his smile, the sureness of his steps, the long lines of his neck. Just as I remembered him. "Cyn?"

"Apollo."

I stretched my hand out to him, but I paused. I couldn't bear it if I reached for him, and it wasn't real. If it was all a dream.

Apollo lifted his hand and glided his fingers between mine. The rough edges of his skin scraped my palm.

I choked on a sob. "Apollo."

He pulled me into his arms and held me in the shelter of his embrace. I breathed in the grassy, bright scent of him and clenched my fingers into the firm muscles of his back. I trembled against him, feeling more likely to break than in any moment of torment or hardship before.

"I thought you'd died."

"I'm sorry." He clutched me tighter to him until his heartbeat matched mine. I pressed my lips against the tender flesh of his neck.

Of all the suffering I'd faced in the past weeks, nothing compared to the ache of beautiful misery in that moment. To have him in my arms was more than I had dared to hope for.

I leaned against him as if I could anchor my soul to his and never lose him again.

We stayed like that for a dozen long breaths.

The light in the meadow hadn't changed at all. Which was strange. Usually in the evening hours, just before the world plunged into darkness, every minute held a different shade of color. "Where are we?" I whispered.

Apollo pulled back from me, grasped my hand, and drew me to sit beside him in the moss. His eyes skimmed the outline of the forest. "I don't know. Somewhere safe, I think." He turned back to me and brushed his fingers down my jaw before grazing his thumb over my lips. "I'm here with you. That's all that matters to me."

I whimpered and felt ridiculous. "Apollo, I'm…" I drew in a shaky breath. "I'm struggling so much. This has been so hard and I'm breaking."

"Oh, love." He pulled me against him again and laid us down against the hillside. "I'm here now."

I wept. My body shook both of us, and he rubbed his broad hand around my back in circles until I finished.

"I'm sorry." I brushed my shoulder across my cheek to wipe the moisture away.

"No. Don't say that." He kissed me and my lips parted. He tasted like sunshine, like joy, like home. His tongue brushed over my lips, and I pushed back harder. I never thought I'd do that again. When we parted, he dragged his knuckles over my cheekbone and pressed his lips against a tear lingering there. "Tell me what you need."

I swallowed and leaned up where I could see his face. He studied me carefully, as if he worried he might do something wrong. "I need a release."

His eyes glimmered, like magic jumped up to the surface of them and his voice dropped to a husky tenor. "I can help with that."

He flipped us so that his body hovered over mine. The solid weight of him pressed me into the plushness of the ground. His hands wandered my form and peeled clothes away. His mouth followed the trail, licking and sucking along my flesh, his teeth scraping over the panes of my stomach.

I dropped my head back and closed my eyes.

Gods, it had been so long since I'd felt safe.

Since touch had felt good.

Since I didn't have to stay in control.

Apollo rolled my pants off me and tossed them aside.

The cool breath of the night air whispered over my bare flesh and goosebumps rose in its wake. But then Apollo covered my body again and the warmth of him seeped into me.

He took me into his hand and brought his lips to mine.

I kissed him hard, our tongues gliding together. Our first kiss was gentle, born from sorrow and reunion. But these kisses were different. They were hunger-fueled and desperation-driven. The roughness of his grip and the eagerness of his pace caused me to groan into his mouth, breaking the contact.

He rumbled a reply that vibrated through my body and my back arched even under his weight.

Gods, it had been so long, and I'd missed him so desperately and felt so hopeless.

His breath brushed against my ear as he whispered. "It's okay, Cyn. You can let go."

I growled my release. Every muscle tensed before I dropped back against the ground. For a moment I lay there and breathed him in as he traced a pattern over my hip.

I opened my eyes, kissed him, and let my lips linger against his. My hand swept down his chest, but he grabbed my wrist gently and pulled it back up. "I'm okay. Seeing you satisfied was enough for me."

An argument sat on my tongue. Apollo drew me into his arms and sighed against my neck, like it was the happiest moment of his life.

A Spark of Death and Fury

I curled against him, my ear against his chest, and the thudding rhythm of his heart seemed to chant *he's alive, he's alive, he's alive.*

"Sleep, love." His voice rumbled against me. "You're safe here."

His words washed over me, lulling me, my body growing heavy.

I kept peeling my eyes back open, meeting his gaze, the surety in it.

I never wanted to lose that moment, or him, again.

Exhaustion won out.

I drifted off in his arms, the warmth of him surrounding me.

As soon as consciousness returned to me, I fluttered my eyes open.

To the room in the Palace of the Four Winds.

No Apollo.

No hope.

I sobbed silently, my shoulders shaking.

Ixion stirred, took a deep breath, and curled in closer to me.

Gods that had felt so real. But it was just my imagination, desperately wanting to believe that Apollo lived, that I'd steal one more moment with him.

I closed my eyes and could feel the warmth of him lingering on me.

There were only two things I'd longed for in the last weeks.

To see Apollo once more.

And for Ixion to make it safely away from here.

The first I'd gotten in a way.

The other, I would die trying to achieve if I had to.

Ixion trembled and I rubbed his back until his breathing eased and he swept back into the cradle of sleep.

25

Artemis

Our group trudged together under the glowing orb of the sun. We'd spent the morning climbing out of the cave, carefully hoisting rocks free to not trigger another slide. Mia—with her magic connected to the earth—studied each shift and stopped us whenever she sensed a rumble within the mountain.

It left us all doused in sweat, coated in dust, and heaving great yawns. The world cooled as we reached the edge of the mountains that Zephyrus lived in, and I trembled. I pulled my coat out and looped my arms through it. Orion had already donned a thick cloak, and he chatted with the young gods, their voices warm hums in the air.

Snow rushed down the side of a slope, like some predator had pounced on the bank, and limbs crackled with the weight as it fell. The sun glistened over the world as we all dropped into defensive positions and whipped weapons out. Mia pressed her fingers into the slush at her feet and tapped into her magic.

Apollo stared ahead of us, his expression not changing

as several dozen gods whose skin glittered with magic appeared before us. One raised her bow.

Apollo didn't hesitate.

He didn't attempt to talk them down like he had with the others.

He dove for her.

The world exploded again. Arrows whipped through the air, Orion's spear flew, the young god's magic trembled into the atmosphere. Apollo fought with a vengeance. Blood splattered his form and stained the snow around him as he employed weapons and his powers of fire and heat to bring combatants down.

A group jumped from behind rocks and landed in front of Orion and me.

"On your right," I screamed.

Orion swung his short spear in a swipe that knocked down the assailant who had been out of his view. Blood peppered the snow-capped rocks.

"Thanks."

"You're not the only one who can watch the other's back." I released four arrows in rapid succession, and they whip, whip, whipped past my fingers.

"And"—he grunted as he sliced his spear through a man who fell to the snow with a squelch—"I'm not the only arrogant ass, either."

I hurled a blade forward, and it hit its target near where Kama swept flame across the sky that swallowed several of the gods. Their screams echoed around. I pulled a second knife free. "Also, not the only person willing to throw it in the other's face."

Orion drew a sword, dodged a blow from a man with sharp silver eyes, and plunged it through him. "Where I come from, we call a stump a stump."

I slapped another arrow onto my bow. "I don't know

what that means, but I refuse to take it any way other than as a compliment."

He chuckled even as a blade hit his weapon and knocked it from his hands. He lifted his short spear off his back and slammed it forward in a fluid motion that knocked the god off his feet, tumbling him into another that Apollo cut down.

"I wouldn't expect anything less than for you to take something however you damn well pleased."

I rolled my eyes, but he smirked at me, and a smile spread across my mouth.

It was probably irreverent to joke like that as we killed.

It was how we coped though.

The deaths weighed on my conscience too.

Gods, I wanted this to be over with. I wished to never take life from another being or use my powers and connections to end lives again.

Mia split the ground open, and Chares called forth a wind that tumbled the few remaining gods into the chasm. Mia smacked her palms together, and the earth followed her motion as it slammed back in place with a crack that shuddered through me.

We all stood breathing heavily, weapons still clenched so tight in fists that our fingers trembled, ankle deep in snow that had turned a glittering crimson.

The adrenaline from the fight drained from my body, leaving me shaky and teetering on my feet. Orion pressed his foot down on a corpse and pulled his long spear free from the body. He frowned at the weapon and the blood that dripped from its point.

There'd be more memoriams lit tonight.

I swallowed and pushed my bow away.

"You there," Apollo said.

A Spark of Death and Fury

A man crouched behind a boulder, and he shrank farther down at Apollo's call.

I clenched my hand around my knife belt, slipped the hilt of a blade between my fingers, and walked up beside my brother.

"Come out." Apollo's voice boomed.

The stranger stood on trembling legs and readjusted his bag as the strap rolled off his shoulder before placing his hands in the air. "Please, don't shoot. I'm... I'm not looking for a fight."

Apollo thrust his bow into the snow. "Strange that you traveled with those who were then."

The man's eyes swept over our group, the six beings covered in gore and ichor. "I only traveled with them to get home. My... my family"—he stumbled over his words—"are in Carens. My brother... he died in the war, and... my mother asked if I would return home." He flicked his hands out and they trembled.

I slid my knife back into its belt.

This was no enemy to fight, just some human who'd got caught up with the wrong travelers.

Apollo drew a blade out and tossed it. "How do we know this isn't a ruse?"

"I'm not even a god."

"You could be lying. We have a mission and can't have spies leaking information."

The man swallowed, his throat bobbing. "I'm no spy. I swear it on Zeus." Apollo glowered, and his words picked up. "Or on whatever deity you patronize... on my mother's life. You can look in my bag." He dropped it to the ground and gestured to it. "There are letters from my family that have my address and verify my story."

Apollo considered him, blinking.

Annoyance pinched through me. He'd intimidated the

man. This human was clearly not a threat, and we should move on.

Apollo cocked his head to the side. "No," he whispered.

He whipped the blade through the air. Shock coursed through me. I had the reflexes of hundreds of nights spent hunting and dashing after creatures though, and I snapped my hand forward. I caught it on the hilt, but Apollo's thrust had been so strong part of the blade rotated and sliced into the meat of my hand. I whimpered through clenched teeth as blood dripped down my wrist.

26

Apollo

"Temi," I screamed as I dropped the blade. The human fell back into the snow and scrambled away from us, but I didn't care about him. "Oh gods. I'm sorry. Let me heal you."

She yanked her hand away from me. The cut was deep enough that the pink of her flesh showed, and blood poured down her arm. "You almost killed that man."

The human sat frozen in horror but unharmed. "We've been doing a lot of that in the last few days." I didn't care about him anymore. I wanted to heal her.

Temi's shoulders rose rapidly with her breath, and her nose flared as tears formed. She looked at Orion. "Could you give us a minute and help this man get back on his way?" Orion cleared his throat and put hands on Chares and Kama's arms, steering them and Mia in the direction of the human.

The group crunched through the snow, and Temi shifted back to me, her lips parted. "You nearly murdered him."

I shook my head. She didn't understand the stakes and

what I had to do. "He could leave and alert others. It's possible he's a spy, Temi. He was traveling with gods."

"So, you… you made yourself the judge and executioner? You would end his life over a hunch, and you don't even feel bad about it?" She ripped a piece of her tunic and wrapped it around her hand. Her gaze remained locked on me with horror written over her expression.

I released a sigh that clouded into the air. "We must do unspeakable things to survive right now. I didn't want to do any of this." My voice came as a growl, and I curled my hands into a fist. "Fate has ripped everything from me. It was Hyacinth who was the good one of the two of us, but he's gone. I will do whatever I must to get him back."

As I reached out to heal her, Temi shoved me with her uninjured hand, causing me to stumble.

I lifted my face as surprise rolled through me, and she growled as she smacked me again, and I faltered a few more steps.

Tears streaked her cheeks, her lips a thin line. "No!" she roared. Her chest heaved for several minutes as the frigid blast of shock seemed to seep out of me and sit in the air between us. She gave her head a shake and her braids rattled against her shoulders. "No," she whispered again. "I will not join you down this path."

"What path?" This was the direction we all headed on together. We knew we'd kill and hurt others in order to rescue Hyacinth and Ixion and defeat Zephyrus. Temi had urged me into taking this action. She was the one who thought we needed to gain the spark and bring down the other gods.

"You want to believe that you can justify killing people who posed no threat to you simply because they impeded your purpose? You think Zephyrus doing wrong—even something as vile as murdering and kidnapping—justifies your malicious choices? Because if that's the case"—her voice broke—"you aren't the man I thought you were."

A ripple of guilt pulsed through me. But this was the path we'd decided to take together. I wasn't the only one killing. "Temi—"

"No." Her voice rose again, and her fingers curled into fists. "I have always believed in you and stood by you despite every stupid decision you've made. But you've fucking lost yourself." She gestured to the dip in the snow where the man had cowered before us. "Name the god who kills humans like it's nothing because it matches his purpose. Name the god who doesn't care about the well-being of mortals." She leaned in close enough to me that her breath brushed over my cheek. "Is it Zeus or Zephyrus, or could it be Apollo now?"

I gasped. Her words struck me like a blast of icy wind.

"Your whole life you've feared becoming your father." She bit her lips and more tears fell down her face that she didn't bother to wipe away. "You get to choose who you are, Apollo. That's always been true. Right now, you're choosing to become the new vindictive, high-god who doesn't give a fuck about anyone other than yourself. We've never hesitated to kill when needed. It's been a part of our existence. But we've only ever done so if the person was a threat. Sometimes we have to do awful things because it's the best choice among terrible ones. But you were going to cut him down. A person who posed no risk and begged for your mercy. Are you going to harm others simply because they stand in your way now?" Her shoulders shook. "I will not remain by you if that's the path you choose."

My mind felt frozen, shocked by her words. I couldn't form thoughts. "Temi, I..."

"I'm going to go find Orion and clean up." She swallowed. "I want you to take a few minutes and realize that man is someone's Hyacinth. If I hadn't stopped you, they would never embrace him again." Her nose flared, and she sobbed out the rest of the words. "You would have stolen that from them. And you don't even feel a pinch of guilt over it."

She licked her lips. "During the war, I struggled with who I am. Am I just a vindictive goddess, destined to destroy humans?" She lifted her chin. "Do you know what I realized? What Orion—a mortal who constantly puts his life on the line for others—helped me see? It's that I didn't choose to be a god or the path fate has set me on. But I decide what actions I take in that." She slammed her hand against her chest. "I am Artemis, goddess of the moon. I will do everything in my power to be the deity who fights for humans and for justice and goodness in this godsforsaken world." She blinked more tears back. "Who are you, Apollo?"

She turned and stormed away. Words stuck on my tongue as I watched her leave, her form growing smaller as she trailed back down the path, before disappearing behind the mountain.

I shifted to face the icy world that glimmered crimson and gold from all the blood. Everything Temi had said was true.

I dropped to my knees in the snow, ice bleeding through my clothing and seeping in, cold and biting.

I had lost myself.

And I'd almost destroyed a life in the process.

I'd hardened myself to believing this was inevitable, that I could steel my heart and embrace darkness if it's what it took to rescue Hyacinth.

She was right, though.

I'd acted as an executioner for a man who had committed no crime.

A Spark of Death and Fury

I'd almost murdered that man who posed no harm to anyone.

We could have brought him with us, or checked his bag, or sent one of the young gods to accompany him home. There were many options. Temi was likely discussing them with Orion and would pick one.

But I moved to kill him without hesitating.

Realize that man is someone's Hyacinth.

If I hadn't stopped you, they would never embrace him again.

You would have stolen that from them.

Oh gods.

I pressed the heels of my hands against my eyes as tears ripped out of me. Gods, what was I doing?

I'd spent my whole life living in fear of my father's shadow. Of the reputation of being a deity. And, recently, of Zephyrus' wrath.

It wasn't Zeus who almost murdered that man.

Or Zephyrus.

It was Apollo.

It was me.

I'd intended to kill him. Would have without a beat of hesitation.

Sobs racked through my body.

I'd become everything I'd ever feared.

The world stretched cold and empty. Fresh snow fell and I wiped my cheeks again as I stood and slipped my hand into my pocket. The cool metal of Hyacinth's ring bumped my fingers.

I pulled it out and let it tumble in my hand. The engraving of the sun and the Hyacinth flower glimmered alongside the stone that symbolized bravery. I'd never even told Cyn that. I hadn't had a chance to, really.

I swallowed and clenched the ring hard enough that it

left marks in my flesh before tucking it back into my pocket.

I'd made this entire journey with the single focus of rescuing Hyacinth and Ixion. But I'd become all that I'd feared and fought against to do so. I'd injured Temi because she did what I should have done. She stopped a wicked god from destroying a human for no valid reason. What she said was true. Gods, Hyacinth had been a human when we'd met. The man I loved so much had already died at the hands of a selfish, vindictive deity.

I'd almost perpetuated that behavior.

Our entire lives we'd vowed to be different, to do better. I'd allowed myself to believe saving Cyn meant the rest of the world could burn. I was wrong. If it wasn't for Temi, I would have just taken a step onto a path I could never come back from.

I marched down the trail and searched until I found a small lake. If the others had used it to clean up, they'd abandoned it already. I wasn't sure where they'd gone.

I stripped my clothes off and shivered in the icy wind.

It didn't stop me from diving into the biting cold of the water.

When I broke the surface, I sucked in freezing air, and the sun moved from behind clouds. The snow stopped and light glimmered over the world in a golden haze. Rays of it reached me and the warmth grazed my trembling muscles.

I closed my eyes and tapped into my powers.

Heat and glittering strength washed through me.

The sun spread across the sky and chased clouds away as golden rays reached out over everything.

After I'd dressed again, I trudged back up the mountainside and leaned into my powers for warmth. It came to me without a struggle this time. Smoke drifted into the darkening sky over a bend, and I crunched along the trail until I reached the fire and the five sitting around it.

Temi whipped her bow out and her eyes met mine.

She lowered the weapon, stood, walked over to me, and raised her chin.

"I am so sorry."

She took a deep breath and turned away before meeting my gaze again.

"Everything you said was right." I clutched my bag tighter. "I know there's no apology that will change my actions."

Orion watched both of us in his surveying manner, the way he did when he prepared to jump into a fight. I steeled myself for Temi's anger, for her rejection.

"You can never do that again."

"I swear, Temi," I whispered as I struggled to choke the words out. "I won't. You were right. I'd lost myself, and I almost ruined everything. I promise you, I'll never do it again. We're here fighting for something better. I'm so sorry I lost sight of that."

She remained still for a minute and then she wrapped her arms around me. I clutched her against my chest and started crying again.

When I stopped, she pulled back and brushed a tear away.

"Please will you let me heal you?"

She licked her lips and her nose flared. A dozen heartbeats passed before she held her bandaged hand forward. I curled my fingers around it, and the magic surged through me. When it was done, I tightened my grip, and she squeezed my fingers in return. A silence echoed between us, but her hand stayed warm on mine. I thought it might break me, having her beside me again, not pulling away.

"Are you hungry?"

I nodded, unable to form words.

She gestured to the fire, and I walked with her, sat before the flames, accepted the dried fruit and nuts she'd set aside for me.

Something within me had changed.

Irrevocably.

I slipped my hand into my pocket and twirled Hyacinth's ring around my finger.

I'd once thought being worthy of Hyacinth meant fighting who I was born to be. Then I'd believed it meant giving into the darkest part of my nature.

It wasn't either of those.

Maybe life was much more complicated than that.

The weight of that settled on me as I leaned closer to the fire.

27

Valerian

I adjusted the silk jacket as I watched my reflection in the mirror and twisted the sleeve around my wrist. Gods, I'd never felt more uncomfortable. A longing to throw on my rough work tunic and spend a day in the stables, breathe the hay-sweetened air, and blend in with the other sweat-drenched workers pulsed through me.

I walked out of the lavish room I'd spent the last few nights in and stepped down the stairs. In some ways, Lord Lucien's estate held more luxury than the palace, which was richly appointed but heavy on history and elegance. Lucien's home seemed to drape finery about for show.

I fought rolling my eyes as my hand glided down the polished surface of the banister. It was an interesting thing, facing my childhood fantasy. In some ways, this opulent estate matched them. In others, the experience had fallen short. It was another crack in my view of the world. I'd spent so much time with King Magnes and his family, that I believed those who held luxurious estates deserved them. A few days with Lucien had disabused me of that notion.

Life wasn't fair and sometimes those who didn't deserve to, prospered.

Outside, the vast back porch overlooked the endless land beyond the estate. The sun eased up in the sky and splashed peach and rosy colors over the rolling hills. The weather was cooler than at home. A breeze whispered across my flesh and goosebumps rose in its wake. Birds sang, filling the air with their trill notes.

It was beautiful.

It was everything I'd ever imagined my father's house being.

I didn't belong here and never had.

A sigh whispered past my lips as I leaned against the bumpy edge of a column. I don't know what I'd expected. It wasn't for my father to welcome me as his long-lost son. Considering the potential this connection had for him, I might have expected more. Maybe I'd even allowed a sliver of my childhood hopes to accompany me on this journey for them to be crushed under the weight of reality.

And Lucien's wife hated me.

I couldn't blame her, really. I was the embodiment of the brokenness of her marriage.

She'd kept her children—my siblings—at a distance from me and wouldn't even sit at the table when I joined. It was as though she believed she could keep them separate from the taint of my status. It had made for an uncomfortable couple of days. I knocked my head back against the column. It ran up to the roof where tiles sparkled in bright colors with streaks of gold shimmering throughout them.

I straightened my jacket, but no amount of adjusting would make it feel right. Enough musing. It was time for breakfast and I should make an appearance. I walked to the dining room. A few of my other siblings ambled into the space, half awake, and they covered yawns with the backs of their hands.

Evander lifted his face. "Valerian."

He said my name like it was a question of my integrity. I bowed and found a seat near the end, at a distance from where most of the family huddled. The others scarcely stole peeks in my direction. They spoke to each other and shifted away from me.

I couldn't blame them. This was their lot, and they had to appease their parents. I was nothing more than a storm blowing through before they returned to their regular life. If they showed me regard for the few days I was here, it might cause them hardship for far longer.

Lucien stepped in; his gleaming emerald eyes dashed around the room and landed on me before tightening. He pulled a chair back on the other side of the table to sit by Evander and started into a conversation. One I was clearly not invited to join.

Asher walked in with his formal jacket on and sat beside me.

"You're back."

He took a piece of bread. "Yes, and ready to return home."

"Any good news?"

He leaned in and whispered. "It looks like Ansair can't afford to damage more trade connections by continuing the war at the moment. I'd call that positive news."

He drifted into his thoughts, and I took a few bites of breakfast, but found my appetite lacking. Other than riding Arion a few times a day—predominantly to keep him from committing mayhem—I'd done little, and I wasn't used to so much sitting around. It left me miring in disquiet.

As the meal ended, Lucien rose and walked over to me. "Let's talk in my office."

This was it. Asher had returned, and I'd minded every step in my visit here. Now he'd sign the paperwork, grant me a title, and I could be on my way, hopefully to never return here again.

Homesickness permeated me. I'd never considered myself to be the type who clung to the comforts of home, but suddenly nothing seemed more attractive than the sweet scent of fresh hay in the stable at Niria, or the ivory edifice of the palace set against the burnt orange of the setting sun, or the brightness of Epiphany's smiles. I hoped to see that all again soon.

Those thoughts flowed through me as I followed Lucien into his office. Asher stopped to wait in the hall, and we'd leave together as soon as I had the documents I needed. Lucien dropped into his seat and waved a hand for me to sit as well. I lowered onto a chair and pressed my hands against my thighs.

My heart picked up. All I needed was one little piece of paper and Epiphany and I could wed. We could start a new life together. Gods, I hadn't let myself hope before this moment. Here we were, though. All the hardship and struggle and even the embarrassment of the last few days had been worth it.

Lucien leaned back against his chair. "I fear I've had some bad news."

My heart plummeted. In the past year, anything shy of death—Magnes, Emrin and Delon, horses who'd suffered miserably during the war, Hyacinth—fell short of the term for me. I suspected Lucien was about to change my opinion on that, however.

I glided my fingers together and kept my posture upright. "Is that so, my lord?"

Lucien lifted a bottle off the desk and loosened the cork.

A Spark of Death and Fury

He poured himself a glass, the amber liquid sloshing about and turning a honey color in the sunlight. He replaced the stopper and took a drink. "I'm afraid my contacts have just received news that your princess is about to be ousted from her position." My body went still. I didn't know what that meant, but it couldn't bode well for Epiphany. Lucien shrugged. "It would seem that Lord Demetri intends to have her arrested for treason. As Demetri is a Carenian himself, and it's looking more likely that he's the future king of Niria, I fear I cannot stand against him. I'd hate to make poor connections. I'm sure you understand. It's not personal."

My arms trembled against the carved wood of the chair. It was the most personal thing that had ever happened to me. My father had rejected me since my birth, of course. But this felt final and real as the same emerald eyes I'd inherited from him glared at me.

More importantly, what did Epiphany face? Surely her cousin planning to detain her was just a rumor, or a lie Lucien made up as an excuse. They couldn't arrest Magnes' daughter, could they?

She had allies. I paused. What allies did she really have? Political advisors that didn't like her, attendants and women who had no influence.

Gods. She had no one.

She was alone.

I couldn't even reach her quickly.

Lucien grinned as he swirled the drink in his glass around.

As if the well-being and lives of so many people—not just myself and Epiphany, but the entire kingdom—didn't rest on the decisions happening now. Like it didn't matter as long as he won in the end.

All my life I'd stepped back, not said what was on my

mind, followed propriety, and disappeared into the shadows.

I'd wanted this man, my father, to see my worth and make King Magnes proud after all he poured into me.

Magnes was dead.

And Lucien never had any intentions of claiming me.

I stood to my feet so fast the chair screeched against the floor. "I'm glad."

Lucien gave me an unimpressed look. "Not really in love with the girl, then? Was this just smart maneuvering on your part?" He cocked an eyebrow. "I'll admit this much. You have worked this all cleverly. Come by that honestly enough."

I wanted to punch him and watch his blood flow down his face and soil his expensive clothing.

But I was raised better than he could comprehend.

"No." I pressed my fingers against the desk. "I'm glad for my sake. I would hate to have the stain of your reputation attached to my name."

Lucien jumped up and his hands curled into fists. "You don't deserve the honor of my name, boy."

"I guess we'll have to agree to disagree but, if nothing else, we can stop pretending to tolerate each other."

He snarled. "You're a bastard who has tried to rise above his station. You've brought your own humiliation upon yourself."

"I may be a bastard by birth." I straightened and the silk jacket slid around my form. "But you're a bastard by your actions. I'm proud of who I am." I glared at him. "Despite from whom I come from. My mother has ten times the honor than you could even fathom. I didn't come here looking for a parent. I'm grateful we don't have to keep this ruse up anymore." He clenched his teeth like he'd take a bite out of me, but I cut off whatever words he formed. "Thank you for hosting me this week. I'm sorry I've proved to be such a burden to you."

I strode out of the office, and the door banged behind me with a finality that felt satisfying. Asher waited in the hall, and he raised his face from where he stood silhouetted in the bright colors of the murals on the walls. "Well?"

"No."

Asher's eyes darted to the office. "I could try speaking with him."

I gave my head a shake. "I don't believe it was ever a realistic aim. He strung me along, and I've likely ruined any connection there might have been." Lucien had once sent a letter to King Magnes stating he would sign the paperwork, but Magnes was gone and Emrin had destroyed the letter. There was no proof other than our knowledge of it which was useless. It was hard not to begrudge Emrin in the moment.

Asher paused for a beat, and the muscle along his jaw jumped. "All right."

"Besides, if anything Lucien told me is true, Epiphany is in trouble. We are two of her very few allies away from home."

His eyes widened incrementally. "Ready to go, then?"

I nodded. I'd been ready to leave since we'd arrived. But now Pip might need us. And there weren't words enough to express how eager I was to return to her. I may not have a name, but I had integrity and cared for her. And I would fight for what was right, no matter the cost.

Lucien didn't understand devotion like that.

I readjusted my coat until it finally felt like it fit and matched Asher's pace as we walked to the door.

It was past time to go home.

28

Hyacinth

Reality slipped away from me like snow melting in spring.

Whenever Zephyrus showed up to harass me, physically assault me, drag me out of the room and down into the windowless space to torture me, when he slit the neck of the guard who fell asleep while watching us, I crept back into the shadows of my mind and allowed myself to disappear.

I didn't know if it was day or night any longer. What was real, even? The last tangible moment that had felt fully solid to me was making love to Apollo in the quiet of that misty forest.

And that had been a dream.

I clung to that memory. The rough feel of Apollo's fingers on mine, the warmth of him covering me. That and Ixion were the only things that grounded me to reality anymore.

Ix had grown quieter. He'd quit asking about the future and jumped every time the door to our room opened.

I would recite a poem, rub circles on his back, and he'd

calm, his body slumping down against mine as sleep washed his worries away for a while.

It was a strange turn of events that I'd gone with Apollo to shield him and ended up shielding Ixion.

I watched the fluttering of the child's lashes, long, dark ones that brushed over the curve of his cheek as he slept.

He was worth all of it.

The pain.

Losing myself.

The likely loss of my life for the last time.

Apollo would be here soon.

He'd see Ix to safety.

I would have spent my life well. Outside of Ixion and the haunting echoes of memories, everything blurred together. I wondered if I'd lost my connection with reality in my attempt to evade Zephyrus.

It didn't even surprise me when his voice drew me out of my thoughts, and I found myself chained to the wall again though I didn't remember leaving the bedroom. The metal of the manacles scraped sores on my wrists, and I leaned back into my mind, away from the physical.

What Zephyrus said caught my attention. "What are you even fighting for, Hyacinth? I suppose you might wish to return to your kingdom now that your father and brother are both dead."

I gasped so hard I choked. The room came fully into shape for me again, the dark stones, the flickering peach of the torchlights.

No. No, that couldn't be true.

Zephyrus probably lied to me to wear me down mentally, since he hadn't managed to physically break me. Zephyrus smiled. The light gleamed against his teeth and warmed the pale color of his skin. "I'm sure you think I lie to you, but let's admit something, Hyacinth." He gripped my arm, and I winced away from him. "I've never told you a falsehood. Though that's certainly not something you could say to me."

That was true. I couldn't remember one time Zephyrus had lied to me. Even when I'd suspected he'd misled me with information about Apollo, that had been the truth in the end.

His other point was accurate, also.

I'd deceived him plenty of times.

Could that mean what he said was true? Father and Emrin were both dead. I'd only seen them a few months before. Yes, Father had aged some, but he was still strong and busy commanding the kingdom. What could have happened to him?

Zephyrus paced back and forth in front of me and tucked his hands beneath his wings. Streaks of light shifted over the forms of his feathers like raindrops slipped down them.

"I can tell from your expression that this is news to you, *Prince.*" He spat my title. "Your Father died of heart weakness. Your brother…" He chuckled. "That was a bit of a twist, I'll admit. I planned to kill him. Instead, he showed up in a battle like a fool."

I stared at Zephyrus, suddenly feeling grounded in my body and the surrounding reality in a way that I hadn't in days. Lies. Emrin wouldn't have been in the battle. He was the crowned prince of the damned kingdom. That made no fucking sense.

Zephyrus' eyes glimmered. "He shouldn't have joined that battle, but stubbornness is apparently a family trait of yours. He spent his short week as king breaking conventions and showing up where he didn't belong."

A sinking feeling dropped through me. That sounded like Emrin in the previous year. Emrin in a war would be a disaster. We were both decent horsemen, but we didn't have battle training. Gods, I couldn't remember the last time I'd picked up a sword. It wasn't even part of our education. I clenched my teeth to avoid expressing any emotions.

Zephyrus started pacing again, his steps echoing through the space. "I considered ending him myself, but him dying slowly and painfully of blood poisoning in a filthy war tent with only your sister at his side made it better than anything I could have coordinated on my own."

The numbness of my fingers ached into my hands. It was as if I couldn't bear the emotions that would go with the story he told and instead felt every pain in my body that much more intensely to counter it. Of all the blows Zephyrus had dealt me, this was the worst.

"You see, Prince, you believe I keep you alive to incite Apollo. That's true. I must kill him to gain the spark because he's the holder of the most magic currently, and you're the easiest way to provoke that. He's sloppy when it comes to his feelings for you. It will make him weak and unfocused."

My nose flared, and I pressed my wrists against the chains. It sent a shot of pain screaming through my body which held back the fear and hopelessness stirred within me.

Zephyrus shifted to face me. "Once Apollo is dead, though, I still have one last task to achieve." He stepped in close enough to me that his lips grazed my cheek. I jerked away and banged my head against the wall. "You fucked with the wrong god when you crossed me. I am going to let you watch the man you love die, slowly and painfully. Then I'll destroy your country before I end you."

I knew I shouldn't engage with him, but panic flitted through me. "Niria is strong." My voice came gravelly.

"Is it? I've already sent nymphs to speak with Lord Lucien, breaking that tie. Your sister is as much of a fool as you are. I thought I may have to face the wrath of her connection with Segion, but she chooses some bastard. It was like toppling a stack of cards." He snapped his fingers. "The tiniest gust and it all falls over."

Tears burned my eyes. The idea of Epiphany alone, trying to deal with the advisors, manage the country, grieving Father and Emrin, and Zephyrus ripping everything from her was a new injury to the countless ones I bore. She had some money, but it would run out. If she lost her home, her place, she could end up destitute.

But no. Valerian would never abandon her. No matter what happened, he would see them both safe. Even if they lost Niria, they'd take care of each other. Zephyrus turned, and I mouthed out a silent 'thank you' to Val.

I'd once judged him over their relationship and picked a fight over it. It had hurt him and her both. How I wish I could apologize once more. I didn't think I would survive this ordeal to see them again, but I hoped they knew how much I loved them both. I wished I could tell Val that I was proud of him and thankful for him. That he was the most worthy person for my sister. In this moment of desperation, I knew he'd be on her side.

"How challenging do you think it will be, Prince," Zephyrus said, stealing into my thought, "to bring down a kingdom with no real leadership? When Niria's allies see how weak the country has become? How it's crumbling from within?" He thrust his lip out. "I don't believe it will be difficult at all. You'll live just long enough to regret the day you crossed me."

I shuddered.

"I think I'll leave you here for the night. I have no reason to take you to your room since there's no boy, right?"

My heart rate picked back up.

No. Ixion would be terrified if I didn't return.

Zephyrus smiled wickedly, like he knew it. "If you've changed your stance on that, let me know. I'll escort you myself."

Ixion might feel afraid, but he'd remain shielded and safe from this monster.

I swallowed. "There's no boy."

"Very well."

Zephyrus grabbed the torch off the wall and walked up the stairs. The light dimmed as he left until I sat alone in the blackness.

The weight of everything he'd said tangled through me, dragging me down. I wept, a sound that echoed back. There was so much to worry about, but that fixed nothing. So, I drifted away from my body, into the eddies of the pool of my mind, until time and reality didn't exist again.

29

Epiphany

My fingers bumped into the tight bun at the back of my neck that tamed my curls. It was a full day with meetings, work, walking in the city to speak with traders, and then a banquet with the high lords. I clinked my teeth together. Everything hinged on this dinner. People were slowly coming around to me, but if I couldn't get the titled families on my side, my efforts would prove hopeless. Giving my heavy navy skirt a shake so it sat more comfortably, I turned and opened the door and then froze.

Half a dozen guards waited in the hallway. Their eyes darted to me as I walked out of my room. Theos stepped forward, and as he bowed his dark hair brushed his shoulders. "With apologies, Your Highness, but we have orders for your arrest."

I stumbled back a step and pressed my hands into the molding of my bedroom door to steady myself. Of all the issues I might face, getting arrested by my guards in my home was not one I expected. A zip of betrayal singed through me.

Demetri.

A Spark of Death and Fury

He had to be behind this.

I had believed that within the palace walls I was safe.

That was an illusion.

Nothing was secure at the moment.

What was worse, being ousted from the palace or being locked away in jail? That wasn't even a possibility I'd considered.

But I was not Pip, the wayward princess, running from her fate anymore.

I straightened my spine. "On what charges and under whose orders?"

Theos, the chief guard, clamped his hands together, his head bowed as if he was ashamed. "We received an official order from the royal advisors on the charge of treason against the throne, Your Highness."

Treason?

Against my father's throne?

He had authorized me standing in his place! That was the most ridiculous charge I'd ever heard.

The guards eyed me uncomfortably, and I took a deep breath. "I will not do you the dishonor of assuming this is something you would have chosen to do. I know you are following orders for the good of this country."

The postures of the men shifted, their navy uniforms glimmering in the sunshine that spilled in through the tall windows behind them. The palace's mausoleum sat amongst the trees beyond. The resting place of so much of my family who had bled and sacrificed and dedicated their entire lives to the wellbeing of this country.

"I thank you for your service. More than a few of you" —I met Theos' steady gaze—"have gotten me out of life-threatening situations, even. You've protected my family and me and, more importantly, this country with your lives. However, I must argue that the grounds for this arrest are unfounded. It will be Nirians that suffer if you follow through on this order. I assure you I observe the highest marks of the law. I'll go with you to speak with the royal advisors, and we can sort this out. In fact, I'm heading in that direction presently."

The guards looked at each other and uncertainty lingered over each of them. It made me furious with the advisors and with Demetri. He'd placed these men who protected the crown with their lives into a deeply uncomfortable position. Despite my outward appearance, it sent a shiver of fear down me. If my guards turned on me, I had no hope. I refused to show anything other than the calm steadiness I didn't feel. Theos bowed. "Forgive us, Your Highness. We didn't wish to follow through on this but—"

"You were given an order, and you did what you needed to. Sometimes we must make hard choices. I completely understand."

I met each of their eyes and the discomfort that glimmered in them, before turning and sweeping down the hallway, anger burning into an inferno in my gut. The guards lingered behind and didn't follow me. When I reached the meeting room, I threw the door open. Every head snapped in my direction, including Demetri's from where he sat in my father's chair.

For a moment, I didn't even feel angry.

I felt an unnatural calm. Like I stood in the eye of a hurricane.

Then fury built again, a blaze that licked its way through my body. If I could, I would draw that flame forth and catch him on fire.

I remembered everything Father and Hyacinth and Emrin had said about leaders.

People didn't respect emotional outbursts.

I took a long, cooling breath and walked over to Father's chair. "You are in my seat, Lord Demetri."

He raised his chin and the stubble along his jaw gleamed with golden highlights. "I didn't expect you to attend today."

"I'm certain that's true." My voice dropped to a whisper. "You sorely underestimated the loyalty of Nirians."

Several of the men looked at Demetri as if curious to see how he would handle the situation.

We stared at each other, caught in a headlock.

Demetri tightened his fingers around the armrest as though he staked his claim, but Joden spoke without lifting his gaze from the papers he held. "Will you honor the Princess, Lord Demetri, by allowing her to have her father's seat?"

A flash of rage brightened Demetri's face, but then he rose and bowed. "Of course." He took a spot farther down the table.

I dropped into the chair and ran my fingers along the engraved wood. Hyacinth had sat here, Father, and his ancestors sat here. They had likely run their hands over the same spot in moments of tension. They exhausted themselves in the service of this country. That realization seeped into my veins and emboldened me.

Demetri apparently had gained a backbone and wanted a fight.

I would fucking give him one.

Dune dropped a stack of papers onto the table. "The first matter today is—"

"The first matter," I echoed, "is that if any of you"—I met each of their gazes before continuing—"take an issue with me and wish to unseat me, you can do it legally and in the light of day before your peers instead of skulking in the shadows, asking honorable Nirians to carry out your dirty work for you."

A few of the advisors looked confused, which was a boon. At least they didn't all stand against me.

But a palpable tension had buzzed its way into the room, like static electricity that whirled around us and prepared to snap.

I was done playing the nice, docile princess.

"Let me make this perfectly clear. Legally, I have every right to sit in this chair for the next few months. Until then, you'll endure my presence, or you will commit treason." I tapped my fingers against the polished table, the clinking sound echoing through the silent space. "Does that turn of phrase sound familiar to anyone in this room?"

A few of the men looked over their shoulders, but others' glares intensified. Several seemed to be angry on my behalf. I wasn't entirely alone.

"I have the authority to remove each of you from your positions and from this moment forward, I will do so if I must. I don't wish to, as my father trusted you and respected your diverging points of view and the perspectives you brought to running our country. The best for Niria is what I want as well." My tone grew so frosty ice could have crawled over the furnishings in the room and it wouldn't have surprised me. "I assure you, I will fight for it."

I sliced my eyes to Demetri whose nose flared but he didn't respond.

"Now let's not delay our work any further. We have the dinner with the high lords tonight and I'm certain many of them will have questions about what we'll discuss today."

After a tense meeting, Joden gestured for me to follow him, and I weaved around those who were leaving the chamber and joined him in the attached sitting room. He twisted his lips up and appraised me, taking in the dark gown. "Did something happen that spurred your speech today?"

I rolled my shoulders back. "Demetri attempted to have me arrested, but it doesn't matter. I handled it."

Joden cocked his head to the side and his eyes brightened with shock. He seemed to consider that for a moment but then nodded as if he'd accepted me managing the situation. "Very well. I have to say, Your Highness, you're doing well and changing some advisor's opinions. However, I cannot impress upon you the importance of this dinner tonight."

Reality hit me.

Demetri had tried to have me arrested before the dinner.

That conniving asshole.

He knew the charges wouldn't stand, but it might hold long enough to keep me from attending this formal meeting with the high lords.

Which would decimate my chances of making a good impression on them.

That rippled through me, leaving me shocked and angry again.

Though I had to give him the smallest acknowledgement that it was a clever move on his part. If evil.

"I'm aware." I paused to steady my voice. "I hear the people in the city are in favor of my leadership."

"The people are only part of the equation. If you do not get the high lords on your side, you'll never gain the throne."

I stared at him, his sharp features and rich clothing. "The *people* make up the vast majority of our population. The widows and those suffering from the fallout from the war should take priority currently."

"I assure you," he said dryly, "the high lords do not care about those matters. Those are women's concerns."

"Women's concerns." I spoke through my teeth. "The women of this country bleed and suffer and sacrifice. We'd be nothing without them."

Joden sighed and his gaze bounced to the intricate carved designs in the stone around the fireplace. "Don't say that at the dinner tonight. That is your opinion, Princess, not a fact."

I gaped. My frustration and helplessness, and fury with Demetri bubbled up to the surface. "I hate you."

Joden's brown eyes sparkled in the sunlight that washed through the windows. He chuckled and slid his hands into his pockets. "Very good, Princess. I think you're finally finding your footing."

He bowed and exited the room.

I huffed a breath and kicked the wall, immediately regretting it when a scuff marred its creamy surface. Damn it.

Nothing to do but meet Isadora and work. The one positive of the week was her help. She was everything I'd expected. Intelligent, quick at making connections, helpful, and a familiar—if not necessarily friendly—face.

It was a balm, but not enough to wipe away the negativity that trickled through me before the dinner. Demetri would concoct some other way to drag me down in the eyes of the high lords. It was the only move he had.

30

Artemis

Orion licked his lips, his cheeks chapped from the blustering winds that beat against us. We'd made it farther into the mountains, and as the light of day bled away, the temperature grew biting.

Apollo had returned to the fold of our group. He chatted quietly with Chares and gestured towards the sun where it sank behind the cliffs and lit their peaks in a veil of hazy caramel. Apollo wore a coat that covered most of his skin, but what was exposed glimmered like he'd dunked his flesh into a vat of golden glitter. Magic hummed over him like a current.

I was glad to see him practicing his powers. His progress was clear enough. More than mine. I bit down hard at that thought as annoyance buzzed through me. I was pleased to have Apollo there, back where he belonged, however.

For a moment, I worried I'd lost him.

I hoped the memory of his choices weighed on him for life, and that he kept his word and would never step on that path again.

Mia squealed as her foot sank into a bank of snow. Kama pulled on her until she popped out. Their giggles bounced around the clearing. Orion and I hung back from the others as we trudged up the trail that the low glow of moonlight dipped into silver and sapphire. Fir trees dotted the banks and slumped under the weight of snow that dripped along their branches.

"Does the ice ever melt here?" I asked.

"Not this high in the mountains," Orion said and then raised his voice loud enough that it reached the group. "We've arrived. The path to the palace is just over the hill there."

Apollo met my gaze as steeliness slipped into his posture again. This wasn't the cold disregard for the world he'd had on the entire trip. His expression was for Zephyrus.

I shifted my arrow bag on my hip as everyone grew quiet, and seriousness swept through the group. Mia and Kama clung to each other as they trundled ahead. Orion's shoulders dropped as he released a breath that puffed out into the air.

"Are you feeling nervous?"

Orion's lips pinched, and his pale skin took on the cool coloring of the dimming world around us. He shrugged.

"You've never really been afraid of death. Which has always seemed strange for a mortal."

Orion clutched his cloak to his neck as another gust of wind swept down the path and whipped snow off trees. "I suppose I never told you the full story of why I joined the army."

There was something heavy in his voice, something that left me apprehensive. My gaze darted to Apollo's firm stance, to the nervous bundle of energy surrounding Mia and Kama who whispered together, to Chares who jumped every time a twig snapped.

"And why was that?" I asked.

Orion shrugged. "I figured it was a fast path to rejoin the family I'd lost."

I stopped walking and heaved in an icy breath. "You joined the army, hoping to die?"

"Ack." He tapped his spear against his shoulder. "I don't know if I'd say *hoping*. It's not an unreasonable thing to expect when joining battles, though, is it? I missed my parents and sister terribly. Still do. It's horrific to be the last person in your family alive."

"I guess I understand."

Orion nodded, but his gaze darted to Apollo.

I suppose I didn't truly comprehend all that Orion had endured. Despite everything fate had yanked from me—my mother, my father, King Magnes, the villagers who raised us, our home—I'd always had Apollo.

But who did Orion have apart from friends and soldiers? I'd seen him as popular, easygoing, and smoothly fitting into every social circumstance. Who did he have that knew the real him? Who did he have that loved him?

A lightness returned to his expression. "Anyway, I joined the army, stayed alive far longer than I expected, and then I met you. So, I suppose there was a purpose in all of that after all."

A smile slipped up on my lips.

He had me.

"So that's why you don't fear death? Because you went looking for it?"

"Well, this is how I see it." He scrubbed his gloved fingers through his pale hair, bumping along the edge of his hood. "What do I have to fear? Worst-case scenario, I die and rejoin my family." He nodded with his chin to the stars that freckled across the rim of the sky. "Best-case scenario, I survive and become a guard for the moodiest goddess that's ever existed."

I scoffed, and he gave me a gentle shove that caused me to stumble a step. I readjusted my bow. "Maybe she won't have you at her temple, after all."

"Maybe she's specifically requested me to join her there, and would be devastated if I told her no."

He was right, of course. I would have been crushed if he had turned the idea down. I'd respect his choices, but I wanted him to return with me. I wanted a future that included us heckling each other, taking hunting trips, and grousing over Apollo's nonsense. The entire future swept before me and gave me a spark of hope. All we needed to do was survive one more day. We'd already endured the attacks of hundreds of gods. Zephyrus was haughty and arrogant which would make him sloppy. We'd defeat him, get Hyacinth and Ixion back, and return to Niria before a new moon graced the sky.

Gods, the idea of that left me speechless. I wanted to wrap Epiphany in a hug, spend an afternoon with Arion, pass a day without having to kill or worry about being killed.

My feet slipped in the slush. "Well, you need to prepare yourself for the second option, I'm afraid. I plan to keep you busy for the next seven or eight decades."

"Eight decades?" He chuckled, and it puffed out like staccato notes into the darkening sky. "You're going to have me working into my old age. What if I want to retire?"

I clicked my tongue. "Yeah, right."

His shoulders shook with a laugh again. "Well, I can imagine worse ways to spend a life than being at the mercy of a stubborn, pain-in-the-ass deity."

"As long as she puts up with your obstinate bullshit in turn, right?"

He grinned. "That's the plan."

The six of us crunched to the top of the path. In the distance, the peaks of the Palace of the Four Winds thrust ivory against the navy of the world. My breath caught. We'd made it. We only needed to go a little farther. Then we'd be home. This journey would be over, and we would figure out our ascension and begin our new lives.

I wanted it so hungrily I could nearly taste the sweetness of it.

The ground shuddered and snow tumbled down the slopes. Everyone crouched and snapped weapons loose as their eyes widened. Mia trembled against Kama. "It's Gaea." She hugged herself, and loose strands of hair whipped around the brim of her hat. "She's after me. She's always hated me having magic connected to the earth. I'm the reason she's here. I should break off from the team and lead her away."

"Mia," Kama exclaimed.

"It's me she wants, Kam," Mia said, her voice firming.

The ground shook harder, and I looked at Apollo. His eyes glowed creamy with the light of the moon that reflected off the snowbanks. He frowned. We were so close to the palace, so close to Hyacinth and Ixion.

Mia fisted her gloved hands. "I can be a distraction and draw her away from everyone."

"We've fought as a unit," Apollo said. "We've mourned and made mistakes as a group. There's no splitting up. We stay together. If Gaea has come for you, then she'll have to get through all of us. We have your back, Mia."

My chest warmed with pride. That was the Apollo I knew—the man he truly was.

It might be easier for us to leave Mia or use her as a

distraction. We weren't the type who chose the simple path. We did what was right, regardless of the cost.

That clicked into my mind like a piece of my identity snapped into place.

Ever since I'd learned of my origins, I'd wondered if it doomed me to leave a trail of destruction behind me. My feet trembled beneath me, and I braced against Orion to stay upright.

I may have been born divine, but that didn't mean I was inherently wicked.

We'd survive this.

Then we'd redefine what it meant to be gods.

The ground cracked and snow slid down into the maw of the earth.

A massive root rose from the pit, snarled branches swirled around until it curved towards us. Carved within the bark of the tree was a woman's face, crunched with derision. Her lips crackled as they peeled apart. "Unwise deities have crossed my boundary." The bark-like browns of her eyes shifted to Orion and then glimmered with a deep green moss color. "Five gods and one son-of-man foolish enough to run with them."

Orion lowered his weapon, posturing as passive, hoping to avoid a fight.

I stepped forward, uncomfortable with Gaea's attention focused on Orion. "We're only passing through."

"Artemis." She hissed my name out and sent a shiver down my spine. "The great huntress blessed with prophecies from the mighty Clothos." She frowned. "The low deities have grown tired of you sky gods, believing the world should bow to you alone."

So, this had nothing to do with Mia, after all.

"A new time comes where the deities tied to the earth

A Spark of Death and Fury

aspire to rule, receive the best dedications, and stop dealing with the destruction the high gods mar the world with."

"If you've aligned with Zephyrus," Apollo yelled, "you've done so to your detriment."

Gaea cackled. "Oh, precious sun god. It's a pity. I wish we could get along as you shine light on the world which draws forth plants. Our realms are interconnected. Unfortunately, you've associated yourself poorly." Her gaze darted to Mia, who trembled and shifted back against Kama.

Gaea hadn't forgotten about her, after all. "Please, listen," I said. "We're not here to take over as the new high gods. The era of the separation between the deities is ending and we plan to usher that forth."

"Your father"—Gaea's body blocked the view of the palace—"was always so arrogant, causing earthquakes, storms, hurricanes. I wonder what destruction his child might produce once she possesses the power of the spark?"

"We aim to gain the spark only to dismantle it. We don't plan to keep it."

She huffed a breath that brushed back my braids like the crisp winds of autumn. "Oh, a pretty story. I think I'll take my chances with those who possess *true* elemental powers." She looked to the three young gods with us who all shrank under the weight of her appraisal. She rose again so that her bark-like form swelled against the night sky. We all grabbed our weapons, yanked spears back, and snapped arrows into bows. Magic glittered over Apollo's flesh.

Gaea dove into the gulf of the earth she'd created and disappeared into the darkness. For a weighted moment everyone remained frozen as our rapid breaths raised our shoulders. Apollo eased over to the hole and trembled as he peered down into it. Then turned back to the group. "She's gone."

He frowned and he had to think of the same thing that skittered across my mind. There was no way she'd disappear so easily after intimidating us like that. There was something more happening here.

"Why would she leave after threatening us?" I asked.

Orion cocked an eyebrow and shrugged.

Unease pulsed through me alongside my heartbeat. There was nothing to do about it, and we needed to find some means to cross the canyon she'd rent into the earth. I eased over to it and peeked down into the ebony depths.

The ground trembled again, and we froze.

A fearsome creature clawed its way out of the hole, dragged itself up to the opposite side of the gap, and dipped its massive paws into the banks. A breath puffed from it and fire slipped out which melted the snow into a puddle that soaked the fur of its golden feet. On its back, the face of a goat growled, revealing razor-like teeth. It whipped around and the head of a lion appraised us with bright eyes. Its tail whirled and a snake with dripping fangs snapped at the end.

A chimera.

The entire group took an unsteady step away from the hole as a second animal emerged out of the pit of the earth.

A bull with golden, sleek horns that sparkled in the moonlight stomped its hooves into the ground. It snorted a cloud that drifted over us. "Don't breathe it," I yelled. "It might be poisonous." I slammed Orion into the snow and smashed my hand over his mouth.

Once the air dissipated, we rose again, and Orion gave me a nod.

Apollo stood with his bow aimed at the bull, an arrow

A Spark of Death and Fury

in place, when a third animal skittered its way up alongside the first two. Its amethyst scales reflected the flaming eyes of the bull, and the clack of its enormous pincers sent shockwaves through me. The creature whipped its tail up where the pointed tip glowed a hot, red color.

Apollo's arms trembled as he lowered his bow. "What the fuck is that?"

"A scorpion," I said.

"The size of a palace."

For a moment, we all froze and stared in horror at the massive animals.

Then the three creatures jumped across the chasm in unison and landed with a rumble of thunder that shook through my bones.

31

Epiphany

Attendants had decorated the dining room lavishly for the dinner with the high lords. The event I'd almost missed thanks to Demetri's scheming. Silver silks rippled over the ceiling and the finest cutlery and gold-rimmed plates were set across the table. Bouquets of flowers bowed in front of gem-studded wine glasses. It matched the people scattered through the space, all draped in richly embroidered fabrics and sparkling jewelry.

This was a reminder that Niria was still wealthy and strong despite all the turmoil.

It brought to mind my mock presentation dinner when Hyacinth had taken the chair I now walked towards. When he'd looked at me with such concern in his eyes. Temi had sat by me and gripped my hand in support. Emrin had teased me about having to wear a robe to match my dress.

That would never happen again.

A ripple of sorrow pierced through me.

I couldn't give into those memories tonight.

I stepped up to the seat at the head of the table and

nodded at all the high lords and their partners. Everyone took their seats, chairs shuffling, napkins placed into laps.

Dinner progressed well enough. I kept a steady conversation up with a man who had wiry gray eyebrows and broad shoulders. He'd been a close friend of Father's as well as the head of a wealthy and well-respected family. He and his wife, who had the seat to his right, were both pleasant and made several gentle remarks on their respect for my family and condolences for losing my father.

The seating arrangements were coordinated by Joden. Demetri sat in the back corner between two people who had deep loyalty to Father. The attendees on either side of me kept a conversation flowing that I added multiple points to, thanks to the advisors' meetings and my time spent with Isadora reading the court documents. The high lords smiled and inclined their heads when I obviously knew what I was talking about.

A spark of achievement glittered through me.

Things were going better than I'd expected.

The dinner wrapped up. Attendants brought out after-meal drinks in sparkling glasses which Demetri lifted and raised his voice. "A toast to the beautiful country of Niria."

The people all turned to face him, hoisted their glasses, and offered remarks of ascent.

He took a sip of his drink, and his eyes gleamed with candlelight. My heart rate picked up even as I lifted my glass. He twirled his goblet between his fingers. "A country that's had fine leadership for many years. Niria has truly stood as the gem on the crown of our continent."

The high lords smiled broadly. The man next to me took another swallow of his wine, as if to cement his agreement.

"Hard times have come, however." Demetri's voice

dropped a cadence. "Gossip now spreads about the country once admired and even envied by others."

The mood in the room shifted, silence punctuating over the glittering finery.

"It's difficult for other countries to hold Niria in the same level of esteem when a woman—a young one with a shaky reputation, at that—sits at the helm."

A few gazes darted to me. Some high lords, however, frowned at Demetri, unhappy with his manners and the turn in the evening. A beat of shame pulsed through me. I wanted so desperately to fight for Niria and hold it up. It was difficult when some people saw me as a liability or even a hardship for the country. I needed to speak but mentally stumbled over words.

Fen licked his lips. "I would say it's more of a mark to the esteemed leadership of King Magnes." He thrust his hands out as he looked around the table. "He had the foresight to educate well all three of his children. I don't believe anyone could have guessed the turn life has given us. Who could have expected us to need a third child to have Magnes' wisdom and education within themselves? Luckily"—he shot Demetri a look so sharp he could have bled from it—"our king had enough wisdom to make sure our country had stability despite the twists fate may throw our way."

Voices rose around the room. A few people thudded their hands against the table and others finished their drinks.

I raised my chin. Regardless of how these families felt about me, they respected Father.

Demetri wobbled his glass back and forth and waited for the group to quiet. "It's true. You've had a wise leader and prosperity for many years. But the gentry from other

A Spark of Death and Fury

countries talk. They fear King Magnes' unruly daughter is going to take his place and ruin this country he cared for so well."

The response was mixed. Some frowned and worry wrinkled their foreheads. A few leaned away from Demetri and clicked their tongues. Others darted looks to me, some encouraging, others uncertain.

I parted my lips to speak, but Demetri cut me off as his voice gained volume. "That sadly isn't the worst rumor I've heard. And rumors—while a nasty business—affect politics, trade, religious ceremonies, and all the interactions countries have with each other." He shrugged as the entire table seemed to stare at him in shock, myself included. This conversation was so far beyond the point of impropriety, he'd thrown it off the cliff.

"It's well known that a stableman from the palace has recently traveled to Carens this past week. A bastard who is trying to extort a title from a gentleman of that country so that the Princess can marry him."

A woman choked on her drink and someone next to her patted her back. Heat spilled over my cheeks, climbed up to my temples, and whirled down my neck. Gazes snapped to me with censure. Rumors floating around were one thing. The cold fact of the situation, sitting bare and trembling amid the lingering remains of an elegant dinner, was another.

I should say something.

But what?

If I denied it, and Val showed up with his title, I'd lose all the integrity I had with these families. Besides, I'd promised to be honest with my people. It mattered to me more than anything.

Demetri clicked his tongue, not noticing or choosing to

ignore how his seatmates glowered at him. "The bastard is the child of a dishwasher. Can you imagine the next person to sit on the throne might be the grandchild of a palace attendant?"

A few uncomfortable chuckles peppered into the silence. Some people studied me with disapproval in their gazes, however. Enough. I sat up straighter. "Spreading gossip at a formal dinner certainly shows how Carens' manners diverge from Niria's, my lord." The man beside me raised his glass and tipped it in my direction. In a way, it almost felt like Father stood at my side and encouraged me. A scowl permeated the man's kind features as he glared at Demetri. Several other people at the table nodded their heads in agreement.

Demetri's eyebrows pinched together, but he smiled.

He'd won that round.

Again.

Damn it.

When the dinner finished, I wished each attendee good evening. Some clasped my hands and gave me encouraging looks, but many scarcely made eye contact with me as they hurried out.

Joden lingered, and once the space had cleared out, I approached him. The royal navy of his jacket sank into ebony shadows with the candles burned down to nubs. The room glowed a low ginger color.

"I'm afraid, Princess, we have two issues."

I forced my muscles to still, to not allow my feelings to permeate through my features. That had been an utter disaster. I'd barely scraped back any sense of dignity for myself. And if Joden thought we only had two issues, he was more of an optimist than me. "What are those?"

"The first, of course, is that the dinner went reprehensibly."

I bowed my head. This meeting had been so important, and I'd lost control of the entire situation.

"The second," he continued, "is that Lord Lucien has denied Valerian's request."

I stumbled back a step. No. He'd agreed to claim him when communicating with my father. I'd expected him to acquiesce for his benefit if nothing else. Everything was falling apart, like sand melting under the relentless pounding of the waves.

"I fear our chances of shifting this back in our favor slip from our grasp," Joden said.

"Surely it's not hopeless."

He studied me for a moment and released a breath. "I'll endeavor to find a solution, but this situation is precarious." He bowed. "Good night, Your Highness." He left me standing alone in shadows as candles slowly sighed their way to extinction.

I stepped out of the dining room and into an empty servant's nook, closed the door behind me, and let tears come as I bit my lip to muffle my sobs. The space sat in darkness. I slid down onto the floor and released hot breaths into the palm I clasped over my mouth.

What could I do?

Valerian was my heart.

But Niria needed me.

If I was forced to choose, I wasn't sure which one I would pick.

I loved both of them fiercely.

Demetri had proven himself to be nothing but selfish and malicious. I couldn't hand this country that my entire family had fought and bled and died for to him.

What would I do about Val, though?

Those thoughts hovered over me as I crept upstairs, still too embarrassed to want to interact with anyone. In my room I unwound the tight style of my hair, peeled off the heavy layers, and removed the crown and jewelry. The one mercy I had was that I'd insisted the dressmaker fashion my gowns so I could remove them myself.

I sat and stared at the wall where shadows danced from an oil lamp until my eyes stung. Ivory moonlight and a cool breeze spilled in through a window I'd cracked open. A clattering noise from outside caught my attention. I stood and pressed my fingers to the pane.

A group of a few dozen horses trotted through the gardens. One rider lifted his face to look at my room. Despite the darkness and the limited view through the branches of the pear tree, I knew who it was. Valerian.

I swallowed hard and turned, donned another dress, and wove my hair into a loose braid. My decision was made before I took time to really think about it. I slipped out of my room, crept along the hall, and stepped down a servants' staircase until I reached the attendants' rooms. My heart beat rapidly as I approached a door and knocked quietly, holding my breath as if I could silence the tapping sound.

A moment passed before it cracked open, and Brina peeked out, her forehead furrowed. "Epiphany." She pulled me into the room. It stretched dark except for where moonlight spilled over her unmade bed. The rest of the space was neatly arranged with her shoes lined up beside a small closest and, on top of that, wildflowers that draped over the edge of a ceramic mug.

"I need to request a huge favor."

She rubbed her eyes and gave me a bewildered look.

"I'm sorry to wake you, but I have to speak with Valerian."

"Has he returned?"

"He has. Do you think you could go ask him? I can't get caught around the stables, especially at night, now."

She fiddled her fingers together. "They don't like for attendants to wander about at dark either."

Oh, right. Gods, I hadn't even considered that. I was so caught up in my own problems I was being selfish. "Of course. I didn't think… Brina, I'm sorry. I shouldn't have even woken you. Forgive me, I'll…"

"I could say his mother wanted him."

"What?"

"If anyone asks, I could tell them his mother sent me. That might help avoid suspicion."

I licked my lips. "Do you mind? I didn't consider before barging down here and waking you up."

She hesitated a moment before nodding. "Let me put something on, and I'll go."

"Thank you so much."

Half an hour later, she returned and unlatched her lock. Valerian whispered, censure sharpening his words. "This isn't my mother's room."

"Can you trust me? You've known me your whole life, haven't you?"

"Brina…" His voice held a warning as the door swung open.

Brina stepped inside, but Valerian hesitated, his arms crossed, his expression lost to shadows.

"Val," I said.

His hands dropped, and he strode forward. "Epiphany?"

I tucked my arms around him. He cupped the back of my head with his hand, grazing his fingers down the bumps of my braid, and buried his nose in my neck.

"I'll just…" Brina trailed off as she stepped out and clicked the door shut behind her.

"I owe her," I said at the same time Valerian asked, "Are you okay?"

We laughed for a moment, the heat of our breaths clouding the air between us. He brushed his thumb over my cheek, back and forth, the rough texture of it scraped and sent shivers down me. I stood on my tiptoes and captured his mouth, kissing him hard, like I could seal us together.

For several long minutes, we held each other and didn't speak. I wasn't sure what words we'd say, anyway. The separation from him had been terrible. We'd both faced awful things while apart, the world crumbling around us.

I sighed and pulled back where I could make out the sparkle in his eyes. "We shouldn't keep Brina's room all night."

"Right. Of course."

I pinched my lips down hard. "I have something difficult to tell you."

"What is it?"

"Things aren't going well. We hosted a dinner for the high lords tonight and it was a disaster." I left off that my relationship with him was half the issue. It didn't need to be said. He had to know I was aware his father hadn't agreed to our plan. "There's a part of me that so desperately wants to leave all this and run away with you."

Valerian remained quiet for a moment, the warm steadiness of his body a comfort. "I'd do that, if it's what you wanted."

"Well, it might be necessary if Demetri takes over the kingdom. We talked about that once… leaving here and finding a different life. Your mother could come with us. Would you seriously consider that still?"

Val kissed my cheek. "Without a moment's hesitation."

I nodded. There was a part of me that wanted to take

A Spark of Death and Fury

that route. It would be easier. Why was I even fighting for this role of stress and disrespect and hardship? Then I thought of Niria, of the woman in the food line who'd trusted me, of every person who depended on our country's leadership and well-being. Of Father and Emrin and Hyacinth. "I have to fight for Niria, though."

Val nodded. His thumb continued to stroke my arm, his gaze intense, even lost in the shadows.

"If..." I tightened my grip and trembled as I fought back tears of desperation and grief. "If it comes down to it, and I have to choose my happiness"—I gave his hands a squeeze—"or the good of this country, I think I have to pick Niria. The well-being of so many people rests on it. And... I can't abandon it."

Valerian's nose flared. The smell of horses and travel whirled around him. I wanted nothing more than to join him, take a couple of stallions and my personal assets and run.

Someone had to fight for our country, though.

"I understand, Epiphany." He lifted my hand and kissed my knuckles. "We've tried."

"I'm not done trying. I need you to know where I'm at, though. If... if the situation grows desperate..." It already was, I was sure of it. "I might have to choose."

He bowed his forehead against mine and grazed his thumb over my cheek. "I support you, whatever you do. Even if I must do so from afar."

I sucked in a shaky breath, and my heart ached. Gods, every moment of our relationship had felt like heartbreak. We'd almost made it. Now we might end up missing each other, right in the darkest part of the night, just before the sun finally crested.

There was so much I had to say to him, and so little time.

He leaned down, kissed me, and swallowed my words back.

I spent another stolen moment listening to the sound of our heartbeats pounding together, wondering if I'd ever get to do so again.

32

Artemis

The beasts prowled towards the six of us. The chimera yawned and fire slipped from its mouth. Poisonous gas whispered up to the sky as the bull snorted. The scorpion swept its tail around, its stinger shimmering an angry red against the glow of the moon.

"Okay," I said, as I gripped my bow. "We can get through these, right?"

Kama nodded and her coppery braid swayed. "We've killed hundreds of gods. How hard can three monsters be?"

Apollo clicked his tongue and drew a blade.

The beasts charged for us.

I whipped arrows out, and they clattered off the side of the chimera like some god had crafted it of stone.

Orion released his spear and the same thing happened.

We exchanged a look.

Holy shit.

How did you defeat creatures that weapons couldn't penetrate?

Kama blasted fire that lit up the sides of the mountain

with wild shadows. The chimera leapt forward and opened its mouth to swallow her flames. His eyes glowed orange with them.

Mia pressed into her magic to cause the earth to tremble. The bull stomped his hoof into the mud and the trembling stopped.

We all tumbled backwards and pressed our feet into the muck of the snow. Uncertainty hung on me. How the hell were we supposed to move past these creatures? They slowed as they came closer.

Apollo's gaze remained on the trio of monsters prowling in our direction as his words came clipped. "We have to get close enough to cut off their heads or strike them a killing blow. Cyn and I faced a creature like this before. It's not easy, but it's doable."

Orion yanked a blade free from his hip.

"You three." Apollo gestured to Chares, Kama, and Mia. "Act as a distraction, keep them busy countering your magic, and the rest of us"—he nodded to me and Orion—"will attempt to end them."

I looked at Orion again, but he just gave a sharp bob of his head before returning his focus to the animals that grew closer with each passing heartbeat. Fur raised on the back of shoulders, and fangs bared.

"Let's go," Apollo said.

The three young gods exploded with the strength of their powers. Earth, wind, and fire magic whooshed through the pass. Flames licked up, encouraged by Chares' gust, and cracks snapped in the ground.

In the scorching heat and driving wind, Apollo, Orion, and I ran towards the fearsome creatures.

They were enormous up close. The bull towered over the peak of the mountain we stood on, and its tail knocked fir trees over as it swung around. I grabbed hold of its leg, and it reared up and thrust me into a pile of snow. I landed with a huff, my breath knocked from me.

Oh fuck.

I jumped back up, ran to the creature again, and weaved between its hooves that shook the ground with each step.

Apollo and Orion attempted to do the same but were also flung away. They both hopped up as Mia's magic trembled down the mountainside again.

We fought for what felt like hours. The crunch of the earth shifting, the heat of flames, the putrid smell of the bull's fumes, the grating, snapping sounds of the animals smashing into the cliffside all blended.

Orion scaled the scorpion. He lifted his blade and the monster rolled. Orion jumped off and the scorpion lifted its tail, the stinger glowing crimson.

"Orion," I screamed as I ran to him.

The stinger dove towards Orion.

And froze just before it reached him.

The animal scuttled off to join the others.

That's when it hit me.

"Apollo," I shouted.

He jogged over and dodged the whipping snake tail of the chimera. Dirt and sweat smattered his face, his curls stuck to his skin, his tunic torn. "Yes?"

"Do you think your shield would hold for a minute so we can talk? I had a thought."

He swiped damp curls off his face. "We can try."

We called the others over and Mia pressed into the earth, reinforcing Apollo's shield with mounds of dirt that the creatures slammed against. The gold of Apollo's magic shuddered with the impacts. I leaned in to the five of them and spoke as quickly as I could get words to form. "They're not trying to kill us."

Apollo's mouth gaped. "It feels a lot like they are."

"No. They probably could have had several of us by now. If they get close to actually killing, they stop. I think they're attempting to drain our magic before we face Zephyrus. He needs you alive to fight him but doesn't want to do it with your powers intact."

Apollo rolled back on his feet and released a breath as his eyes skimmed the dark space beyond the peak we stood on—the place where the palace rested. A chunk of the earth broke as the bull crashed into it. "That makes sense. Zephyrus is always trying to play things to his advantage."

"We need to let you get away."

Apollo's face snapped back up. "What?"

The creatures had destroyed most of the dirt enforcements. Crumbles slid down the glowing gold of Apollo's shield as the creatures slammed against it. "We'll distract them," I said. "You go to Zephyrus before you wear yourself out completely. The rest of us will try to catch up as soon as we can."

Kama nodded as she tangled her fingers with Mia's. Chares' focus had shifted to where the animals pounded against the warbling wall of Apollo's shield. Orion rested his hand on the hilt of his sword and sweat dripped over his forehead. "It makes sense."

A pounding that caused the magic to glitter like it was dissipating drew our attention. Apollo bit his lip. "I'll go."

We studied each other.

I wondered if it might be the last time I'd see him.

No.

We'd succeed.

I knew it.

I pulled him into a hug. "Be careful. And listen, don't let him throw you off. He wants you distracted and emotional. Stay focused. Okay?"

A Spark of Death and Fury

"All right, Temi. I love you."

I squeezed his arms and gave everyone a nod.

Apollo withdrew the magic, and it left with a whoosh. The light dimmed and left us all standing beneath the massive feet of the animals.

"Chares."

He threw a wind that tumbled the creatures back.

We fought again.

Except for Apollo.

He crept down the path, staying low. He looked back once, and I held his gaze for half a dozen heartbeats. I was certain that he could beat Zephyrus.

The five of us returned to our dance of distracting the beasts, dodging their blows, attempting to scale their massive bodies.

After half an hour, a howling sound roared from the canyon. The creatures backed down from us as Gaea rose again, her dark form silvery in the light of the moon that already descended.

"You let Apollo get away," she screeched.

The animals bowed their heads. The chimera curled up, his snake-tail wrapped around his front paws.

Gaea growled, but then her eyes darted to our group, where we huddled together, exhausted and sweat-soaked in the freezing air. She scowled. "Finish them."

She dropped back into the earth.

The three animals turned towards us again.

A different expression colored their faces.

They looked ready to kill.

"Oh, shit," I said.

They prowled in our directions. I bounced my knife in my hand like I could grip it in some manner that would actually make it useful.

"Kama?"

"Yeah?" she said, her voice trembling.

"The chimera's fire can't hurt you, right?"

"Right."

"Okay, you keep it distracted. Chares you focus on the bull. Use you wind to keep it flustered so it can't stop Mia's magic. Then, Mia, when the creatures are distracted use your powers to drop them into the earth and crush them."

"Got it," Chares said.

"As soon as you finish, follow Apollo. We'll all meet at the palace." I pointed to Orion. "You're with me. We'll take down the scorpion."

He jogged alongside me as I grabbed the attention of the creature. I ran up the rocky side of a cliff, dodged around rocks, and slid behind a boulder. Orion landed beside me with a huff, sending snow into the air. "What's your plan?"

"One of us is going to have to act as bait. The other will wait on a rock and jump on top of it while it's distracted."

"I can be bait."

"No." The creature's scuttling movements grew louder, and I clenched my teeth. "You have a stronger knife arm than me. You're more likely to pierce its exoskeleton than I am."

A grin spread across Orion's face. "Aww, Temi."

"Don't," I said. "Just take the compliment."

"And not heckle you about it?" He nudged me in the ribs. "Not a chance."

I snorted. "Go, before the thing finds us."

He smirked at me. His eyes sparkled like the stars behind him where the palest wisp of creamy blue dawned over the horizon. A new day rising.

We only had to survive one more day.

We could do it.

A Spark of Death and Fury

The earth shook and a roar echoed around and then disappeared. They must have the bull down. And with its magic gone, they should end the chimera quickly enough. Gods, if we'd only had a few minutes to think before the fight started it might have saved us hours of exertion.

I jumped up to scramble over the boulders. The scorpion whipped in my direction, its stinger raised menacingly in the air. I sloshed through the snow, dove around the dark forms of rocks, slipped through crevices, and channeled every moment of my life I'd spent creeping through the woods at night.

A boulder shattered beside me. Shards of the rock hit me, and I winced as blood trickled down my arm. The scorpion lifted its pincer to smash another rock, and I dove into a pile of snow. Ice soaked into my clothing. I jumped up and looked for Orion where he stood tucked behind a tree at the top of a peak.

Okay. I only needed to make it a little farther.

I scrambled through small juts of trees and grasped them to swing forward. The creature scurried after me, crushing rocks and vegetation like they were made of sand.

I reached the dip beneath where Orion stood. I flipped around and gasped for air as I backed against the rippling side of the mountain. Ice made the rock under my feet slick.

The creature buzzed with agitation and clacked its pincers as it cornered me.

My muscles trembled.

It just needed to get a little closer.

It took another step, and Orion leapt with the grace of a cat, landed on the creature with a thump, and slammed a sword down between its eyes. The scorpion hissed and thrashed. It came nearer to me, its massive legs cracking the ground beneath me.

Its stinger whipped forward.

I stepped to jerk out of the way but slipped on the ice. My feet whipped out from underneath me, and my head landed with a bang that caused my vision to double for a moment.

The stinger pulsed red as it dove for me.

I lay stunned, unable to move.

"Temi," Orion yelled.

He pounced again, grace in motion, as he landed on top of me and rolled us away.

For a minute I focused on my breaths, clung to his arms, smelled the tang of our sweat, and felt the pounding of our hearts between us.

The scorpion thudded to the ground, the sword still protruding from its head. It jerked and Orion released me as he was yanked back with it. I scrambled to my feet and ran to him. The stinger pierced through his back. His cloak sopped crimson with blood.

"Orion," I screamed. I dropped to my knees beside him.

His body trembled, and he swallowed hard before flicking his pale blue eyes open. "I told you."

My hands hovered above him, frozen in shock and horror. "Told me what?"

"That I'd get a true compliment from you"—he sucked in a breath—"before I died."

That snapped me into action, and I grabbed the massive hilt of the stinger, pulled it out and removed my coat. I balled it up and pressed it against the wound. Orion shuddered as his body convulsed away from me. "You aren't going to die." I pressed harder and blood flooded over my hands, dripped down my arms.

"Temi."

I ignored him. "We need to stop the bleeding. And find

some way to move you off this part of the mountain and…" I licked my lips. "We can… we can…"

"There's venom…" He took a slow, shaky breath and reached for my hand to draw me around where I could see his face, leaving his blood to pour out and stain the ice beneath him. "In the stinger. I probably only have a few minutes."

"No." I clenched his palm tighter. "No… we'll get Apollo and he'll heal you. You'll be okay."

He shook his head slowly, back and forth. Slow ripples of gold washed over Orion as the sun rose, highlighting the pale color of his skin. "I won't, Temi."

"No, godsdamnit." I smacked my free hand against the ice so hard it stung. "You sat by my side in a similar situation and refused to let me die. I'm going to do the same for you."

He winced, and his thumb brushed over my knuckles slowly, smearing the blood. "It wasn't your time yet." He trembled. "It is mine."

"No… No." Tears broke free and coated my cheeks. "You're supposed to put up with my bullshit for another eight decades. That's what we said. And…. you shouldn't have jumped." I choked on a sob. "That hit was for me."

He chuckled, such a quiet sound the wind swallowed it, but he kept brushing his thumb over my hand. "Like I said, it's not your time. You're"—he gasped—"needed for so much still."

"I could make a deal with Hades, like Apollo did. If Hades' magic is back, he could return you as a low deity."

Orion coughed and his body draped farther against the ground. He lifted his eyes, those piercing blue irises that had twinkled as they teased me, and communicated so much without speaking, and seen down to the heart of me. "You know that isn't what I want."

His gaze darted to the heavens, where stars still glittered against the brightening sky.

"You wish to join your family," I murmured.

"That was the plan." His voice sounded so weak, I leaned closer to hear his words. "I didn't realize... that... I would meet you... and I'd have someone... to miss... here... too."

His grip loosened.

"Orion," I whispered. He remained still. "Orion?" I yelled.

He didn't move or tease me or pull his crystal eyes open.

I threw my head back and screamed. Tears tracked down my chin and dripped off it before landing against the crimson blood on his shirt and absorbing into it.

I howled my misery and heartache and fell against the ice, curled my knees against my chest, and rocked as I wept until my throat grew raw.

A silvery essence swept over his body.

His spirit.

Apollo had told me about that happening with Hyacinth. How he could see it when Hyacinth's soul had left him.

I crawled back over to Orion and reached for it, like I could touch him, but my hand passed through it. It glittered. Like the damn stars he wished to join.

I gripped his jaw, and the coarse texture of his beard grated the flesh of my fingers.

"I did not give you permission to break my heart." More tears slipped out of me, and my sobs picked back up and echoed off the side of the mountain as I grieved alone. I brushed over his spirit that swept away from his body.

Then I stood.

"If you want to be among the stars." I sank into my

powers, the cool breathing magic of them, until my muscles trembled with the effort and sweat broke out on my brow. "Then you will be."

The setting moon, nearly lowered behind the mountain, brightened as my powers swept through me. I grasped ahold of his spirit. It felt like summer days, laughter under an ebony sky, and a million twinkling stars. I pulled back to throw with every ounce of energy I had as I commanded the moon and the heavens to obey my call.

His spirit soared until it burst into a dozen stars that sparkled across the sky. The constellation stretched out, a man, his knife belt in place, a bow raised and ready to strike. My body buzzed with energy, a fizzy sensation that filled me up like I could float to the heavens. Like every drop of magic in the universe stood within reach of my fingertips. Something had changed in me, irrevocably. I didn't care.

I dropped beside the pale form of Orion's body and grazed my fingers once more over his beard. "I will never forget you. You do not have to worry about memoriams being lit for you. Or being forgotten." The words came muffled through my tears as my nose flared. "If I have any power as a goddess, any ripple that goes into the future, your name will go down in history with mine."

I brushed the hair back from his brow and touched the grainy surface of his skin.

Then I dropped my shaking body down into the ice and wept like I never had before.

33

Hyacinth

I'd remained more aware than in the previous days. Constant worry over Ixion kept my mind tumbling over things. Standing chained in the dark, it was hard to guess the time, but I assumed I'd been away from him for at least a full day.

He had to be terrified, and I worried he might try to reveal himself.

My wrists pierced with biting pain, and my entire body throbbed alongside my heartbeat. If I clenched my teeth, the iron tang of blood filled my mouth.

I had once thought I'd experienced a great deal of misery at the hands of my advisors in my role as a prince.

I'd been a fool.

I knew nothing of suffering.

That's all my life comprised of anymore.

It was only concern over Ix that kept me grounded, stole me from seeping back into the quiet corners of my mind where I'd learned to retreat. If Zephyrus showed up and offered for me to go to the child again, I might capitulate. Perhaps he'd keep his word and not hurt Ix. Maybe

A Spark of Death and Fury

it would be worth the risk so Ixion could see that I was alive.

But, no.

Zephyrus had already abused him once.

Whoever came for us had to be close.

Ixion only needed to remain alone for another day or so.

That had to be the case.

I didn't think I could bear more.

I focused on the gurgling sound of my breathing, the crackling rattle of the chains as I shifted, the squeaking noises that had to be some sort of rat crawling over the floor.

Staring into the dark left a chasm of space for my thoughts to run to.

Apollo came to me ceaselessly.

Even when my mind darted around to other subjects and grasped onto the painful bitterness of them like I clenched the blade of a sword, Apollo lingered there, golden and bright.

I hoped he was alive.

That soon he'd have Ixion.

Then I thought of Epiphany, and Father, and Emrin.

It hurt to stand there aching and alone, with nothing to do but mull over the fact that I'd lost my last moments with them. Even Pip was probably lost to me. It wasn't likely I would live to see her again.

I didn't know where deities went after their deaths. Having gone to the underworld, it brought me peace for Father and Emrin. They'd reunited with Mother, and all the pain and worries of this world washed away for them.

That left me miring in worry for Epiphany and Niria.

Those three concerns trickled through me.

Ixion, Pip, Niria.

Niria, Pip, Ixion.

They buzzed along my thoughts until I was nauseous with it.

Gods, I wished I could be anywhere but in this blackened dungeon.

It wasn't even the gnawing, relentless hunger or the physical torment that I longed to evade as much as my mind, which seemed to crackle and fall into bitter pieces.

I wasn't certain the damage was repairable.

I worked through passages of ancient languages, poems, mathematical formulas, and problems Niria faced, attempting to unpick them, recite them, roll them around to pass the time and keep my thoughts from flowing out and drowning me.

Despite that, whenever one problem ended, I found myself right where I'd begun.

Alone in the dark.

How many days had passed?

Maybe Ixion was dead, even.

How could I possibly know otherwise?

All I wanted was for this to end.

To stop needing to fight and let my mind drift away.

No.

Ixion, Pip, Niria.

Niria, Pip, Ixion.

Pieces of broken poetry.

Apollo.

Apollo.

Apollo.

A slash of light ballooned through the space and highlighted the craggy surface of the bricks along the wall.

Zephyrus.

I'd lie and tell him I would remove the shield from Ixion. Then he'd take me to him, and I could see if Ix was okay, and reassure the child that I was alive and help was on the way. I wouldn't actually unshield him. He could remain safe. Zephyrus could do what he wanted with me after.

Footsteps echoed down the stairs.

And disappeared.

Perhaps I'd just imagined someone coming.

How much time had passed between that thought and this moment?

Maybe it had been hours, or even days.

I scrunched my eyes closed and forced them to open.

Light still trickled along the wall.

So, I wasn't imagining it.

Zephyrus appeared before me with a gleam in his eyes. He unlocked my manacles and my arms dropped to my side. Blood rushed, cold and sharp, into my limbs as I collapsed with a crack to my knees. It stung so much I wanted to scream but growled through my teeth instead.

"Oh, no, Prince." Zephyrus yanked me back onto my feet. "We can't have you dying yet." He snapped his fingers and two guards stepped out of the shadows, grabbed me, and dragged me across the floor.

My bare foot banged into something and lifted a toenail. The pain pierced through me and highlighted all my other aches and miseries. My vision grew black around the edges, and I slumped down into the arms of the men.

I woke to Zephyrus smacking my face. "No, no," he said. "Your lover is here. You'd hate to sleep through that, wouldn't you?"

My heart galloped.

Apollo was here.

Could it be true?

Or was I lost in my thoughts? Was this all a dream?

Zephyrus grinned at me. It was the most viscous

expression I'd ever seen on a person. I doubted I could imagine a smile that wicked even in my nightmares. So, maybe this was real.

The men who held me yanked me up and dragged me up the stairs.

My mind tangled around what Zephyrus had said, like a vine wrapping up a tree and consuming it.

Apollo.

Apollo.

Apollo.

I only needed to hold on for a few more minutes.

Then Apollo would see Zephyrus fall.

He would care for Ix.

And I could let go.

We made it outside, where the sun streaked the first rays of its light across the icy expanse of the world. I released a breath that shuddered into the air.

I stood barefoot in threadbare clothing. My feet ached and grew numb against the snow.

Without my divinity's protection, it probably wouldn't take long to freeze in this weather.

Zephyrus' guards dragged me out past the porch. They leaned away from a sharp blast of wind despite the thick clothes they wore. Zephyrus sauntered forward, his coat dragging into the snow, his posture imposing as he pulled his wings in tight. "Come on out, Apollo. Gaea has already announced your arrival, so there's no reason to be coy."

Even in the gold of morning sunlight, the mountains sat lilac and frozen beneath the piercing blue of the sky, slick black edifices of rocks capped in mounds of snow.

My heart thundered as we waited.

No one appeared.

Maybe Zephyrus had lost his sense of himself as much as I had.

A Spark of Death and Fury

Perhaps Apollo wasn't really here.

Perhaps he wasn't even alive.

We would stand out here and freeze to death for a ghost.

Zephyrus pulled me away from the guards, exposing me to more of the wind but also to the sun which kissed my skin. I closed my eyes and leaned towards it as if Apollo himself grazed his fingers over me. It was a mercy —to feel his light once more before death.

"You never really cared about those beneath you, did you?" Zephyrus' fingernails bit into the flesh of my arm. I stood unshackled. I could jump on him again, try to kill him. If only I had the energy. Realistically, his hand was what supported me. I'd fall into a pile if he released me.

"You came all this way and you're not even going to show yourself, you coward?" Zephyrus yelled, his voice creating a cloud in the air.

Something flickered from behind a rock. The movement grew and pushed forward against the breeze. A golden glow glimmered in the distance. The winds died for a moment.

Apollo stood there. His eyes darted to me.

"Apollo," I mouthed, unable to find the strength to form the words.

He said my name as well. I wasn't sure if he'd spoken out loud, and the wind had swallowed the sound of his voice. I could imagine it, though, the rumbling depth and gentle tenderness in his tone.

He looked at Zephyrus.

Anger bled over Apollo's expression, like it glowed around him.

The sun widened across the sky, the heat of it bearing down so much it took away the sting of the elements.

Apollo was here.

My husband.

The love of my life.

The man who I would do anything for and who would do anything for me.

All the suffering and hardship and impossible faith had been worth it.

All would finally came to an end.

34

Epiphany

I peeled back the curtains in my sitting room and crumpled the fabric beneath my fingers. Pink spread across the sky, the heavens bleeding. It left me uneasy. Temi had sat with me dozens of times in the gardens I looked at, resting her head on my shoulder and speaking of the future. Now she'd gone to save my brother. Memories of both of them assailed me this morning.

Gods, I hoped they were okay.

I hadn't expected news until they returned, but hearing nothing remained unsettling.

I'd woken up with both of them on my mind and my heart thundering. It was a bad feeling I'd yet to shake.

The windowpanes reflected the dark circles under my eyes. I rubbed my thumb over the tender skin. Face powder could only do so much. The stress of the job, of losing my family, and navigating everything alone showed through like cracks that veined out and left me wondering if I'd shatter from the pressure.

Maybe I didn't have what it took to run a country. A bird swept by and landed in a tree, shaking the branches. A small pang of longing for freedom bloomed in me. The stronger desire to see Niria well washed it away.

I wished Hyacinth was with me.

I was selfish and wretched for even thinking such a thing.

He was in trouble, and I should pray for his sake, not my own.

I supposed, though, we all faced troubles of different kinds.

A knock echoed through the quiet of the room, and I turned around. I'd woken and dressed early, unable to sleep. Some time alone to reflect before facing another grueling day seemed like it might help. I didn't know who might visit me before the sun even climbed its way up the sky.

I smoothed my stiff, navy dress and walked over to the door before cracking it. The man who stood there, his arms behind his back so that the front of his emerald coat stretched against his form, shocked me so much I stumbled a step and jerked the door open with the motion.

"Lord Galeson?"

His cheeks took on a touch of pink, but his eyes held a guardedness I wasn't familiar with. "I thought we'd agreed to abandon titles."

Kindness weaved in with his voice, and the reminder of the connection between us, the respect and support he'd shown me, slowed my racing heart. "I'm sorry. I didn't expect you, and certainly not here."

He chuckled and ducked his head. A strand of his pale hair fell over his eye, and he batted it away. "One of your advisors graciously offered me directions to find you."

I stared at him, unsure of what to say, and then I pulled the door farther back. "Would you like to come in?"

He looked over his shoulder down the long, empty

hallway before he nodded and followed me into the room. As I closed the door, my fingers pressed into the wood as if I might absorb its steadiness. One of my advisors had sent Gale up here to my private living area?

I turned around. "Can I offer you breakfast?"

His gaze tracked over the room, the deep burgundies of the fabrics, the gleaming pottery displayed on carved stands, the massive painting of ebony horses set against an umber background. Some of their legs reared up, and their manes slapped their backs. He shifted to face me, and something sparked in his eyes that I couldn't read. "No, thank you. I plan to see my father soon and we intend to eat."

"Your father is in Niria?" I asked as I gestured to a sofa, which he took.

"He is, yes. I was finally traveling home from Odilla after wrapping up lingering issues from the war. My father planned to meet me farther North, actually, until I received your missive."

I eased into a chair across from him and tangled my fingers together. "My missive?"

His expression grew guarded, and he cocked his head to the side. "Ah. I had... assumed it was from you. I knew it wasn't your handwriting, but I remember"—he offered me a gentle smile, the crystal blue of his eyes turning paler in the light pouring through the windows—"how you don't like to write. The note... well, it sounded rather personal."

I returned the smile, but discomfort wormed its way into me. Someone had sent him a note of an intimate nature that he believed to be from me. "Maybe you'll offer me enough grace to explain the contents of the letter. I've... had so much going on lately. Perhaps I've missed something."

He jumped out of his seat and paced back and forth.

His reaction added to my nervousness. He stopped and pressed his fingers into the gilded trim of the sofa.

"The note I received—which I now understand wasn't from you—made me think you had reconsidered things between us."

I swallowed.

"Call me a fool, Epiphany." A muscle in his jaw jumped and his eyes took on a glint before he lifted them to focus on me again. "But even knowing that you don't reciprocate my feelings, and this was probably just a political need, I was happy to change my route to come see you."

My hands trembled as I took in the weight of what he said, and I clenched my fingers into my skirts to hide it.

His eyebrows pinched together. "I've heard the rumblings of dissent and issues within Niria. Is this what you need, Pip? Do you need a good marriage to secure the country?" His voice dropped to a whisper. "I would accept, even if you only desired it for political reasons."

My mouth gaped.

I couldn't put words to everything swirling through me.

Because yes.

That was exactly what I needed.

Here it was, practically falling into my lap. The high lords had a deep respect for our connection with Segion and their king, who was Galeson's cousin. Marrying him would almost certainly shift their opinions on me taking the throne.

Gods, I needed this so badly.

I could taste the victory of it.

I already had Val's support. He would understand if I made this choice.

But... but it wasn't honest or, maybe most importantly, fair to Gale.

He was a good man.

A Spark of Death and Fury

I'd used him enough.

Niria needed this, though.

Every citizen of this country looked to me for the moment. My cousin would cause issues for our people. He cared more for his pride and comfort than for guiding the nation.

My arms trembled. The scar from the fire when I'd run into a burning building searching for Val peeked out the sleeve of my dress. I brushed a thumb over it.

I'd had no hesitations then.

I knew what was true for me.

A shaky breath wisped out of me.

Would I mess up this moment and spend the rest of my life looking back at it, screaming through the veil of memories, urging myself to make a different decision? The possibility knotted my chest.

I touched the scar once more.

And remembered Hecate.

The fates formed you for greatness.

Being great meant being honest. It had to. How I longed for Father to sit there with me and advise me on what to do. He'd once told me that in moments when I didn't know the right choice to make, to pick the best one I could and hope.

I raised my face. "Gale, I'm so sorry. I didn't send that letter." I stopped speaking for a moment. Joden. He had to be the advisor who wrote the missive and directed him to my private suite. It was the only thing that made sense. He'd found a solution, after all. It would probably disappoint him that I wouldn't take it. I rose to my feet and wished I had curls spilling over my shoulder that I could tangle my fingers into. "I think this was a plan one of my advisors concocted. He meant well. I'm sorry he dragged you back into my troubles. You're coming here was so generous, and what you're offering"—I took a deep breath—"is beyond kind of you. But I can't accept. I want what's best for my country. I won't do it by using you or lying to my people, however."

A sheen spread across Galeson's eyes, but he gave a brisk nod before walking closer and dropping back onto the sofa. I sat again as he spoke. "Do you wish to tell me about the issues? Perhaps I could offer some help."

A tree branch scratched against the windowpane. A gardener needed to deal with that. It was something else I should address, but that wasn't important at the moment. "What you would think of me if I told you the truth."

"Surely, you must know, after everything between us"—he leaned his forearms against his thighs which pulled him closer to me—"that I would not stand against you."

Regardless of his reassurance, it was a risk. He was deeply connected with our closest ally, after all. Segion was the first country to join us in the war—the only country that hadn't hesitated. But I sat on the edge of losing the entire kingdom and Val as well. And I knew Gale's words rang true. He wouldn't betray me.

So, I shared with him the truth.

I was in love with a man who was a bastard with no name.

His father had rejected him again, even after promising otherwise.

At that part, Galeson scowled and crossed his arms.

I continued explaining how Demetri attempted to take over running of the country but didn't care for the well-being of the people in it. He had no training, no idea what it was to be the king.

"So, you can see if I wasn't a fool, I would accept your extremely generous offer. However, I can't use you like that or be untrue to the man I'm in love with."

Galeson remained quiet for several minutes. The silence stretched between us as taut as a bowstring pulled back. He nodded and rose to his feet. "Forgive me, but my father expects to see me within the hour, and I'd like to think about everything you've shared with me. May I ask to impose on your hospitality and stay for a few days?"

Confusion buzzed through me. After all that I'd just said to him, I'd expected him either to leave in disgusted frustration or to discuss it. I stood and walked him to the door. "Of course. You're always welcome here, as a representative of Segion and as a friend."

Galeson clasped his hand over mine for a moment, the touch shocking me, before he turned and disappeared down the hall.

As I clicked the latch back in place, a breath puffed out of me.

I couldn't help but wonder if I'd just let my last hope, my last chance of fighting for my people, walk away.

35

Apollo

If I didn't know Hyacinth's body as intimately as I knew my own, I might not have recognized him.

The man before me struggled to stay on his feet as Zephyrus jerked him up. His thin body was covered in purple bruises and deep cuts that were crusted and oozing from poor healing. A thick, matted beard failed to conceal the sharp juts of his face. Swelling marred the beauty of his features as he stood barefoot in the ice and wind in nothing but filthy, threadbare clothing.

"Apollo," he mouthed.

His eyes, even from a distance, held so much grief.

Anger burned within me.

I'd kill Zephyrus slowly.

I'd rip the skin from his body and snap every bone and puncture every organ he possessed until he begged for me to end him.

The sun flared behind me without me intending to call on it. The heat of it coursed across the sky and caused sweat to drip down my spine.

A Spark of Death and Fury

The world seemed to slow and all I could focus on was Hyacinth.

Broken.

Hurt.

Tormented.

But alive.

Zephyrus smirked and dropped him. Hyacinth fell to the ground and attempted to push himself up, but his arms trembled, and he fell into the slush of ice beneath him.

The sun grew hotter and the snow under my feet melted.

I wasn't controlling it. It was like a dog bent on following its master.

I could draw it down like I had with Zeus. A brutal, but efficient method of ending things.

Cyn was here.

And Ixion I assumed.

"Where's the boy?" I yelled.

"Ask your prince, Apollo. He claims there is no boy."

That's why he looked so terrible.

Why he had no strength.

He'd shielded Ixion.

Oh Cyn, you stupid, loyal, brave man.

Zephyrus turned to Hyacinth and kicked him in the ribs, hard enough that Hyacinth curled into himself. The glow around my skin flowed out, brightening. I ran towards them. Fury built into a flame that licked through me.

The world blurred around me as I moved. All I could see was Hyacinth and the god who would soon regret the day he'd met me. But then I froze. My feet sank in the snow, and my body teetered forward at the sudden stop from that speed.

This was what Temi had meant.

He'd incited me to throw me off, so I failed.

Zephyrus raised his chin. "Not willing to fight for him after all? Do you see this man you chose, Hyacinth?" Zephyrus smirked at me as his wings stretched out. "A selfish coward. This is who you've suffered so much for."

Cyn lifted his eyes.

Standing closer, I could see how they glimmered even past the pain, how the hazel of them transformed to liquid honey in the sunlight that glared behind me.

And the love that still rippled from him.

He was so broken. He should have been thinking of himself.

I closed my eyes and leaned into the sizzling warmth and golden brightness of my magic. It wasn't difficult anymore. It flowed through me like it belonged there, and I belonged to it.

That was true, after all.

I was Apollo, god of the sun.

My heart beat to the rhythm of that giant star.

My body served it as it served me.

It wasn't something to fight.

It was as natural as breathing, if I'd just stop struggling for air.

A memory filtered through my mind of me as a toddler. I fumbled with a little wooden bow and dull arrow that slipped in my sweaty grip and tumbled out of my uncoordinated, chubby fingers.

I dropped them, fell to the ground, and curled my knees up to my chest.

Mother kneeled beside me, her braids draped over her shoulder, her stomach rounded with pregnancy. "Try again, Apollo."

"I can't."

She clicked her tongue, picked up the bow, and placed

A Spark of Death and Fury

it into my hands. "If you believe that, then it will be true. Keep trying until you get it right."

I pulled the string back.

It snapped from my fingers and fell to the grass with a thump. Tears stung at my eyes, and I opened and closed my fists.

"Again, Apollo. You need to learn, so you can teach your sister." She placed her hand over her stomach.

I studied her swollen form, trying to imagine a sister, and what having one would be like. "Won't you teach her?"

Mother's expression wavered, which was unlike her, but she rested her chin on her hand. "You won't have me forever. Don't forget who you are in here." She touched my heart.

"A god?"

"You're a god, but that's not what defines you. It's the choices you make. You will be great one day. Always remember who you really are, underneath it all."

I opened my eyes.

Hyacinth lay injured in the snow.

Zephyrus waited, his wings spread out, his muscles tensed.

I ran.

I knew who I was.

I was Apollo.

God of the sun.

The child of Leto.

Brother of Temi.

Husband to Hyacinth.

I was a man who had made mistakes and jumped to conclusions and harmed others.

I was a man who would do better.

The sun exploded in the sky, golden and vast. It overtook the blue of the clouds and the ice. My magic washed through me like a shock and left me gasping for breath before I steadied again. It was as if an endless well had opened with me; the sun prepared to extinguish itself for my cause if I called for it to do so.

Zephyrus smiled and snapped his fingers.

The wind whipped forth, snow flung around, and my jacket yanked out behind me.

I loosened it to let it fall.

No item was needed for this moment.

Not my bag, or my bow, or jewelry, or written poems.

I'd always clung to things as if they held my heart and memories and future.

I realized now that it didn't matter.

My heart lay shattered on the ground at Zephyrus' feet. No one could take my memories from me regardless of what possessions I maintained, and only I defined who I was.

The magic purred through me, prepared to end Zephyrus.

I needed to get closer so I could hit him without accidentally striking Cyn. The two of them were so close to each other. A wise move on Zephyrus' part.

I continued running and waited for whatever Zephyrus had planned.

Then I slammed into a wall of wind. I hit it hard enough that I winced and fell into the snow. I scrambled back onto my feet. Hyacinth lay within a dozen strides of me. I could nearly touch him.

The wind whirled and whipped up, forming into animal shapes like tigers and lions that bowled towards me. I swung my arm to stop their attack, but my hand passed through their forms.

They pounced and knocked me to the ground.

A Spark of Death and Fury

My head smacked against the ice hard, and I groaned.

The wind creatures continued to slam against me.

I kicked and thrusted my arms and called on fire from the sun.

But what did fire do against the wind?

Nothing.

The ice bit into me and cut my flesh. Blood trickled down my wrist. I rolled over, attempted to gain my footing, but the air creations knocked me down and my face slammed into the snow and busted my lip. A coppery tang filled my mouth.

I jumped up and plowed through the creatures, only for a dozen more of them to knock me down.

"I've got you, Apollo."

I looked back over my shoulder. Chares stood behind a boulder, Kama and Mia shadowing him. He took a deep breath, and the wind animals dissipated. They rolled into a breeze that swept off the side of the mountain and scattered snow into the atmosphere like glitter.

I rose, trembling and rumpled.

Chares clenched his teeth. The wall of air rippled away and brushed curls back from my face. I snarled as I plowed towards Zephyrus.

Warmth filled me as well, though.

I didn't stand alone.

I never really had, if I thought about it.

Love had surrounded me my entire life. Gods, I owed Temi a lifetime of gratitude and apologies.

Zephyrus' wings whipped out, and he flew into the sky. His feathers trembled as he hovered a dozen feet up. He gave a massive beat of his wings that sent a gale of wind pulsing across the mountain, and then deities emerged.

Hundreds upon hundreds of them.

They all vibrated and glittered with magic.

I eased up and clenched my fists.

I stood four long strides from Hyacinth.

He looked worse up close, like he verged on death.

I'd seen him there a few times, but he'd never appeared so beaten and defeated.

Zephyrus landed in front of him. "You show up to fight me with only three children. I'm disappointed, Apollo. Offended almost."

I weighed the situation. The gods stood a distance from us. Endless bodies stretched on either side of the palace as if they'd waited just out of sight. I could strike Zephyrus before they could reach me, but then they'd bring the weight of their forces on us.

I didn't know their powers.

"Tell them to leave," Zephyrus continued. "Face me man-to-man, and I'll ask my friends to back down as well."

Hyacinth sat up behind him and pressed his fingertips to the ground to steady himself. He lifted his head like it took the strength of a lifetime to achieve it. He was the bravest man I'd ever met, and I needed to draw from his courage at this moment. I shifted to Zephyrus. "You don't have friends."

"It would seem you're mistaken about that."

"I'm not," I whispered. "You have those who fear you, maybe even those who respect you. You don't understand loyalty or love, though."

"I told you, love is for fools with no ambitions. Call off your young gods." He nodded to Kama, Mia, and Chares.

"I couldn't call them off if I wanted to." I realized that was true. "They believe in something bigger than themselves. They're willing to die for it, even. Do your friends feel the same way?"

Zephyrus glowered. "I guess we'll find out."

He whipped his wings out again, sending a blast of

wind that knocked me off my feet. "Chares," I screamed. "Mia, Kama, now."

They lunged forward.

The deities converged into a melee. The assembly thundered down the hillside, shaking snow loose in their stampede.

I hoped the young gods would hold their own. They were powerful and devoted to each other. And it was their choice. That's what I'd missed at the beginning.

They believed in a better world and were willing to make the highest sacrifice to fight for it.

As was I.

I drew heat into my hands, flames that danced around my fingertips.

God of the sun thinks the sun can kill him, Hiscu had said. A smile slipped up on my lips as I shot darts of flame at Zephyrus. He dodged the first two, but the third hit his wing, caught feathers aflame, and he hissed.

"You want the spark, Zephyrus?" I pulled more fire to myself, and it laced over my skin. "Come and see if you can get it."

He growled and flung himself at me with a gust that blew out the flames.

His body smacked against mine, and we both dropped to the ground. I gasped as the air pushed out of me, but rolled him over, gripped his arm and called forth my powers until the smell of cooking flesh swept between us. Zephyrus' scream was a howl of a winter wind.

Gods tumbled towards us.

For all his prideful words, Zephyrus wouldn't actually face me alone.

I threw sparks of fire out, used light to blind them, knocked deities off their feet, landed punches.

It wasn't enough.

Too many of them continued to climb onto me.

The howling yelps of immortals dying echoed in the distance where the young gods fought. The earth trembled as it pulled apart, wind whipped around, fire scorched the sky.

I couldn't get free and they were too far away to help.

A dozen deities held down my arms and used their magic to subdue mine. One clenched my face and forced me to look at Zephyrus, who raised a silvery sword that shimmered like he'd forged it of ice. "This was really too easy, Apollo. You'll die as you lived… a disappointment." And the blade plunged towards me.

36

Hyacinth

I shuddered against the ice on the ground and struggled to push myself up to see Apollo.

Apollo.

Apollo.

Apollo.

He'd made it.

He was alive.

And he'd take Ixion home.

The world exploded with gods fighting. Magic shuddered through the air, fire licked across the sky, the earth trembled as it rent open, and wind slammed around. It whisked away the warmth of the sun and the flames.

Deities screamed.

Fell.

Rose again, blood splattered and furious.

The palace trembled.

As if it might break.

Zephyrus and Apollo tumbled together.

My breath caught.

Apollo.

Apollo.

Apollo.

The guards who stood next to me dove for them.

To hold Apollo down.

Zephyrus slid a sword out, a sharp glistening weapon that looked like a ragged piece of glass.

He pulled his arm back.

Apollo fought.

Flames flicked out and burned deities.

The sun pressed down so hard sweat dripped along my forehead and stung my eyes.

Apollo couldn't take them all.

Zephyrus lifted the blade.

No.

Everything froze for a moment.

The roaring of the fight turned into a dull howl that my heartbeat echoed over.

Memories of falling in love with Apollo filled my mind. The gentleness of his expression beneath all the sharp edges and biting banter of him. The taste of his mouth. The warmth of his flesh seeping into mine. How foolish and brave I'd been to get tangled up with him.

A high god.

What was I? A mortal prince and nothing more. I was like a patch of grass that would fade before he even noticed.

I'd once thought that.

My life would have little eternal meaning.

Who would remember a prince who died before his prime, once history rotted out the deeds of men?

Maybe this was my time, though.

My purpose.

Perhaps I was the one who loved Apollo. That would be my legacy. And perhaps it was enough.

The earth had ripped apart in multiple sections.

A Spark of Death and Fury

Melted snow drained down into the chasms created like a massive waterfall.

I remembered standing above the waterfall near home with Apollo as he shook his arms out, which didn't stop them from trembling. We were so young then. The most terrifying thing we faced was not understanding how we felt for each other.

"Do you want me to go with you?" I asked.

He'd lifted his eyes, gold seeping over the irises as his veil had faded some. "No. Yes. Maybe."

"Which one of those is the answer?"

He gasped before answering. "Yes, I do."

I walked beside him, slid my fingers between his, and felt a rightness that I'd never experienced before. Then we'd jumped. I should have known that foreshadowed our entire relationship. One massive, fear-filled leap after another. Apollo had jumped for my sake. And now I could do the same.

Ixion didn't need protection for the moment.

Zephyrus was here, distracted and unable to menace him.

I released a breath and yanked my magic back onto me.

Broken bones knit together, fresh blood tingled down my limbs. A scream burst forth as strength surged through me.

I called forth every plant deep within the belly of the mountain.

Zephyrus' arms shot forward, the blade directed at Apollo's neck.

Vines wrapped around the bastard and yanked him to me.

He yelled as the sword clattered against the hard ground melted snow had unveiled.

The other gods hesitated. Some continued to hold Apollo who fought them. His flames ran up their limbs and his viscous kicks knocked them into the earth.

Others hacked away the plants that trapped Zephyrus. His wings shuddered out as they freed him.

The mob pounced on me to hold me down.

I struggled, but Zephyrus strode up, and slipped a knife from his hip. "Oh, Hyacinth." He glowered. "You are truly a fool."

He swung his blade forward.

A goddess jumped out of the group and threw her body in front of mine.

We tumbled to the ground and her floral scent filled my senses.

Zephyrus' strike stopped mid thrust, like some invisible force stayed his hand.

Apollo continued fighting in the background, making gains. Gods fell to his magic. He snatched Zephyrus' fallen sword and stabbed it through someone's middle.

Zephyrus glowered at the goddess who sat in my lap so that her long hair brushed my cheeks. "Move, Flora."

"Make me," she said, her voice steady, though her arms trembled against me. "Marrying someone for political posturing becomes less convenient when your blood vow comes back to haunt you, doesn't it?" She stretched her body out to cover more of me.

Zephyrus growled. His pale bangs stuck to his sweat-slicked face. "Why the hell are you even here right now?"

"You forget that my closest friend is one of the Fates. She knew when I'd be needed."

"Get the fuck out of the way."

"No," she whispered.

Zephyrus sliced his knife forward, just past her hip, and it struck me in my ribs. The sharp pain of it exploded through me. I'd experienced a lot in the last weeks, but the first injury after my powers healed me always hurt the worst.

He slammed more of his weight, pressing the blade deeper, and I cried out.

Blood gushed, warm and sticky, down my stomach and over my hips.

Oh gods.

Of all the suffering he'd caused me, he'd never injured something vital. Until now.

I pressed my hand to my side where the weapon protruded and pulled back fingers painted burgundy. Blood dripped onto the snow.

My head dropped.

It had all been too much.

I didn't think I could take anymore.

"Get her off of him," Zephyrus barked to the gods.

Some hesitated. Uncertainty rippled through them. Others complied and pulled Flora away even as she bucked and jerked. "Look at this!" she screamed. "Look at who you're supporting and what he's willing to do."

The uneasiness of the crowd deepened. A few stepped back as if to distance themselves.

Zephyrus grinned, though, his eyes glued on me, a gleam in them that reflected the ivory of the palace behind us.

Oh fuck.

His sneer would be the last thing I saw in life.

That seemed brutally unfair.

He raised another blade, and it was almost a mercy.

Each breath I took grew more painful, like a sharp rent opened in my chest. My heart fluttered about as if it struggled to keep pounding.

Zephyrus pulled his arm back.

And froze.

His mouth dropped open as his eyes widened with shock.

A sword like sharpened glass thrust out of his stomach and a dark circle of blood bloomed around it.

Zephyrus gaped. His fingers grazed the edge of the icy blade that split through him.

The weapon sank deeper, and he dropped to his knees.

Apollo stood over him, and he yanked the sword out. Ichor splattered over his face and curls. He kicked Zephyrus and knocked him into the slush of melted snow that his blood poured out into. His voice came as a growl. "My greatest regret in life is not killing you sooner."

Zephyrus parted his lips, but only a low groan sounded before his eyes shuddered closed.

Apollo shifted to face me, and the glow around him brightened. Silver slipped into its color. A shimmer of light flittered above his head and glistened like a bundle of shooting stars. The spark. The crowd gasped and a few stepped back.

Apollo walked over to me, dropped to his knees, and cradled my face into his lap, before grazing his fingers over my cheeks. "Hyacinth."

My breaths came in rapid pants that streaked pain through my chest. Zephyrus was gone. Apollo had ascended. Ixion was safe.

I'd survived long enough for that to pass.

It was all that mattered.

I smiled. "I prayed"—my voice whispered past my lips—"to see you once more."

Apollo shuddered but brought his mouth to mine and kissed me. "Well, I hope you like what you see, Prince, because I'm about to heal you, and you're going to be stuck with the view for a long time."

I smiled, but darkness edged around my vision. "Ixion. He's here… he's…"

"I've got him, Cyn. I've got you. You don't have to be strong anymore."

I shuddered and leaned into him. Blood glugged out of my body with every breath and my head swam.

If there was anyone in the world I could trust to care for Ix, it was Apollo.

I nodded, unable to speak.

Apollo removed the knife from my side. It sliced through me anew and I fluttered my eyes closed as he curled his hands over my wound and his magic washed through me.

Heat.

And fire.

And glittering gold.

Like stars streaking the sky.

Like the sun overtaking them.

Darkness pressed against me.

The desire to disappear into that safe, quiet corner of my mind I'd fought for weeks beckoned.

I didn't struggle against it anymore.

I faded into the warmth and comfort of finally letting go.

37

Valerian

I ran a brush down Arion's massive, glimmering aqua body. He flicked his tail as if he was annoyed, but his expression remained calm. We'd come to some kind of understanding between us, and he—for all his attitude—enjoyed the attention.

He didn't need the grooming, though. His coat shimmered, his seaweed-like hair was clean and untangled. "When Temi gets back, she's going to realize I've spoiled you. You'd better enjoy it while it lasts."

He snorted at me, and I smiled as I placed the brush on the edge of the stall and leaned against the rail. I'd thought returning home would be a comfort. Instead, I felt more like a stranger than ever.

I no longer belonged in the stables, but I certainly didn't fit in the palace.

As much as I worried over Mother, she'd found a place helping Epiphany of all things. I was happy for her—while it lasted, at least. It left me feeling like the only purposeless person in the palace, however.

So, I'd passed the morning tending to Arion after I'd

taken him for a long ride in the distant pastures, far from attendants and stableman and high lords who would barely look at me.

I'd fallen from the favor of friends before as a child.

Somehow it stung worse as an adult.

The door to the stable opened and golden light spilled across the ceiling. I didn't look over to see who it was. No one for me, that was for sure. I fiddled with the sleeve of my silk jacket. It wasn't a practical outfit for tending to Arion, but Asher had pressed the importance of appearances—and I respected him and Epiphany too much to disregard it.

"Princess," a few stablemen said. I turned around where the workers bowed to Epiphany. She wore a navy gown, her crown in place, her hair pulled back at her nape. She nodded to them before walking over to Arion's stall, where he snuffled at her.

"Pip?" I whispered. She reached her fingers through the slats, and I draped my hand over hers to squeeze her palm. "Everything okay?"

It felt like we both waited on circumstances outside our control to determine our fates. Would Epiphany convince the high lords and advisors to change the laws and let her take the throne? Would I remain in her life if they did?

A selfish part of me wished they wouldn't. She'd said she'd run away with me. We could start over somewhere else together.

The part of me that cared about her more, and the welfare of our country, hoped she'd best her cousin.

I didn't know what might happen to Mother and me if they crowned her but wouldn't approve our marriage. However, after visiting my father's estate, I no longer feared that as much. We'd probably have to leave the palace. It would hurt. But we'd make our way. Perhaps fate had been less generous to us in some ways, but we worked hard and respected others. We'd find a place. Even if it became a new home where I would nurse my broken heart.

Epiphany licked her lips. "Lord Galeson is here."

I hesitated. She'd found a solution, then. My body shuddered, and I couldn't fight it. But I could look this woman in the eyes and offer her approval if she came to inform me that they would marry. Gods, this would hurt like hell. I loved her enough to keep that to myself. I'd vowed to support her in whatever way she needed. If this was it, I could do that. "Is he?"

"He wishes to speak with you."

My hand dropped as shock coursed through me. The huffing breath of horses echoed through the space and doves cooed in the rafters above. "What about?"

"He wouldn't tell me," she whispered. "He doesn't know who you are. He just requested to meet with the man I'm in love with."

She raised her eyes, and so much love and fear rippled over her expression.

I wished I could jump over the stall, pull her into my arms.

The stablemen farther down the barn watched us.

I couldn't imagine anything good coming of Galeson speaking with me. What was the worst that could happen, though? He'd call me a selfish bastard? It wouldn't be the first time I'd heard it. If it would offer Epiphany a drop of peace amid the chaos she mired in, it would be worth the cost to my pride. "Of course."

"Are you able to come now?"

"I am."

"My sitting room in half an hour?"

I inclined my head to her, and she turned. The hem of

her dress brushed the hay-lined walkway as she exited to another echo of, "Princess."

The barn fell quiet again. Only the chuffing of the horses, the scraping, clacking sounds of the men working, the slapping of Arion's tail flicking away flies acted as a background to my muddled thoughts.

I shifted to face him. "Do you want to stay here or spend the afternoon in the pasture?"

He cocked his head and gave me an unimpressed look. I couldn't help smiling. "All right." I opened the gate, and he clipped out alongside me. "Maybe you could roll around in some mud. Give me something to do later?"

He snorted like that wouldn't happen, and I patted his side as he trotted out into the wisping green grasses of the pasture.

Then I turned and walked to the palace. Dread filled me. Despite everything I'd faced in the last years, I didn't see myself as brave. I was the opposite, in fact. I was just foolhardy enough to not give up when I probably should.

I stepped inside and nodded to guards who frowned at me. Once I made it to Epiphany's sitting room, I waited. The beaded outline of the molding along the door glimmered, freshly polished at the hands of an attendant I likely knew and had possibly been friends with.

Before the palace staff caught wind of mine and Epiphany's relationship and most attendants stopped talking to me.

It was Pip, though.

I'd do anything for her.

I'd nearly died for her once.

I realized now that, in some ways, dying for someone was easier than living for them.

For Epiphany, I'd gladly do either.

Either way, I knew who I was. I was a good man. I'd

done the most right that I could. Regardless of whatever Lord Galeson had to say, I knew my truth.

I raised my hand and knocked.

Epiphany pulled the door back and gave me an uncertain smile that the lines creasing her forehead belied before she gestured for me to walk in. I straightened my posture, raised my chin, and walked into the room.

I'd never been in it before.

It was a beautiful space, like every room in the palace, rich in shades of burgundy and cream. There were touches of Epiphany in it as well. A blanket too casual for the chamber draped over the back of a chair. A music box sat open on a table, as if someone had started it and forgot to close it.

Galeson stood facing a window, and he turned as Epiphany closed the door. His pale skin lost some of its color. "You?"

I wondered if he remembered me from his first visit to Niria or from that miserable day we'd all learned that King Magnes died. Either way, he certainly recognized me.

Epiphany took a step ahead of me, as if she'd stand between us.

I cleared my throat and bowed, words frozen on my tongue.

Galeson continued to stare at me. "I expected a soldier."

"Rather than a stableman?" I asked.

He chuckled. His gaze darted to Epiphany before returning to me. "No, not that. I just… didn't think you would be someone I'd met."

Epiphany smoothed her fingers down the front of her skirt. "Galeson, meet Valerian. Again."

Galeson's blue eyes stayed locked on me, like he consid-

A Spark of Death and Fury

ered things. "May Valerian and I speak alone," he said to Epiphany, "for a moment?"

Epiphany startled, but I cleared my throat. "It's fine."

Her lips furled inward, and a ripple of uncertainty passed over face before she nodded. "I'll be just through this door here if you need me."

"We won't be long," Galeson said.

She walked out.

For a painfully awkward moment, Galeson and I stood in silence, taking the other in. A clock ticked. Dappled light danced across a wall as tree branches clattered outside the window.

"Tell me you love her," Galeson said.

I hesitated, surprised by his request and uncertain why he'd ask it.

"And mean it." He frowned as he gripped a long leather pouch tight enough that his knuckles lost color. He raised his sharp blue eyes to meet mine. "Swear to me this isn't you using her for your gain."

A breath puffed from me.

I'd spent the entire morning thinking of all I'd lost due to publicly aligning with Epiphany.

I'd lose it all again in a heartbeat.

More, even if it meant her happiness.

"I love her... with everything I have. I'm not sure I remember not loving her."

Galeson's lips pinched. "And if she doesn't take the throne? If she's outcast from the palace? Would you stick by her in that scenario?"

"Of course I would," I said through my teeth, the words coming with heat. There was probably no benefit to express anger with him, but damn it, of all the moments of humiliation, rejection, and judgement, it was this one that licked fury through me. I'd never abandon Epiphany, and I didn't care if she had not a coin or title or name. It was her I was in love with, not her damn position.

Galeson's lips twisted up. "What would you do?"

Sunlight rippled over the doorway Epiphany had disappeared behind. "We're both good with horses. We could start a life together elsewhere using those skills."

"A life of potential poverty if things didn't go well."

Shame burned my cheeks. "That may be true. I would do everything within my abilities to fight that, but there's much I can't control. However, there are things in life more valuable than riches."

If my father had done nothing else, he'd taught me that.

Galeson tapped the bundle in his hands against his thigh and then sighed before walking over to the door Epiphany had disappeared behind and knocked. When she returned, he lifted the pouch, pulled out a bundle of parchments, and unrolled them on the table in front of me before meeting my gaze. "Sign these and you're my brother… legally speaking."

Epiphany stared at the parchment like he'd just dropped a writhing serpent on her sitting-room table. "What is that?"

"Documents my father had drawn up today to claim that he is Valerian's father." He looked at me again. "You'll have to fill in your name, of course. I didn't know it."

Shock coursed through me. The papers sat there, curled at the edges as they slowly rolled back together. Epiphany gasped. "You didn't even know who he was."

"You believe in him," Galeson said, and his voice dropped an octave. "And I have faith in your judgement."

"It's a generous offer, but…"

"It's not that generous." Galeson gestured his ringed hand at the documents. "You'll only receive three percent of my parent's estate. Cut from my portion at that." He grinned at Epiphany, a sparkle of amusement in his eyes. "I don't believe my siblings would appreciate me concocting a plan that took part of their portion."

I stepped towards the table as though to test if this was reality. "You're giving part of your inheritance to me?"

My actual father wouldn't even grant me a title, much less any of his wealth.

Galeson's gaze darted to Epiphany.

Ah. Not for me.

He shrugged. "It's not as selfless as it sounds. You know, Pip,"—they exchanged a long look that made my stomach tighten with discomfort—"my family originally sent me here hoping we'd marry and connect our families, and more importantly, our countries." He lifted his shoulders again and the silk of his jacket rippled with the motion. "King Roenan—who I'll remind you is my first cousin who grew up with me, and therefore pesters me senselessly,"— Epiphany smiled—"desires the connection now more than ever. He is not pleased with the idea of Lord Demetri taking the throne here and potentially drawing Niria away from Segion and into closer ties with Carens."

Epiphany bobbed her head. "Segion has always been our closest ally, and it was my father's wishes for that to endure. You don't have to do anything for that to remain the case for me."

"I know. If I didn't already believe that, us working together during the war solidified it for me."

Epiphany intertwined her fingers. "It's kind of you, Gale." Her eyebrows pinched. "But the likelihood that I'll take the throne is bleak at this point. There's a possibility that you'd bring shame on your family,"—her eyes darted to me, an unspoken apology in her expression—"for no benefit to you."

He looked at her for such a long moment that I struggled to keep my face neutral. His voice dropped to a whisper as he answered her. "Even in that scenario, it would see you safe, with a titled name for your household and some money to add to yours, so hopefully you could establish yourself."

Epiphany bit her lip. "Your parents approve of this?"

"I'm lucky," he whispered, "to have good people for parents. I know you understand that. Besides, we have a solid enough name to endure a minor scandal. My father ran it by my mother first and she agreed the potential benefit is worth the cost to our pride."

Tears broke free and spilled down Epiphany's cheeks. Galeson looked at me and clapped his hands together. "Well, will you sign it?"

I scratched my forehead, all sense of propriety and manners gone with the shock. "I… I will. If you're certain, Lord Galeson."

He gave me a wry look. "You should probably just call me Gale. After all, we're about to be family. Right?" He didn't give me time to answer before turning to Epiphany. "And I have an idea on how to secure your throne if you'd allow me to make suggestions."

Epiphany went to her desk for a reed and ink and walked back over to us. Her fingers curled around the tools that would seal both of our fates. My heart raced as she handed them to me. She turned towards Gale. "I'm listening."

38

Artemis

Silver sliding over my arms, hovering over my body and along my legs, pulled me out of crying.

I lifted a hand and the light blurred with my movements.

The spark was back.

The reign of the high gods had returned.

I was pretty certain I'd ascended. My magic whirled through me in a way it never had before, like it had fused with my blood and swept down into my bones.

Had Apollo gotten the spark?

Or Zephyrus?

The fear of those questions snapped me into action. I cleared my throat hard, and it ached. I wiped my puffy cheeks with the back of my arm and slung my pack on. Bending down beside Orion once more, I cupped his cheek. "I'll be back."

I took in the chalkiness of his skin and his pale hair that fluttered in the breeze.

He looked nothing like he did in life, all his expressiveness and giant smiles gone with his spirit.

I swallowed down more tears, snatched his short spear, and trundled out on the path to the valley where the Palace of the Four Winds sat surrounded by hundreds of gods.

Oh, shit.

My feet slipped over the ice as I ran.

My head ached from hitting it, and my body trembled from the magic I'd exerted, but I was needed.

The moon still glimmered above, like she'd remained with me during my time of grief instead of sinking for the day. When I made it lower on the trail, the glare of the sun brightened, so that it swallowed the sky, taking the beauty of the moon with it.

As I reached the muddy and broken yard, I whipped my bow out.

But then I let it drop.

The fighting was over.

Gods bowed to Apollo, who kneeled before Hyacinth.

I hesitated as I took in the prince's appearance. Blood coated his torn, stained clothing, and a thick beard covered his jaw. I jogged over to them, where the three young gods stood guard. Chares had a gash on his face and Kama seemed to shift her weight to one side like she limped, but none of them appeared to have sustained life threatening injuries.

Their bodies shimmered with the silver light that bathed Apollo and reflected the glittering spark that hovered above him.

He kissed Hyacinth's cheek and grazed his thumb along his jaw as his body curled over him.

Then I remembered what Clothos had said to me.

WHEN YOU LOSE *what you've gained*
 And arrive at a fight too late

A Spark of Death and Fury

Your brother will ascend only to bow

WHEN THE SUN *overtakes the moon*
And the trio stands guard
That is your moment to rise

I GASPED. She'd known I'd lose Orion. She could have warned me. No wonder Apollo hated her. Tears pricked my eyes again, and I batted them away.

I still didn't know what my moment was exactly, but I could feel the weight of it with each step that brought me closer to Apollo.

He lifted Hyacinth in his arms and the prince's head lolled against Apollo's shoulder, but his chest rose with breath.

He was alive. Relief flooded through me.

"Apollo." His golden eyes snapped to me. "What are you doing?"

"I have to go find Ixion, and I'm not leaving Cyn here."

"But... what about the gods?"

Apollo's gaze drifted to the masses that still bowed, though some began to stand with wary expressions on their faces.

"It's not my priority."

"Apollo..."

"I have other things—" He stopped speaking. "Where's Orion?"

My lip trembled, and my eyes filled with tears.

The stone of his expression washed away. "Oh, Temi."

"Not now. Later."

He gave me a long look full of sympathy and shared

pain before nodding. "I'm going to find Ix. Mia and Kama, will you stay with Temi? Chares, come with me?" He turned and walked into the palace as Chares trailed him before I had time to argue.

I shifted back to the crowd.

THAT IS *your moment to rise.*

OH.

This was it.

I met Kama and Mia's eyes and then stepped forward to face the assembled gods as the duo trailed behind me.

I cleared my throat and raised my voice so that it poured out of me as smooth as moonlight on a clear night. "We may not have met yet, but my name is Artemis, goddess of the moon, sister of Apollo, and daughter of Poseidon."

The gods shuffled. Some nursed their injuries.

Today they learned they could die.

We now held the spark.

The ability to end them easily.

That wasn't our purpose, though.

"We don't intend to start a new reign of high gods. In fact, we've come to undo that." A god near me with cautious gray eyes pinched their lips. "We will dissipate the spark and return it to the humans to whom it belongs."

Gasps rang out. Someone called, "Who is to stop another from rising over us again?"

I looked at Kama and Mia and down at my clothes. We all stood splattered in blood, weapons in our grip, still standing after facing hundreds of gods, a handful of

A Spark of Death and Fury

deadly monsters, Apollo's vindictive father, and loss, after loss, after loss.

"We will. If you don't believe we can manage it after everything you've seen today and all I'm sure you've heard about us,"—I tightened my hold on Orion's spear—"try us."

A tense pause echoed through the clearing.

"If, however, you want what Zephyrus claimed to stand for." I paused and met as many gazes as I could. "If you're looking for a future where we are all on equal footing, where we each return to working with the elements we were born to direct, and stop all the infighting between us, then leave here peacefully and go home."

Whispers trailed through the wind like snow taking flight. Many gods nodded, but some narrowed their eyes and raised their chins so that the sun overhead brightened their faces.

"However, if that isn't a future, you can bear…" I dropped lower, into a fighting stance. The echo of Orion's absence, of him not covering my side and me not automatically falling into awareness of his weak spots, rang through me. "Come stop us yourselves."

Another shuffle. Feet squelched into the ruined earth. A flag draping from the eaves of the palace crackled in the wind. Kama and Mia shadowed me like pillars of wrath as they glared at the crowd.

No one moved.

I straightened my spine. "Let me make this clear. If anyone leaves here thinking to stir trouble in the future, know that I will find you,"—my voice hardened until it became ice, slicing against the wind—"and I'll end you." I reached for my powers until the silver light around me glowed bright enough that it stung my eyes. "I am Artemis, goddess of the moon, and also of the hunt. I have no fear of tracking down deities and slaughtering them if needed. My hands are covered with blood, and I'm not afraid to add some more."

For a moment, the wind whipped about, snagged over bloodied tunics, tangled long hair.

Then the gray-eyed deity near me bowed. Others followed, prostrating their bodies.

The first god rose again and locked their sharp eyes onto me. "I pledge myself to you, huntress goddess and your brother."

I parted my lips to argue. We weren't asking for pledges or vows. We only wanted everything returned to balance. Kama grabbed my arm to stall me. Her voice came as a whisper, so quiet I struggled to hear her. "Don't. They need someone to look to for now. Let it be you rather than another Zephyrus."

I bit down hard but gave a quick nod as the gods echoed the first deity's words. Then the group dispersed. Many shimmered before they disappeared. "Will you two keep watch?" I asked. "I need to find Apollo."

"We will," Kama said.

I turned and stepped into the shadowed entrance of the palace. A glittering glass chandelier dominated the massive foyer. As I walked through the structure and took in the austere beauty of it, I wondered how some could have so much and yet still want more. My footsteps echoed as I trailed down a hallway. I'd never allow myself to become that. I'd swear it on Orion's memory that I'd hold the course.

Muffled sobs echoed on the other side of a door. I pressed it open slowly and my hands tightened on the spear. Apollo knelt on the floor. A child who glowed silver wept in his arms as though he'd cried for a long while, his cheeks puffy and red. His eyes darted to me, he screamed, and clutched against Apollo, who whirled around, a knife in his hand.

Apollo released a breath at the sight of me. "It's okay, Ixion. This is my sister, Temi."

Ixion sniffled, and Apollo continued rubbing his back as he held him up.

His focus drifted to the bed, where Hyacinth lay, his chest rising and falling. "Will"—Ixion hiccupped and wiped his nose with his hand—"Papa be okay?"

"Papa?" Apollo asked before following Ixion's gaze to Hyacinth. "Oh..." The muscles in Apollo's jaw jumped, the light around him brightened, and his eyes turned pure gold. He whispered. "I don't know, Ix. Temi and I are going to get you both home and we'll do everything we can do to help him. Okay? Are you ready to go?"

He sniffled. "Are the bad gods gone?"

"I think so," Apollo said, and then looked at me. "I sent Chares to clear the palace."

"Kama and Mia are holding the entrance."

"Good. There's a stable here and carts. We should get one." He looked over his shoulder at Hyacinth. "We're going to need it."

"Two," I whispered.

Apollo turned back to me, his brow furrowing.

"I..." My nose flared, and I struggled to speak. "I want to bring Orion home."

Apollo released a breath. "Of course." He brushed his hand over Ixion's curls and the child leaned against him. "Would you let Temi take you, so I can carry your Papa?"

Ixion studied me for a moment then grasped Apollo's face with his small hands. "She's good, isn't she? You told me Papa was good, and you were right."

Apollo's eyes took on a sheen, but he nodded. "She's good."

I walked up and opened my arms for him. He hesitated again before draping against me and wrapping his legs around my hip. I shifted Orion's short spear under my arm, ready to pull it out at a moment's notice, and stepped into the hallway. Ixion fiddled one of my braids between his fingers. "Papa said Apollo would come to rescue us. And he did."

I nodded, unable to properly respond. Hyacinth had obviously paid a high price to protect Ixion. I knew Apollo well enough to know that he held it together because he had to, but worry and sorrow echoed through him.

I understood.

Once we'd cleared the grounds and loaded up two carts with supplies, pilfered food, and a pair of horses each, Apollo laid Hyacinth into one and bundled him with blankets.

"Come on, Ix," I said. "We can drive the other carriage."

Ixion's golden eyes widened with panic. "No," he screamed. "No." He struggled to get out of my arms, and I released him, uncertain of what had caused his reaction. "Don't take Papa away from me."

"Hey," Apollo said as he scooped Ixion into his arms. "It's okay. We're not taking him anywhere you aren't going. Do you want to ride with him? Help him stay warm?"

Ixion nodded as he sniffled. He scrambled out of Apollo's hold and clambered into the carriage where he tucked against Cyn. Kama, Chares, and Mia watched with crossed arms and Apollo appeared ready to cry, but he only gestured for us to continue forward.

When we reached the ridge where the broken lines of the earth marked the graves of the monsters the young gods had defeated, my stomach pooled with dread. I

A Spark of Death and Fury

jumped off the cart and turned to Apollo. "Would you come with me? I don't think I can carry him alone."

Apollo looked nervously at where Hyacinth lay sleeping, but then spoke over his shoulder to the three young gods. "Stand guard. We'll only be a minute. Keep Ixion shielded from us when we return. He's seen enough death."

The word sent a chill down my spine, and I batted my eyes hard to combat more tears as I started walking.

How much could a person cry in one day?

Wasn't there a limit?

I walked up to the gulch where we'd fought, and Orion had died.

The massive scorpion still laid dead at the mouth of the chasm. Its imposing form stretched stark against the silver and gray of the cliffs.

Orion's last moments echoed through my mind.

How he'd jumped to protect me. How he'd killed the damn creature only for it to end him, anyway.

If this monster hadn't attacked us, he'd still be alive. He had lived through so many battles and fights to succumb to this fucking thing.

Anger coursed through my body.

I ran up to the scorpion and shrieked before kicking it with enough force that it shuddered.

But that wasn't enough.

It would never be fucking enough.

I kicked it again, and again, and again.

I screamed.

Apollo yanked me away from it and pulled me into his arms like he'd become a cave to protect me. "Shh, Temi." Hot tears streaked my face as he squeezed me so tight it almost hurt.

"How... how could he make it so far and die in the

end? Gods damn it. I told him not to come. He was a mortal. And... And he died saving me." My voice turned into a mewling whisper. "He died taking a hit meant for me, Apollo."

Apollo said nothing. He just drew me in tighter and squeezed the air from my lungs. For a long time, we didn't move until finally I pulled back and nodded at the dip in the mountain's side. We walked around the scorpion to find Orion, still and cold.

I whimpered at the sight of him there.

It had somehow seemed like a nightmare or a worry I'd worked over so many times that it felt like reality. But seeing him broken and unmoving, it hit me.

I'd never talk with him beneath a moonlit sky again. Never tease him and feel his elbow nudge me in the ribs. Never see his eyes sparkle as he prepared to pull some shit that was borderline questionable.

More tears fell. Gods, did I hate it. I hated the hurt. It ached so badly I almost wished I had never met him solely to not experience the pain.

All the chaos of my brain stopped at that, like a winter wind suddenly stilling, leaving only the clarity of the soft forest noises.

No.

That wasn't true.

I would never wish to not know him. No matter how painful it was.

The grief meant that I'd cared for him. And I would hold that forever.

"Do you want me to do it?" Apollo said tenderly. "I could possibly manage. Or maybe get Kama or Chares to help me?"

"No. It's important to me I help."

Apollo eased over, and I joined him. We lifted Orion

and carried him down the path, before loading him gently, reverently, into the cart.

Apollo drew the sun down, and my neck prickled, my attention drawn to the sky where the moon beckoned to me.

Ah.

My time had come.

For all of Orion's teasing me about being the goddess of the moon, he'd never gotten to see it come to fruition.

I whispered to that lunar body, felt the glittering silver of my magic rush through me, and pulled the ivory form into the sky.

We plodded into the night where the velvet dark of the heavens spread. A new constellation glittered, the bow pointed at the moon, as if it reached for it.

I could almost hear Orion chuckle. *Instead of a heretic star worshiper in the halls of your temple, you have one competing for attention with your moon.*

My heart warmed and ached at the same time. We carried forth under a night sky that I would never see the same again.

39

Epiphany

I fidgeted with a bracelet on my wrist. My head ached from the weight of my crown. A bead of sweat dripped down my spine. The chatter of the high lords in the dining room buzzed like a nest of bees just beyond the door.

Gods, this was it, and there was no going back.

Galeson stood to my right, his chin raised, the emerald green of Segion's colors in every detail of his outfit from his jacket to the jewels he wore on his fingers.

Valerian stood to my left dressed in a similar outfit in navy. He remained the quietest of the three of us, his face schooled into neutrality.

I knew he felt as nervous as I did, though.

Tresson walked up and bowed before me. "They're ready, Your Highness."

"Thank you." I swallowed and met Galeson's gaze.

He gave me a nod, his expression certain. His eyes lingered on me for a moment and a touch of warmth reached his cheeks. "It's going to be fine."

I couldn't find words, but bit my lip before smoothing out my skirt and pulling the doors open.

A Spark of Death and Fury

The dining room stretched as beautiful as ever, fresh silks lining the ceiling, the rich tang of wine in the air, and hundreds of high lords standing at the table. Demetri stood behind a dozen others, glowering at me.

As the three of us went out together, a few people gasped. Father would not approve of the breech of propriety. I suppose we gave them a shock. I stood before my chair at the head of the table while Valerian walked up to the chair to my left and Gale took the seat next to his. To my right, Gale's parents stood as honored guests. People studied us, our seating arrangement.

A few whispered.

Propriety be damned, I guess.

I inclined my head and struggled to not clench my hands, which had grown clammy, as everyone found their seats.

The dinner took a moment to pick up. The group mired in silence as attendants passed out blackened fish and briny olives. Asher, who sat in the middle of the table next to Joden, began a conversation about the battles and how they affected the economy. He offered several generous comments about Segion's connection.

Gale's father accepted the opening and lifted his glass in his direction. "Thank you, Lord Asher. Segion has long been honored to have such strong ties with Niria. As many of you know, King Roenan is my brother's son, and we've frequently discussed that Niria and Segion are so close that we're nearly siblings. It's the very reason, when Niria called on us for military connections, we did not question or hesitate. We value Niria like it's our own country."

Several of the high lords patted the table in agreement while others swallowed drinks. Demetri narrowed his eyes at Galeson, his father, and me as if he attempted to see through our plot.

Gale's father took a swallow of his wine before he continued. He smiled and met Galeson's eyes before continuing. "The true reason for celebration tonight, however, is the engagement of Princess Epiphany."

The room quieted again. A woman with long earrings cleared her throat.

Galeson looked at me, his expression steadying even as my heart raced about in my chest. His Father continued. "To my son, Lord Valerian."

Gasps echoed off the high ceilings. Demetri tossed back his drink. Joden's lips pinched, while Asher offered a supportive nod. A chair wobbled like it might topple, and the people sitting nearby steadied its occupant.

Galeson smiled like he didn't recognize the chaos running through the room and he threw his arm around Val's shoulder to pat it. Val sat so motionless he may not even have breathed. "I was glad to hear this news," Gale's Father continued his speech and broke into the buzz of conversation. Everyone hushed again. "For King Roenan has wished for a tighter alliance between our countries. As I said before, Segion never hesitated when Niria needed help. It only makes sense that we should have deeper bonds between our leaders."

He paused, letting that fact sit in the room. It stood as a reminder that no other country had aligned to our cause without at least some hesitation, Carens included. He nodded to Galeson who sat straighter as he picked up his father's speech.

"I counted myself lucky, during the war, to work with your princess." Galeson offered me a smile, too intimate for the moment, that surpassed the careful maneuvering and show they'd orchestrated. "And I was glad to find she was a competent and hardworking representative of your country. The way she managed through the losses of her father and brother…" He paused, and the guests dropped their faces. An echo of sorrow whipped through us all and settled on me. "Speaks to her character and abilities. Segion looks forward to continuing our alliance and is delighted that our family shall now have a connection with your queen."

The group at the table considered him, uncertainty hushing through the space. Galeson's father took a bite of his fish and swallowed before speaking again. "Of course, King Roenan has heard rumors you plan to consider installing a Carenian on King Magnes' throne."

He said the word with disgust laced in his voice, his eyes flicking to Demetri as if it offended him to find the man sitting at the table. Demetri parted his lips like he might speak, but Gale's father began before Demetri could. "I suppose if you snubbed King Magnes' family, and King Roenan's as well…" Gale patted Valerian's shoulder again, who's mouth gaped as if it just dawned on him that legally he was in fact related to the King of Segion now. "I suppose a move like that may sour relations between our two countries greatly."

The mood of the room shifted. Eyes darted to Valerian, as if everyone considered him in a new light. The ruse fooled no one, of course. They all knew that Galeson's family claimed him for a political move, not because of actual bloodlines. That didn't matter as much as what the implications of those relationships meant.

Suddenly the people in the room who couldn't bother with me a week before saw King Magnes' child, King Roenan's cousin, and the potential behind a union.

Galeson's father looked at me and raised his glass. "So, I offer congratulations to Princess Epiphany and Lord Valerian on their engagement. May their marriage have as happy a connection as our two countries have shared."

A beat of hesitation.

Then some lifted their glasses and congratulations echoed through the space. The dinner carried on, conversation sweeping forward. Many high lords and their partners asked me for details about our wedding plans. Others skirted around discussing what our connection with King Roenan's family might mean for trade. The entire group acted as though this was the blessing of the century to have me sitting in my father's spot, engaged to Valerian. The very thing that had horrified them the week before.

It was over.

We'd won.

When my gaze landed on Galeson's, I paused and smiled. He was a good man. I owed him a great deal.

He raised his glass to me and took a long drink.

After the party ended—Demetri being one of the first to leave, his face distorted into a scowl as he stormed away—Valerian and I walked out of the dining room together.

Gods, this would be our new life.

We could have conversations again, go horseback riding, spend an afternoon in the sitting room.

I didn't know where I'd actually find the time for any of that, but the fantasy of it alone was enough to buoy my spirits. The evening had ended triumphantly, and now Val walked by my side. His shoulders were rolled back, the sparkling emerald of his eyes fixed on me like I was the only thing of interest in the world.

Heat pooled through me.

For a moment, I didn't think I could be happier.

Tresson walked up and bowed. "Your Highness, my lord." Valerian startled at him addressing him that way, and I bit back a smile. He'd get used to it. "There's a letter for you."

A Spark of Death and Fury

I accepted it and flipped it over to find a hastily made seal that had smudged down the edge of the parchment.

Tresson strode away, and Valerian and I stood alone in the hall. I ripped it open. The letters blurred together like someone had scratched them off quickly and my head ached trying to make sense of them. "Would you read this?"

Valerian took it, and his eyes skimmed over it. "It's from Temi."

My breath caught.

"Pip, I hope this letter finds you well and I'm sorry I send it so hastily. It's coming in the possession of a god who can travel instantly, as not all of our party is able to. I write to say I will see you by the week's end if our pace holds steady."

Val stopped reading. His voice grew thick with feeling when he picked back up. "Your brother is with us." His hand holding the parchment trembled, and his words came as a choked whisper when he finished. "He is alive."

I released a sob and pressed my palm against my waist.

I stumbled a step before bumping into the wall and sliding down it until I sat on the floor and dropped my face into my hands.

Until that moment, I hadn't truly believed it.

Hyacinth was alive.

Tears poured down my face, and for the first time since before the war, they were tears of joy.

Valerian slid down beside me and drew me into his arms. We wept together as we clung to each other and released the tension that had held us captive for months. Finally we breathed in a drop of hope.

40

Apollo

Our group lumbered along in silence as we came down into the warmer valleys of the southern countries. Mia and Kama rode with Temi, and Chares sat by my side, content to lean against the rail and keep his thoughts to himself.

Ixion remained in the cart next to Hyacinth, who hadn't woken yet. Whenever I checked on him, he still breathed and the pounding of his heart thundered against my hand. The previous night I'd laid beside him and never fallen asleep as I kept touching his pulse, my fingers lingering over the warmth of his flesh, and then the unfamiliar scratch of his beard.

I didn't understand why he hadn't woken. Was it something my magic did? Or the weapon Zephyrus used? Or…. or?

The lack of sleep and the worry ate away at me. It left me achy and snappy.

So, it was probably a positive thing that Chares wasn't in a chatty mood.

Sun spilled over the hills and swept across the valley

before us in washes of gold. It made the world intensely beautiful.

I wished Hyacinth could see it.

I longed to feel his hand warm and steady in mine. Watch his eyes turn amber in the light.

A sigh slipped out of me, and Chares looked in my direction but didn't comment.

"Papa," Ixion shrieked. "Oh, I'm glad you're awake."

"It's all right, Ix." Hyacinth's voice rumbled, and I yanked the horses to a halt and tossed the reins to Chares so I could jump into the cart beside them. Hyacinth rubbed Ixion's back as the child clung to him.

I bent down, and Ixion pulled away.

"Cyn," I breathed and reached out to brush a thumb over his cheek. He jerked away from me, and his eyes dilated before he fluttered them closed.

Ixion whimpered beside me, and Cyn reached out for him.

It was as though he didn't see me.

"Hyacinth," I whispered. He leaned farther from me. His muscles tensed like he waited for someone to attack him.

I wished I could go back in time and slow down the moment I'd killed Zephyrus. Make him suffer more.

"He needs water." Temi had walked up, and she looked at the three of us uncertainly but thrust a waterskin in my direction.

Right. Of course. I accepted it, and her fingers gripped my hand before she released the pouch. I gave her a nod and turned to offer it to Hyacinth. "Can you drink?"

He didn't move or speak.

"You've been asleep for several days. You need water, love."

Ixion frowned at Hyacinth. "Papa," he whispered. "Drink some water."

"I'm not thirsty, Ix. You have it."

"I've had a lot. Have a sip."

Hyacinth hesitated before he shifted towards him. Ixion thrust his hands out to me, motioning for the pouch, and I handed it to him. Hyacinth took a quick swallow and then pressed it back to Ixion. "That's enough."

"There's plenty of water now, Papa."

Hyacinth's eyes dragged closed again, as if he couldn't keep them open. My heart thudded about, and I reached for him but paused. My touch didn't seem to be a comfort. The glitter of his magic washed away from his flesh, like it drained from him.

I jumped forward and pressed my fingers against his pulse. His muscles stiffened when I touched him, and he shuddered.

He was alive.

But... but...

"He's shielding me," Ixion said. His brown eyes shimmered. The gold color of them was lost again. "He wants to keep me safe."

"Cyn." I touched his leg, and he curled into himself. His brow furrowed like he expected pain. "You don't have to shield Ix anymore. Zephyrus is dead, and I'm here. We're on the way home."

Hyacinth didn't respond, but Ixion did with tears that streamed down his cheeks.

My eyes darted between the two of them. Then to Temi and the young gods, who watched us with uncertain expressions.

My mind whirled, trying to understand.

"Apollo," Temi called and gestured with her chin for me

A Spark of Death and Fury

to join her away from the group. Everything in me wanted to stay beside Hyacinth, but something in her look compelled me. I jumped down and walked with her over to the lacy gray leaves that began the meandering of the forest. The silver shimmer of the spark that hovered near me glowed along the forms of the trees. I planned to disperse it once we made it home. But it was a good safety precaution for our trip.

"Yes?" I said.

"Hyacinth..." She bit her lip. "He's been through a lot."

"I know."

She reached out and squeezed my arm. "He needs time."

I sighed as heartache and frustration bubbled in me like she'd shoved me under the surface of my feelings, and I tried to kick for air. "Right."

"Let's get him home. Perhaps that will help."

"Of course."

The next few days passed in even terser silence. Temi grieved Orion. She often slipped off under the light of the moon to weep. Once I followed her and held her as she sobbed and let her tears wet my tunic.

I didn't know what to say.

Maybe sometimes words didn't matter.

The young gods finally found space to process the loss of Nero, as well, and remained quiet and withdrawn.

Hyacinth continued sleeping most of the time and refused to eat or drink when he woke. Ixion coaxed small sips or bites of food into him.

It wasn't enough.

Certainly not with him being as good as mortal with his divinity transferred to Ixion.

I longed to have him wake up—truly wake up—and

see that he was safe now. Ixion was protected. He could let go.

Nothing I said or did broke through to him.

By the time we'd reached Niria under the pressing globe of a moonlit sky that Temi had called on to aid us with extra light, Cyn's body had grown weak again.

"Temi, can you let the gate guards know we're here and remove any attendants from the halls?"

Temi frowned at me. "Why?"

I wanted to cry but lowered my voice to a whisper that drifted beneath the chirping of the crickets. "He couldn't stand the indignity of being seen like this."

Temi gave me a look full of sorrow and squeezed my arm, before jumping back on her cart and going ahead of the group. The three young gods hovered around, acting as sentries who would not hesitate to protect us.

A ripple of gratitude swept through me.

I owed them my life.

More than that... the life of my husband and Ixion as well.

When we made it through the gates, Chares pulled a sleeping Ixion into his arms, and I lifted Hyacinth, who jerked his face away from me. Tears broke free, streaked down my face, and landed on his cheek. "Oh, love." His skin looked sallow, even under the dim light of the moon. "Is it selfish of me to ask you to come back once more?"

He didn't answer or open his eyes or give any indication of life aside from the rise and fall of his chest, and I shuddered.

We made it into Hyacinth's room, to the tall windows and elegant furnishings. The luxurious touch all the details held.

I remembered the first time we'd made love in that space.

A Spark of Death and Fury

The way he touched me, like he could hold the sun in his hands.

We both should have known it would end up burning him.

Leaving him a husk.

I laid him on the bed, and the door burst open. It roused Ixion, who Chares tucked in next to Cyn. Temi blocked the person. "Epiphany." She drew her into her arms. "Wait. Before you come in, Hyacinth's been through some things. We need to talk."

Her voice fell into a hum as she pulled Pip out into the hallway. When they returned a few minutes later, Epiphany, who stood in a dressing gown, her hair splayed over the bright color of it, gasped and pressed her fingers to her lips.

I wanted to shove her out of the room.

Demand that she leave.

Not that it was fair.

Watching her take in Hyacinth, seeing the color drain from her face, gave me fresh vision to look at him all over again. His pale skin and sharp juts of his cheeks, the thick beard he never would have tolerated, the way he curled into himself, his eyes that stared blankly ahead.

I had been so focused on keeping him alive and getting him home, I'd refused to acknowledge just how unwell he appeared.

The next day, the royal physician came to see him.

He shook his head as his lips pinched. "Give him some time."

So, we did.

Months of it.

We coaxed Ixion out into the world again. Valerian took him under his tutelage, taught him to ride, and tutored him. A sparkle came back to the child's eyes. When he'd return to us at night, I'd draw him into my lap and tell him stories of adventures, memories of Ares, snippets of poems Hyacinth had taught me.

And all the while, Hyacinth faded and faded and faded.

I left only once with Temi and Arion to the mountain peak that overlooked Niria, where we dispersed the spark. We watched the silver drain from our coloring and our skin return to the shimmering glimmer of the low deities, felt the nausea of earth sickness fade alongside it, and then sat in silence as the moon rose in the sky.

I didn't even attend Epiphany's wedding, though I made sure the sun shone for it.

Instead, I stayed in Cyn's room.

Watching my husband.

The love of my life.

Slowly.

Slip.

Away.

GUARDS USHERED Temi and me through the pulsing crowds of Niria. Rejoicing hummed through the air. Officials had announced that Princess Epiphany would soon be crowned queen. The country had a lot to celebrate. Pip had married, and Niria's divine prince had returned along with the sun and moon deities who'd chosen to make their center of protection in the capital. Trade had improved with Segion and other allies, and after a difficult year, money flowed through the country again.

Of course, the people didn't know about Hyacinth.

How he still would barely eat.

Scarcely made eye contact.

A Spark of Death and Fury

Never held a conversation with anyone outside of brief words to Ixion.

How the sun god they rejoiced at having in their country had led him down a path that had destroyed him.

People clapped and waved their hands, jeweled bangles clattered on their wrists, flags—recently adjusted to include the sun and the moon alongside Niria's symbols of roses wrapped around a sword—whipped about in the wind. The sky shimmered a gentle blue.

The last time I'd walked through the Nirian crowds like this, I'd done so beside Hyacinth.

I'd sneered at him and judged him and treated him terribly.

Tears bit at my eyes. Temi slipped her arm through mine and squeezed me against her. I patted her hand. She'd lost a great deal as well.

I didn't understand how everything could finish like this.

How had we fought and bled and sacrificed only for us to end up so broken?

"I'm glad you came with me." Temi leaned in where her words could reach over the cheers and jingling music of the crowds.

"Epiphany thought it might help." My voice dropped to a whisper. "Maybe if there is no one around who reminds him of… everything that has happened… and if she changes his environment maybe he'll eat something."

Temi's brow furrowed.

She didn't speak false words of comfort.

We'd never given each other bullshit like that and despite all that had altered, despite our new status—because even with the spark dispersed, the other deities had somehow dubbed us, unofficially, as the reigning gods—that hadn't changed.

The truth was, Hyacinth refused to stop shielding Ixion, rendering his body essentially mortal. If he didn't eat or drink more, he wouldn't live much longer. I clenched my teeth to fight a whimper as pain streaked through my heart.

Temi gestured to the temple as we approached it. "They've made some major renovations."

I nodded and followed her up the steps. My mind wasn't on the temple, though. It was on Hyacinth, the vacant look in his eyes when I'd told him goodbye earlier, his sunken cheeks and chapped lips.

We continued walking past the entrance where workers had pulled down the grand statue of Zeus. Some new sculpture sat half-finished and covered in a massive cloth. We moved farther into the building and through a door that separated the chamber from the main part of the temple. An altar defined the center of the room, and two thrones rested back against a curved wall. Above one seat, a silver moon shimmered. Behind the other, a golden sun stretched its long rays out where they ended in yellow gems.

I groaned.

Temi smirked. "I'm so glad I got to be here to see your reaction."

"This is terrible."

"Worth it, for Niria's sake, right?"

"Yes."

Because I'd promised Hyacinth I would do everything I could to protect his kingdom. I didn't know it would cost me my heart and soul. I didn't know it would take him from me.

Diamonds decorated the surface of the ceiling, like the night sky glittered above our heads. I recognized the constellation of the hunter, his bow pulled back. Temi lifted her face, her eyes glistened, and I swallowed past more feelings. "Will it not hurt?" I whispered. "To always see that?"

Temi kept her gaze on Orion's stars. "It will hurt. But I think that's good." She leaned in closer to me, the sandalwood smell of her filling my senses. "It means he's not forgotten. That he was loved, and his life had meaning. Even if it hurts to remember. It's good to feel that pain because it means he mattered."

I nodded, lost for words for a moment, before I squeezed her against my side. She patted my chest and pulled back. "Do you want to return to Hyacinth now?"

I hesitated. I did, but this clearly held importance to her. "Go ahead. Show me the rest of this horrendous place. I know you're eager."

She grabbed my arm as another smile spread over her lips and drew me farther into the temple.

Later, when I returned to the palace, I walked through the pasture and my ankles sank into long grasses. Butterflies drifted through their blades. One landed on the seedy head of a plant and fluttered its golden wings for a moment, before taking to the air again.

In the distance, Temi joined Valerian to chase Ix, his miniature bow clamped between his fingers.

"You'll never catch me," Ix cried, his voice trailing to me in the wind.

Valerian chuckled as he reached him, pulled him up, and swung him around.

Epiphany and Hyacinth sat beneath the shade of a massive tree. A small table filled with refreshments stretched between them. Cyn, even though he faced away from me, thick blankets draping over his lap, scarcely responded to the scene unfolding before him. He sat in a chair affixed with wheels that the young gods built for him.

I could imagine his vacant stare, his unmoving expression. A chill ran down my spine. Epiphany whispered something to him, and he didn't respond or move at all.

Before I reached them, Ix trotted over to Hyacinth and dropped by his feet. "Papa, would you recite a poem for me?"

Hyacinth startled, his blanket shifting over his lap.

"Of course I will." He patted the boy's hand.

I stopped walking and closed my eyes as he began speaking. Without being able to see his too-thin form, the sharp lines of his face, the blankness playing out over his once-vivid eyes, and only hearing the rich resonance of his voice as he shared a poem from his childhood, I could almost feel the presence of the man he once was and imagine he still stood there. His hazel eyes turning amber in the sunlight, his eyebrows pressing that v-shaped dimple between his brows as his lips twisted up, preparing some retort for me.

The poem came to its end and the last warmth of his voice died under the creamy clouds. Ix leaned in and hugged him before he ran out to the pasture again. I walked over and took the chair beside Hyacinth's.

Epiphany crouched down in front of him. "Do you want any wine, Cyn?"

He stared out as if she didn't even stand there.

She met my gaze, and a sheen swept over her eyes. She'd had no success, then. I whimpered, unable to swallow the sound back.

41

Hyacinth

There is a place where dreams blend, reality breaks, and everything is as real as nothing. I lived in that place.

I was certain Apollo had come to the Palace of the Four Winds.

Defeated Zephyrus.

Rescued Ixion.

But then why did Ix still call out for me? Why did I still need to shield him?

Apollo's arrival must have been an imagining born of my broken mind. Zephyrus had finally pushed me too far.

Or maybe none of it was real to begin with.

How did I even know I was a prince? That I'd loved the sun god? That I was to inherit a kingdom?

Perhaps none of it was true.

It sounded like a story.

Broken figments of a shattered mind that rattled together like a wind chime as it glistened in the sunshine.

Apollo had once felt so present.

Father and Epiphany and Emrin and Valerian had too.

Maybe that's why I saw some of them now.

My mind had finally crumbled, and I lived in the dreamscape. My thoughts had wandered for what felt like months, but recently I lived in one dream almost all the time. In it, I'd returned to Niria. I slept in my richly appointed bed next to my husband. I sat in a meadow that overlooked Valerian and Epiphany interacting like a couple in public.

A dream, but a beautiful one.

Only Ixion kept me anchored to the world and made me question the doubts I had over the integrity of my mind.

He would ask me to tell him a story or recite a poem, and I'd brush my hands over his curls, feel the hum of my magic against my palm, and lean into the warmth of his hug.

He was still here, and he needed me.

I couldn't just disappear.

But I was lost.

Only Ixion could call me back in fragments.

Epiphany spoke. I couldn't tell if it was real or not. After all, Zephyrus had said my father had died and, yet, I'd had a lengthy conversation with him that morning. He'd seemed fuzzy though, just out of focus.

"I don't know where I am anymore," I'd said.

Father squeezed my shoulder. His hair was the rich brown it had been in my childhood. "You'll find your way, son."

"But what if I don't?"

"You will."

Maybe Epiphany wasn't real either. Perhaps Zephyrus still had me locked in that basement, enduring unspeakable torments, and my mind had created this rich dream to retreat to. I didn't want to risk breaking it by interacting. Pip seemed so present and clear, however. She differed

A Spark of Death and Fury

from how I remembered her, too. She wore her hair pulled back into a tight bun, a crown on her head, and a dark dress that made her appear older.

Something had changed in my resolve to not interact. I'd fought for so long and was so tired of it.

Better to know if it was authentic or not.

Maybe I'd grown brave enough to finally face my death.

"Do you want any wine, Cyn?"

The question hovered in the air. I knew others were around us though I couldn't name who or focus my attention on them. Everything was too stimulating. The blue of the sky too bright, the whinnying of the horses too loud, the scraping of the grasses by my ankles too intense.

I peeled my dry lips apart. "I'll take some, Pip. Thank you."

I waited for the illusion to burst.

For the world to narrow back to the dungeon, to torture and pain and hopelessness. Epiphany sobbed and reached a shaky hand out to offer me a glass.

This was the moment of truth. I curled my fingers around it and touched the softness of her fingers. She didn't disappear. The cool bite of the glass pushed into my palm. I took a taste, and the bursting flavor of the wine flooded my senses. When it hit my stomach, it rumbled like I hadn't eaten in weeks.

Epiphany was actually here.

Could it be possible that this was reality?

Epiphany wiped her cheeks with the back of her hands. "Let me know if you need anything?"

I bobbed my head but feared speaking anymore. This would all go away in just a moment, I was sure of it. If I lost it again, it would break my heart. I didn't think I could endure it.

More people came into focus. Valerian walked out of the stable leading a burgundy-coated mare with a cream nose. "Ix," Val called, "come meet your new horse."

Ix shifted around Temi and his eyes grew wide. "She's mine?"

"All yours." Val chuckled. "Only if you promise to take excellent care of her."

"I will. I promise." He bounced on his toes. "Can I ride her?"

Valerian patted the saddle. "You can."

Ix spoke to Epiphany. "Will you ride with me, Aunt Pip?"

She smiled, and color swelled over her skin as she looked at Valerian, who nodded. She bent down and took Ix's hand in her own. "I can't, actually." She pressed her free fingers over her waist. "I'm going to have a baby, and my physician thinks it's best if I stay off horses for now."

Ix squinted at her stomach and then snapped his gaze back up. "Will this baby be my brother or sister?"

"They'll be your cousin."

Ix's face brightened. "I always wanted a baby. Thank you, Aunt Pip."

Epiphany and Valerian laughed.

My heart warmed, but this felt, again, like a dream of a happy future I'd never get to experience.

My hand shook as I set the wineglass onto a table beside me. Drops of the burgundy liquid peppered the surface. That didn't happen in dreams. Or did it?

"I once told you." A voice I knew so well my heart ached spoke. I'd felt his presence as he sat in the chair beside me earlier but hadn't looked in his direction. I never did in this dream. I wasn't that brave yet. If I turned and didn't find Apollo there, if I realized this was only a figment of my imagination, it would break me. I kept my eyes ahead as he continued talking, and the deep hum of his voice rolled through me. "I'd said that I would look out for Niria, no matter what happened between us. That I would help remove my father and start a new era. I want you to know," he whispered, "before it's too late... that I will keep that promise to you."

There was so much pain in his voice. I longed to reach for him.

He wouldn't be real.

He wasn't there.

Apollo kept speaking. "And I'll be good. My entire life, I ran from being my father. Wanted to not disappoint Temi. Wanted to make you proud. I've realized that the onus of who I am is on me, though, not anyone else. Regardless of what happens between us,"—he paused for a moment, and I thought he'd disappeared until he spoke again—"I'll use the rest of my life protecting and, if necessary, fighting to keep innocents safe."

Wind ruffled over my skin. Gods this all felt so real. "Selfishly, though," Apollo continued, "if I could, I'd stay with you in the forest frozen in twilight and fog from a dream I had. I'd hide you from everyone there, and the world could fuck itself. I'd still give everything up to have you."

My throat tightened.

The forest.

Where we'd made love.

That safe place that only he and I had shared.

I turned towards Apollo. There he sat, hunched in his seat, his expression the picture of misery.

"You remember the forest?"

He snapped his face in my direction. "I... umm... I had a dream where we were in a forest together."

Looking at him hadn't made him disappear or grow

fuzzy like all the visions I'd had of him during my torment. Perhaps this was happening. "I had that dream too."

Tears poured down Apollo's cheeks and dripped along his neck. "Did you?"

I shuddered. "It was the only thing that anchored me at that moment. I was... losing myself. I think I have lost myself, after all. I never know what's real or not anymore."

Apollo stared at me like he didn't know what to say. This was nothing like a dream where he was golden and bright and sure. This was gritty and heavy. I lifted a shaking hand towards him but then stopped.

Like I had in the forest.

If I touched him and he wasn't really there, that would be it for me.

He reached out and laced his fingers between mine, the scrape of his calluses sliding down my skin. I sobbed. "Apollo?"

"Yes, Cyn. I'm here."

"I didn't know... I'm not sure where here is."

"We're in Niria. You're home again."

"Ixion?"

"See for yourself." He nodded to the pasture where Val lifted Ixion onto a horse and Temi called to Arion, who pranced around her like a puppy.

My lip quivered. "I thought this was all an illusion... imaginings I'd made up... to disappear into." My hand shook harder, and Apollo tightened his grip. I leaned into it and never wanted the moment to fade. "I didn't believe I'd ever make it home again. But then... Epiphany was here so vividly. It felt real. And then you mentioned that dream. How could you even know about it?"

Apollo licked a tear off his lip. "You've faced... so much. It's over. You're home now. You're here with us."

I stared at Valerian, whose jacket rippled in the wind as

he steadied Ixion. For several minutes, we didn't speak. Tears spilled down my cheeks, and I held onto Apollo like he was a rope holding me from plunging into an abyss.

"Did you know," I whispered, "I once imagined that I was Icarus, flying towards the sun? I thought I'd burn and fall, but I desired you so badly, I didn't care."

Apollo's voice came choked. "I suppose that came true."

It hurt to hear the pain in his words. To know that he still blamed himself. But it also made everything feel that much more true. Maybe I'd actually survived. Maybe I was actually home.

"For some time, I've wanted to fade. I've longed to disappear into whatever comes after all of this." I turned to face Apollo. Gods, he was still there wearing a tunic in such a way that would look sloppy on anyone else but only highlighted the beauty of his form. "I'm so broken, Apollo. I don't know what I have left. If you're really here with me, if this is real, then I want to find it again."

He garbled a sob and dropped on the ground before me. "Cyn, I need nothing but you, just as you are. However that is, in whatever state, I'll be happy to have it."

I scraped my thumb over his knuckles lightly, as if indulging too much, would make everything fade. "This may be all there is. I can't seem to... remember who I am."

"This is enough," he said through his tears.

"I don't know if this will actually get better." I lifted my face to find his eyes—brown but somehow shimmering like gold—boring into me. "But I'll try."

Apollo laid his head on my lap, then pulled back. It startled me to have so much of his touch. For him to be so there and present. I loosed my fingers from his grip and brushed them through his hair to stall him. This felt so new and uncertain. I didn't want him to move away from me, though.

"Don't you think it's sad that flowers die at the end of their season?" I asked.

The question hovered in the air between us. Apollo swallowed and rolled back on his heels. "Yes, that's sad."

"Sometimes," I whispered, and my eyes darted about all the millions of details of the world before they landed on him again, "the most beautiful blooms come after the hardest winters."

"Those are the best flowers, I think."

I trailed my fingers around the glass of wine. "Do you have your lyre with you?"

"It's in my knapsack."

I forced a smile. "Then that's a yes. You still keep that with you all the time, don't you?"

"Most of the time. Not always, anymore."

In the field, Temi had mounted Arion and joined Ix, who she encouraged into a gallop.

"Hey," Valerian called, "don't start by teaching him bad habits."

"He's out of luck," Temi yelled over her shoulder, mischievousness in the pinch of her face. "He has me as an aunt. He's going to learn all kinds of bad habits."

Valerian crossed his arms and blew out a breath, but chuckled.

Gods, if this was real, if I was actually here and life was this good, I would fight for it. I'd proven to myself that I could endure so many things. I could face finding my way back again too.

"Would you play for me?" I asked.

"You want me to play music for you?"

I stretched my fingers out slowly and just touched the edge of his jaw. I winced when his flesh scraped against mine but didn't pull away. "If you help me, then I'll do everything to find my way back again."

He lifted his hand, as incrementally as I had, and placed it over mine. "Cyn, I'll do anything for you. I'll play music, and read you poems, and gather you flowers, and"—his voice grew into a grizzle of a sound—"shove you off a damn cliff if it would help. You did that once for me."

A real smile spread over my face. "You chose to jump."

"Yeah, you're right. And I'll jump a hundred more times for you. A million, even."

My heart felt like it would burst. *This is real, this is real, this real*, it seemed to beat out. "Ixion is truly safe?"

"He is."

I was scared that wasn't true. That my mind tricked me. That I'd leave Ixion unsheltered. Everything felt so authentic, and I couldn't keep the fight up any longer. My muscles tensed, and I drew the magic back to me. It swept through my body, wound around my bones, flooded my veins.

My addled brain cleared, and everything came back into focus. Apollo was still there. "Music?" I garbled the word out.

Apollo stumbled up. He choked on a sob as he nabbed his bag and pulled the lyre out along with a small bundle. "I have something else for you, if you want it."

He unfolded the cloth until it revealed my ring, clean and sparkling in the sunlight. He offered it out to me, and I picked it up and grazed my fingers over the etchings of the sun, the Hyacinth flower, and across the glittering green stone.

I released a breathy, silent cry and pushed it back onto my finger.

Apollo sat on the grass before me. He began to play and—once his tears dried up—sing, letting his voice join the fluttering flowers and blue skies and Ix's laughter that peppered the world.

I lifted the wineglass and took another sip before cradling it in my hands. The flavor of it bloomed intensely in my mouth, but I didn't move my gaze from Apollo.

For the first time in a long while, a tendril of hope snaked through my chest, as golden and pure and gentle as a ray of the sun.

Perhaps it would never be perfect.

Maybe we'd lost too much along the way.

But maybe, with time, it could be good.

The song ended, and Apollo lowered the instrument onto his lap.

"Would you play another?" I asked.

He picked the lyre back up but didn't take his eyes off of me. This was the man I loved with my whole heart. He'd fought for me. If this was real, I would fight until I found him again.

Maybe fate, for all the hardships it had thrown my way, offered me a chance to do so.

Apollo's fingers glided over the strings as he started into another song.

Epilogue

42

Apollo

I stretched out on the grass and pulled my lyre free from my bag. I leaned against the hillside and strummed my fingers over the strings as lazy clouds slipped across the pale blue sky. Once I'd imagined this being all I'd want out of life. No responsibilities, no pressure, just days filled with music and freedom.

A chuckle bubbled up past my lips. It was rare for me to have this kind of time anymore. Between my weekly temple duties, my role with the sun, working alongside Temi to manage—and occasionally quell uprisings—among the gods, supporting Hyacinth in his role as one of Epiphany's advisors, and family responsibilities, my days remained full.

Anyway, if I were to take a day off, I wasn't likely to spend it playing music in a graveyard. I eyed the mausoleum ahead of me. That was more Temi's scene with her close friendship with Hecate. I could hear her scoffing at that and smirked as I remembered our conversation from that morning.

"I heard you and Hecate took your own journey this week. Is terrifying royalty your new pastime?"

She'd scowled. "Trying to remind Ansair of which gods stand with Niria. Epiphany worries they are preparing to start trouble again." She tapped my finger against the armrest. "If you get a chance, could you ask Ixion if he's sensing any whispers of war from them?"

"No problem."

I wasn't sure if Ixion would make it tonight and, if not, I'd need to go see him tomorrow. But that brought me around to why I spent my day wasting time in this quiet corner of the palace's grounds, instead of attending my duties.

Tonight would be hard for Cyn.

A dozen years after his traumas at the hands of Zephyrus, most days were good now. But this particular event—important though it was—always triggered him. I didn't know when he planned to arrive here for it, but he wouldn't face it alone. Bringing Hyacinth to mind reminded me of our conversation from the night before and I smiled.

He'd dropped on the floor in front of me, rested his head on my leg, his eyes on the fire as he groused about the advisors.

"Do you want Temi and me to cause an eclipse during the meeting?" I traced my fingers through his hair that he kept longer than he used to, the soft waves rippling over my fingers. "Or I could catch a chair on fire. Something dramatic?"

He'd scoffed. "Not everything can be handled by fire."

"Not everything." I'd kissed his cheek. "But a great many things, in my experience."

He'd laughed and turned around to capture my mouth

with his and forget about the advisors in favor of something more pleasurable.

The warmth of that memory buoyed me as the sun slowly sank down the sky. Epiphany walked up, her gait slow due to the late stage of her pregnancy, Hyacinth and Valerian shadowing her. Cyn met my gaze and the pinched expression he wore faded.

He stepped over to me, and I jumped up and drew him into my arms, breathed in the sweet jasmine scent of him, and kissed his cheek as he melted against my shoulder. "Hello, love."

"Apollo." He breathed my name against my neck.

I rubbed his back and felt muscles loosen.

"There are my two favorite rascals," Valerian cried as Brina walked up with his and Epiphany's four-year-old twins in tow. They jumped and raised their arms to him, and he scooped them up and whirled them around so that they shrieked.

Branches in the forest clattered as Arion crashed through the brush with a smiling pair on his back. Arion's body glimmered even as the sun dipped below the tree line and left the sky a plummy periwinkle. Temi wore her bow across her back and her silver gown drifted out behind her. And Adamantia, Val and Pip's eldest, had her dark curls free, the greens of her irises sparkling with mirth and freedom.

Temi dropped down and spoke with Epiphany before nodding to me. I pulled Hyacinth tighter to me and released the golden light of my magic. For a moment it was just the two of us, swirled in the light of the sun. Hyacinth chuckled. "This never gets old, golden boy."

"Being in the light of the sun?"

"Being with you."

I smiled and kissed him as the magic faded.

A Spark of Death and Fury

Temi glittered silver as she pulled the moon into the sky. Night sailed across us and gave the air a chill, then Temi led the way across the clearing to where she'd built Orion's monument, a large, low, rectangular slab carved with all the adventures he'd had. It started with him as a child, holding his sister's hand, cows bowing their heads to eat grass. It ended on the back with the scorpion he'd saved Temi from.

Epiphany stepped over to Hyacinth, and he parted from me to join her. I opened my bag and pulled out candles, beautifully crafted ones that smelled of vanilla. Hyacinth handed one to Epiphany and she placed it on the stone. I lit bits of parchments with my magic and passed them to everyone.

Epiphany touched the wick of the first candle I'd laid out.

For their father.

Hyacinth added another and lit it.

Their mother.

And another.

Emrin.

The group all quietly added different candles. The lights bobbed like a hundred fallen stars and glimmered like lightning bugs dashing around. I added my contribution, remembering Ares' kindness, Delon's boisterous laughter, and Mother's steady strength.

Temi pulled a final candle, as she always did.

Unlike the pristine ones everyone else put out, hers was a crude, squat one she formed with her own hands. She placed it in the center, and I walked up beside her to offer a light.

She set the wick aflame, the glow of it sparkling alongside the others, a peaceful field of stars.

Orion.

We watched as the lights slowly glittered away, until smoke fizzed against the navy sky. Epiphany left to sit against a tree, and Temi followed her. Valerian and Hyacinth stood speaking with me when the shrubs parted.

"Ixion, you made it," I said.

Ixion walked into the clearing, his hand intertwined with his partner's. Dia was a nymph with silver eyes who had a softer spot for Cyn than me, though she loved us both as we loved her. In Ix's other arm he held their infant, Peiri, and the glimmer of the baby's magic glowed against his swaddling wraps.

Hyacinth melted at their arrival and his shoulders dropped as he walked over. "Ix."

"Hey, Papa. We've brought a guest who's been eager to see you."

"Sorry we're late," Dia said. "He's had a fussy evening."

"I know how that is." Hyacinth smirked mischiveously at me. "Getting Apollo to make it on time for anything is near impossible."

I scoffed as a smile so sincere and sweet it whirled through me spread over Hyacinth's face as he spoke to Peiri. "Hello, little one. Were you crying because you missed your Papa today?"

Ixion handed Peiri to Cyn, supporting the child's head until he had him transferred. "He needs another day in Papa's gardens. He slept better than he ever has that night."

"Bring him tomorrow, if you'd like. His grandfather can play him music,"—Hyacinth smiled at me—"and his papa can walk him until he's worn out."

I kissed Peiri's head, the softness of his skin always surprising me. "We'd be glad to have him anytime. By the way, Ix, have you heard any rumblings from Ansair?"

A Spark of Death and Fury

Cyn shot me a look. "Let's talk politics another time." Peiri smacked his flower bud lips and Hyacinth smiled again, entirely taken in. "Tonight is a family night."

I rolled my eyes. "Says the prince."

Hyacinth clicked his tongue and bounced Peiri as he started to wake. "Come now, little one. I'll recite you some poems and help you sleep for your parents tonight." He gave Ixion a wicked look. "As soon as you can speak, I'll teach you some of your father's favorites from when he was a boy."

Dia laughed and walked with Val and Hyacinth as he carried the baby over to Epiphany and Temi who cooed at him. Ixion clapped his hand around my shoulder and leaned into me to whisper. "If Papa asks, I didn't bring it up tonight, but you don't need to worry over Ansair. They're firmly in their place right now. No rumblings of war."

I chuckled and patted his arm. "Good man."

He wrapped his arms around me. "Love you, Father."

My heart galloped. Raising Ares' son, stepping into his shoes, had been an honor. Sometimes it still left me surprised that this was my life. That all these good things belonged to me. I felt like a man in possession of a treasure chest, staring at a pile of gems, uncertain of what to do aside from admire them.

Ixion's voice took on a more wary tone as his eyes darted to Hyacinth. "How's Papa doing with this?"

"He's okay. It's a hard day, but this year is better, I think." Hyacinth smoothed his fingers over Peiri's curls. Yeah, I'd worried about him, but he seemed all right.

Later, when Epiphany and her family had returned to the palace, and Ixion and Dia said goodnight and promised to drop by the next day, Hyacinth walked up beside me and brushed his nose against my cheek. For a moment he said nothing and quietly breathed against my skin. I rested my hand over the dip of his back and felt the warmth of his body against mine, the way his heartbeat slowed.

He kissed my cheek. "I'm going to head home."

"I'll come with you."

"No." He nodded to Temi. "Stay with your sister a while longer. This is an important day for her. If you don't mind, though, I'm going to go. I'm tired."

"Of course. I'll follow behind soon?"

He smiled, squeezed my hand, and turned to walk out of the clearing. I remained until Temi left not long after. Directing the sun and the moon kept us both on early schedules—me for raising the needy star, hers for drawing the moon back down.

I crunched through the path that ran from the palace grounds, through the woods, until it reached the clearing where our cottage sat. It had taken several years before we'd moved out of the palace to this simple place with ivory walls that glowed blue in the moonlight and a red-tiled roof that stretched demure under the blanket of night.

We hadn't added fences or deterrents to keep others away. Yet humans rarely visited. Children sometimes dared each other to make it to the clearing which Cyn found endlessly amusing. Despite my close interaction with the people of the city in the last dozen years, the story of my, Temi, Orion, and the young gods' slaughter across the continent had spread and grown.

I'd now—according to legend—single handedly slain ten monsters. Temi had killed a dozen vengeful high gods with a single arrow.

Total bullshit. We'd barely survived.

We had, though.

And the myths surrounding our adventures gave the humans—those who didn't know us well, at least—a pinch of fear and a hefty dose of respect for us. Enough to keep Hyacinth's and my little cottage peacefully avoided.

Wind rustled through the clearing and tangled the flowers of Cyn's garden together. The plants covered every inch of the lawn. Different varieties bloomed throughout the year, and I knew the names of all of them.

Not because of personal interest.

Hearing Cyn discuss them, however, watching his eyes brighten, working alongside him to pull weeds and plant new bushes, was probably the happiest part of my life.

The windows sat in shadows, no peachy flicker of lamps lit. I stepped around to the back of the house where Cyn had planted—as he called it—his 'Temi garden' of flowers that only bloomed at night. Creamy moon flowers rattled together on their vines, and blue creepers stretched along a trellis.

No Hyacinth, though.

I walked back around to the front and into the cottage.

Cyn's tall form, the lean, muscular shape of him stretched silhouetted in a doorway. I removed my bag and let it drop to the ground with a thunk.

I'd learned a few things about Hyacinth since we'd escaped Zephyrus' wrath.

I never entered a room without making noise to announce my presence. I didn't slip up behind him or touch him without making sure he could see my movements first.

Those things still sometimes triggered him, shoved him back into that vacant space he'd nearly succumbed to.

He turned and offered me a smile. His eyes caught a hint of moonlight that pooled in through the door. Then he shifted back to the room he faced and rested his head on the sill.

I closed the door and walked up behind him, my movements slow despite him knowing I was there. I waited for him to lean back against me and then I wrapped my arms around his waist. "Why are you standing here in the dark?"

He sighed as his body leaned against mine, and he remained focused on Ixion's room, the carefully made bed, the jacks arranged on the windowsill, the bow that rested in the corner. All the little details of his childhood that lingered.

"He's too young to have a baby don't you think?"

I considered that as I pressed my lips against Hyacinth's neck and kissed his pulse. "We weren't much older when we got him."

Hyacinth groaned but clasped his hands over mine.

"Besides," I said. "He'll be a great father. He's had an excellent Papa to learn from."

Hyacinth's shoulders dropped and he turned in my arms. "He's had two excellent fathers… three, actually." He smiled and for a moment we didn't speak, but the memory of Ares flashed through my mind. The form of him silvery in the moonlight on a night much like tonight when he'd visited to forewarn us of everything to come, attempting to protect us.

"Are you ready for bed?" I asked.

Hyacinth nodded, and we clasped hands to walk across the living room. A fireplace decorated with the upside-down stalks of drying flowers defined the space. Next to Hyacinth's chair, a table sat with a reed and ink pot and parchment with some poem half written on it. We crossed the space without light, our house so familiar it was unnecessary, and stepped into our bedroom.

The windows had no curtains—they weren't needed

with how private our home was—and moonlight spilled over our bed, while Cyn's roses danced against the windowpane.

Hyacinth pulled his robe off and brushed his hands down the silk of it, before hanging it up in the closet. He shrugged his shirt off and my heart picked up as I took in the broad line of his shoulders, the warm tan of his flesh turned a liquid blue in the near-darkness, the rise of his breath.

He was alive and here with me.

I doubted I would ever cease being grateful for it.

I had lost him, and lost him, and lost him.

Now I had him.

For as long as we both lived.

I hoped I would be the one to lose him one more time in the end instead of the other way around. It would hurt like hell, and I was sure it would probably break me. I didn't want him to be left alone, though. For now, we had centuries still stretching ahead of us and I intended to treasure them.

I pulled my tunic off, draped it over a chair and walked up behind Hyacinth before letting my chest graze his back and sliding my hands around the firm planes of his stomach.

I waited until the tension in his body loosened and then kissed his shoulder, tasted the sweetness of his flesh, and drew our bodies flush together.

He turned, tilted my chin up and captured my mouth with his as he stroked a finger down my neck.

We stumbled towards the bed and our limbs tangled together as we hit the mattress. His body tensed in a more pleasant way as he pressed his hips against mine, clutched his fingers into my back, grazed his teeth against my shoulder causing the flesh to tingle.

I rolled us over. My knees created divots in the bed on either side of him as I brought my lips to his neck.

His body went rigid, and I jumped up.

It had been a long time since intimacy between us had caused that reaction, since he'd felt trapped or terrified when my body covered his.

"I'm sorry," he whispered.

My heart thundered, my body still hungry and wanting, but I sat back on my knees. "You have no reason to be. We can stop."

"I don't want to. I just need a minute." He closed his eyes and took several long breaths. I waited with my hands resting on my thighs. I would follow his lead, but if he wanted to stop, we would.

He opened his eyes and pulled himself up to kneel beside me before dropping his forehead to my shoulder. "I'm sorry again. I'm ruining the mood."

I ran my hand around his back. "You are the mood, Prince. You can't possibly ruin it."

He sighed and his breath whispered down my chest, causing my nipples to harden. "Today brought up a lot of memories." I tucked my chin against his shoulder as he continued speaking. "Sometimes I don't know why you continue to put up with me, golden boy."

I leaned back and grinned. "Put up with you? You're my ambrosia, Cyn. If you ever decide you want to leave, let me know where we're going, and I'll pack our bags."

He laughed, the lightness of it reminding me of the young man I'd met and fallen in love with. We'd seen each other through so damn much. My favorite version of Hyacinth, though, was the one by my side. The one I got to love through beautiful days full of laughter where he tended to his flowers while I played songs for him on the lyre. And the one where I got to love him through the hard days where he shuddered at my touch and withdrew and struggled to come back to me.

I loved him exactly as he was.

I loved his soul.

His essence.

To have him was a treasure.

He grazed his palm along the length of my neck and pressed his mouth to mine hard enough that it ached. He sucked my lip between his teeth and leaned his body closer to mine.

I pulled him onto my lap and groaned into his mouth.

He ground against me and then wrapped his hands around the hardness of both of us, glided his hand up and down, and captured my gasp with another hungry kiss.

For a moment the world washed away.

The hardships.

The memories.

The fears.

It was just Cyn's body warm and desiring against mine.

Cyn's breath tickling my ear.

Cyn's heartbeat pressed against my lips as I trailed my mouth over his chest.

Then he shuddered, wilted against me, and his entire body trembled as he reached his end. The sight of it was always enough to bring me over the edge as well.

I did as I'd always done since we'd met.

Fell.

Jumped.

Released myself to him.

For a moment we leaned against each other, and our heavy breaths echoed through the room.

I jumped up and grabbed a towel to clean us both up and chuckled. "You'd think we're boys who don't know how to pace ourselves."

He dipped his head. The moonlight poured over the kingly lines of his profile, the sculpted edges of his form. "I think our days of boyhood are long behind us."

I curled my fingers behind his neck and pressed a kiss to his cheek. "I don't care how old I grow, you make me feel like a young man every time I stand in the same room with you."

A smile slipped over his lips. Those lips I loved to taste, to watch curl up with laughter, or pinch into a scowl when I teased him.

"Come on, love, let's get some sleep."

We lay down and a long time passed as the stars twinkled against the midnight sky.

Hyacinth's shoulders rose with steady breaths.

But I knew that body.

Better than my own, even.

I knew the subtle hitch of his breath when he actually slept.

I ran my fingers along the edge of the blanket and stopped when I reached his arm, making sure he was aware of me before I hugged an arm around him. "Why are you still awake?"

His voice came gritty and low. "Just a lot on my mind."

"Want to share?"

He sighed and leaned in closer to me. "One day we'll be gone, and only legends of us will exist."

I hummed against the waves of his hair. "That's true."

"I think people will only remember me as the mortal foolish enough to get involved with a god. The tragic prince who died."

My heart ached at his words and for a moment I couldn't form a reply. After half a dozen heartbeats I pulled him tighter against me. "They'll remember me as the god selfish enough to cause you all that pain."

His hand clenched around mine, his ring, with its emerald stone and sun and flower etchings, bit into my fingers. "I love you, Apollo. You once told me you'd suffer it all a thousand times again to have one day with me."

I kissed the edge of his shoulder. "I still mean that."

"So do I."

"Well, maybe the myths about us will be awful. I'll be the selfish, conceited sun god, bent on a path of destruction, dragging my lover along with me. You'll be the handsome young prince who captured the attention of the gods and paid the ultimate price for it. But it doesn't matter."

Hyacinth pulled away from me and rolled over where he could face me, his eyebrows drawing together and forming that v-shaped dimple between them that I still loved. "You don't think so?"

"No. Because one day we'll be gone. A memory. Others can make of us whatever they want." I lifted his hand and kissed the edges of his fingertips. "I know the truth of us."

"What is that?"

I smiled and traced over the sharp lines of his jaw, along his chin, up over the plushness of his lips. "Once, many years ago,"—he grinned as I began like I used to start stories for Ixion—"there was a half deity prophesied to be the god of the sun. He hated his fate and ran from it, right into the arms of a prince who, at first, he thought he loathed." Hyacinth chuckled. "He discovered along the way that man was his heart and soul. The deity brought hardship and loss to the prince, though and had to live with the many mistakes he made."

"Does the prince get to interject in this story?"

"He's a prince, he can do what he wants."

Cyn laughed. "The prince didn't know what all he entangled himself with when he wrapped up with the sun god. Even after everything, he didn't regret it. For he'd found his soul as well and he loved that god just as he was, mistakes and all."

He grew quiet and our heartbeats thundered together.

"So, let the people tell their stories and myths," I whispered. "We know the truth of us. Our story is a tragedy but if you peel all the layers back there's one thing remaining."

"What's that?"

"It's a story of a god who loved a prince until it nearly undid them both. Who still loves that man with every breath of his body. And who is okay with becoming a memory if it means the prince is in it."

Hyacinth huffed a quiet laugh before he nestled against me. I traced my fingers gently across his arm until his breathing began to hitch. I smiled and curled around him, felt his body next to mine, and knew I meant the words.

For all the good and bad I'd done…

For all anyone might remember me for…

It was my love of Hyacinth that pattered around in my chest, the desire to see the sun turn his eyes into honey candy that motivated me to raise it each day, his body my spirit rested in.

One day we'd both be gone.

Only memories remaining.

Tales we'd have no way to shape or define.

The truth of us lay here, though.

There was nothing, not vengeful gods, or death, or loss, or hardship, or brokenness, could take that from us.

I kissed his cheek gently and he readjusted and tangled in beside me.

Gratitude slipped through me again.

I'd once been a god.

Aimless and lost.

Until this man had rooted me.

I had so much time left to do this again.

To feel his body warm against mine, to listen to the cadence of his voice, wrestle through grief and pain, and experience the endless well of love that ran between our two souls before it ended.

And our story… well, that could be for someone else to tell.

I already knew the truth of it.

Apollo & Hyacinthus

"You are fallen in your prime defrauded of your youth, O Hyacinthus!" Moaned Apollo. "My own hand gave you death unmerited—I only can be charged with your destruction.—What have I done wrong? Should loving you be called a fault? And oh, that I might now give up my life for you! Or die with you!"

Behold the blood of Hyacinthus, which had poured out on the ground beside him and there stained the grass, was changed from blood; and in its place a flower, more beautiful than Tyrian dye, sprang up.

And Sparta certainly is proud to honor Hyacinthus as her son; and his loved fame endures.

-Excerpt from Metamorphoses, Book 10
    By the poet, Ovid
    Translated by Brookes More

Author's Note

It has been a tremendous honor and joy to take Ovid's short collection of verses about Apollo and Hyacinthus and form it into four heartbreaking, passionate, brutally beautiful books.

I didn't know when I skimmed through a collection of Greek myths a few years ago—and stumbled over a painting of a grief-stricken Apollo holding the dead Prince Hyacinthus in his arms—how deeply I would soon know, and love, these characters.

I hope they would feel I've done their stories justice.

(And I hope Ovid would endure my alterations. These boys needed a happy ending after everything we put them through.)

This series is special to me in a way that is evading words and it's making me sad to leave this world and these wonderful characters.

I hope you loved this world, these characters, and these stories as deeply as I have loved crafting them.

Thank you for your support. Without readers, I

Author's Note

couldn't continue to publish these books and they wouldn't exist.

That's a magic of its own, in a way.

Thank you for allowing Apollo, Cyn, Temi, Pip, Val, Orion, and Arion to become a part of your life. I hope they enriched yours as much as they did mine.

-Nicole, August 2022

———

Bonus content for this book can be found at:
   www.authornicolebailey.com/FATEbonus

Acknowledgments

For the readers who messaged me after reading the acknowledgments from A Shield of Fate and Ruin to say I owed you a better apology than what I offered there, I hope the epilogue acted as a better balm for broken hearts than I could ever offer here. Thank you for reading these books, the messages, and the continued support. It's priceless.

To my husband, thank you. You know I stole one thing Apollo says to Hyacinth in the epilogue from you. Your love shines through so many of these characters. I love you.

Milly, you corrected an egregious error on my part in this book and I thank you tremendously for that. I don't have words to express how much I appreciate the work and love you poured into editing this series. I know you emotionally bled as hard as I did and loved these characters as much as me (while still pushing these books to be the best they could.) Your fingerprints are all over these books, and I cannot thank you enough.

Natalie, nothing I say will be sufficient. You were more brutal with the line edits of this book than I was with the characters in it. And somehow you kept me laughing all the way through it. (I'm leaving that "and" at the start and you can't do shit about it.) On a serious note, you vastly improved this book and have made me a stronger writer. More importantly, your friendship is priceless to me. Thank you.

To my early readers who sent me typos and errors you

found through this series, thank you. You helped these books shine and I so appreciate each of you!

To Stefanie Saw, they always say 'don't judge a book by its cover' but I would be fine with someone judging this series by them. They are beautiful and I feel honored to have your artwork covering my stories. Thank you.

Printed in Great Britain
by Amazon